D0012293

"BLACKTHORN & GRIM IS GOING TO BE A SERIES TO WATCH."
—*RT Book Reviews* (4½ stars)

Praise for
Dreamer's Pool

"Distinctive voices and darker themes interlace in Juliet Marillier's *Dreamer's Pool*. It's an enchanting tale grounded by her damaged and compelling protagonists, Blackthorn and Grim, who rise above adversity to become a formidable team."

—Jacqueline Carey, *New York Times* bestselling author of *Poison Fruit*

"*Dreamer's Pool* is a fabulous read, a rich tale that resonates of deepest myth peopled by well-drawn characters who must sort out their personal demons while unraveling mysteries both brutally human and magical."

—Kristen Britain, *New York Times* bestselling author of the Green Rider series

"Marillier's fascinating narrative, based loosely on Irish myth and centered on women's empowerment, never slips into sentimentality or untoward sensuality, delivering a tasteful feast for the imagination."   —*Publishers Weekly*

"The best thing about this novel (and there are many good components) is that it's the opener for a series featuring the taciturn Blackthorn and mysterious Grim." —*Library Journal*

"Marillier's *Dreamer's Pool* is a tall, deep draft of mystical Irish brew that will fill your mouth with its satisfying magical flavor and leave you thirsting for the next to come."

—*Fresh Fiction*

"A simply gorgeous story with wonderful, intriguing, and complex characters. . . . This is a tale that will tug at your heart and, like the fable that it draws upon, linger in your head and soul for days afterward. I cannot wait for the next installment in this series."

—Karen Brooks, author of *The Brewer's Tale*

"An unbelievably and expertly written story that weaves magic, danger, love, and strong characters all into one fantastic story!"   —Feathered Quill Book Reviews

continued . . .

Dreamer's Pool

A BLACKTHORN & GRIM NOVEL

Juliet Marillier

A ROC BOOK

ROC
Published by New American Library,
an imprint of Penguin Random House LLC
375 Hudson Street, New York, New York 10014

This book is a publication of New American Library. Previously published in a
Roc hardcover edition.

First Roc Mass Market Printing, November 2015

For more information about Penguin Random House, visit penguin.com.

ISBN 978-0-451-46700-3

Printed in the United States of America
10 9 8 7 6 5 4 3 2 1

Penguin
Random
House

To the daughters of Papatuanuku

acknowledgments

My thanks to the team at Pan Macmillan Australia: Claire Craig, Libby Turner, Brianne Collins and my publicist, Eve Jackson; and to Anne Sowards and her team at Penguin Group (USA). I'm grateful to my wonderful agent, Russell Galen, for his ongoing support and his enthusiasm for the Blackthorn & Grim project. To my daughter, Elly, a big thank-you for helping me with some gnarly plot puzzles.

In early 2014 I attended a druid camp in my homeland of New Zealand. There I met a group of folk who were down-to-earth, insightful and at times hilarious. I came away refreshed in mind and spirit. This novel's dedication arose from friendships formed during that time, and is also a recognition of my link to the place of my birth and up-bringing. I acknowledge the influence of both on the final shaping of this story.

A high-profile abduction case was in the news when I was writing *Dreamer's Pool*, and undoubtedly played a part in Blackthorn's driving need to see abusers of women brought to justice. The courage of the three women involved in that case was remarkable. May their lives from now on be full of kindness and opportunity.

Lastly, to my loyal readers all around the world: Your passionate enthusiasm for my work helps me keep going, and I can't thank you enough.

chARACTER LiST

Approximate pronunciations are given for the more difficult names (*kh* is a soft guttural sound, as in the Scottish
loch).

Laois / Laigin (Leesh / Lain)

Blackthorn:	a prisoner
Grim:	a prisoner
Poxy:	a prisoner
Dribbles:	a prisoner
Strangler:	a prisoner
Frog Spawn:	a prisoner
Slammer:	a prison guard
Tiny:	a prison guard
Mathuin:	chieftain of Laois in northern Laigin
Conmael:	a fey nobleman

Ulaid

Muadan:	chieftain of southern Ulaid
Breda:	Muadan's wife

Dalriada

Oran:	Prince of Dalriada
Ruairi: (*rua*-ry)	Oran's father, king of Dalriada. His court is at Cahercorcan.
Eabha: (*eh*-va)	Oran's mother, queen of Dalriada
Lady Sochla: (*sokh*-la)	Eabha's sister, Oran's aunt
Sinead: (shi-*nehd*)	her personal maid
Feabhal: (fa-val)	Ruairi's chief councillor
Master Cael:	a senior lawman
Master Tassach:	a senior lawman
Oisin: (a-sheen)	a druid

ORAN'S HOUSEHOLD AT WINTERFALLS

Donagan:	Oran's body servant and friend
Aedan:	steward
Fíona:	his wife
Eochu: (och-u)	stable master
Niall:	head farmer
Brid:	head cook
Teafa: (ta-fa)	a young seamstress
Lochlan:	head guard
Garalt:	guard
Fergal:	guard

WINTERFALLS VILLAGE

Fraoch: (frech)	smith
Ornait:	his mother
Emer: (eh-ver)	his younger sister
Iobhar: (ee-var)	brewer
Eibhlin: (ev-lin)	his wife
Scannal:	miller
Deaman: (da-maun)	baker
Luach: (lokh)	weaver
Becca:	a friend of Emer
Cathan:	Becca's first love
Brocc:	sheep farmer
Cliona:	sheep farmer
Pátraic:	lad from the brewery

SILVERLAKE VILLAGE

Branoc:	baker
Ernan:	miller (deceased)
Ness:	Ernan's daughter
Mór:	a villager

Cloud Hill / Laigin

Lord Cadhan:	chieftain of Cloud Hill in northern Laigin
Flidais: (flid-is)	his daughter

Domnall: (*don*-al)   senior man-at-arms, married to Nuala
Eoin: (ohn)   man-at-arms
Seanan: (*shan*-aun)   man-at-arms
Ciar: (keer)   Flidais's personal maid
Mhairi: (*mah*-ree)   maidservant
Deirdre: (*dee*-dra)   maidservant
Nuala: (*noo*-la)   maidservant, married to Domnall

                            Others
Lorcan mac Cellaig: king of Mide (a historical figure,
                            circa 848)
Abhan: (a-van)   a traveling horse trader

                            And not forgetting
Snow: Oran's horse
Star: Donagan's horse
Apple: Flidais's horse
Storm and Sturdy: Scannal's cart horses
Tinker and Treasure: Abhan's cart horses
Bramble: Flidais's dog

1

BLACKThORN

I fished out the rusty nail from under my pallet and scratched another mark on the wall. Tomorrow would be midsummer, not that a person could tell rain from shine in this cesspit. I'd been here a year. A whole year of filth and abuse and being shoved back down the moment I lifted myself so much as an inch. Tomorrow, at last, I'd get my chance to speak out. Tomorrow I would tell my story.

In the darkness of the cell opposite, Grim began muttering. A moment later the door down at the guard post creaked open. How Grim could tell the guards were coming before we heard them was a mystery, but he always knew. The muttering was a kind of shield. At night, when the place belonged to us prisoners, he spoke more sense.

A jingle of metal; footsteps approaching. Long strides, heavy footed. Slammer. Usually, when he came, we'd shrink back into the shadows, hoping not to draw his attention. Today I stood by the bars waiting. My time in this place had broken me down. The person they'd locked up last summer was gone, and she wasn't coming back. But tomorrow I'd speak for that woman, the one I had been. Tomorrow I'd tell the truth, and if the council had any sense of right and wrong, they'd make sure justice was done. The thought of that kept me on my feet even when Slammer went into his little routine, smashing his club into the bars of each cell in turn, liking the way it made us jump. Yelling his stupid names for us, names that had stuck like manure on a boot, so we even used them for one another, Grim and I being the only exceptions. Peering in to make sure we looked sufficiently cowed and beaten down.

"Bonehead!" The club crashed against Grim's bars. "Stop your stupid driveling!"

At the back of his cell Grim was a dark bundle against the wall, head down on drawn-up knees, hands over ears, still muttering away. Funny thing was, if Slammer had opened that cell door just a crack, Grim could have killed him with his bare hands and not raised a sweat doing it. I'd seen him at night, pulling himself up on the bars, standing on his hands, keeping himself strong as if there might be giants to kill in the morning.

The guard turned my way. "Slut!" *Crash!*

I wished I had the strength to keep quite still as the club thumped the bars right by my head, but the three hundred and fifty-odd days had taken their toll, and I couldn't help wincing. Slammer didn't move on to the cell next door as usual. He stopped on the other side of the bars, squinting through at me. Pig.

"Got something to tell you, Slut." His voice was a confidential murmur now; it made my skin crawl.

Slammer liked playing games. He was always teasing the men with talk of messages from home, or hinting at opportunities for getting out. He was a liar. They all were.

"Something you won't like," he said.

"If I won't like it, why would I want to hear it?"

"Oh, you'll want to hear this." He put his face right next to the bars, so close I could smell his foul breath. Not that it made much difference; the whole place stank of unwashed bodies and overflowing latrine buckets and plain despair. "It's about tomorrow."

"If you're here to tell me that tomorrow's the midsummer council, don't trouble yourself. I've been waiting for this since the day I was thrown into this festering dump."

"Ah," said Slammer in a voice I liked even less than the previous one. "That's just it."

Meaning, I could tell, exactly the opposite. "What are you talking about?"

"Now you're interested."

"What do you mean, *that's just it*?"

"What'll you give me if I tell you?"

"This," I said, and spat in his face. He was asking for it.

"Euch!" He wiped a sleeve across his cheek. "Filthy whore!"

Filthy was right; but not the other. I'd never given myself willingly in here, and I'd never been paid for the privilege. The guards had taken what they wanted in those first days, when I'd still been fresh; when I'd looked and felt and smelled like a woman. They didn't bother me now. None of them was desperate enough to want the rank, skinny, lice-ridden creature I'd become. Which meant I had nothing at all to offer Slammer in return for whatever scrap of information he was teasing me with.

"That's the last time you'll spit at me, Slut!" hissed Slammer.

"You're right for once, since I'll be out of this place tomorrow."

He smiled, but his eyes stayed cold. "Uh-huh." The way he said it meant I was wrong. But I wasn't. I'd been told my name was on the list. The law said a chieftain couldn't keep prisoners in custody more than a year without hearing their cases. And with all the chieftains of Laigin here, even a wretch like Mathuin, who didn't deserve the title of chieftain, would abide by the rules.

"You'll be out, all right," Slammer said. "But not the way you think."

Oh, he was enjoying this, whatever it was. My mouth went dry. Over in the cell opposite, Grim had fallen silent. I couldn't see him now; Slammer's bulk took up all my space. I forced myself to keep quiet. I wouldn't give him the satisfaction of hearing me beg.

"You must have really got up Mathuin's nose," he said. "What did you do to make him so angry?" Perhaps knowing he wouldn't get an answer, Slammer went right on. "Overheard a little exchange. Someone wants you out of the way *before* the hearing, not after."

"Out of the way?"

"Someone wants to make sure your case never goes before the council. First thing in the morning, you're to be disposed of. Quick, quiet, final. Name crossed off the list.

No need to bother the chieftains with any of it." He was scrutinizing me between the bars, waiting for me to weep, collapse, scream defiance.

"Why have you told me this?" A lie. A trick. He was full of them. I willed my heart to slow down, but it was hopping all over the place like a creature in a trap.

"What, you'd sooner not know until I drag you out there in the morning and someone gives you a nasty surprise? Little knife in the heart, pair of thumbs to the throat?"

"You're lying."

"Better say your prayers, Slut." He moved off along the row. "Poxy!" *Smash!* "Strangler!" *Crash!* "Frog Spawn!" *Slam!*

Across the walkway, Grim was standing at the front of his cell, big hands wrapped around the bars.

"What are you looking at?" I snarled, turning away before my face could show him anything. The three hundred and fifty-odd marks stared back at me from the wall, mocking me. Not a count to freedom and justice after all; only a count to a swift and violent end. Because, deep down, I knew this must be true. Slammer didn't have the imagination to play a trick like this.

"Lady?"

"Shut your mouth, Grim! I never want to hear your wretched voice again!" I sank down on the straw pallet with its teeming population of insects. Even these fleas would live longer than me. I wished I could find that amusing. Instead, the anger built and built, as if the swarm of crawling things was inside me, breeding and multiplying and spreading out into every corner of my body until I was ready to burst. How could this be? I'd held out here for one reason and one reason only. I'd endured all those poxy days and wretched, vermin-infested nights, I'd listened to that idiot Grim mumbling away, I'd seen and heard enough to give me a lifetime of nightmares. And I'd stayed alive. I'd held on to one thing: the knowledge that eventually I'd get my day to be heard. Midsummer. The council. It was the law. Curse it! I'd done it all for this day, this one day! They couldn't take it away!

The crawling things broke out all at once. From a distance, detached, I watched myself hurling objects around the cell, heard myself shouting invective, felt myself hitting my head on the wall, slamming my shoulder into the bars, ripping at my hair, my mouth stretched in a big ugly square of hatred. Felt the tears and snot and blood dribbling down my face, felt the filth and shame and utter pointlessness of it all, knew, finally, what it was that drove so many in here to cut and maim and, eventually, make an end of themselves. "Slammer, you liar!" I screamed. "You're full of shit! It's not true, it can't be! Come back here and say it again, go on, I dare you! Filthy vermin! Rancid scum!"

It was catching, this kind of thing. Pretty soon everyone in the cells was shouting along with me, half of them yelling at Slammer and the other guards and the unfairness of everything, the rest abusing me for disturbing them, though there wasn't much to disturb in here. Crashes and thumps told me I wasn't the only one throwing things.

All the while, there was Grim, standing up against his own bars, silent and still, watching me.

"What are you staring at, dimwit?" I wiped a sleeve across my face. "Didn't you hear me? Mind your own business!"

He retreated to the back of his cell, not because of anything I had said, but because down at the end of the walkway the door had crashed open again and the guards were coming through at a run. It was the usual when we got noisy: buckets of cold water hurled in to drench us. If that didn't work, someone would be dragged out and made an example of, and this time around that person would have to be me. Not that a beating made any difference. Not if Slammer had been telling the truth.

I got a bucket of slops. There was a bit of cursing from the others, but everyone stopped yelling, not wanting worse. The guards left, taking their empty buckets with them, and there I was, dripping, stinking, bruised and bleeding from my own efforts, with the buzzing insects of my fury still swarming inside me. The cell was a mess, and with wretched Grim over there, only a few paces away, there was nowhere to hide. Nowhere I could curl up in a ball with the blankets over my head and cry. Nowhere I could give way to the terror of knowing that in the morning I would die, and Mathuin would be alive and going about his daily business, free to do to other folk's families what he had done to mine. I would die with my loved ones unavenged.

I scrabbled on the floor, searching among the things I'd hurled everywhere, and my fingers closed around the rusty nail. Those marks on the wall were mocking me; they were making a liar of me. I hated the story they told. I loathed the failure they showed me to be. Weak. Pathetic. A vow breaker. A loser. With the nail clutched in my fist I scratched between them, around them, over them, making the orderly groups of five, four vertical, one linking horizontal, into a chaotic mess of scribble. What was the point in hope when someone always snatched it away? Why bother telling the truth if nobody would listen? What use was going on when nobody cared if you lived or died?

I waited for death. Thought how odd human nature was. All paths were barred, all doors closed. There was no escaping what was coming. And yet, when the guard known as Tiny—a very tall man—brought around the lumpy gray swill that passed for food in this place, I took my bowl and ate. We were always hungry. One or two of the men caught rats sometimes and chewed them raw. I'd never had the stomach for that, though Strangler, in the cell next to mine, always offered me a share. In the early days we used to talk about food a lot; imagine the first meal we'd have when they let us out. Fresh fish cooked over a campfire. Muttonfat porridge. Roast duck with walnut stuffing. Carrot and parsnip mashed with butter. For me it was a chunk of bread and cheese or a crisp new apple. When I thought of that first bite my belly ached and so did my heart. Then I'd got beaten down and worn out, like an old mattress with the stuffing gone to nothing, and I didn't care anymore. Same with the others; we were grateful for the swill, and thankful that Tiny didn't rattle our cages and scream at us. So, even when I was looking death in the eye, so to speak, I ate. Across the walkway, Grim was on his pallet, scooping up his own share and trying to watch me and avoid my eye at the same time.

The long day passed as they always did. Grim muttered to himself on and off, making no sense at all. Frog Spawn went through his list of all those who had offended him, and what he planned to do to them when he got out. It was a long list and we all knew it intimately, since he recited it every day. The others were quiet, though Poxy did ask me at one point if I was all right, and I snarled, "What do you think?" making it clear I didn't want an answer.

I sat on the floor, trying out the pose Grim seemed to find most comforting when under threat, head on knees, arms around legs, eyes squeezed shut. The day before you died was the longest, slowest day ever. It gave you more time than you could possibly want to contemplate all the things you'd got wrong, the chances you'd missed, the errors you'd made. It was long enough to convince the most hopeful person that there was no point in anything. If only this ... if only that ... if only I had my chance, my one chance to be heard ...

Another round of swill told us it was getting on for nighttime; a person wouldn't know from the windows, which were kept shuttered. It was a long time since they'd last let us out into the courtyard. Maybe Mathuin's men didn't know folk could die from lack of sunshine. Our only light came from a lantern down the end of the walkway.

Frog Spawn's ravings slowed, then stopped as he fell asleep.

"Hey, Slut!" called Strangler. "Place won't be the same without you!"

"Our lovely lady," put in Poxy, mostly mocking, a little bit serious. "We'll miss you."

"Don't let the vermin take you without a fight, Slut," came the voice of Dribbles from down the far end. "Give 'em your best, tooth and nail."

"When I want your advice," I said, "I'll ask for it."

"Wake us up when they come for you," said Strangler. "We'll give you a proper send-off. Worth a bucket or two of slops."

Grim wasn't saying anything, just sitting there gazing across at me, a big lump of a man with a filthy mane of hair, a bristling beard and sad eyes.

"Stop looking at me," I muttered, wondering how I was going to get through the night without going as crazy as Frog Spawn. If there was nothing I could do about this, why was my mind teeming with all the bad memories, all the wrongs I hadn't managed to put right? Why was the hate, the bitterness, the will for vengeance still burning in me, deep down, when the last hope was gone?

Finally they all slept; all but Grim and me. The lantern burned low. Soon we'd be in darkness.

"Lady?"

"What?"

"Maybe you can ..."

"Maybe I can what? Fly through stone walls? Charm the guards with my feminine wiles and make a miraculous escape? Wave a wand and turn them all into toads?"

He was silent.

"I can't fix this, Grim. I wish I had a magic charm to set the world to rights. To see evil-doers punished and good men rewarded. To see the innocent protected and the guilty judged. But it doesn't work that way." I looked across at him hunched on his pallet. "I hope you survive," I said, finding that I meant it. "I hope you don't have to wait too long for ... whatever comes next." I vowed to myself that when the end came I would be strong. No pleading; no tears; no cries for mercy. I would not give them the satisfaction. "You should try to sleep," I said.

Another silence, then Grim spoke. "I'll wait up. If that's all right."

"Suit yourself."

Time passed. If I'd had even a skerrick of faith in gods of one persuasion or another, I'd have prayed to them to make a lie of Slammer's words, or if that wasn't possible, at least to give someone else the chance to do what death would prevent me from doing. Never mind my own so-called crime and the need to prove my innocence. Mathuin must be brought to account. He must be stopped. He must be made to pay.

But I did not believe in gods, not anymore, and there was nobody else. When I died, my vengeance would die with me. There was no justice in the world.

Maybe I could use the rusty nail to slit my wrists. Better to make an end of myself than let Slammer or one of the others butcher me like a pig for the table. More dignity in it this way. But no; I'd blunted the nail with my wild scratching, and it wouldn't even break the skin. I contemplated sticking it in my eye. But that wouldn't be final enough, and I doubted I had the resolve anyway. I could smash my head against the bars, harder than before, but I'd probably only knock myself senseless and come to just in time for that little knife Slammer had mentioned. Hanging was too slow. By the time I'd ripped up my skirt and made a noose, then managed to tie it high enough, Grim would have made enough racket to fetch whichever guard was sleeping outside the door down the end. Which made no sense, when you thought about it; rush in to stop a person killing herself, so you could do the job for her in a scant—what—six hours or so?

"How long till dawn, do you think?" I murmured.

"A while yet." Grim's voice was held quiet, too, so as not to wake the others. In this place, good sleep was a gift not to be taken lightly. He muttered something else.

"What?"

"I'd go in your place, if I could."

I hadn't thought the big man had it in him to surprise me, but I'd been wrong. "That's just stupid," I said. "Of course you wouldn't. All men are liars, and you're no better than the rest of them."

A silence, then. After a while he said, "I would, Lady. The way I see it, your life's worth something. Mine'll never amount to much."

"Bollocks. My life, the one I had, is gone. Even if I walked out of here right now, a free woman, it would still be gone. There was one thing I wanted: justice." Sounded good; wasn't the whole truth. "Two things. Justice and vengeance. I don't mind dying so much. My life's a poorer thing than you imagine. But I do mind dying with that man unpunished. That fills me up with fury."

"Lord Mathuin?" Grim's voice was not much more than a breath, and in that moment the lantern flickered and went out, plunging us into darkness.

"One more day. Was that too much to ask, one poxy day?"

This time the silence stretched out so long I wondered if he had fallen asleep. But then his voice came again.

"How will I . . ." A long pause. "I don't know how I'll . . ."

"How you'll what?"

No reply.

"You don't know how you'll what, Grim?"

"Nothing. Forget it."

The night wore on, and in the cells it was quiet. Was it getting close to morning out there, or was I only imagining that? At a certain point I began to shiver and found I couldn't stop, even when I curled up on the pallet with the blanket wrapped around me, a grub in a meager cocoon. The shaking was deep down, as if frost was creeping into my bones. My teeth chattered; my joints ached like an old woman's. My good intentions, of standing up bravely before they did whatever they were going to do to me, vanished away in the face of my wretched, trembling body. Maybe, when a person was truly terrified, mortally afraid, there was no hiding it, not even for the best dissembler in all Erin. "Hey, Grim!" I forced the words out. "Talk to me about something warm, will you?"

"Big woolen blanket," Grim said straightaway. "Flame red in color. Wrapping you up from head to toe, with only your face showing. Roaring fire, throw on a pinecone or two for the smell. Bowl of barley broth. Mulled ale with spices. Curl your hands around the cup, feel the warm in your bones." A pause. "Any better?" His voice sounded odd.

"Yes," I lied. "Keep it up."

"Out of doors," Grim said. "Big field of barley all ripe and golden, sun shining down, yellow flowers in the grass. You go down to paddle in the stream, and the water's like a warm bath. Ducks swimming by with little ones. A dog running about. Sky as blue as—as—"

"Forget-me-nots," I said. "Grim, are you all right?"

"Fine," he mumbled. "All out of words now."

A sudden rattling at the door down the end. If I'd been cold before, now I was frozen. They were here. Already, they'd come for me.

"Wake up the others. That's what they said."

"No, Grim. Let them sleep."

The door creaked open, as if someone was trying not to make too much noise. The light that came through was not the light of day, but the glow of a lantern. Out there it must still be nighttime. They were robbing me, not only of mid-summer day and the council but of half the night before as well. Typical of this piss hole and the foul apologies for the men who ran it.

Slammer was at the bars. I stood by my pallet, the blanket around me, trying to breathe.

"You got a visitor."

"A what?" How many stupid tricks could he inflict on me before this was all over?

"A visitor. Make yourself tidy, and be quick about it."

I was dreaming. Nobody had visitors in here, and especially not me. Who was there to come? Unless it was Mathuin wanting to gloat, and he'd hardly do that at a time when all sensible folk were in their beds fast asleep.

Slammer was unfastening the door of my cell; swinging it open. "Hurry up," he said. "Haven't got all night."

A lie. It had to be. The only reason they'd let me out of here was so they could kill me without anyone finding out, or at least anyone that mattered. Nighttime would make that easier. I'd be neatly buried in some corner before the sun was even thinking about rising.

"Slammer." Grim spoke in a tone I had never heard before; it sent a chill right through me. "You're top of my list. When I get out of here, I'll hunt you down, I swear it. Before I'm done with you, you'll be in such little pieces nobody will know you were ever a man."

"Hah!" Slammer was scornful. "When you get out of here? By that time you'll be an old man, Bonehead, a dotard dribbling into your beard."

"Shut up!" mumbled a sleepy voice from farther along the cells.

Slammer seized me by the arm and hauled me out of my cell, then along the walkway beside him, blanket and all. There was nobody at the guard post and the door was ajar. We were going outside. Out into the open air, under the night sky.

"Get a move on," Slammer said.

I snatched a glance at the moon and stars as he hustled me across the courtyard. The open space made me dizzy. I sucked in a breath of air, but all I could smell was my own filthy body. No sign of the other guards; no sign of an executioner. Maybe Slammer had requested the privilege of doing it all by himself. He was pushing me ahead of him now, into some kind of outhouse—I had a sudden image of myself being hauled up on a rope like a pig for the slaughter—and then there was the bright light of two lamps, and a man sitting at a table looking at me, and the shock of realizing that maybe Slammer had been telling the truth.

"Thank you," the man said, rising to his feet. "Leave us now."

"Woman's a miscreant," Slammer protested. "Not safe—"

"Nonetheless."

"Against the rules," Slammer muttered.

The man—long-legged, dressed in a fine hooded cloak—suddenly had a little jingling bag in his hand. He counted out some coins. "I doubt that I'll be in any danger," he said, "but you're welcome to stay just outside the door. We'll call you when we're done here." The bag was put away, still jingling, and Slammer went out and closed the door behind him.

"Sit down, please," said my visitor, as if we were a pair of high-born folk meeting for a little chat.

I sat down on a bench; I was still shivering. The tall man seated himself opposite me and slipped back his hood. This was a person of striking beauty, and almost certainly fey or half-fey. I had seen enough of his kind, in my old life of long ago, to recognize the signs: the widely spaced eyes, the broad brow, the proud, chiseled features. His manner suggested privilege, certainly, but it was lacking in the arrogance of men like Mathuin of Laois. Facing him across the table, I was sharply aware of my lice-ridden, scabby body in its ragged apology for clothing. What in Morrigan's name was this elegant creature doing here? He could hardly be my executioner.

"You don't remember me, do you?" he asked, lifting his brows as if at some private joke.

So he was going to play games too. I had never seen him in my life before. "I don't know you, and I don't know why you're here." After a moment, because he had not called me Slut, I added, "My lord."

The stranger sat there examining me for a while. I made sure I looked him in the eye. If I was pathetic and wretched, draggled and filthy, that was not from any fault of mine. I was damned if I'd leave this place looking beaten, even if that was the way I felt.

"Your case was up to be heard today, yes?"

I managed a jerky nod. *Was.* So he knew. "The guard told me that plan's been changed."

"Did he tell you the new plan?"

"A quick and covert disposal at dawn. No due process, no hearing, no case." What business was it of his? "Are you going to tell me who you are?" I blurted out. "Did Mathuin send you?" Unlikely; a fey nobleman would hardly act as messenger boy for a human leader.

"I have a proposition for you," the man said. "If a name will help you trust me, I will give it. I am Conmael."

It meant absolutely nothing. I couldn't for the life of me imagine why the fellow would have any interest in what happened to me. As for offering my own name, I'd had one when they'd locked me up, and another one before that, but I wasn't going to share either with a complete stranger. "What proposition?" Under the circumstances, only one kind of proposition was of any interest, and that was one that would see me survive the dawn and stand up before the council as I'd expected. How this Conmael would achieve such a thing, and why he'd bother, was quite beyond me. Lies, all lies—what else could this be? "I'm growing weary of tricks," I said. "These days, I lose my temper quickly."

Conmael smiled. He folded his hands on the table before him. His fingers were long and graceful; he wore a number of silver rings. "It is no trick," he said. "Nor is it an unconditional offer of freedom. But you can leave this place safely, no longer in fear for your life, provided you agree to my terms."

Despite everything, my heart leaped at the word *freedom.* I clamped down the sudden elation. He wanted something from me, no doubt of that. I couldn't imagine what it might be, since I had nothing at all to offer. The whole thing was deeply suspect. I might be exchanging my present hell on earth for something even worse. *But you'd be alive,* said a little voice inside me. "Terms. What terms?"

"You had a calling before ill luck visited you. A profession, a direction in life. Yes?"

If he thought I was going to talk about the time before, he was wrong. That was past, over, forgotten. All that remained was Mathuin, and vengeance.

"You have certain talents by which you can provide for yourself and do good in the community."

"Had. Not have. That time's over. That woman's gone."

"If you were free now, this moment, what would you do?"

"Why would I tell you that? You could be anyone. You could be in Mathuin's pay."

"I am in no man's pay. Answer my question, please."

"I'd do what I thought I'd be doing until the guard kindly brought me the news that my execution was imminent. I'd stand up before the midsummer council. Explain what it was that got me locked up. Tell them what Mathuin does. Tell the story of the young woman who fell pregnant with his child when he took her by force, and how her husband abandoned her when he found out, and how she asked me to help her get rid of the child. How I spoke out publicly against Mathuin, and found that there were a dozen other women whom he'd treated in the same way. How he locked me up for smearing his name." Mathuin should be brought to account for his behavior, most certainly. But it was not this wrong that burned in me, crying out for vengeance. It was a far older evil. I would not tell of that. When the chieftain of Laois had imprisoned me, he had not known who I was. I'd planned to tell him when I spoke out before the council. "I want that man exposed for what he truly is. I want him punished. Mathuin is not fit to be chieftain."

"And afterward?"

"What do you mean?"

"After you expose the chieftain of Laois as an evildoer and have him removed from his position of power, what then?"

"Don't mock me!"

"Answer the question, please. Dawn is fast approaching."

"Then nothing. All that matters is . . ."

"Vengeance?" Conmael's voice was very quiet. "This is not simply a case of standing up for those women, is it? It's more, far more. It's a burning need to right a personal wrong. An old wrong."

I stared at him, and he gazed back, eyes blue as deep water, handsome features perfectly composed. "How can you know all this? Who are you?"

"A friend. Someone who would rather not see you destroy yourself."

"Destroy *myself*? It's Mathuin who's doing the destroying."

"If you want me to help you, you must set your need for vengeance aside."

"Then the answer is no." If I could not make an end to Mathuin's ill-doing, what point was there in anything?

Conmael was silent for a little. Then he said, "Life is a precious gift. It seems you set a low value on yours. Consider what you could do with this opportunity. You could help people. Free them from pain and suffering. You could heal your own wounds."

"I'm not after personal redemption. I want justice. I want that man to admit to his misdeeds. I want him to pay the price."

"Refuse my offer, and you'll be the one paying the price."

"What do you want from me?" My temper was hanging on a fast-fraying thread. "Get to the point!"

"Ah, so you will hear my terms, then?"

"I'd be stupid not to." Letting him set out his conditions, whatever they were, would at least keep me out of the cells a bit longer. Was that the first trace of dawn light coming in around the edges of the door?

"Very well. I'm offering you a chance to be safely out of here before they come for you. You'd leave the district and travel north to Dalriada. There'd be help along the way, and a place to stay when you got there. After that, you'd need to earn a living doing what you did before. There's always a need for skilled healers."

"Travel north. When?"

"Straightaway."

As I made to speak again, to say I couldn't go anywhere because I had to appear at the council, Conmael gestured me to be quiet. "There are three conditions you must agree to meet before I grant you this opportunity. Firstly, the considerable skill you possess must be used only for good. You will not let bitterness or anger draw you down the darker ways of your craft. Secondly, if anyone asks for your help, you will give it willingly. I do not mean solely those who come to you for assistance with their ailments, but anyone at all who seeks your aid."

"And thirdly?" It occurred to me that I could be as good a liar as anyone. What was to stop me from agreeing now, and once I was out of here, doing whatever I pleased? I might yet live beyond dawn and see Mathuin brought down before nightfall. My heart began to race.

"Thirdly, you will not seek vengeance. You will remain in Dalriada and stay away from Mathuin of Laois."

That, I could not do. But I bit back the *no* that sprang to my lips. "Is there a period of time attached to this ridiculous proposition?"

Conmael gave a cool smile. "Seven years," he said. "That is the term for all three conditions."

I opened my mouth to say yes, but he got in first.

"You understand what I am, I believe. Although you may not always see me, I will be watching. You will not break the terms without my knowledge. Each time you do so, one further year will be added to the seven."

"*What?*" Morrigan's curse, I'd be lucky if I managed seven days, let alone seven years! Walk away and leave Mathuin behind me, his crimes not only unpunished but not even reported? Agree to every single request for help? As for using my gifts for good, all the good had been beaten out of me long ago. My spirit was as stained and foul as my reeking, vermin-ridden body. But then, what did it matter if I was bound to his stupid plan for my whole life, provided I saw Mathuin brought to justice first?

"Mathuin has done ill deeds," Conmael said. "He's also a powerful chieftain who enjoys the support of many fellow leaders. You are a prisoner, without family, without resources, with no home to go to and no friends to help you. Even if you did stand up at the council, even if you did make these accusations before the assembled chieftains, who would take your word against Mathuin's? All you would achieve is your own destruction. So let us set a limit on the number of times you may break the rules. Five, I think."

"Or what happens?"

"Or you find yourself back here, filthy, worn down, defeated, with the executioner knocking on your door. And this time, no reprieve."

I gaped at him. "Are you telling me you can turn back time?" He was fey, no doubt of that, and the fey had powerful magic. I had seen it, long ago. But this—the fellow must be out of his mind.

Conmael's gaze was wintry. "Try to exact vengeance now, and you will surely fail. You are no fool; in your heart, you know that is simple truth. Exercise patience and self-control for the period I have set out, and you may have some small chance of success later. My proposal is your only way forward. It would be a mistake to believe I cannot, or will not, do exactly what I have told you."

"You're proposing that instead of being Mathuin's prisoner I should be yours."

Conmael rose to his feet. "That comment shows a willful misunderstanding of the situation. I thought I'd made myself quite clear. I'm offering a home, safety, an opportunity to do some good. I'm giving you the chance to remake your life. You'd be the first to say what a wretched, broken thing it has become."

I found myself unable to speak. Conmael moved toward the door. Almost dawn. He put his hand on the latch.

"Wait!" My mouth was dry. "Supposing I agree to this and stick to the conditions, what happens after seven years?"

He turned his head toward me. His face was grave. "Then you are your own woman again, and free to make your own choices." He opened the door, and there was Slammer, waiting. "We're done here," Conmael said, and before I could get another word out, he had stepped past the guard and was gone from view.

"Wait!" I called. "Yes! I say yes!" I rushed out the door and into the immovable form of Slammer.

But there was no reply; only the plangent note of a bird as it flew across the brightening sky: *Fool! Fool!*

Conmael was nowhere to be seen.

2

GRIM

She goes out and the door shuts behind her. Gone. Not coming back. Not ever. Don't rightly know how I'll go on without her. Don't know how I can keep on breathing through the dark. As long as she's here I'm still alive, deep down. As long as she's here I've got a job to do. Someone to look after.

When they kill her, I'll know. I'll feel it like she does, the moment, the snuffing out. After that it'll be dark all the time. Nobody to hear me. Nobody to see me. When she's gone, I'm gone.

"Shut it, Bonehead!" someone yells from down the other end. Didn't think I'd been making any noise. Put my head down on my knees, stuff a fold of blanket up against my mouth, push the words in. Squeeze my eyes tight. Stupid. You can't see the sunrise in here anyway. But I do see it: the sky getting brighter, the guards holding her still, the knife flashing in the sun. She'll be brave. She's been brave from the day they threw her in here. Standing up for me. Talking me through the dark. Snappish and foulmouthed, but alive. So much alive. Like a flame that never goes out, no matter what. Looking over at me and seeing, not a big lump of nothing, but a man.

Door creaks. Keys jingle. I start the words to shut the bad things out.

"Get a move on, Slut!" Slammer snarls. Then, "For the love of all the gods, Bonehead, knock it off!" And, a wonder, I hear her steps along the walkway and the clang of her cell door. She's back.

Slammer leaves her. I wait till the door down at the end shuts behind him. Lift my head; try to keep my voice steady. "Lady? You there?"

"Shut up, Grim."

"Who was it? Did they . . . ?"

"Are you deaf? I said shut up."

I do as she says. When that door opened, light came in. I heard a bird singing. It's got to be nearly dawn. Why did Slammer bring her back? I want to ask, *Does this mean they're not going to kill you after all?* But they are, or she wouldn't be hunched up in there, trying not to cry. I can't see her, but I know that's what she's doing. Who came to visit her? She always said there was nobody. Maybe that's a lie. Maybe there's a husband, a lover, a sad mother or father out there. "Lady?"

She sighs, a little sound in the dark. "I was offered a lifeline and I was too stupid to take it. Too slow, too cautious. Missed my opportunity. Nothing's changed. The sun will come up, just the same as it does every day, and what happens will happen." She goes quiet for a bit, then says, "If you ever get a second chance, Grim, grab it with both hands. Don't hesitate for a moment, you hear me?"

"If I could hold a tune," I tell her, "I'd sing you a song."

"Spare me."

"What song would you want, if I could?"

"Believe me, I wouldn't."

"If it was me going out there, I wouldn't want one of those trumpet-call, flag-waving things. I'd want a lullaby. I'd want to be sung to sleep quietly."

"What are you trying to do, Grim, turn me into a blubbering heap? Don't sing, I beg you. I don't want a march, I don't want a ballad, I don't want a dance. And I really, really don't want a lullaby."

"Good," I say. Funny; my effort to stop her crying has left my own face all tears. "Because I'm the worst singer you ever heard. Even Strangler's a better musician than me."

"Not crying, are you, Grim? A big bad fellow like you?"

"Me? Nah."

I'm just saying this when there's a crash like the end of the world, and all of a sudden I'm lying on my back with everything coming down around me, and somewhere above me, above the heap of rubbish that's weighing down my chest and legs and half covering my face, there's open sky. Everyone's shouting.

Takes me a while to get myself out; for a bit I think my leg might be broken, but no, I can move all right. Place is all chunks of stone, bent bars, splintered wood, like a huge storm has hit it, but there's no rain coming down, no wind roaring over, just that sky calling me to climb up and get out, quick, before the guards come. Scrabbling noises tell me the others have the same idea, and now here's Poxy clambering toward me across a mountain of rubble, his face all over dust, and after him comes Dribbles, making sobbing noises as if he can't catch his breath.

The bars of my cell are bent all out of shape; I squeeze between them into what's left of the walkway, and there's Lady, white as a ghost, muttering something about not hearing her say yes. Making no sense at all. Need to get her out, quick. Where the guard post door was there's a big heap of stones. Roof's broken open up above my cell. From behind us, down the other end, comes an awful muffled screaming. I look that way and all I see is a tangle of bars and stones; the whole place has come down on Strangler, Frog Spawn and the others. Not dead, though. At least one of them's not dead.

I grab Lady's hand and pull her over to the spot where the roof's open. "I'll boost you up," I tell her. "Crawl across the roof and climb down on the western side. Then run. There's woods not far off." As I'm bending to get hold of her so I can lift her up to the gap, I see it: Slammer's hand sticking out from under all those stones, with a knife in it.

"But—" Lady's protesting. I make sure she's got hold of the edge of the broken roof, then push her up so she can scramble out.

"Shut up and run! Don't look back!"

She disappears through the hole. I'm not hearing much from outside, no shouting, no hammering, nobody rushing to the rescue, and that's mostly a good thing; if they're slow to come, she'll be in the woods before anyone spots her. Away. Safe. I'll have done my job.

Poxy doesn't look too badly hurt. I boost him up high enough to haul himself out. He's hefty, even on the gruel diet. Then I lift up the bundle of skin and bone that's Dribbles, and Poxy leans down through the hole to grab his arms and pull while I push from underneath. Can't see Dribbles getting far, out there.

"Look after him, eh?" I say to Poxy, but the boys aren't talking; just getting up through the hole's been enough of a stretch. They're out of sight, and I head back to the other end, where everything's come down in one god-awful mess.

It's Strangler doing the screaming. No sound at all from the others. It'll take me too long to dig them out, and if they're still alive, they won't be in a fit state to run anywhere. But I can't leave Strangler without at least trying.

Big block of stone leaning up against his cell; can't see him, only the bars broken and sticking out, and a pile of rubble behind.

"Strangler! Coming to get you! Try to keep quiet, will you? Don't want the guards in here."

"Bonehead! Shit, this hurts!" Strangler's voice is all pain.

I try to shift the big block, which is nearly as tall as I am and too wide to get my arms around. I move it a whisker and a pile of stuff falls on me. I look up and see that if I shift this any farther, the other half of the roof's going to come down and Strangler and me will be flat as griddle cakes. Can I tunnel in below maybe, slip him out like a ferret from its hole?

"Hang on, Strangler. Listen, can you move? Can you get down on the floor?"

He tries, it hurts, he starts to scream and bites it back.

"If you can get down low I might be able to pull you out under here. There's a gap, just small. But you always were a skinny runt of a man. Look, here, I'm sticking my arm through. Can you feel it?" This is taking too long. I can hear someone shouting out there. If the guards spot us going over the roof, they'll be onto us before we get a chance to run.

A hand touches mine. He's there, he's made it.

"Good man. Can you give me both hands? This is going to hurt a bit."

The gap's small. I'd get a child out easily, but a man's another matter. An injured man, even worse. There's a broken bar sticking out halfway through, and pieces of the stone wall balanced on one another like some kind of toy, all set to fall at a wrong touch. This could kill him.

"Got you. Deep breath, Strangler. I'll try to make it quick and clean."

He lets out an unearthly shriek as I haul him through. I'm going to hear that sound forever, in my nightmares. Then he's out, lying facedown beside me, his chest heaving. He curses me with every foul word he knows, which I take as a good sign.

"Got to get out," I tell him. "Up there. Now."

"Others," Strangler whispers. "Are they . . . ?"

"Some out already, some . . . gone." I jerk my head toward the wreckage of the other cells. "Come on, we've got to move."

"Shit. My back."

He can't walk. Whatever happened, it's hurt him too much to let him even stand for long. The roof's pretty high. Had planned to boost him up, same as the others, then jump for the edges and haul myself after him. Change of plan needed. People shouting outside now, and it's day. Something I haven't seen in a long while: blue sky.

"Just leave me the knife, Bonehead," says Strangler, eyeing Slammer's weapon, which I've stuck in my belt. "Go on, climb up, save yourself." And when I gape at him, he asks, "Your Lady get out all right?"

"Lady, Poxy, Dribbles," I tell him. "And now you and me. Don't argue, put your arm around my shoulders, here." I crouch down and lift him onto my back; he screams again. "Sorry, Strangler. No choice. Try to keep quiet, will you?"

"Give me the frigging knife."

If he thinks I'm going to let him kill himself right in front of me, he's got me all wrong. I head back toward the gap with Strangler draped over me like an outsized shawl. If he can hold on long enough, maybe I can do this. Block of stone in the middle; second block on top.

"What in the name of . . ." groans Strangler.

"Keep still and try not to fall off," I tell him; then I step up on the two blocks, with him still over my shoulders, and reach up toward the gap. Someone's trying to open the door now, and not having any luck; no surprise, since it's blocked by a heap of stones with a dead man underneath. I start to wonder what we'll find outside.

"Shit, Bonehead," Strangler protests, which is fair enough, since it's pretty certain I'll drop him when I jump.

"Hold on," I say, and reach up with both hands. Not quite high enough to get a grip on the edges, but not far off. I stand on tiptoes; I'm only an inch or two short.

"Bonehead!" someone hisses from above. The two of them are still there, Poxy and Dribbles, and Poxy's got a bit of rope, gods only know from where, but I'm not asking questions; I'm setting Strangler back down, tying a loop around his chest and praying hard. My heart's going crazy. Strangler's sobbing, begging me to stop trying to save his life.

"Now!" I call when the knot's done. The rope tightens; I boost Strangler up toward the hole. His screams cut through me. He can't hold on to anything—strength all gone—but we get him up and out, and I'm left in Mathuin's lockup with a bunch of dead men for company.

I don't wait. I jump, hook my elbows over the side of the gap and hang there, pretty sure a big chunk of roof will break off and crash down with me attached. I take a breath, tighten my belly, think of Lady out there on her own. I pull myself up. I'm on the roof, or what's left of it, with Strangler sprawled beside me. Poxy's disappearing off the western side. I didn't expect them to wait for me and they haven't. Strangler's face is a nasty shade of gray in the morning light. Feeling a bit the worse for wear myself.

Down below guards are milling around, but nobody's spotted us. They're all working on getting the door open. No sign of a storm. The sky's cloudless, the wind's only a breath. What's happened is freakish. When I give myself time to think about it, this is going to scare the shits out of me.

"Right," I murmur to Strangler. "Over that side, down the tree, then a sprint across farmland to the woods. I'll carry you. But you have to keep quiet." I remember the layout pretty well; I've thought about getting out a lot, down there in the dark. This place is outside the walls of Mathuin's fortress, which is up the hill behind us. And it's clear of the village. Nobody in a place like that wants a bunch of thieves and murderers a hop and a skip away from their little ones. Have to hope it's too early for sentries to be up on the fortress walls, ready to pick us off with a well-aimed arrow or two. "Not far. Then we'll get you some help."

"Hah!" wheezes Strangler. "Give us the knife, I'll help myself."

"Shut up. Here."

I get him up on my back again, then go crab-wise across the roof. I try to walk soft-footed but it sounds like there's a giant stomping around up here. The guards don't come. We struggle down the big oak tree and stagger away across the fields, where sheep and cows take a look at us, then go on grazing. Morrigan's curse, it's so open out here. Feel like a mouse or a shrew, creeping from one hidey-hole to the next with owls and hawks up there ready to swoop. Every shadow's a threat; every rustle in the grass is an enemy. Strangler goes quiet. He gets heavier and heavier. But we make it into the woods. We go deep in, where the oak roots are old and tangled and the leaves grow so thick it's all shadows. No sign of Lady. No sign of Poxy and Dribbles, either. Hope that means they all got away safe.

"All right?" I say to Strangler, who's lying prone beside me. "Sorry I had to hurt you; only way to get you out."

But Strangler doesn't answer, and when I take a look at him, I see that he's staring straight upward to the light coming through the leaves, and he's lying with his arms out and his hands open, like a child sleeping. Only he's not sleeping, he's dead.

3

ORAN

"You disappoint me," my mother said.

Such directness was typical of her. My father was more likely to show his opinion of me by lifting his brows and tightening his lips. This occurred, for instance, when I failed to show adequate enthusiasm for such activities as hunting, hawking, and combat practice. I had learned to acquit myself adequately at all three; I was no fool. A future king of Dalriada must be as capable at blood sports as he was at, say, strategic thinking.

My parents had never understood my passion for poetry, my love of lore, my fondness for observing birds and animals about their natural activities, and my corresponding distaste for the business of impaling them on arrows or skewering them with spears. They saw this as a weakness in me, an unfitness for the destiny that lay before me, a destiny that was mine whether I liked it or not, since, inadequate as I might be, I was the only son they had.

"At two-and-twenty, you might at the very least attempt to show some interest in the matter," Mother went on. "Your manner hints at something . . . not quite right. Something . . . amiss."

"With respect, Mother," I said, though my patience was wearing thin, this being a subject we had edged around many times in the past, "if you mean what I think you mean, you are in error. I understand the need to father an heir, and when the right woman comes along, I will marry and procreate as you wish. If you find fault with my demeanor, it is not because I hanker after some young man, Donagan for instance, but because the notion of a strategic marriage fills me with unease. The thought that so significant a matter could be decided on the basis of a formal letter from Father to some ruler in a distant kingdom, and that I might not see my bride in the flesh before she arrives for the betrothal . . . it feels deeply wrong to me." In the ancient tales, marriages made for purposes of power and alliance often went awry. The stories that stirred me were those of lovers who met by chance and knew at first sight that they were made for each other. A man like me might wait a lifetime for such a story.

"You speak like a green girl of thirteen, Oran, not a grown man. Sometimes I despair of you."

"I know, Mother."

"At eighteen, Lady Flidais is perhaps a little older than is quite ideal, but in view of her pedigree we can overlook that. And there are obvious advantages to your father of an alliance with Cadhan. His holdings may be small, but his connections are beyond reproach. I met Flidais once, when she was a child of six or seven; a charming, well-behaved little thing. Her father's letter suggests she has retained those qualities. Cadhan describes her as exceptionally comely, accomplished in the domestic arts and of a sweet and gentle temperament, which I must say sounds rather suited to your tastes, Oran."

"I have read the letter, Mother."

"So?"

I suppressed a sigh. "Such a missive is written for one purpose only, to persuade the recipient that the woman in question is a paragon of all the virtues and has a face and figure to rival those of ancient goddesses. It's hardly likely to say the girl is short and dumpy with pimples, and bone lazy to boot. Or that she doesn't much care for the idea of marrying a man whom she's never clapped eyes on. Even if that is the truth."

"There's a picture."

"So Father mentioned. Are you suggesting a picture cannot lie just as effectively as a letter?"

"Oran, you would madden the most patient of mothers! At least look at it."

She reached across the table and laid the little wooden oval in front of me. Since I could hardly screw my eyes shut like a three-year-old refusing to eat his mashed turnips, I looked.

The tiny painting had been executed with great skill. Such images frequently have something of a sameness, as if the artist can conjure only one face, and varies it with changes in the style of the hair, the clothing, the background. But the girl depicted here was very much herself. Her hair was worn loose, flowing down over her shoulders in waves as dark as a crow's wing. Her eyes were a deep blue and gazed directly from the portrait, giving me an uncanny sense that she could see me. The letter had said *sweet and gentle*; this heart-shaped face with its small, straight nose and not-quite-smiling mouth suggested the description might not, after all, be a lie. On the girl's lap was a tiny white dog, a delicate thing with spindly legs and large ears; she held it with some tenderness. The artist had chosen to show the two of them against a background of oak leaves.

"A pretty thing," observed my mother. I was not sure if she meant the portrait or the girl herself. I only knew that now that I held the painting in my hand I did not want to give it back to her. "You know, of course, that once you marry you'll have your own household; no new bride wants to be under the eye of her mother-in-law. You'll move to Winterfalls. That should be pleasing even to you."

I opened my mouth to say she should stop making assumptions, then shut it again. At some point I would have to give in. My parents were right: I did have to sire a son and heir, and at two-and-twenty I was past the age when a man was expected to get on with such things. What chance was there, really, that I would find the one woman who was my perfect complement, my other half, my long-dreamed-of true love? My mother had told me often enough that I had my head in the clouds. To be a dreamer at the age of ten was acceptable. At fifteen one might almost get away with it. In a man of two-and-twenty it was starting to verge on risible.

And this girl, this woman in the picture . . . There was something about her, something that went far beyond the obvious beauty, the tender pose, the artful execution of the image. Unless the artist was an exceptional dissembler, the subject of his work was a rare creature.

"All your father is asking," Mother said, evidently taking my silence for a mulish refusal to listen to her wisdom, "is that he may reply to Lord Cadhan's letter telling him you are interested."

"No," I said, rising to my feet. Before she could say anything I added, "I'll write the letter, and it won't be to Lord Cadhan, it will be to his daughter. As for being interested, I'll wait until she replies before I decide that."

I had the satisfaction of seeing my mother completely lost for words. I poured her a cup of mead from the jug on the table. Only after she had gulped down several mouthfuls did she find her voice again.

"Your father would have to read the letter. He would need to approve it."

"No. It will be for no eyes but hers."

"I see." Mother's face showed a peculiar blend of shock and hope.

"However, I have no objection to Father writing a covering letter to Lord Cadhan; I'll seal my own missive and give it to his scribe to enclose." I paused to draw breath; assessed that look on her face again and decided to press this rare advantage. "When Flidais's reply comes, we'll discuss the matter further. A condition of my agreeing to marry would be that I move to Winterfalls as soon as the decision is made. The hand-fasting would take place there." In my own home, on my own ground. Winterfalls, near Dreamer's Wood, was surrounded by forest and lake. It was a place of birds and creatures, peace and tranquillity. My heart began to race. My mind soared into a realm of dreams. This was foolish indeed; both letter and portrait were probably lies. Well, my letter would be all truth, and I'd see what Flidais made of that.

Two turnings of the moon passed before my father received Lord Cadhan's reply; spring was turning to summer. Enclosed was a sealed message bearing this inscription: *To Prince Oran of Dalriada. Personal and Private.* I took it away to my apartments unopened. My heart was beating with such violence I wondered what would happen if these negotiations did bear fruit, and I came face-to-face with the woman of the portrait. I would, perhaps, drop dead from sheer excitement, proving to be the ultimate disappointment as a son.

Only once the door was closed and bolted behind me did I break the seal and read the words within.

I do not know how to address you, she wrote, *since we have never met. You have the advantage of a picture—I have seen the artist's rendition of my features, and I believe it to be true to life—but I know only that you are two-and-twenty years of age and in excellent health. I would have written a formal letter of the kind my father's scribe has taught me to construct, but that would be an inadequate response to the beautiful words you sent me. My mother wanted to open your sealed message. It was only the words* Personal *and* Private *that prevented her from doing so. As it was, she sat beside me while I read it, which did rather diminish the pleasure. Later, I took your letter out of doors and read it again in the shade of my favorite oak tree, with only my little dog Bramble for company. (There is a story to Bramble's name—don't you find there are stories everywhere if you look for them?— but I will save that for another time.)*

It is odd that my mother, who believes me old enough to travel far from home, marry an unknown prince and in time, perhaps not so very much time, bear his children, was concerned that a sealed letter might contain material shocking to my tender disposition! I assured her that your missive included nothing of the kind. It was, I said to her, full of courtesy and goodwill. I did not mention the poem. That is between you and me.

What you wrote was lovely. I read it over to Bramble several times and she agrees. I would like to write my own poem in return but I confess to feeling somewhat shy about it. Perhaps next time. Will you write to me again before a final decision is made about the marriage?

*I liked the description of Winterfalls. There is a
forest near here where I love to walk, just me and
my maid with Bramble. My little dog is very well
trained and knows not to bark or run about after the
wild creatures. Shy deer live there, and scampering
squirrels, and frogs in the hidden ponds. I think you
would like the place, Prince Oran. Perhaps
Winterfalls is something similar. I hope so.*

*My father is writing a reply to your father. From
what little he tells me, I gather we are at the stage of
"considering" the proposition. Do you sometimes
feel as I do, as if you were a commodity to be
traded? If my whole future were not in the balance,
that might make me laugh.*

I hope you will write again soon.

Flidais of Cloud Hill

Your letter warmed my heart, I wrote. *Please
take all the time you need to make up your mind.
My father is so delighted that I am at last prepared
to consider marriage that he will be easily persuaded
to wait a little before things are quite settled. I hasten
to assure you that I have no objection to the general
idea of being a husband and father; only that I have
read too many old tales, and they have made me
wary. I wanted to wait for the right woman. I wanted
to be quite sure each of us could make the other
perfectly happy, not only while we were young and
hale, but through all the years of our lives.*

*I believe that in you I may have found that
woman. I believe—you will think me foolish—I
knew it the moment I saw your picture. Too many
old tales, indeed. That is what my mother would
say. But I spoke to Donagan, who is my body
servant and friend, the brother I never had, and he
said I had been wise to wait. He reminded me that I
love wild creatures and am fascinated by their ways,
and suggested that trusting my instincts would serve
me well. So perhaps I am not so foolish.*

Should agreement be reached on our marriage, I

*understand I would ride to Cloud Hill for the
betrothal and stay on awhile. This, dear Flidais,
would allow you ample opportunity to show me
your forest with its scampering squirrels. I do not at
present have a dog of my own—my beloved old
hound, Grey, died last autumn, and thus far I have
not had the heart to replace him. Perhaps you would
allow me to share Bramble. If you do me the honor
of agreeing to be my wife, we might in time acquire
another small dog as companion for her. Were you
going to tell me Bramble's story?*

I will tell you a secret, she wrote. *Bramble is not
the kind of purebred dog people expect a lady like
me to own. I found her in the woods one day,
entangled in blackberry bushes, her poor skin
covered in bleeding scratches. She was crying most
piteously. It took me and my maid some
considerable time to extricate her. While we worked,
Bramble was so patient and good, despite her fear.
She knew that at last she had found friends in a
dark world. So she was rescued and given a new
name, and she has been my constant companion
ever since. You will laugh at me, but I have
wondered if Bramble came from the realm of the
fey. Sometimes her eyes take on a particular look, as
if she is gazing right out of our world and into a
place I cannot see. Do you believe what some folk
say, that the fey still walk the land of Erin, but only
show themselves when they choose? Or do you
think me foolish for giving credence to any such
idea? My maid says I am fanciful, but she likes it
when I tell her stories of those ancient times.*

*Oran, are you a tall man or short? Fat or thin?
Fair-haired or dark? These things weigh nothing in
the final decision, you understand. Only, I would
like to know.*

4

BLACKTHORN

One thing was certain: there'd be no sleeping in warm barns or begging crusts from local farmers until I was off Mathuin's land, and even then I'd have to find some way of cleaning myself up before I let anyone see me. These filthy, sodden tatters were all the clothes I possessed, and there was no concealing my matted, crawling locks and my bruised and stinking body. All very well for Conmael to say *Make your way to Dalriada*. Dalriada was far away, and even if I'd had so much as a paring knife or fishhook, I was too weak to do more than pick a berry or two from the bushes as I passed. I was the kind of vagrant who made folk hustle their children indoors and bolt the door behind them. Which I could understand, since if I'd been a respectable sort of person I'd have been doing exactly the same thing.

There was little doubt in my mind that what had happened was Conmael's doing. The sturdy-looking roof suddenly caving in on a fine morning without a breath of wind; the door conveniently blocked so the guards couldn't come rushing in; nobody stopping me as I clambered over the roof, climbed down, and crossed open ground to get to those woods—that had to be fey work. Conmael must have heard me calling after him, saying I wanted out after all. Or maybe he knew what I wanted without being told, just as he seemed to know a whole lot more about me than any stranger possibly could. It made me feel queasy. And now here I was, free at last, but bound by his poxy conditions unless I wanted to find myself right back in Mathuin's lockup, waiting for the executioner. Could he do that? After what had just happened, I had no wish to put it to the test.

The first night out saw me making camp—if you could call it that—under oaks, on rising ground. Midsummer, hah! It was freezing. Everything I had on was damp, including the blanket I'd had wrapped around me when Slammer and his cronies threw that bucket of slops to shut me up. I'd been drinking from streams, crouched like some feral creature, wary of capture, but all I'd found to eat were those berries, and they'd been dry and shriveled, not even good enough for sparrows and shrews. The idea of getting to Dalriada on my own was laughable. One more day like this and I'd be too weak to walk ten paces.

All I'd managed to do was find a hollow and hunker down in it with the clammy blanket over me. As the darkness deepened and the night birds started up a mournful chorus, I decided Conmael was nothing but a meddler. In the old tales, the fey were full of tricks. A curse on the man, I shouldn't have trusted him an inch. He'd taken me out of one hellhole to drop me right in another.

It was too cold to let myself sleep. The chill would carry me off before starvation got a grip. Grim would have solved the problem by performing his nightly exercises, pulling himself up on a branch of the oak or walking on his hands awhile. Even thinking about that made me tired. He'd used some of that strength to get me out; bade me run and not look back. But what about him? What about the rest of those poor sods?

A soft noise in the dark. I sat up, peering over the edge of my hollow. Had that been only a creature padding by, or had I caught the tread of a human foot? Earlier in the day I'd stopped on a rise, and when I'd looked back I'd seen men with dogs, searching along the road; men in Mathuin's colors. Morrigan's curse, I was shivering so hard my nest of foliage was trembling all around me.

No sound now, but light; somewhere not far away, someone was making a fire. The warm glow of it touched the mossy trunks of the oaks and turned the foliage to a rich tapestry: green silk, gold thread. The fire called me as a dryad calls a lovelorn shepherd or a mermaid a lonely fisherman. A wonderful smell came wafting my way: was that chicken soup? My mouth watered.

Now someone was approaching, not furtively but in measured fashion. "You can come out." Conmael's quiet, authoritative tone. "Unless, of course, you prefer to sit there and freeze to death."

No contest. I dragged my cramped limbs up to stand and hobbled out.

"Come this way," the fey man said, offering a supportive arm.

I did not ask whether the fire might draw pursuit after me. If Conmael could make the roof of Mathuin's prison cave in, I imagined he'd have no trouble casting some kind of invisibility charm over us for as long as he needed to. Who knew what he could do?

By the gods, the warmth of this little fire was good! And yes, there was a pot of soup warming on it, and a dry blanket that he passed me to wrap over my wet things, and another blanket, folded, to sit on. I sat, swathed, and thought how dangerous it was for a person to become so weak she might do almost anything for a fire and a full belly.

Conmael filled a cup from the pot and passed it to me. "Careful," he warned. "Don't drop it."

I willed my shaking hands to take control; lifted the cup to my lips; took a mouthful. Shut my eyes in utter bliss. I could almost understand those old stories in which folk exchanged their first-born child for a bowl of broth.

"And drink slowly," he said, "or you'll make yourself sick." Then, after a moment, "But I don't need to tell you that; you're a healer. And now you'll need a healer's name. I imagine you won't be wanting to use either of your old ones."

"You imagine right." This was the best meal I had had in my life. Ever. If that was because it was fey food, and if that meant drinking it changed me into a toad or whisked me off to another world, too bad. I was going to finish every drop and probably lick the cup clean afterward. Somewhere in the back of my mind was the question of names, and how he knew I had two, but right now it didn't seem to matter.

"There's bread," said Conmael. "Take just a little at first—here."

When he passed me the chunk of oaten bread, I had to blink back tears. In the lockup, when the men had dreamed of roast pork, sausages and plum pie, I had longed for fresh, honest bread.

"Thank you," I made myself say. The first bite transported me to that place Grim had described: barley fields in sunshine, yellow flowers, bare feet paddling in a stream. I had indeed become weak, to be thus overwhelmed by simple things. "Blackthorn," I said, trying to get control of myself. "That is the name I choose." It felt right; it had in it the idea of what I was now, walking under a shadow and all prickles.

"Mm-hm."

That was all he said until I had finished both soup and bread, and had warmed up sufficiently to stop shaking and begin yawning, the food and the fire conspiring to draw me toward sleep. Then my companion spoke again. "I have a bag here for you, with a change of clothing and some items for the journey: a knife, a flint, way-bread and so on. When you reach Winterfalls there will be other supplies ready. Not much; only sufficient to get you started. And you'll be wanting to bathe. My folk will bring warm water shortly, and will ensure that you have privacy. That is for tonight only, Blackthorn. From tomorrow you'll be relying on your own resources."

I understood he was not planning to stay, which was just as well if I was supposed to strip and wash here under the trees. Out of the myriad urgent questions, I chose what seemed the most important right now. "Winterfalls. I don't know the place—where and what is it?"

"Winterfalls is a holding in the northeast, near the coast of Dalriada. It's the residence of Prince Oran, only son of the Dalriadan king. Quite a young man, I understand, and establishing his own household for the first time. There's a sizable settlement there and many small farms. They don't have a local healer, so there'll be no shortage of work."

"Are you telling me I'll need to live in this settlement?"

Conmael smiled. "You loathe that notion so much, Blackthorn?"

"Let's just say it would add to the difficulty of keeping your conditions."

"I know you better than you realize," he said. "There is an old cottage some miles from Winterfalls settlement, on the edge of a wood. The local folk can walk or ride there quite easily; there's a path through Dreamer's Wood and another that skirts it. The place will be highly suitable for you, though it's run-down. You'll need to do some work on it. People can get to you if they need help, but you'll have plenty of time in your own company. There are the makings of a garden; the house was tenanted by another wise woman some years ago. You'll be able to gather wild herbs in the woods. And my folk are nearby."

"To keep an eye on me."

"To watch over you."

"And to slap another year on the sentence if I make even the tiniest error."

"You think my terms harsh. But you have received your life back in return. Besides, learning can be very harsh indeed. And long. You know that already."

"Conmael."

"Yes?"

"Did anyone else get out of that place? When you did what you did?"

When he did not answer straightaway, I wished I'd kept my stupid mouth shut. After a while he said, "My interest stretches only as far as yourself. What became of those incarcerated with you, I have no idea." He gave me a very direct look, then added, "I did not believe you could surprise me, Blackthorn, but you just did."

"What, because I asked after my wretched cellmates?" What if Grim had lifted me up to the light, waited until I was safely out, then fought an impossible battle, one man against ten, twenty, thirty of Mathuin's men-at-arms? The whole wretched bunch of them, Strangler, Frog Spawn and the rest, might now lie crushed beneath those stones. Conmael had made it happen and he didn't even seem to have thought about that. "For them, maybe death was a kindness," I muttered. An hour ago, before the fire and the soup, I would have believed my own words. Now, I was not quite so sure.

"I'll leave you." Conmael rose to his feet. "Enjoy your bath. It will be safe to sleep by the fire here. You will not see my people, but they will guard you." He did not wait for me to reply, but with a sweep of his grand cloak simply vanished.

Perhaps the bath had been there all along; if not, invisible hands had delivered it at some moment when my gaze was elsewhere. A wooden tub stood on the opposite side of the fire, steaming in the chill night air. Beside it, on a large flat leaf, was a handful of soft soap and a scrubbing brush. Nearby stood a neatly strapped pack that, on being opened, proved to hold the promised change of clothing—plain attire, of good make but unobtrusive—as well as a comb, a flint and a knife that would allow me to gut a fish, skin a rabbit, strike a spark and put up a defense against attackers. There was the wherewithal to catch the fish or trap the rabbit, and also a parcel of hard-baked way-bread, a water skin, and a little leather bag containing a moderate supply of coppers. Conmael had been thorough.

The bathwater was not going to get any warmer. Besides, if I delayed it might disappear as the giver had, the fey being fond of playing tricks. I did check the area first, in case Conmael had lied about this being private, but it seemed my only audience would be owls in the foliage above or night insects about their business—my naked flesh, foul though it currently was, would probably bring clouds of biting things. Another reason to get on with it.

Ahhh. No words could describe the first hot bath in more than a year. I soaked and scrubbed until the water was black with dirt and my skin was tingling. I washed my hair, but the matted locks were beyond combing out. At some point I'd have to take to them with the knife. Not now; I was so tired I risked cutting off an ear by mistake. I dried myself on the spare blanket, put on the clothes—oh, the pleasure of warm, dry wool against my skin—and threw my old ones into a heap. They'd have to be disposed of be-

fore I moved on. Had those men with the dogs been looking for me? Would Mathuin make a fresh attempt to silence
me? Or was I insignificant to him provided I stayed out of
his way?

If I stuck to my bargain with Conmael, those questions
would stay unanswered for seven years. Unless, that was,
someone tracked me down before I got to Winterfalls and
the safety of this cottage he'd spoken of. Conmael's invisible henchmen could hardly be planning to guard me all the
way there—hadn't he said I'd be relying on my own resources from tomorrow?

I dealt with the fire, spreading the ashes up over the
coals, hoping it would burn long and slow to keep me warm
until sunrise. Then I settled with the luxury of one thick
blanket underneath me and one on top, and a shawl around
my shoulders and under my head. Within the space of a
few breaths I was asleep.

I woke next morning to find the fire still glowing under its
ash blanket. Nothing else had been disturbed, but the bath-
tub was gone. Fortified by my night's rest, the good food and
the warmth, I concocted a meal of way-bread soaked in hot
water—Conmael had left me his cooking pot. I burned my
old clothing, then covered the fire with earth and moved on.
It was a fair day and I made good progress, keeping to the
cover of woodland where I could, and going by lesser paths
in more open areas. It was not possible to stay entirely unseen, for there were folk working in the fields, making the
most of the fine weather. But Conmael's gifts meant I was
unobtrusive now, just one countrywoman among many, and
the shawl was handy for covering my matted hair.

It was late in the day, nearly dusk, when I began to suspect someone was following me. Whoever it was, they were
doing a good job of it, keeping a certain distance away,
maintaining a watch, staying out of sight. Someone with a
light tread; someone wood-crafty. But surely not Conmael's folk, who would make no sound at all. A pox on this! I
had almost persuaded myself that Mathuin's men had lost
the trail or given up on me. It seemed not. Who else would
be bothering to track me?

Well, two could play this game. No stopping for the

night; no camp; no fire. I would not make myself an easy target for anyone. Never again. And I would not call upon Conmael's folk for help; my pride had not been entirely beaten out of me. I would make myself into a shadow, and I would find this tracker before he found me.

I walked through the dusk and into a moonlit night. The sounds of daytime—cows lowing, the turning of a water wheel, a dog barking—gave way to the hooting of owls, the sudden, heart-tearing cry of some small creature in a predator's grip, the rustling of a cold wind through the leaves. And, from time to time, the very small sounds made by someone who was trying hard to go undetected. The snap of a twig; a soft clearing of the throat; a creak that might or might not be a creature moving in the undergrowth.

The plan had been to keep going; to tire my pursuer out. The farther I went, the more convinced I was that there was only one man following me. It was now well into the night and the fellow was still there. The flaw in my plan became apparent. Rested, warm and fed, I had set out in the morning with new heart, ready for anything. Now I was reminded that a person does not so quickly recover from a long period of deprivation. I was, quite simply, worn out. If I tried to keep on walking until daybreak, I'd end up tripping over a tree root and breaking my leg. And while Conmael would perhaps come to my rescue, I had absolutely no desire to put myself further in his debt.

Well, here I was in a passable camping spot, on a hillside overlooking pasture land, with some bushes for cover and a bit of an overhang for shelter. The plan would have to change. I needed sleep. So, hunker down without a fire and keep the knife within grabbing distance. On balance, it seemed likely anyone who had taken the trouble to track me so far was not intent on a simple job of murder. As I unrolled my blankets and nibbled a piece of dry way-bread, I realized I'd probably got this all wrong. The invisible follower might be human, but he wasn't carrying out Mathuin's orders. He was surely in Conmael's pay. His job was not to hunt me down and kill me, but to make sure I got to Winterfalls in one piece.

The more I thought about this, the more likely it seemed. And, now that I had settled in one spot, I could not hear the tracker at all. Perhaps I had exhausted him. Or maybe I had finally lost him. Either way, I'd have to take the risk and sleep for a while or I'd be in no fit state to go on in the morning.

I huddled as far back beneath the overhang as I could and wrapped myself in blankets and shawl. Under the waxing moon, the fields were a silver tapestry scattered with the dark knots of trees and the shining patches of stream and pond. I reminded myself that I was free now; that the aches in my weary body were good ones, brought about by walking on the fields of Erin under an open sky. No degree of exhaustion could ever compare with the spirit-sapping weariness of a year in the vile confines of those cells. Every day in there was a day too many. As I drifted off to sleep, I told myself I would never, ever let myself be locked up again.

I woke to find a little fire burning not far away. Conmael's folk again. No offerings this time, but the warmth was welcome; it eased the worst cramps from my limbs, and I was able to eat a hot breakfast before I moved on. No sign at all of the tracker, though the ground near the fire was disturbed, making me wonder if he had been right up here, a hop and a step away from where I'd been sleeping. I could not find any clear footprints, but someone had certainly come close. When the fey had brought the bath, they'd left no traces at all. I walked on with the knife stuck in my belt. A big dog would have been useful. If Conmael returned, maybe I'd ask for one.

Another day's walking; a night camped in woodland. The tracker was still with me, soft-footed as a wary wild creature, betraying his presence only in the smallest ways. Skillful; persistent.

By late afternoon on the next day, the weather had turned wet. If I'd had a home to go to, certain shelter ahead, I'd have kept on walking, knowing I could be under a roof by dusk with a hearth fire and dry clothing. But my body was not strong as it had once been, and I was traveling an unknown path. I headed deeper into the woods and found a shallow cave that opened onto a small clearing among elder trees. There was evidence that others had camped here before me: a rudimentary hearth fashioned of rocks, a place where the stream had been dammed to form a shallow pool, and in the cave, a stack of wood. The rain fell steadily; my clothing was wet. But this hearth was protected by the rock shelf above it, and I would be able to make a fire and dry things out. As for the tracker, he'd have a choice: emerge and show himself, or stay out there and get soaked through.

When I'd kindled the fire and was building it up, I saw him. He was only a darker patch under the trees, motionless. Then a gust of wind brought down a small branch, and he flinched as it landed close by him. I peered through the curtains of rain, but already he'd shrunk back from view. Not coming out, then. Well, it wasn't my problem if he died of an ague. I'd never asked him to follow me.

I'd caught a fish earlier in the day, and now I made it into a kind of soup with a handful of greens I'd gathered along the way. What I did not eat now I would have in the morning. I made a makeshift frame to hang my damp clothing on, but with the tracker so close I was not prepared to strip. I draped my shawl and stockings over the frame and set my boots in the warmth. I was beginning to think the pack Conmael had given me had a fey charm of some kind on it, for the rest of my belongings, including the two rolled-up blankets, were quite dry.

The fish soup smelled appetizing. My supplies included a bowl, a spoon and a cup, all fashioned from a strange pale substance, neither pottery nor bone, but smooth as silk to the touch and carved with little creatures—hedgehog, owl and fox—peering out from a twine of ivy. They were far too fine for the likes of me. I filled the bowl, draped one of the blankets around my shoulders, then settled by the campfire to eat.

Beyond my place of shelter the rain was coming down in remorseless, drenching sheets. I watched the stream broaden and the little dam overflow its confines. My fire was the only light in the darkening woods; the moon would not show her face tonight. I gazed toward the spot where I had last seen the tracker, but it was too dark now to make him out. If he had any sense at all he'd back off, leave this dogged pursuit and find himself somewhere dry to sleep.

Such pigheaded persistence. It reminded me of something. It reminded me of . . .

Morrigan's curse! Surely not. Why in the name of all the gods would Grim follow me miles across country, and if he did, why would he act as if he was on some kind of secret mission? No, it couldn't be. I squinted out through the rain again. Had those glimpses of the tracker matched the hulking lump of a man who'd shared my imprisonment day in, day out for the last year? Why would he do this? It couldn't be him. But in my mind I saw Grim performing those exercises in the near dark of the cells, every single night, every endless, mind-numbing night, hauling himself, pushing himself, keeping himself strong as if tomorrow would be not another day in the dank horror of Mathuin's prison but a day of challenge and hope and heroism. For pigheaded persistence, Grim was the man.

"Danu save us, Grim," I murmured, remembering the way he'd lifted me out of the place. After it happened, after we saw open sky above us, that had been the first thing he'd done. "That day you were waiting for really did come."

What now? I might be wrong. I might call out only to see a complete stranger, armed and dangerous, heading up the hill in response to my kind invitation. But if it was him, and I didn't call out, I might go out there in the morning and find a sodden corpse, dead from cold. I hated obligations. I didn't want to owe Grim anything—wasn't my agreement with Conmael bad enough?—but I couldn't turn my back on him. There was no way I'd have got out through that broken roof by myself.

Right, then. I'd need to make it quite clear that all I was offering was a share of fire and food for tonight, and a spot to sleep out of the rain. He could explain why he was here, and I'd tell him I didn't want company on the road, either open or covert. And in the morning we'd go our separate ways.

I stood up and yelled through the downpour. "Grim! If that's you, get yourself up here out of the rain, you stupid man! What's the point of escaping if you're only going to drown?"

No answer that I could hear, but there was some movement down there under the trees. A shambling shape, like a troll or giant from an old story, made its way slowly out and up the hill toward me. Even as I set the little pot back on the fire, I slipped my knife from my belt. Grim free might be quite a different man from Grim behind bars. Who knew what acts of violence he might have in him, what old offenses might be preying on his mind, what wrongs he might believe needed righting? One well-aimed blow with his big fist and I'd be gone. He'd sleep by my fire, help himself to my belongings and be on his way, and the sodden corpse wouldn't be him, it would be me.

"Hurry up!" I snapped. "Get that cloak off, you're dripping everywhere. Move in by the fire, here."

He was shivering with cold; his clothing must have been soaked right through. This sorry specimen wasn't going to be making any explanations until I got him warm and dry. I'd never called him Bonehead the way the others had. Right now the name seemed perfectly apt.

"Listen," I said, putting the knife back in my belt. "Forget modesty, we've seen the worst of each other already. I'll turn my back, you take those clothes off and wrap this blanket around you. Let me untie that—"

"No ..." It was a feeble protest; his attempt to push my hands away was equally pathetic.

"All right, do it yourself, then. But hurry up; the longer you keep those wet things on, the longer you'll take to warm up. Tell me when you're decently covered again." It was beyond ridiculous, after that place, for there to be any need for privacy between us. The things we'd seen in there made a mockery of the niceties of life outside. On the other hand, we *were* outside now, and I at least would have to teach myself, all over again, how to behave around ordinary people, the kind of people who didn't realize places like Mathuin's lockup even existed. With my back to Grim, I got the way-bread out of my pack and broke off a good-sized piece. Then I waited. And while I waited it came to me that small courtesies like this should not be dismissed. That the ability to give a person a few moments' privacy was a worthwhile thing; it was to offer the gift of respect.

"Lady?" Grim's voice came eventually, deep and uncertain. "You want this pot stirring?"

"Can I turn around without offending your modesty?"

"Blanket's a bit small. Nice and warm, though."

I turned. Had things been different I might have smiled, but I had too much on my mind to be amused by the spectacle of a very large man draped curiously in an inadequate length of cloth. "Black Crow save us," I muttered. "You'd better have the other one as well, here."

"You'll be cold—"

"I have a perfectly good shawl and my clothes are dry. And I have a full belly. Sit down here and eat, it'll help warm you up." I poured the remaining fish soup into the bowl, stuck the spoon in and handed it to him. "And this." I put the way-bread down beside him.

"You don't want me eating your supplies—"

"Shut up, Grim. Not another word until it's all gone. That's an order."

He ate; I busied myself draping his sodden garments over bushes and stones around the fire. His prison rags were gone; at some point during the three days since our escape, he had acquired a set of plain clothing, trousers, shirt, tunic, cloak, boots. If he had a pack or weaponry, he'd left it out there in the woods.

The food was soon gone; it would be way-bread for breakfast. I hoped the fish would be biting again tomorrow.

"First good meal I've had in days," Grim said. His voice was markedly steadier, but he was avoiding my eye. "Thank you, Lady."

One thing needed sorting out quickly. "I've got a different name now. Blackthorn. Don't call me Lady."

There was a pause; then he said, "Blackthorn. That's a healer's name, isn't it? A wise woman's name."

"That's right. It's what I was, a long time ago. But Blackthorn's not my old name, it's a new one, from the day we left that place."

"Mm-hm. Good choice. It suits you."

"Prickly and difficult."

Another silence. "Not how I'd put it, but yes, that too."

"Grim."

"Mm?"

"I've got a bit of a story to tell you. About what happened that day. But first, who got out? Apart from us, I mean?"

The silence stretched out so long, this time, that I thought he was not going to answer at all. Then he said, "Poxy and Dribbles. Got out and away as far as I know."

"Nobody else?"

"Just them and us, Lady. I mean Blackthorn. Have to get used to that."

No, he wouldn't, because after tomorrow morning we'd never need to see each other again. "You've got some questions to answer," I said. "But first I'll tell you the story." As simply as I could, I told him about the fey benefactor who had come from nowhere and had offered me freedom provided I went to Dalriada and didn't come back. I explained that I had promised to go back to my old craft and use my skills to help people. Conmael's other requirements, I did not share; there was no need for Grim to know. But he did deserve an explanation of the strange event that had killed our cellmates. "I don't think Conmael cared at all who was hurt or who died," I said. "Only, for some reason, that I should get out before Mathuin's men came to make an end of me. Thank you for helping me that day."

"That was nothing," he mumbled. "Just wish I could have got the others out too. All of them." And after a moment, "I don't trust the fey, and you shouldn't either. Full of tricks. They say they're helping you, and all the time they want something from you. You need to be careful. Why would this fellow do that when he was a stranger to you?"

"I have no idea. But I can look after myself."

We sat there awhile without talking. The rain was easing off; I hoped the morning would be dry so I could move on quickly.

"Grim?"

"Mm?"

"Why did you follow me? Why are you here?"

His only response was a shrug.

"Come on, Grim, you can do better than that. Why come after me, and why be so secretive about it? For a while there I thought you were Mathuin's men. You scared me."

He shot me a glance, then looked down at the ground
again. "Thought you weren't scared of anything."

"There's a difference between being afraid and letting
people see that you are," I said, pushing back an old memory that threatened to surface. "Grim, answer the question,
will you? You must have somewhere to go, your old home,
your old work. But here you are, sitting by my campfire,
eating my food. Why?"

Nothing; he just sat there hunched over in his blankets,
head bowed. From time to time a shiver ran through his
large form.

"Come on, Grim."

"Stupid," he muttered. "Thought you might need help.
Protection, you know? On your own, suddenly back out
here, no resources, weakened after so long locked up . . .
Seemed as if I might make myself useful."

I made myself count up to five before I answered. "That
was kind of you. But completely unnecessary. I'm well able
to fend for myself, and thanks to Conmael's people I didn't
start the journey with no resources at all. I appreciate your
concern, Grim, but I'm not in need of a bodyguard or a
traveling companion. In fact I prefer to be on my own. You
were in that place too; you'll surely understand."

"I'll be off, then." He made to get to his feet.

"Don't be stupid! You're not going anywhere until
you've had a night's rest and got your clothes dried out. In
the morning you can head off on your own business and I'll
be on my way north." One part of my question remained
unanswered. "Why didn't you just come up to me and ask if
I needed help? Why track me? Though I have to say, for a
big man you're quite good at it." I knew nothing of his life
before we were locked up; neither of us had ever spoken of
those times.

Grim sighed weightily. "Because I thought you might
say what you just said. That you didn't need me."

"If you'd heard it earlier, you could have saved yourself
a lot of effort. And stayed dryer."

"I should go." He tried to get up again.

"Stubborn, aren't you?" Something about this was really
bothering me, but I couldn't quite put a finger on it. What was

I missing? "You're not going off tonight in the rain. Especially not wearing my blankets. And if you weren't too tired to think straight, you'd see how ridiculous you're being. Settle down and get some sleep, and in the morning there's to be no running off before I wake up, understand? I have a job for you before you leave."

"What job?"

"Cutting this off." I gestured toward my matted locks.

I had his full attention now; he looked horrified.

"No! Why would you want that?"

"Why wouldn't I? It's disgusting. Washing it was no help at all."

"I could comb it out for you."

"Hah! If you believe that's possible, you'll believe anything. I want it chopped off close to the scalp. So no disappearing, all right?"

"If you say so."

It was only later, when we had banked up the fire and settled ourselves to rest a discreet distance apart, that he came out with it. "Lady?"

"You mean Blackthorn."

"Sorry."

"What, then?"

"It's just . . . it's just, I've got nowhere else to go. I thought . . . I did think . . ."

I opened my mouth to retort, *Then you thought wrong*. But the clouds parted for a moment, admitting watery moonlight, and a bird called, deep in the woods, and I realized that if I had spoken those words aloud, I would have added another year to the seven I owed Conmael, and lost one of my five chances. This was a cry for help if ever I heard one. A pox on the man, how dare he do this to me? With an effort, I spoke in calm, even tones. "What did you think, Grim?"

"Thought you'd say no. But wondered if you'd surprise me. Hoped you might let me come with you, and . . . and keep guard. Keep an eye out for trouble." After a moment he added, "There's a few things I can do. Handy things." And a little later, "But you wouldn't be wanting someone like me around. I understand that."

And suddenly my mind was awash with contradictions, too many of them to make sense of in the middle of the night. One thing was certain: I was going to be stuck with a traveling companion, for now at least. "We'll see," was my inadequate response. "In the morning, we'll see."

5

GRIM

Turns out she doesn't know the way. Just walking north by whatever tracks she finds and hoping she'll end up in Dalriada. Which maybe she would, but not as quick as with me helping.

The first morning, she makes me cut her hair. Makes me toss the pieces of it in the fire. That's hard. But, in a way, funny; her hair always was like flames. In that place, I'd look across and see it all glowing red, and I'd think of the things a fire gives you: warmth, light, a feeling like being home.

It's good sitting by our campfire at night, out in the woods or in a cave or wherever Blackthorn, as she calls herself now, decides to stop. Just the two of us all quiet, and the crackle of the flames. Our little patch of brightness in the big dark. It's good being free, and it's good being with her, and it's even better having a job to do. Seems like she does think I can be useful to her. Even though they called me Bonehead, meaning stupid.

After I cut her hair, I do mine to match. Couple of days later I get her a kerchief off someone's washing line, but she makes me put it back. In time, she says, she'll earn a living at her craft—I guessed already in that place that she was some kind of wise woman, with all her talk about plants—and she can pay for her own kerchief if she wants one. Anyway, she says, she likes the wind in her hair, what's left of it. Makes a change after being shut up so long. I keep quiet about where my new clothes came from. Wonder what she thinks I should have done—tapped on some farmer's door, looking like the wild man of the woods, and asked if they needed an honest worker?

We cross over the border from Mathuin's land to the next chieftain's. I have to tell her we're safe; she doesn't know the area at all. We climb to the top of a hill, and I point back south to the place we've come from, lost in a haze and too far away to see clearly. We've just crossed a bridge, and I make sure she knows that's got us out of Mathuin's grasp. Chase us over here, and he'd get himself in a lot of trouble with his neighbor. Most places you go, there's some kind of war on, a little war between rivals. About whose cattle can graze where or who's supposed to keep bridges mended, that kind of thing. Probably no different in Dalriada, but I don't say anything about that.

"You're sure?" she asks when I tell her where we are. "That really is the border?" I see her thinking, *How would he know that sort of thing?*

"It is. Now turn this way." I show her the view northward: rolling hills, patches of farmland, lakes and forests and a range of higher hills lying purple-blue in the distance. It's a pretty sight. "You're looking across the kingdom of Mide," I say. "Those hills, the big ones, they mark the border with Ulaid. And Dalriada's in the far north. Don't know about your place, Winterfalls. But we can worry about finding it when we're closer."

"You're a fountain of knowledge, Grim," she says, and almost smiles. "How long do you think it will take to get to Dalriada?"

"No hurry, is there?" We've been managing all right, what with fishing and trapping and her knack for boiling up handfuls of weeds and making something tasty out of them. The way-bread's running low, but she seems to think that fellow, Conmael, might provide more if we need it. Seen nothing of him so far, and I'll be happy if it stays that way. Never did trust the fey. More trouble than they're worth, tricky and meddlesome. Mind you, he did get her out, and for that reason I can't hate him. But because of Strangler and the others, it's hard not to.

Blackthorn's thinking. There's a little crease between her brows. "I suppose not. And life on the road surely beats what we had before. Still, I'd like to get on. The nights are only going to grow colder, and our supplies are limited."

"I can get you a cloak. Good boots. Just say the word."

"I'll manage with what I have," she says. "Not that I haven't stolen in the past to keep body and soul together, once or twice, but we won't do it if we need not. Maybe I'll find some work as we go." She thinks a bit more. "The trouble is, I've forgotten the ways of ordinary folk, Grim. Forgotten how to say the right things, play the right part. Conmael seemed to think I could slip right back into being a village healer. But I'm not sure I can. Part of me has turned wild, and another part's turned dark as endless night, and I'm not going to change back just because someone says I must."

Dark as endless night? Her? Seems like being shut up in that place has made her blind to herself. And even out here in the open, with good things all around, she's still in the shadows. "Give it time," I say. "Another reason not to rush, maybe."

"I'd like to get there before autumn. He said the cottage was run-down. It would make sense to attend to that before the storms set in."

"We'll be there in time."

She gives me one of her looks, as if she doesn't quite believe me. "You sound so certain."

I don't have any answer to that. Inside, certain is just what I'm not.

A few days later, we're coming along a track between grazing fields when we hear shouting and screaming up ahead. Blackthorn looks at me; I look at her. Whatever this is, it's trouble, and we don't want it. But before we can work out a shortcut that'll take us around the spot, a lad comes in sight. He's sprinting toward us as if a monster's on his tail. Face a nasty shade of green. "Help!" he wheezes. "The cart— Fergus—trapped—"

I'm back in the cells, hearing Strangler's voice from the

ruins, thinking how useless my help turned out to be. And
I'm back in the other place, the place I can't get out of my
head, no matter how hard I try. I'm fighting, I'm falling, I'm
wondering how a god who's supposed to be merciful can
stand by and watch this. I want to shrink down and hide. I
want to be invisible. But I'm out here in the open, and
Blackthorn's right next to me, and there's no getting away.

"Help us, please!" gasps the lad, pulling on my sleeve.
"The farm—too far—Fergus . . ."

We go back with him, running. When we get there it's a
sorry sight, a cart overturned, sacks of grain spilled everywhere, and a man pinned underneath. He's alive, at least;
he's groaning in pain, and in my head it's Strangler all over
again. Folk are trying to free the horse, and more folk are
trying to lift the cart at the same time, and everyone's in
everyone else's way.

Blackthorn and I don't need to talk, don't even need to
look at each other. I pass her the knife, she snaps out a couple of orders and cuts the harness away. Once the horse is
free, I squat down and get my shoulders under the back of
the cart.

"When I give the word, slide him out quickly and carefully," Blackthorn says to the other fellows. "Wait until I
say, or you'll do him more damage. Ready, Grim?"

I grunt a yes, then lift. Needs to be high enough for the
wheel to come off the ground, with enough room for them to
pull the fellow out clean. "Now," says Blackthorn. Sliding,
scraping, a yell from the man as they move him. I hold until
she says, "He's out, Grim," then I set the thing down again.

Blackthorn said she'd forgotten how to act around ordinary people, but she does just fine. Tells them she's a healer;
takes a good look at the man and says he's got a leg broke
and maybe ribs too. Makes a splint with sticks and kerchiefs.
Talks to the fellow quietly while she puts it on, gets him
calmed down. Snarls at a woman who's panicking, shuts her
up quick.

I break down a gate to make a stretcher. One of the fellows helps me lift the injured man on—he screams—and
we walk him to the farm. Folk are looking at me a bit oddly,
but not saying much. Blackthorn's not being talkative either. Still, when we get there she gives more orders, and

folk run about fetching what she needs. I stay close, but I make sure I'm not in her way. This fellow, the one with the broken leg, is the farmer, Fergus, and the woman who was making all the noise is his wife.

The splint Blackthorn made comes off and she puts on a better one. I get another job: holding the leg in position while she binds the thing right so the bone will mend straight. Fergus's wife gives him some strong drink beforehand, which helps a bit, but not enough to keep him still while we get everything lined up the way it should be. A couple of fellows help. Fergus's screams run right through me. It's hard to hold firm, keep my eyes open, swallow down the dark.

"All right?" mutters Blackthorn, sparing me a glance as she wraps her bandage around leg and splint. Some tricky twists and ties there; not sure how she's doing it, but I can see it's tight and strong. Seems like she hasn't forgotten much.

"Mm." Has to be all right. It's not me lying there wondering if my leg will ever be good enough to let me farm again. And she needs me; that helps.

"Good. Well done, Fergus, nearly there." My guess is, that's the hard part for her, saying words of comfort, being gentle. The other part, ordering folk around, taking charge, fixing things, that seems to come easy enough.

When the leg's done she gets Fergus sitting up and puts a strapping around his chest. Rib broken, she thinks. Settles him to rest, propped on pillows. Tells the woman how to make up a draft for the pain, and how long to leave the splint on for. Orders Fergus not to do any work until then, if he wants to be able to use his leg again. Says it all in a rush, as if she doesn't want to give them time for questions.

She doesn't need me anymore. I go outside, find a spot where nobody's in sight and bring up my breakfast under a bush. Can't seem to stop. I'm still retching even when there's only spit and bile left to come. When I'm done at last, my eyes are streaming, my chest's heaving and my mouth tastes like a cesspit. Funny, that. You could say I saved one today, or helped save him, and that evens the score. But it doesn't. I could save ten, twenty, fifty, and it wouldn't make up for Strangler lying dead in the woods, and Poxy and Dribbles butchered on the road, left there like pieces of meat for me to stumble over after Mathuin's men had done their foul work. That's a part of the story Blackthorn's never going to hear. Strangler's buried in those woods, a stone's throw from the lockup, and the other two I laid to rest in a quiet field with a nice big willow for shade. But I've got them all on my back, and the others from long ago. It's like a scale that can never balance. A weight that'll never lift.

I find the well, draw up a bucket, splash my face and take a drink, hoping the foul taste will go. And here she is beside me, bag on her back, staff in her hand.

"We're moving on," she says.

Fergus's wife said something about food and drink before, but I don't mention this. "All right. I'll get my things."

I fetch them, and Fergus's wife gives me a little bag. "Some provisions, since your woman won't take any payment. Would have liked her to stay on a night or two, seeing as he's so poorly. But I didn't ask; she said you two have to move on."

"That's right." I put the little bag into my pack. "Heading north."

"Good luck to you," the woman says. "You saved my husband's life today. I can't believe what you did. Lifting that cart all by yourself—that's a feat beyond any ordinary man."

Nothing to say to that. I shoulder my pack and pick up my staff.

"Sure you don't want work here?" An older man, perhaps her father, comes to the door behind her. "Strong fellow like you, you'd be welcome. With Fergus laid low, we could do with the help." A pause. "And there's no healer between here and Maedan's Bridge."

I shake my head. "Got to be moving on," I say. I wonder if they'd be so keen to keep us if they knew where we'd just come from.

"Good luck to you, then," says the man. "Long way to go?"

"Long enough."

We walk on in silence. Blackthorn's in a hurry. She keeps looking over her shoulder as if she wants to set space between us and the farm as fast as she can. It's only when

we're away from the fields and up into some scrubby woods
that she slows down and draws breath. I don't ask questions. A lot later, when we stop for a rest by a stream, she
says, "I saw that woman giving you something."

"Mm-hm." I fish the little bag out of my pack, open it
and find a purse of coppers, which from folk like them is a
lot. And there's a slab of bread and cheese, wrapped in a
cloth. I pass the purse to Blackthorn and divide the food in
two.

"Keep them," she says, handing the coppers back. "It's
your reward, not mine."

"Ours," I say, giving her a share of the bread and cheese.

She opens her mouth to make a sharp remark—I see
this in her eyes—and shuts it again without a word. We eat
in silence. I tuck the purse back into my pack.

"Next market we pass, I'll buy you a kerchief."

Blackthorn's got nothing to say to this. Instead she asks,
"Why were you sick? After everything we've seen, what
could be so hard about watching a man get his leg splinted?"

"Got eyes in the back of your head, have you?" It comes
out as a growl, and it shuts her up, at least for now. One
thing's sure: the story of Strangler and the others is going
to stay where it belongs, deep down where nobody can
hear it. Nothing will hurt her. Nothing will harm her. I'll
hold to that if it kills me.

6

ORAN

I was with Donagan in the yard when my father's messenger came to Winterfalls. Knowing he would not send a rider in haste unless the matter was urgent, I told my companion to continue the task at hand, which was to check on the progress of the stable extension. I sent the messenger off to the kitchens for refreshment and took myself into the house to read the missive in my private quarters, alone. It could not be a death, a grave illness, a serious accident; news of that kind would not come in writing, nor would it be delivered by anyone but a senior councillor.

I sought to identify the cause of my churning belly and thumping heart, and deduced that I was terrified Flidais's father had gone back on his word and decided to marry his treasured daughter to another, despite our families agreeing to the match. With Father's letter in my hands, still sealed, I bade myself behave like the prince I was and not some foolish youth. I looked at the picture hanging above my bed, and the calm eyes of my beloved gazed back at me as if to say, *Do not fear, Oran. All will be well.* I opened the letter.

There were the usual preliminaries; those I scanned quickly. Ah! Here was the meat of the message. It threw me into a whirl, for it was nothing I had expected, news that was indeed urgent, but not in the way I had dreaded.

The disturbances in the southwest have now become such a threat, my father wrote—or rather, his scribe wrote for him—*that Lord Cadhan fears for his daughter's safety. He requests that you do not travel to Cloud Hill to meet Lady Flidais as planned. Instead, he suggests that the lady should ride north to us more or less immediately, accompanied by her attendants and an escort of men-at-arms. Lord Cadhan believes his holdings may come under direct attack. His wife wishes to stay by his side and support him through what may well become a significant conflict. Oran, I do not know whether his reading of the situation is accurate. However, I must offer Lady Flidais the sanctuary of our home. Since Cadhan and I have reached agreement on the terms of your marriage, your mother believes my reply to him should include the suggestion that the formal betrothal take place as soon as Lady Flidais has recovered from her journey. This should send a strong message to Cadhan's enemies that he has friends in high places, though, in truth, both distance and my existing alliances make it unlikely I could provide much in the way of practical support to him in this matter. The king of Laigin is overlord to both Cadhan and his troublesome neighbor; it is for him, not me, to intervene in their dispute should that become necessary. But this betrothal will, at least, reassure Cadhan that his daughter is safe and that her future remains secure.*

Custom requires two turnings of the moon to pass between the betrothal and the hand-fasting. Allowing for the significant time it will take Lady Flidais's party to ride to Dalriada, you should still be able to have Winterfalls refurbished to your satisfaction before your bride moves there—she would, of course, be with us at Cahercorcan until

*the hand-fasting. It seems unlikely Lord Cadhan
and his wife will be present for the occasion of their
daughter's wedding, which is unfortunate, but I see
no other alternative.*

    *Please attend court immediately, as arrangements
must now be made in some haste. In particular, a
response to Lord Cadhan's message must be
dispatched within a day, and as you have proved
stubborn on other aspects of this marriage, I want
us to be in complete agreement as to that message's
content. I will expect you tomorrow.*

My father's signature sprawled across the page above
his scribe's neat rendering of his name: Ruairi, King of Dalriada. King first, father second, always. One day I would be
king. And Flidais would be my queen. If we had children, I
hoped I would make time to listen to their hopes and fears,
share with them my love of poetry, teach them the secret
ways of wild creatures, let them follow their dreams. But
perhaps, when I became king, all those things would be lost
to me. Perhaps, the moment I donned the crown, I would
cease to be the man Flidais had agreed to wed and turn
into a younger version of my father.

A tap at the door, and Donagan let himself in.

"Something wrong?" my body servant asked.

"Not exactly. Here." I passed him the letter. Donagan
was no ordinary serving man. He had been with me as
companion and attendant since we were twelve years old.
His father was one of my father's councillors; his mother
was one of my mother's personal attendants. We had
shared an education, both in book learning and in sports
and games; we had done everything together. I trusted him
more than anyone.

I could not seem to gather my scattered thoughts. While
he stood there reading, I paced the bedchamber, picking up
small objects and setting them down, folding my arms and
unfolding them. I thought of Flidais in peril, Flidais under-
taking a long journey on which she might at any time be
attacked by her father's enemies, Flidais coming here under circumstances more likely to make her tearful than joy-
ful. What woman would want to be betrothed without her

parents present at the ritual? What woman wanted to be sent off to her marriage in fear and haste? Could our letters, tender and honest as they were, really be sufficient to make up for my failure to visit her, to meet her in the flesh and talk to her before she left home?

On the other hand, this crisis meant I would see her soon, and that filled my heart with a sensation like sunlight, like gold, like a warm bright fire. She was coming here! I imagined the betrothal at Cahercorcan, seat of the Dalriadan kingship. The cavernous hall; the shadowy corners; my father's advisers lined up in their formal robes; my mother taking charge of everything, including poor Flidais. Then I imagined the ceremony as it might be at Winterfalls. Outside, perhaps, in the garden on a sunny day. Only our trusted attendants would be present. I would pick flowers for Flidais to wear in her hair. Bramble would wear a little garland around her neck.

Donagan cleared his throat and I came back abruptly to the here and now.

"How serious do you think it is?" my companion asked, rolling the missive and setting it down on my writing table. "The conflict in the south?"

"If it were very serious," I said, still pacing, "I imagine Father's tone would be different. But it must be serious enough, if Cadhan wants to send his daughter away. One thing I do know."

"What's that?"

"The betrothal won't be at Cahercorcan, and nor will the hand-fasting. Flidais is not the kind of woman who enjoys grand formal occasions, lavish feasts, complicated entertainments. I'm quite sure of that. Her party can ride direct to Winterfalls. We'll have both events here, as well as the waiting period in between. Provided Cadhan doesn't send an army of folk, we should have room for all of them. If we require additional serving people I will throw myself on Mother's mercy."

Donagan gave me a familiar look. While he did not say it, I knew he was thinking, *Your imagination is running away with you, Oran.* "You'll want your own family to be present for the hand-fasting," he said.

"In fact, I'd be delighted if they absented themselves

entirely. It would be so much easier. But yes, my parents must be there, of course; I can hardly deprive them of the opportunity to see their only son wed at last. As for the aunts and uncles, the cousins, the nephews and nieces, the court officials, the hangers-on, if they want to ride here for the event, I won't turn them away."

Donagan went on looking at me, not offering anything.

"What?" I used my most princely tone, the one that sent servants scurrying. It had no effect whatever on my friend.

"If I may make a suggestion," he said, giving me his half smile.

"You'll do so anyway, I have no doubt." I heard myself sounding like a spoiled child—perhaps, when Donagan had first come to live with me, I had indeed been one—and added more mildly, "Please do. But remember, Flidais hasn't grown up in a king's court; her father is a local chieftain. She's a woman who likes solitary walks, poetry, music, quiet conversation."

"I know that very well, Oran. You've spoken about nothing but the lady since we moved to Winterfalls. As that was well before midsummer, I believe I've been hearing her praises sung for nearly two turnings of the moon. My suggestion does not relate to Lady Flidais's preferences, but to how you might best present this to your father."

"I'm listening." I studied Flidais's picture while Donagan talked, wondering how well Bramble tolerated going on horseback.

"Offer a compromise: ask for the formal betrothal to take place here, but agree that the hand-fasting should be at court." When I made to interrupt, he raised a hand. "Hear me out, please. You're the future king of Dalriada. You must be wed at court; it's expected, and nobody is going to listen to your protestations about Lady Flidais's sensitive nature. I'd be surprised if your future wife weren't expecting a ceremony befitting her new status. And who knows, if this territorial dispute dies down soon, her parents may even be able to travel in time to attend. They would most certainly expect the hand-fasting to be at Cahercorcan."

"Is that it?"

"You should approach this with subtlety, Oran. Don't let your feelings overwhelm your sense of what is appropriate."

"Appropriate? You must know my mother would take charge of the whole thing, bully Flidais into agreeing with whatever she wanted, make this into a grand spectacle."

"I believe that is what most mothers do when their sons marry. And you are an only son."

"Don't laugh at me, Donagan. This is important to me."

He put a hand on my shoulder. "I know. But I do believe you have a better chance of convincing your father if you approach this in a spirit of calm compromise. You might use this argument . . ."

The following day, I sat with my father in the royal council chamber and presented my case. Not alone, sadly; my father had six councillors, and all of them were present. Over the years I had come to view these advisers as more hindrance than help. Decisions were made far more quickly and easily in their absence. Here at Cahercorcan, the trappings of nobility sometimes strangled one's capacity for rational thought.

"Father, I hope you will consider that Lady Flidais has not grown up at a king's court, and may at first be overawed by the scale and formality of Cahercorcan. Not only that— she will travel from her home under circumstances quite different from those she expected: in haste, in fear of attack, and without her parents to accompany her, though I imagine there will be a chaperone, perhaps a kinswoman, as well as other attendants. Flidais's letters show her to be a young woman of some sensitivity. I believe accommodating her and her party in the smaller, quieter household of Winterfalls would be a far kinder choice. And it would mean Flidais came straight to what will be her new home. We would, of course, travel together to Cahercorcan for the handfasting when the time came."

On reflection I had seen the wisdom in Donagan's arguments. Provided Flidais had time for rest and recovery at Winterfalls for those two months, she would cope with the stuffiness of my father's court for the hand-fasting ritual and subsequent celebration. I would support her; I would make sure my mother did not bully her.

Father scratched his beard, then glanced at his chief councillor, Feabhal. "There's a question of propriety," he said.

"Indeed, my lord." Feabhal fastened his chilly gaze on

me. "Prince Oran, housing the young lady under your roof before the two of you are hand-fasted might be seen in some quarters as . . . unseemly. Inappropriate. I'm sure you understand."

"I'm not sure I do, Feabhal." I made sure my own gaze was steady. "If you are suggesting my behavior would be anything but perfectly seemly, you offend both me and Lady Flidais. Winterfalls is a spacious residence. The lady will have her own private quarters; they are even now being prepared. And if she does not bring a chaperone, no doubt the queen can find any number of aunts or cousins to do the job of safeguarding her virtue. If that is what you mean."

Feabhal cleared his throat but did not speak.

"Nobody would dream of suggesting you would act anything but correctly, Prince Oran," said one of the other councillors quickly. "It's more a matter of what folk might think."

"Let them think what they will. A virtuous man is beyond gossip." I found myself on the brink of laughter, and forced my features into an appropriately princely expression. "Father, the territorial dispute faced by Lord Cadhan—did he provide details?"

"Some. Why do you ask?" I had my father's full attention at last.

"Cloud Hill lies in the far north of Laigin, does it not? On the border with Mide, which is ruled by one of our own kin."

"Distant kin," my father said. "But yes, Lorcan is a family connection of sorts. That particular area of the border has seen many disputes over the years. Raids, challenges, petty wars. More or less inevitable, since it's fine grazing land."

I had studied the maps, counting the miles between Cloud Hill and Winterfalls over and over. "I deduce that Lord Cadhan's territorial issue does not relate to cross-border incursions from Mide, since we know Lorcan to be a peaceable leader whose authority is seldom challenged. I suspect the threat comes from a certain powerful chieftain named Mathuin, whose holdings lie to the south of Cadhan's."

"I had come to the same conclusion," my father said. "That is not something Cadhan would put into a letter, of course."

"Mathuin of Laois is a known troublemaker."

"What foundation have you for such a claim, Prince Oran?" The scorn in Feabhal's voice was ill-concealed. His opinion of me had never been high.

"I have learned a great deal from this present wise company, Feabhal." I looked around the council table, making sure I met each man's gaze in turn. "Some, I know, believe I am too fond of music and storytelling. A man can learn much from monks, scribes and scholars. From wandering bards and druids: folk who travel widely and keep their ears open. I have heard that Mathuin is intolerant of opinions other than his own. He has his ways, sometimes brutal ways. If he wants something, he takes it without waiting to seek advice or weigh up the consequences. I have heard, also, that the king of Laigin shows some reluctance to become involved in disputes between his chieftains."

"Interesting," my father said. "But you understand that we cannot send forces south to help Cadhan with whatever difficulty he's in, whether it's of Mathuin's making or someone else's. That could ignite full-scale war. We must limit ourselves to offering Lady Flidais sanctuary, which is all Cadhan has requested. Let's not complicate matters, Oran."

"I'm not suggesting we take up arms in Cadhan's support, Father. I know such an action would have far-reaching consequences, and might set you in conflict with your existing allies. But someone might have a word with the king of Laigin. Someone to whom any ruler would be prepared to listen."

They had caught my drift now. "You're not speaking of Lorcan," Father said, "but of his father-in-law, the High King. We might send a confidential message to Lorcan; he might then have a quiet word in the right quarter. And pressure might be put on Mathuin to cease and desist from whatever he is doing to Cadhan."

"A long bow to draw, perhaps. But it could be effective. Mathuin has some supporters among his fellow chieftains, but nobody really trusts the man. He's viewed as autocratic and unpredictable. His overlord is considered weak."

"You've been studying hard, Prince Oran." Feabhal managed to make this sound like an insult, and this time my father noticed.

"To good effect," he said. "I have heard something of the same criticism. I will consider your suggestion seriously, Oran, though there's always a difficulty with these sensitive matters; it would be far better if I could speak to Lorcan in person."

I seized the moment. "He will, of course, be invited to the hand-fasting. He's a kinsman, isn't he?"

My father favored me with a smile, which was a rare occurrence. "Indeed," he said. "You show some perspicacity in this matter, Oran. I welcome that. When the opportunity arises I will have a word with Lorcan. As for the matter of where Lady Flidais should be accommodated, that decision must be made immediately. I should send a response to Lord Cadhan today by the swiftest messenger I can find. I don't believe the issue needs further debate. If you want to house her at Winterfalls from the start, so be it. But speak to the queen, obtain her approval, and make sure you ask her about a suitable chaperone for the young lady."

"Of course, Father. I will do so straightaway." I resisted the urge to leap up and do a little dance of triumph. Silently I thanked Donagan for helping me prepare my argument. It was true about the bards and druids, the scribes and scholars; but I had not thought of using them.

"I'll have my scribe draft the reply. Oran, I will need you again once it's ready. The rest of you are dismissed."

"Yes, Father." I hesitated. "May I enclose a brief message for Lady Flidais?"

"Go and talk to your mother first. If you've time to write a letter as well, do so. Be sure it really is brief."

My dear Flidais, I wrote, I have just come from a difficult meeting with my mother. I will spare you the details. Mother only wants the best for us, but she is a formidable woman and somewhat inflexible in her opinions. However, her delight in our impending marriage has mellowed her. My love, I was horrified to learn of your father's current difficulties. Please stay safe on your journey north. I

*will be counting the days until you reach
Winterfalls. As my father has said in his letter to
Lord Cadhan, your party is to come straight here,
not to court. This makes your journey a little
shorter, since my home is situated some twenty
miles south of Cahercorcan, which is a grand
fortified place built on a promontory overlooking
the northern sea. I am making your new home ready
for you, dear Flidais, and I dream of walking in the
woods with you and Bramble, and sitting by the
hearth reading poetry. My mother will be sending a
small army of additional serving people to
Winterfalls, though I have my own very capable folk
here. She is including a rather fierce aunt as
chaperone. I offer my apologies in advance—Aunt
Sochla will find she has nothing to do, I believe.
Dear Flidais, Father has asked me to keep this
short, and I will. Please be safe on the road, and
know that my heart travels with you.*

Oran

7

BLACKTHORN

It turned out I could still patch people up pretty well. The beatings and abuse, the degradation and filth hadn't been quite enough to drive out what I'd learned long ago in that life I didn't want to think about. The part I couldn't do, or not for long, was talk to folk, be courteous to them, take an interest in their little woes, accept their groveling *thank-you*s with a smile.

It got me wondering how I'd ever managed to deal with my own kind before. I surely couldn't now. All I wanted was to be left alone. If I couldn't have vengeance, if I couldn't bring Mathuin down, I wanted simply to exist, somewhere quiet, somewhere beyond the well-trodden paths, somewhere I wouldn't need to think about anything except getting water from the stream, gathering mushrooms or berries, making a fire to keep myself alive through another night. Seven years I had to stay alive, or there was no purpose to any of it. Curse Conmael for setting this burden on me!

And as for Grim, why in the name of all that was holy hadn't he stayed with those people at the farm? I'd seen the way they looked at him. How often did folk meet a man with the strength of a giant? He'd have been given work there, sure as sure, if only he'd asked them. Work, a home, money in his pockets. Wasn't that what he wanted, a job, a purpose? I wasn't offering either.

But he came on with me, a big lump dogging my footsteps, and I couldn't send him away because I'd made my promise to wretched Conmael. Besides, it seemed Grim really did know the way to Dalriada—how, I couldn't imagine and wasn't planning to ask, since I'd learned long ago that his past was under the same sort of lock and key as mine. And while I could fend for myself perfectly well, there was no disputing that Grim could do some things a lot more quickly and easily than I could. Gathering firewood, for instance, or building a shelter. If we'd been attacked on the road or in our camp, I could have defended myself up to a point. But his presence meant nobody was even going to try. And he could pay his way, more or less. After that first time, with the cart, he found plenty more opportunities to earn a few coppers or a fat hen or a loaf of fresh bread.

It was more difficult for me. Often enough, we passed farms or settlements where a healer was needed. It might be a woman straining to give birth to a babe set awry in the womb, or an old man rattling and wheezing in his death throes. Conmael's agreement had turned me into a coward. I feared to offer help, lest folk take advantage. I knew quite well how one request for aid could turn into many. *Oh, please help my child, he's struggling to catch his breath.* So herbs were steamed in a pot, and a poultice was applied to the chest, and common sense advice was given about keeping the little boy warm and clean and feeding him light, nourishing fare. Next thing it would be, *Couldn't you stay one more day, just to be sure?* Or, *My neighbor's little girl has the same sickness, you'll look at her too, won't you? And by the way, the old fellow down the road is poorly as well . . .* And so it would go on. If a person had promised never to say no to such requests, she might find herself trapped somewhere for life, unable to keep the rest of the bargain, which was to go to this place called Winterfalls.

Not that I was looking forward to getting there. The cottage had sounded all right, but once folk knew there was a wise woman in residence again, it would be visitors all day whether I liked it or not. If I did my job adequately, as it

seemed I still could, they'd keep coming no matter how
snappish and contrary I might be. Conmael had trapped
me neatly. I couldn't even regret saying yes to him, since if I
hadn't, I'd have been dead and forgotten by now. And even
when things had been at their darkest, when anger had
been like a rat gnawing at my vitals, when grief had shut
down my heart, I'd known death was not the answer.
There'd always been vengeance to keep me going. There
still was, provided I could find enough patience to last me
seven years.

I practiced on Grim. There was the day he found a fair
like the one he'd spoken of, and went off with his bag of
coppers in his pouch while I stayed away, sitting under a
tree keeping myself to myself and half wishing he'd never
come back. But he did, a bit the worse for wear, having
drunk a fair quantity of ale, and he brought me the kerchief
he seemed to think I wanted. I thanked him and made myself wear the thing, which I guessed was the most eye-
catching he'd been able to find in the whole encampment:
bright poppy red with a border of blue flowers done in
wool embroidery. Just the thing for crossing country unno-
ticed.

Despite the interruptions while one of us did some work
and earned the pittance that was all most folk could afford
to pay, we made reasonable progress. I judged it to be close
to the festival of Lugnasad, harvest time, when we came up
over a pass and looked north across the region of Ulaid. To
the east I could see the gray expanse of the sea, under a sky
of building clouds that promised rain by nightfall. That meant
another miserable wet camp, unless we reached farmland and
happened on a barn whose owner wasn't going to wake us
up and demand a day's labor for the privilege of shelter.
Ahead, over those hills and valleys, way off in the misty distance, lay the kingdom of Dalriada. Somewhere up there
was Winterfalls and the end of my journey. Just how far we
still had to walk I wasn't sure, and nor was Grim, since he'd
never heard of Winterfalls until I mentioned the name. He
did know Dalriada was in the far northeast of Ulaid, so we
still had a way to go. All the same, getting over the mountains felt like some kind of achievement. I found myself hop-

ing Ulaid was full of folk who didn't need help, or preferred not to ask for it. Found myself, stupidly, wondering if the cottage Conmael had mentioned might turn out to be a sort of gift. Hah! The complications of this whole thing—the offer, the obligation, the guilt, the choices in it—were enough to make a person's head spin. It was both gift and burden. Because nothing came for free, ever.

"Better be moving on," said Grim. "Storm's coming."

It was coming fast. The clouds were a dark stir in the sky; the distant sea was a slaty sheet. The wind poked chill fingers through the warm clothing Conmael's folk had given me. I had not seen my fey benefactor since that night. I wondered, sometimes, if he'd become bored by the whole thing, or forgotten me. I considered testing this theory by heading off on my own in whatever direction I chose. But the price of being wrong on this particular point was far too high to take chances. If I got to Winterfalls, and if the time stretched out to a year, two perhaps, with still no sign of Conmael, then maybe . . .

"Woods down there," Grim observed, leaning on the staff he had cut from a fallen oak branch. "Best shelter we'll get."

By the time we reached the wooded lower slopes, it was raining steadily. A rumble of thunder, not so far away, sent us along a track into dense oak forest. Here the canopy kept off the worst of the rain. But our clothing was already soaked. The storm had turned day to dusk; there was no choice but to make camp somewhere in these woods.

It took longer than I liked to find a spot, near some rocks, with a busy stream gushing past not far away. There was a cave of sorts, a place where we'd be able to keep a fire burning. We had a routine now, as folk do who travel long paths together. I built a hearth from stones while Grim gathered fallen branches and sticks. I kindled the fire; Grim filled the water skins and got out the makings of a meal. Supplies were low. It was some time since we'd visited a settlement or farm, and we were down to a few dried-up mushrooms and the remains of a bag of oatmeal Grim had earned by helping move a particularly difficult bull from one farm to another without anyone being hurt.

While he boiled the oatmeal in water over the fire, I foraged for wild onions near the stream; going farther afield in such bad light would have been foolish.

Wet clothing was always a problem. No matter that we'd lived opposite each other in the lockup for a whole year, and seen such horrors that a naked body had no more power to shock either of us. The fact was, we weren't in there now, and some things didn't feel right. After that first night, when I'd called Grim up to the campfire and made him strip so he wouldn't perish from cold, he'd never taken his clothes off in front of me. He'd always go and do it somewhere out of sight, and if there was nothing dry to put on he'd make sure he was well covered with blankets. As for me, if I had to change I'd simply ask him to turn his back. It was a small enough thing, and I wondered sometimes why we bothered, after everything. Shyness? Shame? Could have been a bit of both, or something else. It went along with not using those names for each other, Slut, Bonehead, when everyone else had. Back then, it had marked out a kind of alliance. It had said that even when you'd seen a person scorned and beaten and degraded, you could still show them courtesy.

I didn't say any of this to Grim, of course. He understood it in his own way, without needing my words to complicate things. There was an enforced closeness about traveling together, one of the reasons I'd have rather been on my own. Courtesy and respect, and a bunch of other things, kept us on opposite sides of the fire even when we were shivering under our blankets. It stopped us from asking each other about the time before that place, and what had led us there. Family, friends, home: none of those. A lot of the time we said nothing at all.

We ate our meal hunched over the fire. The wettest items of clothing we draped over sticks and bushes. The rest we wore, along with the blankets. My joints ached. I longed for a hot bath. But, fey as he was, Conmael wasn't the kind of being who could be summoned when you wanted him and asked for three wishes. More likely he'd be the one doing the summoning.

About the meal, the less said the better.

"It's hot," I said, curling my fingers around the cup. "That's something."

"Mm-hm." Grim had almost finished his share. He was a big man, and always hungry. It made me wonder how he'd managed in that place, where we'd learned to be grateful for watery gruel. How he'd stayed so strong. Strong enough to get three of us out, and then himself.

"Be good if we don't need to stop too much from here on," I said. "We must have enough coppers now to buy our food if we can't catch it along the way."

"Mm-hm." A silence. Then, "We'd be wanting to keep some set by," Grim said, staring into the fire.

This statement bothered me for several reasons. "Why do you say that?" I asked.

"We'll be needing things when we get there. You'll want healers' supplies. And a lot more, if this cottage is in a bad state of repair. Enough to get us on our feet."

That this made good sense didn't make it any less troubling. It wasn't just his easy use of "we." It was the assumption that the two of us might have some kind of life together after we reached Winterfalls. The implication that, in some capacity, Grim would be staying. I thought of things I could say, brutally true things, and discarded them one by one. He'd asked me for help, that night in the woods. He'd said he had nowhere else to go. If I didn't want seven years to become eight, I had to be careful.

"That makes it all the more important to get on quickly," I said. "If Conmael thinks I can set up as a healer at Winterfalls, then I suppose I can, one way or another. Maybe this Prince What's-His-Name will dispense some largesse. Though that's doubtful. I imagine there's a court physician for him and his nobles, and my job will be tending to the folk the prince's healer thinks himself too good for."

Grim gave me a look but said nothing.

"What?" I snapped.

"Got a low opinion of yourself."

"Did I say that?"

"Didn't have to." He drew breath. "You don't want to start believing those things, you know. What they used to say, in that place. The names. The . . ."

I waited.

"It's all lies. You know that. But when they keep on saying it, over and over, when they make you say it yourself, when they . . . It's hard not to believe it. It's hard not to think you're the lowest of the low. For some of us, maybe it wasn't lies, maybe it was the truth. But it was never true for you."

For a bit, I couldn't think of anything to say.

"Sorry," said Grim. "Shouldn't have talked about it."

"You can't know that," I said, setting down my cup and holding my hands out to the fire. Why was it so hard to get warm? "You know nothing about me. I might be all those things they said."

"I do know."

At least he hadn't invited me to share my life story. If there was anything he and I had in common, it was the understanding that we wouldn't trespass on that forbidden ground. "Your faith in me is without any basis in fact," I said.

"Faith's faith," said Grim.

It was too dark and cold to do anything but sleep, so we slept, or I did anyway. Grim wasn't much of a sleeper. Freedom hadn't changed that. In that place, he'd catnapped during the day, when the guards were elsewhere, though he'd always woken when they were coming. His uncanny awareness had alerted him even when he was asleep. At night we'd talked, sometimes, and when we weren't talking he'd gone through his routine. I'd fallen asleep to the sound of him breathing hard as he performed some impossible exercise, and when I'd woken, whether it was morning or still night, he'd always been awake before me. Sometimes standing at the bars, as if he was waiting for me. Sometimes lying on his pallet staring at the roof. But never sleeping.

We'd become used to waking fast in there. Mostly, at night, they left us to ourselves. But sometimes Slammer would take it into his head to come in and stir us up, and it didn't pay to get caught off guard. Times like that, Grim would shout to warn us and we'd scramble up and get to the back of our cells.

Still, I wasn't expecting to be shaken rudely awake now, out in the middle of nowhere in a thunderstorm. I jumped up, but my mind was still half trapped in the dream I'd been having, a bad one involving Mathuin of Laois.

"What?" I growled, clutching the blanket around me. Danu save us, it was cold!

"Someone down there." Grim was almost swallowed up by the darkness. The fire was down to ash-coated coals; his knife caught the last of its light, gleaming in the shadows. "In the woods."

My common sense fled. My mind filled with Mathuin, his men-at-arms, his thugs here to make an end of us and rob me of my last slim chance to see justice done.

"Step out and show yourself!" I shouted, before Grim grabbed me and clapped his big hand over my mouth. For a moment I fought him—a pointless exercise—and then a light appeared in the woods below our camping spot, and another, and a third, and it became plain that our visitors were not Mathuin's folk but Conmael's.

Grim let me go only to push me behind him. He planted his feet squarely, the knife ready in his hand.

"Grim," I said. "They're friends."

"Hah!"

"Grim. Leave this to me." And when he still made no move, "Trust me. Please."

He grunted, stuck the knife in his belt, folded his arms.

Conmael was coming up the rise. Behind him walked three others of his kind. All wore hooded cloaks, and each had the noble nose, broad brow and lustrous eyes typical of the fey. A person who had not encountered such folk before might perhaps think this an unusually handsome, if somewhat odd-looking, family of human brothers. Anyone who knew their lore, or who had lived close by a place where their kind dwelled—a cave, a hollow hill, an ancient forest, a mysterious lake isle—would recognize their true nature.

I stepped forward, trying to set aside the awareness that I was inadequately clad, tousled from sleep and freezing cold to boot. "Conmael," I said, shivering despite my best efforts. "What brings you here in such inclement weather?"

"A desire to make sure you do not drown where you sleep," he said smoothly. "The stream is rising fast. I wish you to reach your destination." His gaze went briefly to Grim, then returned to me. "No longer alone, I see?"

His manner set me on edge. I spoke through chattering teeth. "Last time we met you said you'd leave me to get on with things. What's changed? I'm keeping my side of the agreement." Had I managed to miss a request for help somewhere along the way? Reduced my remaining chances to four and added another year to the sentence before I'd even reached Winterfalls? That would be cruel. But perhaps that was the game, with the term of the agreement always stretching just a little further than I could reach. Such a trick would be typical of the fey.

"Speak up." Grim's voice was a rumble of aggression.

Conmael's brows rose. "My conversation is not with you," he said, "but with your mistress. Shouts and blows may have won arguments for you in the past, fellow. They are pointless in the current situation."

The flicker of anger already in me flared abruptly to a full-sized blaze. "Keep your remarks to yourself!" I snarled, painfully aware that although the insult had been aimed at my companion, Grim was standing strong and quiet beside me while I raged. "If that's the best you have to offer, we'll be better off without your interference!"

Conmael gave an airy wave of the hand. "If that is your wish, of course. It merely occurred to me that the stormy weather might be slowing your journey and making it less comfortable than it need be. I provided only scant supplies for you. By now, surely you have need of further resources."

I opened my mouth to tell him we were fine on our own, thank you, but Grim got in first.

"Dry clothing for the lady. Fresh bread, a round of cheese. Two more blankets and a second knife. That should see us to Winterfalls."

I was stunned into silence.

"My offer was not made to you," said Conmael.

"Consider Grim's request my request," I snapped. "Provided there is no payment required in return, that is. I'm not talking about a handful of coppers here. No payment of any kind. My obligation to you is already heavy. I'd rather go cold and hungry than add to it."

"You're sure that's all you want? Bread, cheese, dry clothing and a blanket or two?"

"And a knife," said Grim levelly.

"And a knife, but perhaps not just yet," Conmael said, eyes still on me, "since your guard dog seems likely to plunge it into me the moment I turn my back."

It seemed to me that under the circumstances Grim was doing a remarkable job of keeping his temper. "I'm willing to accept the offer of some necessities, Conmael," I said, hugging the blanket around me. "But I can't believe you came out here in the rain just to ask us if we needed help. Your folk are surely capable of leaving us a basket of bread and cheese any time they're so inclined."

"Your campsite will be flooded before dawn," said one of Conmael's companions. "Unless you care to swim out, you should move." He held up the lantern he was carrying to reveal that the stream had risen significantly. Perhaps he was right about a flood, perhaps not. I had no wish to put it to the test.

Now I felt not only cold, tired and angry, but stupid as well. We'd made a foolish error. In the dark, with little knowledge of the terrain around us, we had no choice but to accept these folk's help.

Conmael spared me the indignity of having to ask. "Strike camp," he said, "and we will lead you to a more suitable spot, dry and sheltered. The necessities you requested will be ready for you there." A carefully judged pause. "I did explain before that I wish to help you, Blackthorn. There is no need for every encounter to be a battle."

"It was your manner that made it so. I hope you and your friends will do me the courtesy of absenting yourselves while I get dressed."

They set down their lanterns and faded back into the shadows. Within the space of two breaths I could not see them at all. It was deeply disconcerting: not just the suddenness, but the feeling they might still be there watching, only invisible. On the other hand, the spectacle of me or Grim unclothed was hardly going to cause any excitement.

"I'll hold up a blanket for you," Grim said now. It seemed he, too, suspected we were still under scrutiny. "Better be quick, it's cold."

We put on our damp clothes. We bundled up our supplies. As soon as we had our packs on our backs, Conmael and the others were there once more, raising the lanterns, lighting a path through the woods. Not the track we'd come in by, since it was already deep in water, but another that snaked up around the rocks, then curved down under the trees again. An unpleasant thought came to me: that we were being led far astray, into a realm beyond the human, and that there would be some kind of trick attached. Perhaps Conmael had decided seven years of tending to the aches and pains of my own kind and staying away from Mathuin would not be enough to teach me whatever it was he thought I still had to learn. Perhaps both I and hapless Grim, whose only crime had been to follow me when he wasn't wanted, would now be condemned to ten years, fifty years, a hundred years in the world of the fey. A hundred years doing Conmael's bidding. If it was anything like the tales, I'd be sent back into the human world the same age I was now, and find that not only was Mathuin dead and gone, but his grandchildren were too. So much for justice.

I stumbled, and Grim's hand shot out to keep me from falling.

"All right?" he muttered.

"I'll cope. You?"

"I'll do. Wish I knew what the fellow was playing at."

Conmael was walking up ahead of us. He did not turn, but his voice came clearly, for all the moaning of the trees in the wind and the relentless voice of the rain. "Blackthorn knows the nature of this game. Whether she chooses to share the details with you is her business."

"She told me." Grim's voice was granite hard. "And it didn't make a lot of sense."

"To you, maybe not."

There was a silence as we climbed, then Grim said, "I understand why you would save Blackthorn. But why couldn't you do it without killing the others? It wasn't their fault she got shut up in there."

Now Conmael did stop. He turned to face us, his high-boned features touched by the lantern light. "You expect me to justify my actions to you?"

"It's a fair question," I said.

Conmael shrugged. "I had a purpose. I achieved that purpose. Perhaps, if someone had asked them, your fellow prisoners might have chosen a quick and painless demise over a longer stay in Mathuin's custody."

"Quick? Painless?" Grim's words were like blows. "Didn't wait around long enough to check, did you?"

"You would prefer that I had left Blackthorn to Mathuin's executioners? Don't tell me that given the choice between her and the others you wouldn't have chosen to save her."

"Stop it," I said, hating the look on Grim's face. He hadn't told me the whole story about that day, about what had happened after I got out. Something dark was in his eyes now; it was in the set of his jaw. "It's past now. Just move on."

"Broke the whole place down, didn't you?" Grim wasn't going to let this go. "If you could do that, why couldn't you get her out without killing anyone else? If you've got magic, you should use it better."

"Grim. Walk on."

"Just saying."

There was no crossing over to the Otherworld. There were no tricks, as far as I could tell, though I was hardly in an ideal state to detect them. Conmael and his companions led us to the edge of the forest, where the light from their lanterns revealed a shelter cunningly fashioned around the trunk of a massive oak. It was woven from branches and foliage, with a low opening well screened from the weather. The neat space inside was carpeted with dry grass, and on this were set a cloth-covered basket that smelled of freshly baked bread, a pair of folded blankets and two bags. Conmael hung his lantern from a low branch.

"It will soon be day," he observed, glancing up at the sky. The storm was clearing, the rain was easing. A fresh westerly wind made the strange little hut seem altogether appealing, even if the place was somewhat inadequate to shelter the two of us, Grim being an unusually big man. "You will need more sleep before you move on. We will leave you now. Your supplies are here." Conmael gave Grim a fleeting glance. "All that you requested."

"Thank you," I said, making an effort. Winterfalls was still a fair distance away, judging by what we'd seen from up on the pass. I'd best keep my wretched tongue under control until we got there and sorted ourselves out. "When might I expect to see you again? It's good to be warned if one's about to drown. But I'm hoping you won't make a habit of visiting in the middle of the night."

"When there is a need, you will see me," Conmael said.

"My need or yours?"

He smiled. "Let us see how this unfolds. I bid you farewell. Travel safely." And just like that, he and his friends were gone.

The basket did indeed hold fresh bread and a round of cheese, as well as a flask of mead. The bags contained a change of clothing for me, and—somewhat surprisingly— another for Grim. There was also a knife and, of course, the blankets.

"Very nice," observed Grim, holding up a generously sized woolen tunic in a fetching shade of blue. "Doesn't feel right to put them on, though. Or eat the food. You know those stories? Fey food that sets a geis on you, fey garments that burn your skin all away. That fellow, that friend of yours, I wouldn't trust him an inch. Whatever he's up to, it's no good."

"He did save my life."

"All the same."

"Well, if you want to stay in those wet things and nibble on the last dried-up mushroom for breakfast, fine with me. I'm going to risk the geis and the poisoned clothing spell. I've eaten Conmael's food and worn his gifts before, and I still seem to be all right. Turn your back, Grim."

"He wouldn't hurt *you*," Grim muttered as I stripped off the damp clothes and wriggled into the dry ones. But when it was his turn he put on the trousers and shirt and tunic and wrapped the warm cloak around himself, and everything fit as if made especially for him. That turned him very quiet. We shared the food without talking, saving some for the journey. It was only as we settled to sleep—it was not yet dawn—that Grim said, "I don't like owing that fellow anything at all. He'll want payment one way or another. His kind always do."

But I was snuggled in my blanket on the dry grass, warm and comfortable, and I fell asleep before I could answer.

8

GRIM

Last part of the journey's easier. We've got good food and warm clothes, and that helps keep our spirits up. Be happier if we'd earned those things with the work of our own hands. Heard too many tales about fey gifts and fey promises and how they turn a man's life upside down. There can't be good in it. Hard to weigh it up. A puzzle. Conmael saved Blackthorn from the executioner. That's big. It's big enough that I should forgive him plenty. But I don't like him and I don't trust him. His kind don't think the way we do. They don't have feelings, if the tales are true.

Anyway, he doesn't come back, so we travel on without him. Lonelier country here in the north, mountains and lakes and dark forests. Not so many farms and not so many folk on the road. That suits the two of us. Some days we go from dawn to dusk with hardly a word spoken. Just walking on, stopping for a rest or a drink or a bite to eat, then walking on again. There's a peace in it that has me wishing we'd never get to Winterfalls, but a day comes when we reach a crossroads with a marker. Letters scratched on a big stone slab, and arrows pointing off north and west.

"Winterfalls," says Blackthorn, looking up the road to the north. It doesn't surprise me that she can read. I reckon hers might be quite a story. She turns to look along the track to the west, leading to a soft woodland, all kinds of green. "Winterfalls," she says again. "Through Dreamer's Wood."

"Which way?" I ask. I can see the northern track is the main one—it's broad and well kept and seems to run fairly straight. The path through Dreamer's Wood is prettier. Looks like the kind of way that could lose itself quickly.

"The northern one's quicker, I'd guess," says Blackthorn. "But the cottage isn't in the settlement of Winterfalls. It's on the fringe of Dreamer's Wood. That's what Conmael said. So we're going that way." She gives me a glance. "Looks as if we're nearly there."

I wait for her to say it: *Thank you for helping me get here, Grim; now you can go your own way.* But she doesn't, just turns and heads off along the westward track. I hurry after her. If this place turns out to be a ruin, I'll fix it up nice and neat. Mend the roof, dig new drains, put a good bolt on the door. See that the fire draws well, the shutters fit tight, the privy's dug deep. Make it into a proper home.

We get closer to the wood and a funny feeling comes over me, the same as when that poxy Conmael and his cronies were around. I look at Blackthorn, but she's walking on as usual, lost in her own thoughts. Probably thinking it'll be good to stop moving at last. We've walked through the best part of summer. Soon those trees will be turning all colors, their leaves like a beautiful big fire. As red as that hair of hers. Seems like this might be the right sort of spot for her, funny feeling or not.

We reach the trees, all kinds, some I know the names of and some I've never seen before. Strikes me as odd how quiet it is in there. Even the birds aren't chirping much, though it's a sunny day. One step ahead, the path will be in shadow. And something tells me I don't want to take that step.

"What?" says Blackthorn, but she's stopped walking. We stand there looking ahead along the path into Dreamer's Wood. Little branching foot track goes off on the right, just wide enough for one person to walk. You wouldn't go that way with a horse and cart or a herd of cows. It's a slow, up-and-down, in-and-out sort of track. Thing is, though, it doesn't go through the wood, but around the edge of it, in sunlight. Might be the path to the cottage, might not. But if we follow it, sooner or later we'll get there. That's what I'm thinking, but I don't say any of it. She's the one in charge.

"This way," Blackthorn says, backing up and taking the smaller path. "No need to go into the wood." Then, dropping her voice as if she thinks someone else might be listening, "Did you feel it?"

"Felt something. Don't know what it was."

"Mm. Well, let's find this wretched cottage."

We walk on a bit, and I hear birds singing in the fields, see them too, picking over the remains of a barley crop. But if there are birds in the wood, they're staying quiet. Scared of the place, maybe, same as I am, though I'm not going to tell her that. Not much use as a minder if I fall into a jelly over something I can't even see; something I can't put a name to. Dreamer's Wood. Wonder who the dreamer was and what happened to him?

"Quiet in there," says Blackthorn.

"Mm."

"Makes a change from that place. No shouting. Not even chirping. Peaceful."

I don't say anything.

"The silence might take a bit of getting used to," she says.

I'm thinking the silence will keep me awake. Make more room in my head for the bad things. Need to work on that. Need to stay strong. "Anything's better than Slammer," I say. Then I recall that Slammer's dead, crushed under a broken wall with only his hand sticking out, and I wonder if he had a wife, children, a life outside that place, or if screaming at us was his whole life. I wonder what happened to make him so crazy.

We walk halfway around the wood and there's the cottage, half under a stand of willows.

"Morrigan's britches," mutters Blackthorn, stopping in her tracks. "What a wreck."

But I'm not seeing a wreck, I'm seeing what the place could be with a bit of love and care and hard work. Patch the roof, mend the shutters, see to the drains, everything on my list and more.

"Nothing that can't be fixed," I say.

"Of course," puts in Blackthorn, "Conmael's folk would do it, if I asked them. It would probably only take a click of the fingers to set the whole place to rights."

When I don't answer, she takes a long look at me.

"What do you think?" she says, as if it matters.

"Not up to me, is it? You're the one Conmael wants to live here."

"All the same," says Blackthorn, "what do you think? What would you do if you were me?" And when I still can't find anything to say, she adds, "Come on, Grim."

Trying to put myself in her head is enough to turn me dizzy. "You want to be on your own," I say, hoping I won't disgrace myself by shedding tears. Big man like me, ridiculous. "After that place, that's what you want most."

"Go on." Her face gives nothing away.

"So the easiest thing would be to call Conmael and his folk, and ask to have the cottage fixed up and all the supplies you need laid on," I say. "You could lock the door behind you and keep out anyone you didn't want."

A silence. She's waiting for me to say more. Getting the words out is like swimming in porridge. Feels like a test. "But if I was you, what I'd be wanting most was to do things for myself, without magic to make it easier. Mend the outside, fix up the inside. Make sure that well's free of rubbish. Dig a garden, maybe get some chickens, take the time to explore and learn about things. In that place of Mathuin's, it was always other folk deciding things. Big things like you getting to have your hearing, and little things like the chance to take a piss without Slammer looking on and making comments. I know you've made a promise to Conmael, and there's no changing that. But if I was you, I wouldn't be wanting any more favors from him and his folk. I'd be wanting to do things myself."

Blackthorn smiles. When she smiles it's like the sun suddenly comes out, when you've been thinking the day's going to be all gray clouds. "I'll be needing a bit of help," she says. "Only until the place is fixed up. Just so we're clear. You're right—I like being on my own."

I see myself the way she might be seeing me: useful, since she's hardly going to be climbing up on the roof to mend the thatch or lifting stones to fix those walls. Useful but sad, because I can't hide how much I want to stay. To a stray dog, every crumb's precious. "Mm-hm," I mumble, not trusting myself with words right now.

She's studying the tumbledown dwelling. "A fire and a brew, I think," she says, "then we can see what needs doing. Come on."

9

ORAN

The wait seemed endless. It mattered not the least that I had seen the maps, that I knew the distances. I understood that even if they changed horses every few miles and were favored with exceptionally fine weather, Flidais's party could not arrive at Winterfalls until some weeks after Father's reply to Lord Cadhan reached its destination. It was a long ride. Flidais was a young lady, not a warrior. She would need to take her time over the journey, despite the urgency suggested by her father's last communication. I knew I must be calm and wait. But I could not. I strode from place to place, from task to task, until Donagan took me aside, sat me down and suggested I should exercise better self-control.

"If you keep on this way," my friend and servant said, "you know what will happen."

"What?" I heard the edge in my voice, and moderated my tone. "I have no idea what you mean, Donagan."

"My guess is that someone will report back to the queen, and that your mother will descend on Winterfalls to check on your health. If she does not like what she sees, she may decide to change the plan. To receive Lady Flidais at court instead, or to move here and take charge of your household herself. The queen will not be impressed if she believes you . . . unhinged."

"Unhinged!" I shouted, leaping to my feet. My gaze met that of the painted Flidais, whose sweet image had changed me forever. I saw in her eyes that she still loved me, but that she thought I was being just a little ridiculous. "I'm sorry," I made myself say. "It's just so hard waiting. Everything's ready, or will be, the house is prepared, the arrangements are progressing, and there's nothing for me to do but stamp about the place getting in everyone's way."

"How about a ride?" Donagan said. "Perhaps as far as the wood, or farther if you like. The weather's good; we may as well make the most of it. We could go through the village, see how the local folk are faring. They like it when you do that. Unusual for a prince perhaps. But you're not like other princes. That, no doubt, is why Lady Flidais warmed to you."

Winterfalls settlement lay just beyond the southern boundaries of my home farm; the main road to Cahercorcan ran through the village. We rode there, just Donagan and me, thereby breaking my father's rule about never going anywhere without at least two guards in attendance. As a man settled in his own household and soon to be wed, I considered it unnecessary to abide by such rules. Besides, both Donagan and I could hold our own in a fight, should it come to that. Not that the local people were likely to attack either of us, since we were long known to them as summer tenants of the royal residence. I had known since I was a child that the place would one day be my home and that these would be my people, since it was customary for the prince of Dalriada to live at Winterfalls from his marriage until such time as he became king.

I'd never been overfond of formality—that was one reason I did not want Flidais to go to Cahercorcan, a place bound by etiquette, precedence and protocol—and I had made it my duty to get to know the folk of Winterfalls well, to understand their daily lives, their work, the things that were important to them. Sometimes that meant disregarding the rules for princely behavior that other folk—my mother, for instance, or Feabhal—set such store in. I wanted to be as good a leader as I could be, and it seemed to me folk would not follow a leader who knew little of them.

That made our ride through the settlement slow paced.
Folk came out to greet us, to ask questions, to congratulate
me on the forthcoming betrothal, for everyone knew Lady
Flidais was on her way north. The women, in particular,
seemed almost as excited about this as I was. Many expressed delight that the ritual was to take place here at
Winterfalls, not at court. I realized I would need to arrange
things so the folk of the settlement and the farms could be
present, if not for the ceremony itself, then most certainly
for the celebrations that would follow. A bonfire, I thought,
and dancing. I spoke to Fraoch the smith, who was accustomed to exercising his well-muscled arms not only in the
crafting of iron goods but also in playing the bodhran at
weddings, fairs and festival days. He knew which musicians
were the most skillful and the most reliable; he knew which
dances folk would like best for such an event. I spoke to
Iobhar the brewer, Deaman the baker and Scannal the
miller. Iobhar gave us ale, Deaman gave us a wheaten loaf
and Scannal asked me to have a word with his grandmother.
She told me a wise woman had moved into the old cottage
out by Dreamer's Wood, and that folk said she'd a sour
temper on her but could give a body a cure for anything.

This was something of a surprise. The wise woman must
be a very recent arrival, or someone in my own household
would have made mention of her. There was a physician at
Cahercorcan, of course, with several skilled assistants. But
Cahercorcan was a good twenty miles away. There was no
healer at Winterfalls, either in my own household or in the
village. There had not been for a while. I remembered the
cottage as damp and deserted, its previous inhabitant dead
and gone so long ago that only the very oldest folk remembered her name.

We thanked the people for their gifts, wished them good
day and rode on, letting our mounts have their heads once
we were clear of the settlement. On our own we were not
master and servant, but simply friends. The day was fair, the
air clear, the sun warm. With my body stretched and my
mind occupied, I felt at ease for the first time in many days.

"Black Crow save us," remarked Donagan, pulling up
his horse as we crested a rise some time later and looked

down toward Dreamer's Wood. "Someone's wrought a minor miracle."

I rode up beside him and saw that this was true, and that the someone was in plain view, tying down thatch on the refurbished roof of the old cottage. A big man. A very big man, moving about with the ease of a lad.

"Who is that?" I asked, not recognizing the fellow.

"I don't know him," said Donagan. "Maybe this wise woman brought him with her. Whoever he is, he's transformed the old place, from the looks of it."

Without further discussion we rode down the hill and headed toward the cottage, which might almost have been an entirely new construction, so thoroughly had it been repaired. The work extended to the garden, where the crumbling drystone walls had been set to rights and the tangle of weeds cleared. A freshly dug patch of earth lay ready for winter vegetables. The pathway had been swept clean of leaves, and there were garments flapping on a line. As we approached, I saw a flash of red, and thought perhaps someone had slipped away under the trees behind the cottage.

The burly thatcher spotted us and made his way down his ladder. His movements were deliberate, unhurried. Nonetheless, by the time we had drawn up our horses on the path, there he was, feet apart, arms folded, waiting for us. The fellow stood head and shoulders above the tallest man I'd seen in my life. He had the look of a fighter, the head shaven, the nose crooked, the eyes small, the neck and shoulders bullish. His was a face only a mother would think handsome. He said nothing at all, simply stared at the two of us.

I glanced at Donagan, and he dismounted.

"Good day," my friend said. "My name is Donagan. This is Oran, Prince of Dalriada; I am his servant and companion. We heard the cottage was newly occupied. A healer, they're saying in the village. A wise woman."

The giant grunted in response. It could have meant *Yes*, *No*, or *Move away before I do you an injury*.

"Winterfalls is the personal holding of the Dalriadan heir," I said, feeling sure my most princely tone would fail to impress this person. "This cottage is in my gift." And when the man still failed to find words, I added carefully, "That means it's up to me who lives in it."

He stirred now. "What are you saying, that Blackthorn can't stay here?"

"*My lord*," muttered Donagan.

The giant gave him a look.

"You address Prince Oran as *my lord*," Donagan said.

"It's all right, Donagan," I said. When facing a man who could probably kill me with a quick flick of the wrist, being addressed with proper respect seemed unimportant. "May I ask your name?"

"Nobody's stopping you," said the giant, shifting his feet a little.

Another silence.

"May I speak with your mistress?"

The man's jaw tightened. A pulse beat in his temple. "You mean Blackthorn? She's off gathering herbs," he said. *"My lord."*

"Keep a civil tongue in your head," said Donagan, his tone icy. "You're speaking to the prince of Dalriada."

I got down from my horse. The district did need a wise woman, and the lady had done nothing amiss, save possibly absent herself rather than engage in a conversation with me. "We've interrupted your labors," I said, giving the very big man a smile. "You're doing a fine job with the thatching, that's clear. And the rest of this—is it all your work? The place looks transformed."

The giant spoke. "What you said. About the cottage. Blackthorn can't stay here without your say-so, is that the sum of it?"

"My lord." Donagan looked about to explode.

I ignored him. "That is the sum of it, yes; even a tumbledown ruin generally belongs to someone. All these lands are mine. But I didn't say the wise woman couldn't stay. Only that I would like to speak with her."

"You can speak to me."

"Not without a name, at least."

"Grim."

"And you are her servant?" At the expression on his face, I added, "Brother? Husband?"

He narrowed his eyes at me. "Traveled here with her.

Fixed the place up for her. I look after her. That enough for you?" After what seemed to me a carefully judged pause, he added, "My lord?"

"Thank you, Grim. You don't expect Blackthorn back soon, then?"

"She's her own mistress. She'll be back in her own time. My lord."

"You say you traveled here—where did you come from?" If this Blackthorn was going to stay in the area and tend to my folk, I'd need to know at the very least that she could do a good job of it. If she'd left a position elsewhere, there must be a reason.

"South."

I held his gaze, playing him at his own game.

"Laigin," Grim added eventually. "I'll tell Blackthorn you came by. You want to check on her, ask the folk she's been tending to. They seem happy enough. My lord."

For him, this seemed a long speech. At the end of it he glanced, not too subtly, toward the ladder.

"Thank you, Grim. You'll be wanting to get on with your work."

A grunt.

"Please ask Blackthorn to come to my house one day soon, at her convenience. There's certainly a need for her services in the district. But best if the matter's put on a more formal footing."

"Formal?" His eyes narrowed again. He balled his hands into fists. Substantial fists. "What does that mean?"

"Nothing you need concern yourself with."

"What does it mean, *my lord*?"

Donagan took a step forward; I halted him with a gesture. "I like to be sure my folk are adequately compensated for their work, and that they carry out that work as well as they can. No more than that. It may also be useful to Blackthorn to know our procedures for airing grievances and settling disputes. A monthly open council, held on the day of full moon, which you are both welcome to attend."

Another grunt. Grim's distrust was written all over his plain features.

"You're surprised that I take an interest in my people's welfare?" I asked. It was a wonder Blackthorn had found any work here at all, with this bristling mastiff on her front doorstep. But she'd been doing her job and doing it well, if the word in the settlement was correct.

"You ask a lot of questions," Grim said. "My lord."

"That's because I want to hear the answers."

"Never met a prince before. But the way I see it, too much power twists a man. Leads him down dark ways. No reason to trust you, my lord. What you've said is that you've got power over Blackthorn. You can turn her out of here when you like. Make her do your bidding. Her and me, we don't like that."

"You can't speak to the prince that way—" began Donagan.

"Ask Blackthorn to come and see me," I said, keeping calm. "Come with her if you wish. Not all princes are the same, Grim. If you mean well at Winterfalls, you'll be treated well." I let my gaze run over the cottage again. "There should not only be work in these parts for your ... companion, but for you too, I'm certain."

"I'll tell her." Grim turned away, heading for the ladder. The set of his shoulders suggested an anger far deeper than his words had conveyed.

Donagan seemed about to say something.

"We'll ride to Dreamer's Pool," I told him, mounting my horse. "Sample the food and drink we were given. Then home."

We followed the little track that skirted the wood. The cottage and its surly minder were soon out of sight behind us. Not far along the track, another narrow way branched off under the trees, leading to the heart of Dreamer's Wood, and this we followed. The place was as eerily quiet as ever. Even the birds seemed muted here, as if they dared not lift their voices. The only sounds were the gurgling song of the stream that ran alongside the path and the whisper of the wind in the trees.

Folk said there were fey beings living in Dreamer's Wood, though nobody had ever seen one. They said it was a place where remnants of an ancient past still lingered. It was no wonder people skirted the wood, entering only if they had to. The village folk feared what they did not understand. They feared magic, and the fey were known to be full of magic.

As a child, I had wanted to believe every word of this. It had never occurred to me to fear Dreamer's Wood. The place had drawn me, and when we had stayed at Winterfalls I had spent long mornings sitting in the mysterious shade, dreaming of old tales and hoping a fey being would appear and perhaps engage me in conversation. Later, when my father had appointed Donagan as my companion, I'd ceased those solitary vigils. Donagan had been tolerant for a boy of that age. But I had known he thought my fancies childish. Besides, I had never once seen more than hedgehogs and rabbits in the wood.

The horses sensed something, no doubt of it. I felt the tension in Snow's shoulders as she went forward, though she was obedient to my directions, as ever. Donagan's Star twitched her tail and turned her head one way, then the other.

"Can't say it would be my first choice of a spot to sit down and enjoy a bite to eat," my companion said.

"It's quiet," I said. "And we might run into the elusive Blackthorn. Didn't our friend Grim say she was gathering herbs?"

"If she's anything like her minder, she won't take kindly to being run into. You should have corrected that fellow's manners, at the very least. If you let folk speak to you like that, you're in danger of losing their respect."

I glanced across at him. "With Grim, there was no respect to lose. If I learned anything about the man, apart from the obvious fact that he's strong and able, it was that he doesn't like being answerable to anyone. Did you see the way he was moving about on that roof? It made me wonder what he was before."

"Before what?"

"Before he was this Blackthorn's minder, or companion, or assistant."

"He's surely hiding some kind of secret or he'd have been readier with his answers. His manner almost suggested he wanted you to turn the two of them out."

We reached the pool and dismounted, looping our reins

over a branch. The horses did not drop their heads to drink or to crop at the long grass. The two of them stood still and silent, side by side.

Donagan got the provisions out of his saddlebag and we sat down on the grassy bank to eat and drink. Deaman's bread was very good; Iobhar's ale washed it down well. Chewing with enjoyment, I noted the things I loved about this place, and imagined sitting here with Flidais by my side, sharing them with her. The stillness; the way Dreamer's Pool had a kind of glow about it, not only the sunlight filtering down through the autumn canopy but a light that seemed to come from within, from the water itself. The tiny insects that danced on the reflective surface of the pool. The neat curls of the ferns that fringed the water, the glinting droplets hanging there. The pebbles on the shore, smooth and shining, each different, each beautiful. The place was a poem in itself. She and I would come here with Bramble. We could pretend that this was our own private place where nobody could find us. Here, we could forget that one day I would be king of Dalriada, and that she would be queen. We could be no more than a pair of lovers enjoying each other's company. My mind drifted further, and I drew it back sharply. I would not dishonor my sweetheart, even in my daydreams.

"Let Aedan see this Blackthorn for you," Donagan offered. "It's appropriate for your steward to deal with such matters. I'm taking it that all you want is to be sure she has the appropriate skills and experience, and that she and the fellow will look after the cottage. It sounds as if the people are happy with her."

"Donagan?"

"Mm?"

"Whom would a young lady like Flidais want to attend her, supposing we were fortunate enough to be blessed with an infant? A court physician, or a wise woman like this Blackthorn?"

Donagan gave me a sideways look. "Are you speaking of a confinement? You can hardly expect me to have any expertise in that. It's a matter for women." After a moment he took pity on me and added, "I believe your mother would say you need not concern yourself with such things at this point, if at all. And she'd add that if you insisted your child be born at Winterfalls, and not at Cahercorcan, she would ensure the court physician took up residence here well in advance of the expected birth. As an alternative, you might engage your own physician, who would be permanently attached to your household."

"What do the women of the village do?"

"Without the services of a midwife," Donagan said, "I imagine that they assist one another, and that some of them die. Their infants too. It's unsurprising that they've embraced Blackthorn, unknown though she must have been to them."

With a sudden chill I realized my attempts to be the friend of my people had been sorely lacking. How could I have overlooked something so important?

"Don't look so stricken," Donagan said, packing up the remnants of our meal. "This woman's here now, and as for your future wife, you have plenty of time to put arrangements in place. You'll be able to ask Lady Flidais in person what she'd prefer. Though I suggest you do not do so the moment you see her; she might take that to indicate you are overeager for the marital bed." I felt a flush rise to my cheeks, and saw him grin. "A joke, Oran. Only a joke."

"It is no laughing matter." I rose to my feet, gazing across the still waters of the pool to the trees beyond. I had glimpsed that sudden spot of red again, perhaps a scarf, perhaps a head of vibrant hair among the haze of grays and greens, perhaps a bright bird passing. It was gone now. Maybe Blackthorn liked visitors even less than her henchman did. "We'd best be on our way. I can't imagine how I overlooked this. I must set it to rights without delay."

"If taking action on the matter will stop you from stamping around in a state of constant anxiety, it can be only good," observed my friend. "Shall we ride?"

I would have written to my father as soon as we returned home. But a messenger had come during our absence, and there was a letter from Flidais. It had been carried north by a series of riders, and under the lady's instructions it had been delivered not to court but directly to me. I left Donagan to help the groom with our horses and retreated to my bedchamber, wondering if a time might come when my sweet-

heart's communications did not turn me into a shaking
bundle of nerves, and considering whether that would be a
good thing or a bad. I knew what my mother would say.

I broke the seal, which was not Cadhan's, and unrolled
the parchment.

> *To Oran, Prince of Dalriada,*
>
> *I write this in some haste to let you know that I
> and my attendants are now safely across the border
> of Ulaid. We are enjoying a few days' rest in the
> household of the local chieftain, Muadan. I have
> never traveled so far from home before, Oran, and I
> admit I find it deeply disconcerting. I feel somewhat
> set adrift, though folk have been very kind and have
> gone out of their way to make me welcome. I am
> glad that my maidservant Ciar is traveling with me,
> along with several women from my parents'
> household. That means I am bringing a little of
> home with me, though I am so far away.*
>
> *I am anxious about the safety of my father and
> mother and of all our people. Riding away and
> leaving them felt wrong, though I know this was
> what my parents wanted.*
>
> *When I feel sad I remind myself that when I
> reach Winterfalls you will be there, and I think of
> sharing poems and songs and long walks in the
> woods, and that brings the smile back to my face. I
> will be pleased when this endless journey is over.*
>
> *Bramble is much disturbed; at night she burrows
> under her blankets and refuses to show so much as
> the tip of her nose. I think my little dog longs to
> reach Winterfalls as much as I do!*
>
> *My host, Lord Muadan, has offered the services
> of his messenger to bring this letter to you, which is
> most kind of him. I will seal and send it now. I hope
> that I will not be far behind it, dear Oran.*
>
> > *Flidais of Cloud Hill*

My heart beat fast. She was in Ulaid! That meant only a
matter of days before her party reached Winterfalls. Of

course, she might decide to spend a while enjoying Muadan's hospitality. The horses would need to be rested, or fresh mounts obtained. I recalled that Muadan loved to hunt, and kept a pack of wolfhounds for the purpose. Bramble would hardly be comfortable there.

I bade myself be calm. I was the head of my own household; I was the heir to the Dalriadan throne. Such a man did not greet his intended bride in a lather of nervous sweat, with trembling hands and a mind wiped clean of rational thought. I must not let love make me foolish.

I stood by the window looking out across my grazing fields, and made a list in my mind of what preparations still remained to be completed before my sweetheart's arrival. The list was not very long—thanks in part to my enthusiasm, and in far greater part, I suspected, to the efficiency of my household, the place was all but ready. There was a riding horse to be brought down from Cahercorcan, a wedding gift to Flidais from my father. Some further improvements to the bathing arrangements were still to be made. And the matter of the wise woman. But Donagan was right: that was not truly urgent. This Blackthorn would present herself at my house in due course, as I'd requested, and I could have a word with her then.

10

BLACKTHORN

The day we'd moved into the cottage, I'd had to make a decision. The place had one main room with a hearth and a couple of shelf beds, and a falling-apart lean-to at the back. The only place for a healer to conduct her business was in that main room, and it was plain I'd be sleeping there as well. Which had left the question of Grim. I'd already told him, somewhat against my better judgment, that he could stay awhile and work on the repairs, since there was so much needing to be done on the place.

I hadn't wanted him leaping to any conclusions about what that might mean. Not that he'd ever suggested we might become any more than traveling companions. But he was a man, and my experience of men suggested I'd better make it quite clear where we stood. So, right at the start, I'd told him he'd be sleeping in the outhouse. It was a low structure of stone, separated from the cottage by a weed-choked garden patch. In fact the outhouse had survived the years better than the cottage itself, with its earthen floor reasonably dry. It only needed the cobwebs brushed away and a new door and shutters fitted. A few boards, a supply of fresh straw, a couple of blankets—it would be more comfortable than many places we'd slept in during our journey. Compared with Mathuin's lockup it was a palace.

At the time Grim had made no comment, simply taken his pack and his blankets out there and found some old sacking to hang across the doorway until he could get started on the work. The cottage had to come first. We'd found the place full of cold drafts. The chimney was blocked by the dried-out corpse of a blackbird, the roof leaked, the shutters were hanging broken or gone altogether, and the whole place stank of mold.

But that had changed quickly enough. Grim had put in long days on the repairs, making the place clean and comfortable. If he was not up a ladder or digging a hole or planting something, he was off bartering some of our small stock of coppers for tools or seeds or other supplies. The local folk started offering him work, helping to get a harvest in or dig a well. They paid him in coppers or food or other items we needed. But he never did more than a day or two for them; mostly he worked on the cottage. Grim wasn't a man who gave much away, but as the place changed I saw him changing with it, walking straighter, holding his head higher, readier with a smile.

I thought it likely the little house was more of a home now than it had ever been in the days of the last wise woman. Grim had lime-washed the outside and adorned the newly thatched roof with a row of fanciful straw creatures. He'd mended the broken furniture. He'd dug the garden and planted seeds. I'd added roots of this and that, which I'd gathered in the woods. Conmael had chosen the spot well; there was a good supply of herbs in season if a body knew where to look for them.

Folk came to consult me, at first warily, then, as the word spread, with more confidence. People have a natural fear of a wise woman—the taint of magic hangs over my kind, a remnant of a time when we did more than prepare herbal remedies, strap up broken limbs and help women give birth. The need to see so many people and to stay courteous left me ill-tempered and weary at the end of the day. Grim was good at having a brew ready when I needed it.

But the sleeping arrangements soon became a problem. Me in the cottage, him in the outhouse—it had sounded all right to me, for as long as he hung around. We'd been there some while when I got up in the night, went out the back to relieve myself and fell over Grim, who was rolled up in a blanket, sleeping across the cottage doorway. He woke with a start, apologized and headed off to the outhouse before I could say a word.

The next morning he was up and working before I stirred. I didn't ask him about the night before, and he didn't mention it, but I knew him pretty well after our time locked up together, and I could tell something was bothering him. I could see the signs, though he was working hard not to show them. A clenching and unclenching of the fists; the pulse beating in his temple; his lips moving as if he were constantly having a conversation with himself. Signs I hadn't seen for a long while. I didn't want to think about what it meant. If he'd taken himself off after we escaped and gone his own way, I wouldn't be needing to waste time worrying about him now. I had enough responsibilities with my promises to Conmael, my job to do and the effort of being pleasant to folk I cared nothing about. I didn't need the big lump of a fellow weighing down my thoughts into the bargain.

But there he was. And I found out, after I'd taken the walk to the privy by night a couple more times, that while he was in the outhouse he wasn't sleeping, he was curled up muttering to himself, same as in Mathuin's lockup. I didn't look in on him, because that would be breaking an unspoken rule about privacy. But I knew he'd be crouched down at the back, in a corner, trying to be invisible. Trying to shut out the bad things, to keep the shadows at bay. The nonsense words were like a spell or charm. An incantation. Fill his mind with them, and he need not hear Slammer crashing his stick on the bars or yelling insults. He need not hear Poxy or Dribbles or me screaming as we were beaten, or worse. Even here, long days and longer miles from that hellish place, Grim's nights were full of those sounds and sights. He hadn't slept at night in that place. He'd kept the darkness away with his relentless exercises, and when he hadn't been doing those he'd been talking to me. When I'd been asleep, when everyone had been asleep, he'd probably kept on talking anyway, until morning came.

Once I'd worked this out, I wished I hadn't, because it meant I had to find a solution, and I didn't much like the only solution that presented itself, which was that I should invite Grim to sleep in the house. There were two parts of me arguing with each other and I couldn't shut up their voices. One said, *He didn't ask you for help this time, so you don't need to do anything. He's never complained about the outhouse.* The other said, *You were in that place too. It turned you upside down and inside out. He helped you escape and now he's mending the house for you. You owe him.* And the first voice replied, to my shame, *I never asked him to do either of those things.*

It ate away at me until I had to do something. But I needed to go carefully or I'd only make matters worse.

We were sitting by the hearth—the fire burned well now that he'd unblocked the chimney—as evening shadow spread itself over the wood, turning the green and brown quilt of daytime to a soft blanket of purple and gray. Grim had made rabbit stew with dumplings, one of the best meals I'd tasted for a long while, and I waited until we were finished eating before I asked him.

"Grim?"

"Mm?"

"Must be cold in that outhouse."

A pause, then, "Roof over my head," he said. "Not complaining."

I drew a couple of long breaths. "You don't sleep, though, do you?" I asked, hoping this would not send him back into silence.

"Never did sleep much. Once, maybe. Long time ago."

"Mm. You need your rest. Working so hard."

A silence; Grim stared down at his clasped hands. "Keeping you awake, am I?" he said eventually.

I found myself wishing he would shout at me, berate me for my selfishness, point out that with him slaving away on my behalf the least I should do was give him a proper place to sleep. His patience made me angry; it filled me with a guilt I had no room for. Wasn't this hard enough already, when my own nights were haunted by Mathuin? "Might almost be better if you were," I found myself saying. "My dreams don't make the best company."

A grunt was all the response I got. But I was used to him, and I knew it was no dismissal, but an acknowledg-

ment that he understood. Which annoyed me even more—
I didn't need understanding, I didn't want folk making
allowances for me, I just wanted them to go away and leave
me alone so I could make quite sure I didn't forget the only
thing that really mattered: making Mathuin pay for his
crimes. Getting through the seven years so I could ensure
that happened. Not wasting my anger on the folk who
came to my door seeking love potions and cures for the
pox and poultices for boils in awkward places. Not wasting
it on Grim. Saving it for the man who had destroyed my
life, and who would keep on doing the same to other folk
until I stopped him.

"Thing is," said Grim, and his voice was just above a
whisper, "I don't do so well on my own. At night. Day's all
right, sun shining, work to do, and you're in and out of the
house."

I said nothing. I heard how hard it was for him to admit
this.

"Loneliest place in the world, sometimes, that place of
Mathuin's," Grim said. "Even with the noise, the screaming,
Frog Spawn going on and on with his list, and Slammer . . .
A fellow could be in there, with all that around him, and
feel like he was at the bottom of a well, in the deep of a pit,
somewhere nobody would ever find him. Nighttime, worse.
Even when Frog Spawn was quiet, even when the guards
were off sleeping, I could hear it. See it. Everything. All the
things, from the first day, they never went away. Not for a
single heartbeat."

I nodded, though Grim was not looking at me, but into
the fire. I didn't remind him that we were out now, and safe,
and that those things were gone. "You could have killed
Slammer or Tiny," I said. "Any time they had you out of
your cell, you could have done it in a moment."

A long silence, then he said, "Thought of it. A lot. Before
you came I might have done it. They'd have made an end of
me, after, and it would all have been over. Different when
you came. If I'd done that, you would have been on your
own."

There was nothing to say to this. Nothing at all. I'd have
survived without his hulking presence in the cell opposite.
I'd have managed without his voice measuring out the

hours of night. My anger would have kept me alive. But he had made a difference. The big ugly fellow who'd insisted on calling me Lady even when I was lower than the low had been . . . not a friend, because a person like me didn't have friends, but . . .

"Maybe it'll go away one day," he said, lifting his head, looking over at me. "Do you think? When we're old folk?"

Suddenly I wanted to cry, which was beyond ridiculous. "We're old already, the two of us," I said. "Old inside. Old and tired."

"Thing is," said Grim, "when I did sleep, it was because you were there across the way. Knew I had a job to do, a reason not to string myself up and make an end of it. A reason not to attack Slammer and get myself killed. Still got a job to do, only . . ."

"Only you can't always remember that when you're on your own at night?"

"That's about the size of it. Big soft fool, I am."

Words came to my lips, words I knew would hurt him terribly, although they were the truth. Some part of me, a long unused part, stopped those words before I could say them. "Grim. We've seen so much, the two of us, we've been through so much, it's stupid to concern ourselves with what folk might think if we both sleep here in the cottage. If being able to see me when you wake in the night will mean you get proper rest, then we'd better make sure you can, for now at least. There are two beds; we'll use them. Only one request: you might make some kind of screen, so we don't have to do that whole silly exercise of one holding up a blanket while the other gets dressed in the morning."

"You wouldn't be wanting folk to think badly of you," Grim said, but I had seen the change in his eyes, the dawning hope. "Wise woman and all. Doesn't seem quite right."

"They can think what they like. Why would I care? If they choose not to make use of my services because they think I'm a woman of easy virtue, that's their problem."

"What about the prince? Oran of Dalriada? If what he said was right, about the cottage being his to let us live in or not, he might take it into his head to throw us out."

"I doubt a prince is going to take a personal interest in

who shares the local healer's sleeping quarters. He'll surely have weightier matters on his mind."

"An idea," Grim said. "I could keep my bedroll out in the lean-to. It's dry now I've mended the roof and put in the new door. Bring it in last thing at night, put it out first thing in the morning, before anyone's here but the two of us."

"If that soothes your finer feelings, Grim, by all means do so." *It's not an invitation to creep into my bed in the middle of the night*, I thought of saying, but decided it was unnecessary. We were beyond weary, the two of us; worn out by what had befallen us, sickened by it. If anyone were to creep into anyone's bed, it would not be because of the desire a man feels for a woman, or a woman for a man. It would more likely be the terror of an infant waking from a nightmare and reaching for the comforting familiar.

"What?" I said, sensing Grim's eyes on me.

"You were smiling."

"Don't assume anything from that. Disturb my sleep and you'll be straight back into the outhouse."

He kept on at me about Oran, Prince of Dalriada, and the time the fellow had come riding by with his serving man and stopped to talk. That was the day I'd made sure I wasn't home, since I'd had no desire for people of his kind to ask me for help with their aches and pains. How was I to know the fellow owned the cottage and the land around it, as far as the eye could see? When I'd watched them ride up, what I'd seen was wealth, privilege and power. I'd seen a man like Mathuin of Laois, and I'd slipped off into the woods before he could start asking awkward questions. Before he could impose his will on me or ask me for something I wasn't prepared to give. I loathed his kind. They were all the same. Too much power made people arrogant and unfeeling. It turned them cruel. It blinded them to right and wrong.

Time passed and this prince didn't favor us with another visit. Nor did he send one of his lackeys to ask why I hadn't done as I was bid and come to report. Maybe he was impressed by the job Grim had done to the old dump of a place. Maybe word had got back to him that I did an adequate job of providing what folk needed when they were sick or hurt.

As for Conmael and his folk, there was neither sight nor sound of them, though I couldn't walk far into Dreamer's Wood without feeling the presence of the Other. Maybe the fey weren't there right now, but something was; something old and strange and powerful. I was careful, gathering herbs or bark or mushrooms, to do it in the right way, with words of thanks. Each night I set a crust of bread and a cup of mead on a flat stone outside the back door. Grim never said a word about that. He went into the wood too, for fuel or other materials, but he came back out as quickly as he could. Perhaps he said his own words of thanks. I never asked.

There came a spell of unusually warm weather, a touch of summer in late autumn. The plants in Grim's garden patch spread their leaves to drink in the sunlight, the birds sang in the fields, and I took it upon myself, in the absence of folk seeking my help, to wash a number of filthy garments while I had a good chance of getting them dry. Grim carried buckets of water from the well; we heated it one pan at a time, over an outside fire, and I scrubbed until my shoulders ached. Grim helped me wring out the clothing and hang it on the line, then headed off to a job he'd promised to do for Scannal the miller, loading sacks of flour onto a cart and taking them somewhere.

Nobody was around, so I took the opportunity to have a good wash myself, using the remains of the hot water. Once dry and dressed, I tried to restore order to my wet hair. That day when Grim had cut it seemed a long time ago. Now there were strands down to my eyes at the front, and the rest of it was all over the place. Generally I avoided looking anywhere I might catch sight of my own reflection, but I got the odd accidental glimpse in a pool or bowl of water, and the woman I saw was not only aged beyond her years, she was unkempt. I could ask Grim to do the job again, of course. It had felt good, the day he'd hacked off the whole stinking mess of it, as if I was shedding some of the foulness of Mathuin. But winter was coming, and if I had to meet up with the prince of Dalriada sometime, it might be better if I wasn't near-bald. So I combed my hair and let it dry in the sun. Soon it should be long enough to tie back out of the way.

I was starting to chop vegetables when I heard the scream. A woman's voice, coming from somewhere in Dreamer's Wood. "Help! Help!"

Curse Conmael and his wretched agreement. And why did Grim have to be away just when I needed him? I threw things into a bag, slung my shawl around my shoulders, put on my boots, stuck a knife in my belt. I ran out the back door and into the wood, because I'd made a promise and I had no choice.

The screaming had died down to be replaced by other sounds: men's and women's voices, horses neighing, a shrill yapping. Seemed a whole party of folk had made its way into the wood without my hearing a thing earlier. Had I been so absorbed in my bathing that I had missed them entirely? What if this was an attack, a fight? What if I showed myself only to end up the way I had in Laois, accused of a crime and shut up to rot in a cell?

I hesitated under the trees. The woman was not calling for help now. Did that mean I need not announce my presence? Could I turn my back and slip quietly away home?

Too great a risk. I could not afford to get it wrong. I walked forward. The voices were coming from down by the pool; I could hear folk moving about. And now I was close enough to see them. A number of men dressed in uniform colors of gray and blue, someone's escort, most likely. A number of horses, saddled and bridled but tied up as if the party had stopped to rest. And there on the edge of the pool, people clustered around something on the narrow strip of level shore. Someone was sobbing.

I broke into a run, and as they saw me several of the men laid hands on their weapons.

"I'm a healer," I said, not caring if my annoyance showed. "I live nearby. What has happened here?"

Several people spoke at once, some of them babbling in distress; I could make nothing of it. The small crowd parted, letting me through to where a young woman lay prone, unmoving. A man was kneeling beside her, trying to revive her. Another woman—not much more than a girl—sat hunched over, a short distance away. Where the others were weeping, wailing, trying to offer explanations, this one was quite silent. Under the cloak that was draped over her shoulders she was wearing only a shift, and it clung damply to her body. Her dark hair hung in a drenched tangle over her narrow shoulders and her face was parchment-pale. It was a warm day; perhaps a swim had seemed a good idea.

"I'm a healer," I said again, squatting down next to the man. "My name's Blackthorn. Is she breathing?"

He shook his head. I put my fingers to the woman's neck, but even before I touched her, I knew it was too late. Her features had a shadowy look that was all too familiar. This was an empty shell, the spirit flown. She'd been young; perhaps no older than her dark-haired companion.

It had to be said. "I'm sorry." I rose to my feet. "I can't do anything for your friend. She's dead."

There were gasps of shock from the ladies; one of them looked as if she were about to faint. Under the circumstances, unhelpful. I noticed, then, that one of the men was also soaked; he was stripping off his tunic, while one of his friends stood waiting with dry clothing. The man kneeling beside me had turned pale. An older man brought a blanket, which he laid over the dead girl. He helped the other fellow to his feet.

"A sad accident," the older man said to me. "Thank you for coming to help, even though it was too late." To the fellow in the wet clothing, he said, "Eoin, you did your best. She was already gone."

I glanced at the shivering girl and decided there was a further requirement for my services, whether I liked it or not. "This lady seems cold and distressed," I said to the older man, who seemed to be in charge. "My house is not far away. It's warm there. She could rest awhile, get dressed in privacy . . . I could provide a restorative draft." I glanced at the body under its blanket. "You'll need to make some arrangements."

The man opened his mouth to answer, but the girl spoke first. She was a comely thing, small and pale, her face delicately formed and her eyes of an unusual deep blue. That fall of dark hair, when dry, would add to her beauty. "How far—how far is it to Winterfalls?" Her voice was shaky.

"To the village? Not far."

"To Prince Oran's residence."

I should have realized where they were heading. There was the fine clothing, the silver on the harness, the substantial escort. "Just beyond the village. You could be there very quickly."

"Lady Flidais," put in the older man, "with your approval, I'll send a couple of men on ahead and let the prince know what's happened. I'm sure he will want to ride out to meet you. You've had a terrible shock. If you go to the healer's house, you can wait for him in comfort. If you wish, of course."

Lady Flidais looked up at him. For a moment her lovely face looked quite blank. "What . . ." she began, then her voice faded. She cleared her throat. "What about . . . Ciar?"

"We will stand guard, my lady, until the prince arrives. I'll have a couple of the men make a stretcher to carry her to Winterfalls."

"Oh," said Lady Flidais, as if she had barely understood. "Yes."

Under other circumstances I might have slapped her cheek to break the trance, but I refrained. "My lady," I said, "you need warmth and rest. I'm Blackthorn, the local healer." I doubted very much that she'd heard my name earlier; she'd looked as if she was taking in very little. "My cottage is close by. If your attendants can collect whatever you need, a change of clothing, your personal items, we'll walk there now."

The girl seemed unaware that she was only half-dressed, and wet besides. One of her women was fussing with a brooch, pinning the gaping edges of the cloak together before the men-at-arms could get too much of an eyeful. While they organized themselves I spoke again to the older guard. "Is the prince expecting you?" Not that it was any of my business who or what Prince Oran was expecting, but if his visitors were going to get themselves drowned more or less on my doorstep, I wanted to be sure no responsibility would attach itself to me.

The guard managed a smile. "I'll wager you're the only person in these parts who didn't know the prince's new bride was on her way to Winterfalls."

My stomach gave an uncomfortable lurch. I *had* known, vaguely, that Prince Oran was to be wed to some lady from the south. Pressed hard, I might have recalled someone mentioning the name Flidais. I took another look at the lady, who had an attendant on either side supporting her. "You mean *that* is the prince's bride?" Once this had left my lips I realized it might be taken as offensive. I was surprised that this wilting flower was a princess—or was soon to be one, by marriage—because I had thought a princess would be stronger. More courageous in adversity. Foolish of me. "No offense," I added quickly. "She is very young."

"Prince Oran is also young, or so they say." The guard was about to add something more when a forlorn cry rang through the wood, making the little hairs on my neck stand up on end.

"Bramble," said one of the women. "My lady, you've forgotten Bramble."

The cottage that had seemed so spacious was overfull of folk, and they were chattering like magpies. I didn't like them here, I didn't want them here, but since I'd offered my help, I was stuck with them.

The fellow in charge, Domnall, had turned out to be competent. He'd ordered some of the men to make a stretcher, others to keep guard over the spot where the accident had happened, a small party to take a message to the prince. That left me with Flidais, her attendants and six men-at-arms who'd been given the job of watching over us. Until the prince of Dalriada sent someone to convey his future wife to the comforts of Winterfalls, it was up to me to look after her. In the back of my mind was a question whose answer I did not want to consider. Who had called for help, the girl who had ended up dead, or one of the others? By failing to rescue that girl in time, had I already made the seven years of my bond to Conmael into eight?

Not only did I have a house full of people, I also had a dog. If such a pathetic scrap of nothing could be called a dog. I fully understood why Lady Flidais might have wanted to leave it behind. The animal was a bundle of nerves. It cringed in terror when anyone came close, as if it expected a beating. As for the lady, she sat staring at nothing, her body all shivers even now that she was indoors and wrapped in a blanket. She and the dog made a sorry pair.

I took charge. Told the guards to go outside. Built up the fire, heated water for washing, found more blankets. Made sure the lady was warm, dry and adequately clad. Sent one of the women—the tall one—out with a jug of mead and some bread for the men-at-arms.

The dog had gone to ground under a bench. One of the women—the gray-haired one—fished it out and brought it to its mistress, thinking, no doubt, that it might comfort her. A trace of a smile touched the lady's wan features as she reached for her pet, and I thought, *Ah; this is the answer. This will bring her back to herself.* A moment later Flidais shrieked, making me start. The dog had sunk its teeth into her hand, drawing blood. She dropped it unceremoniously on the floor, and it fled back into hiding.

"You," I gestured toward the nearest woman, "take that animal outside. If there's a leash, find it."

The woman—this one had long dark plaits—extricated the dog from its bolt-hole; it went rigid in her grasp, limbs splayed. "Lady Flidais won't want to be parted from Bramble," she said. "Not once she's back to herself."

A creature like that seemed to me a waste of time and space. Its only purpose was to be cosseted. Why in the name of the gods had they brought the thing all the way from the south? "Just make sure the animal's not underfoot, then. And keep the leash on," I said. "Lady Flidais, I'll make you a restorative brew. Try to breathe slowly, it will help."

The story came out in bits and pieces as I found the herbs and prepared the mixture. The party had been in high spirits, knowing Winterfalls was so close, for they had made a long journey from the south. When they'd entered the shade of the wood, Lady Flidais had said she would like to bathe, so she would be cool and fresh to greet her future husband, and Ciar, her maidservant, had agreed to go in the water with her. The men had been persuaded to turn their backs while the two young women swam—the rest of the party had had no inclination to strip off and join them. The impression I got, without anyone quite saying it, was that Lady Flidais was not the conventional type of noblewoman.

"And then," said the gray-haired woman, "they both got in trouble and went under, and one of the men waded in after them. Lady Flidais bobbed up and managed to swim to shore on her own, but Ciar—by the time he got her back up to the surface, she was . . ." She glanced at Flidais and fell silent.

If I were choosing a spot for a swim, it wouldn't be Dreamer's Pool. But perhaps these travelers from far away had not felt the oddness of the place.

I put a cup of the restorative brew in Flidais's hands. "Drink, my lady," I said. "This will make you feel better." After a moment, I added, "I'm sorry for your loss." I felt only the sadness that attends the death of any young, healthy person, but if my words were any sort of comfort to the lady, what matter if they were precisely true or not? Her demeanor was troubling me. Yes, she'd had a terrible fright, but by now I'd have expected her to be coming out of that trancelike state and starting to weep or rail at the gods. Or at least to have something to say. She'd asked a sensible question back at the pool, unless my memory was playing tricks, but since then she hadn't spoken a word.

But then, if the drowned girl had been her body servant, perhaps this was the loss not of a lackey but of something closer to a friend. I crouched down next to the lady. "Your maidservant—had she been with you long?"

She turned her big blue eyes on me. "A year." Her tone was flat.

"We departed in haste," said the dark-haired attendant. "Under the circumstances, our riding skills weighed more than our abilities to dress hair or mend garments. Ciar was a good rider."

But not such a good swimmer, I thought, if she drowned so quickly. The cry for help could not have been hers, or surely I would have reached the pool to find her still alive. I had brought folk back from near-drowning before, folk who had stopped breathing but still had a pulse. Ciar had been well past that point.

I turned my attention back to Lady Flidais, who was taking reluctant sips of the draft. There was a little more color in her cheeks now. "You left home in a hurry, my lady?" I asked, not because I wanted to know, but to get her talking again. Cloud Hill, they'd said. Why did that name sound familiar?

"My . . . my father's holdings are under threat," Flidais whispered. "We had to get away quickly, yes. I don't want to talk about it."

An awkward silence ensued. The lady sipped her drink. Her attendants had run out of things to say, or at least, things they were prepared to say in my presence. That didn't stop them having a good look: at the sleeping arrangements, at the bundles of drying herbs and the plaits of garlic and onions hanging from the roof, at the jars and bottles and bags containing various substances I used in my craft. At the boxes Grim had made to hold my supplies, with their carved lids, and the basket he'd woven for firewood. At the neat pegs to hold clothing, the well-scrubbed hearth, the rush-strewn floor. Whatever these ladies might think of me, nobody was going to say I was a slattern. A healer kept things orderly; couldn't do her job otherwise. When wise women appeared in the old tales, they were often toothless hags living in caves festooned with dangling bones and full of wriggling things in jars. As hags went, I was a youngish one, and though I had lost a tooth or two in that place, I could still bite hard. If my story was ever told by the fireside, it wouldn't send folk to bed with good dreams.

As for the wriggling things, my work was mostly cleaning wounds, stitching up cuts and mixing drafts for the flux. It was delivering babies and sitting by the beds of the dying. On occasion, folk did ask for what might loosely be called spells. I'd had two requests for love potions and one inquiry about bringing down ill on an old enemy—that one I understood all too well. I'd talked the love potion girls out of the idea with a few truths about the nature of men. As for the fellow who wanted to punish his enemy, I'd told him I did not deal in such matters, and that he'd be better off taking his grievance to the village elders, or to Prince Oran—that was if the prince bothered to listen to the troubles of ordinary folk. The man hadn't wanted to take no for an answer. Offered me an incentive in the form of silver. I'd held on to my temper by the merest thread. In the back of my mind, I'd wondered what I was supposed to do when helping one person meant inflicting ill on another. Would refusing add another year to my seven? On balance, I thought not. The first thing Conmael had asked me to do was use my gift for good, not ill; to carry out my work in the manner a true healer should. It could be said that refusing the man *was* helping him. Helping him to see the error of his ways. Helping him avoid worse trouble. At least, I hoped so.

A knock at the cottage door; I was jolted out of my thoughts. It was one of the guards. "Lady Flidais, there are riders in sight; I think it may be the prince and his party."

Flidais rose to her feet, passing her cup to one of her women. Lifted her chin; straightened her back; squared her shoulders as if preparing for a battle. It seemed she wasn't such a wilting lily after all.

"Mhairi, my cloak," she said, and I heard the effort she was making to keep her voice steady. "Deirdre, my shoes. Nuala, keep Bramble out of the way until someone brings her traveling basket. I wish to greet the prince in an appropriate manner. We'll do so outside." The women scurried into action, obedient to her commands. Cloak on, shoes on, dog tidied away. Damp hair quickly pulled back with a scarf, which Mhairi—the tall one—tied up in what appeared to me an elegant manner, not that I would know about such things. Flidais stood perfectly still, allowing them to prepare her. Then she moved toward the door, and I thought she was about to leave without a second glance, taking all of them with her, giving me back my space and my silence. But at the last moment she turned to look at me. The blue eyes blazed with determination; the delicate jaw was set firm as a warrior's. "Thank you for your assistance," she said.

I nodded, saying nothing. I admired her courage. At the same time, her tone—haughtily dismissive, the voice of a fine lady addressing the least of underlings—set my teeth on edge, and if I had let myself speak, something unforgivable might have come out. I was angry with myself as much as with her. This shouldn't matter. After everything, it shouldn't matter in the least.

"You will be compensated for your trouble," Lady Flidais added; then, without waiting for a reply, she swept out the door with her ladies after her. Deirdre—the one with plaits—turned back before she left. She had the little shaking dog in her arms, and on her face there was a look of genuine apology.

"Thank you, Mistress Blackthorn. We've caused you a great deal of disturbance, and you've been so kind and helpful."

"Just doing my job," I said. Which was the truth, though not all of the truth. *Just doing my job because otherwise I'd be dead and Mathuin would never face judgment. Now take yourselves and your business out of my house so I can shut the door on you and breathe again.* Which was less than fair, since it wasn't this woman's fault that her mistress had taken it into her head to ride to Winterfalls by the slow route and stop for a swim along the way. I wondered if it had occurred to Lady Flidais that her maid's death sat squarely on her own shoulders?

They were gone. Out of the house, at least. Morrigan's curse, I hated being among folk! Noble folk in particular; their pretensions were like a burr in the clothing, a constant, scratching annoyance. Even their serving folk had airs and graces. Just as well I wouldn't be tending to Lady Flidais in the future. There'd no doubt be some court physician in Prince Oran's residence to look after her kind. The ordinary folk I could just about tolerate, in small doses.

The house was mine again, at least until Grim got home, and he knew how to keep out of my way. I tidied up and put the kettle back on, thinking to sit in the quiet until he returned. Dimly I heard horses outside, voices, folk moving about. They'd be away soon; I might go out then, and see if the garden had sustained any damage from the tide of uninvited guests. Grim would be less than pleased to lose any of his new plantings.

Someone knocked on the door. Bollocks! Why couldn't these folk leave me be?

I was inclined to wrench the door open and snarl in the face of whoever it was. I took a breath, then walked over and opened it with restraint.

A man stood there, tall, russet-haired, youngish, dressed like a courtier. Vaguely familiar.

"Mistress Blackthorn?" he inquired.

Fool. Who else would it be? "I am Blackthorn, yes."

"My name is Donagan. I am Prince Oran's companion."

Ah. I'd caught a glimpse of him that day when I'd fled into the wood and left Grim to deal with our unexpected visitors. The memory did not bring warm feelings.

"The prince has asked me to thank you for your assistance to Lady Flidais and her party. He wishes to compensate you for your services." On his palm, he held out a little drawstring bag in pale kidskin.

I wanted to refuse it. Why, I wasn't sure. Stubborn pride? The knowledge that I had only helped because of the promise? My dislike of chieftains and princes and fine ladies? I opened my mouth to deliver a withering retort, and at that moment I saw Grim approaching along the path, his pace easy.

"Thank you," I said, taking the little bag. I almost dropped it—the thing weighed twice as much as I'd expected. Grim would indeed have thought me foolish if I had told the prince's lackey to keep his money. "I wish I had arrived in time to save the woman who was drowned. When I got to the pool she was already gone."

"So the men-at-arms told us," Donagan said. "Still, Prince Oran appreciates your kindness to the lady. He passed on his regret that he could not thank you in person."

Donagan must have made up that part himself—what prince would say such a thing? I made no comment, just stood there waiting for him to go. But he didn't seem in a hurry to move on.

Grim came up, not rushing, stopped a couple of paces away with his gaze on Donagan, put down the sack he was carrying, didn't say a word. He didn't need to, since everything about him said, *What do you think you're doing here?*

"Grim," said Donagan in a friendly enough tone. "Prince Oran's been hearing good reports of your work in the district." And when the two of us only gaped at him, he went on. "It seems you're skilled not only in thatching but in several other crafts."

"Do what I can," Grim mumbled, then shot a glance at me. "Has something happened here?"

"Story to tell," I said. "Later."

"Prince Oran may well wish to make use of your skills in the future," Donagan said, looking at Grim. "And yours," he added hastily, glancing at me.

"We have work already," I told him. "Plenty to keep us busy."

"Ah, well." Donagan was unruffled. A courtier, skilled at keeping things running smoothly. "Thank you again, and I'll bid you good day."

Grim managed a grunt; I gave a nod. Donagan strode off to his horse, which was tethered under the trees at the far side of the garden.

"What was all that about?" asked Grim as we watched the king's man ride away.

"Come inside and I'll tell you. How were the flour bags?"

Grim gave me a funny look. "Heavy." He cast his glance over the garden; he sniffed like a hunting dog. "Folk have been here; not just him, a lot of folk. And horses. Just as well I fixed the wall around the vegetable patch. Here, a bit of this'll be good in the brew." He leaned over the drystone wall and plucked a few sprigs of basil, a few leaves of thyme. "Good pile of horse dung over there. I'll dig it into the new patch."

"Brew first. Dung later, if you insist."

11

I've come home with a story to tell. But Blackthorn's got her own story and it's bigger than mine. So instead of talking I sit down and listen.

It's odd all right, a girl drowning with a whole crowd of folk around her, even if their backs were turned. Seems that's what happened. Blackthorn says it's just as well it was the maid who drowned on Prince Oran's land and not this woman he's marrying, since that's the sort of thing wars get fought over. That sounds a bit hard to me, but most likely true. The maid was a person like me, well, maybe not so low, but far below Lady Flidais. The sort of person who can die and nobody cares much, except her closest family, that's if she's got any. I tell Blackthorn this and she says with some folk, not even the family cares, but yes, she knows what I mean, and she thinks Lady Flidais and her women won't spend much time mourning this girl who's died.

As for taking a swim in Dreamer's Pool, that turns me cold. If Conmael and his kind don't live in the wood, then something else does, something that isn't animal and isn't human. Last thing I'd be wanting, knowing it was watching, would be to strip off my clothes and get in the water. Not that I would anyway, seeing as I can't swim. But the thought of it gives me the creeps.

Haven't said this to Blackthorn, but if our cottage hadn't been outside the wood, if it had been in there under the trees, I might not have stayed, even for her. Something wrong in that place. Can't put my finger on what it is. Any time I go in for firewood or herbs or water I feel it, like an itch on the skin or a buzzing in the ears. Something different. Something not right.

"I wonder how she'll do as queen of Dalriada," Blackthorn's saying, talking to herself more than to me. "I can't say I took to the girl. But I have some sympathy. Especially if Prince Oran is anything like Mathuin."

"He's young."

"That doesn't make him good."

"Doesn't make him bad either," I say.

"What would you know?"

"Seemed all right, the day they stopped here. Him and his man."

"Didn't they only pass by to find out who'd moved in here? You hardly had the chance to judge his character."

"True enough," I say. "But there they are, just over the fields, and we're stuck with them. Maybe this Oran will be a good husband to the lady and maybe he won't. That's not our business."

Blackthorn gives me a look. "It's hard, sometimes, not to make things your business. Like with Mathuin. If I'd stayed quiet, let the bad things keep on happening, I wouldn't have been locked up. If I'd kept quiet all my life I wouldn't have been in Laois at all."

I don't say a thing. Blackthorn never talks about the time before, and nor do I. For us, the story starts when she was brought into that place and we were prisoners together. I know she fell foul of Mathuin because she spoke up about the wrongs he was doing, taking women against their will, getting them with child, nobody saying a word because of who he was. But before that, nothing at all. Until now.

"That's my problem," she says. "I never did learn to keep my mouth shut. And I can't now, if the same thing happens here—Prince Oran doing the wrong thing by his folk, I mean. Conmael made me promise to use my abilities for good, not ill. That means speaking up if something isn't right. A wise woman is supposed to be . . . wise."

"Might be wiser to keep quiet," I say. Wouldn't take much to get us thrown out of here, on the road again, nowhere to go. Her with more and more years owing to Conmael; me just a burden to her. Or worse. We might find ourselves locked up again. "It's a healer these folk need, not a . . ." Can't find the right word.

"Conscience?" Blackthorn smiles, but it's not a happy sort of smile. "Don't look so worried, Grim. Maybe Oran's a paragon of virtue, a prince among princes. And maybe he'll be so busy preparing for his wedding that he'll forget all about us." She spots the purse they gave her, on the table where she's left it. "They seemed keen to pay me for my efforts, though I couldn't save the girl. Have a look."

When I loosen the string and turn the bag upside down, what spills out onto the table is a shiny stream of silver pieces. I came home proud of the money I earned from Scannal today, but this puts my ten coppers in the shade. I whistle; Blackthorn mutters an oath.

"Talk about upside down and back to front," she says. "A small fortune for failing to save a girl from drowning."

"Paying you for your kindness." Seems plain to me. "Helping his young lady. Cares about her."

"He's probably never seen her in his life before," says Blackthorn, sweeping the coins back in the bag. "He won't give a toss about her. All that'll matter to him is her father's connections. See if I'm not right."

I've got a half bag of flour, thanks to my day's work for Scannal, and there's a rabbit hanging, snared last night. I make a pie, throwing in the vegetables Blackthorn's cut up. While I do it I'm going over the day, my day, not hers. A good day's work, hard enough to keep out bad thoughts for a while. Scannal's not much of a talker, which is the way I like things. Trusts me with his horses and the cart. Big strong horses, gentle as lambs, the two of them. Sturdy and Storm, their names are. Handle the load of flour bags like a dream. That's the best part, driving the load from the mill to this other settlement, place called Silverlake, over to the east. Back along the road Blackthorn and I came in on, then take a fork to the left, and a few miles on, there it is, lovely spot, scatter of houses by the water, few fishing boats out on the lake, sun shining, trees all red and gold. Birds everywhere, swans, ducks, others I don't know the names of. Scannal's said the baker's place is a bit farther on, and I stop in the settlement to ask the way. A woman tells me how to get there. She's got two little boys, and they stare at Sturdy and Storm with big round eyes. I give them turns on Storm's back, not moving along, just sitting.

The woman tells me a bit of a story. Scannal hasn't supplied this baker before. Silverlake has its own mill, but no miller, because the fellow's died in a nasty accident. Found one morning crushed under his own grindstone. She says even if there was someone in Silverlake or surrounds who knew how to do the job of milling flour, which there isn't, they wouldn't be wanting to take over. Everyone thinks the mill's got a curse over it, or a ghost in it, or both. The woman points out where it is, up on a rise behind the settlement. Then she remembers what I've asked, and shows me the path to Branoc's place, which can't be seen from where we are. I have to drive the cart farther along the lakeshore.

"Better be getting on," I say, making sure the children are out of the way of wheels and hooves.

"We'll be seeing you again, then," says the woman, giving me a look up and down that's a surprise to me.

"Maybe," I say. I climb up and take the reins.

"Drop by on the way back and I'll give you a bite to eat," she says. "Big man, big appetite, I bet. Branoc won't feed you. Doesn't care for visitors. All by himself in that old place and seems to like it that way. Mind you, he does bake fine cakes. Like something from the Otherworld, they are. A body could spend a lifetime trying to make cakes like them and not come anywhere close."

I nod my head, not saying if I'll drop in later or not; then I'm gone. Out of the settlement, along the lakeshore, and up to a house that must be the baker's, since this is the end of the track.

It's an odd-looking place, sort of cobbled together, with a roof that needs rethatching and a damp look to it. There's a yard where I can turn the horses, and a barn with a big door. I'm guessing that'll be where he wants the flour bags. Nobody about, so I back the cart up there and call Storm and Sturdy to stand fast. I hop down. Before I can make another move a man comes round the side of the barn with a pitchfork in his hand, all ready to run it through me. I don't bother to tell him what a bad idea that would be. I make myself hold still.

"Come from Scannal's," I say. "Brought your flour. Where do you want it?"

Pitchfork man gives me a good look over, not the way the woman in the village did, but as if he doesn't like what he sees but thinks it's too big to tackle on his own. From what the woman was saying, Branoc lives alone, so this must be him. He's long and gangly, dark-haired, with a look about him that says he wants me gone soon. "In there," he says, jerking his head toward the barn door. "Wait."

The door's got big bolts across it. Fellow must be scared someone'll steal his bread-baking secrets. I go to help him with the bolts and he snaps, "Leave it!"

I back off. *Bonehead*, a voice says inside me. I wait. I've been planning to feed and water the horses while I'm here, but now I'm thinking I'll take them back down to the shore first.

Door's open. Not much to see in the barn. Seems it's only for stores, and the baking's done somewhere else. A couple of full sacks, some sickles and forks and spades, barrels of this and that. Buckets, ladles. There's a sort of loft, too dim to see properly, and a ladder going up through a trapdoor. Steep.

"Where do you want them?" I ask, loading the first sack onto my back. "Up there?" I hope the answer's no, though if it was me, I'd be storing my flour upstairs out of the damp.

"I will carry them up later," Branoc says, surprising me—who'd want to be clambering up and down that flimsy ladder with a weight over his shoulder, if he had someone to do the job for him? "Place them by the wall, there, and be sure to stack them neatly." He takes the ladder down and carries it outside. Helpful, since that'll make it easier for me to get the full bags over to the spot where he wants them.

I'm used to being treated like I'm nothing, so I keep my mouth shut and get on with the job. Branoc—a foreigner, I'm guessing, not only from his name but from the way he talks—watches me for a while, not offering to help. After a bit he wanders off to do something across the yard, and I keep carrying one sack after another into the barn. It's a lot of flour. With luck it'll be a while before I need to come back.

I finish off, making sure the sacks are lined up straight, grabbing a broom to tidy up after myself. Don't want any fuss about the payment, which I'm supposed to collect for Scannal. While I'm doing this I hear a few noises from upstairs, clunks and scrapes, and when Branoc comes back over I say, trying to be friendly, "Should bring you a cat next time."

He gives me a narrow-eyed look. "A cat? Why would you do this?"

"You got rats up there. Heard them running around. Big store of flour, you wouldn't want it spoiled."

"Your work is finished, yes?"

"Mm-hm." I get myself out of the barn. I've annoyed him, not sure why. But some men don't need a reason to get angry. I know that better than most. "I'll be on my way, then." I fiddle with the horses' harness, waiting for him to give me the money. All he does is shut the barn door and shove the bolts across. "Scannal asked me to collect his payment," I say when he's done it.

He stomps off to the house. I hope he's fetching what's due. While he's away I get the horses and cart all ready to go. Hoping I won't have to hammer on the fellow's door and demand the money. Hoping I won't get into a fight. Thinking about Blackthorn and the cottage and the garden, and knowing I can't get angry or I might lose everything.

Turns out all right. Branoc comes striding back from the house and gives me a bag of coppers. The weight tells me it's more or less the right amount, but I shake the coins out and count them anyway. Then I get up on the cart and head off, knowing he's going to watch me all the way down the hill, making sure I'm gone. Though why I'd be wanting to hang around I can't imagine.

Down on the shore I get out the bread and cheese I've brought and when Storm and Sturdy have had a drink I give them their oats. We eat. I look out over the lake. If I lived in such a pretty spot I wouldn't be bad-tempered like this baker. I'd be getting on with my work and thinking how lucky I was.

Horses make light work of the trip back. I drop the cart at Scannal's and give him the payment, and he gives me my share and the half bag of flour.

"This yours?" he asks me as I'm heading off, and he's got Blackthorn's red kerchief in his hand, all floury from the back of the cart where he's picked it up from a corner. Must've got tangled up with something in the wash and ended up in my pocket, though I don't recall it being there. Must've dropped it when I was unloading the flour bags.

I take it and stick it back in the pocket. Needs a good wash before she can wear it again, not that she does wear it much. I bid Scannal good day and walk home.

All this is in my head now while I cook the pie. I want to tell Blackthorn about my day. But she's gone outside. She's sitting in the garden, still as a stone, staring ahead of her. Wanting to be on her own. Wanting quiet. Needing to be left alone. So I keep on cooking, and later when she comes in we eat the pie without saying much. She's had enough of folk cluttering up the house, fine ladies especially. She's tired of chattering voices. And upset that a girl drowned and she couldn't save her. Not that she says so, but I know anyway. So we sit by the fire awhile, and outside it gets dark so we go to bed, and somehow my tale never gets told.

12

ORAN

"Give her time," Donagan said. "She's young, she's far from home, the circumstances of her arrival were unfortunate. This is a girl of eighteen, Oran, not a seasoned traveler."

Donagan was helping me get ready for bed. This was part of the regular duties of a body servant. Since I was an adult man and perfectly capable of taking off my clothes and putting on a nightshirt unassisted, we were doing what we usually did at this hour: sitting in my bedchamber sharing a jug of mead and talking. Or rather, I had been talking and my companion had been listening, until now.

"But she won't even see me," I said. I understood his argument; I had already made allowances for Flidais's distress, her exhaustion, perhaps a sudden attack of homesickness. "She's been shut up in her quarters since she first got here. Two whole days. I should be helping her recover, comforting her, reassuring her. We're to be married, after all. She's barely spoken to me."

"After what happened to her maidservant, you should be glad she did not say she wanted to go straight back home." Donagan was looking at Flidais's portrait; her image gazed back at him, eyes full of love and sweetness. I had been startled, when I'd first seen her in the flesh, how like she was to that picture. It had all been there: the perfect heart shape of the face, the deep blue of the eyes, the delicate mouth and neat, straight nose. It had all been there but the look of love. Instead, her face had worn a wary expression, as if she were trying to take my measure. Perhaps I did not live up to her expectations. Perhaps she thought me ugly or weak-looking, too tall, too short, too soft, too . . .

This was foolish. What had I been hoping for? I could not say, save that after our letters, I had not anticipated that she would be so . . . cool. Even allowing for the unfortunate circumstances, I had thought she might summon a smile, not the conventional smile of a formal greeting, but a special smile just for me. I had thought, when later I gave her the poem I had written for her arrival, that she would read it straightaway, not pass it to one of her waiting women with scarcely a glance. I had not expected that she would shut herself away from me as if she were thinking better of her choice.

"She'll be fine by the betrothal ceremony," Donagan said. "I'm sure of it. Women have these ups and downs, Oran. They're creatures of a hundred moods."

"But the letters. The confidences, the poetry . . ." I made myself stop. Donagan had not read any of the letters, either mine to Flidais or hers to me, and I had no intention of sharing them with him or indeed anyone. They were private; secret; a precious bond between my sweetheart and me. I believed in the letters. I believed in true love, the kind from ancient tales. If I said this to Donagan, he would call me a child. "Perhaps she is hiding from me," I mused. "Perhaps she cannot bear to face the truth."

Donagan gave me one of his looks. "What truth?"

I grimaced. "That she doesn't love me after all? That she finds herself obliged to wed a man who disgusts her?"

"Your thoughts are leading you into a maze that's entirely of your own invention, my friend. I suggest you drink a lot of mead, then have a good night's sleep. Who knows, the lady may be in quite a different mood tomorrow. Or the day after. Or the day after that." When I failed to reply, he went on. "You're spending too much time fretting over this. If you want my advice, you'll leave Lady Flidais and her women to their own devices and turn your attention elsewhere. Has it escaped you that your mother and father will be here in a few days? Winterfalls will be full to the brim with folk. Tomorrow might be a good day to call your household together and rally them with a few uplifting remarks. Afterward you might make a personal tour of inspection: the accommodation for the king and queen, the sleeping quarters for their serving folk, the stables . . . If you wish, I can draw up an itinerary."

"I believe I might just manage to retain that in my mind." Hearing how this sounded, I added, "I'm sorry, Donagan. I am somewhat on edge, I admit it. Navigating uncharted waters."

"You will find your way even without a map," Donagan said with a smile. "Most men do."

When he was gone I sat by lamplight with parchment, ink and pen before me and Flidais's picture on the wall, looking down on me. I had thought to craft a new poem for my beloved, capturing my love for her, my uncertainty, my hope. But I could not write. The words that should have poured forth from my heart were silent. I was mute; the river of my imagination had turned as dry as dust. I sat a long while, knowing that Donagan's advice was wise and sensible, recognizing that all I needed to do was give Flidais time.

In the end I did write, but not to my beloved.

> To Eabha, Queen of Dalriada,
> Mother, greetings. Lady Flidais has arrived safely at Winterfalls and is recovering from her long journey. Indeed, I have seen very little of her since she came here, as she is still too exhausted to leave her private quarters. I have ensured that her party is being well looked after in every respect.
> On the journey to Winterfalls, Flidais witnessed the accidental death of a member of her party. She was seriously distressed by this unfortunate event, and this has contributed to her current state of nervous collapse.
> I write to advise you of this since, if Flidais is not fully restored to herself within the next few days, I believe it may be wise to delay the formal betrothal.

*I understand the difficulties this would present, and
I hope it will not be necessary.*

   *I will send a message immediately if the
arrangements change. Otherwise I will expect you
and Father and your party in seven days, as
planned.*

*Your obedient son,
Oran, Prince of Dalriada*

I sealed the letter without reading it over. I imagined
Mother opening it. I imagined her irritation when she saw
that I had not done as a prince should and had a scribe
write it for me. I thought of her displeasure at the inconvenience—and it would indeed be inconvenient, with my father's responsibilities at Cahercorcan. Perhaps there would
be no need to send it. Maybe by morning Flidais would be
restored to health, and able to walk or ride out with me, so
I could show her and Bramble the places I had described in
my letters. If not that, she might at least be well enough to
sit with me in my library. I could read to her. I could give
her the betrothal gift I had chosen with such care.

I lay awake, pondering the tumult of emotions that had
coursed through me since my beloved's arrival, and thinking that too great a fondness for old tales had perhaps addled my wits. What had I expected, that she would throw
herself into my arms? Speak words of love before a whole
crowd of folk? Had I imagined she would address me with
the same fluency she'd shown in her letters, even after her
exhausting journey and the shocking death of her maidservant? Flidais was a flesh and blood woman, not some princess from ancient myth. I'd been thinking like a child, and a
selfish child at that.

Tomorrow I would do as Donagan had suggested. I
would call my household together and tell them how proud
I was of the fine work everyone had done in preparing
Winterfalls for this change. I would run through what was
expected for the visit of my parents and their substantial
entourage. Then I would talk to Aedan about the plans to
include the local community in the betrothal celebrations; I
would make sure the folk of the village and farms had been
consulted.

But before I did any of that, I would go to Flidais's quarters and speak with her. Exactly what I would say, I was not sure. I must hope that, when the time came, the right words would come with it.

I slept fitfully and woke with an aching head. So much for Donagan's theory about the mead. I could not possibly visit Flidais at this hour. The light beyond my window was the earliest pale wash of dawn. But I would be unable to settle to anything else until I spoke with her.

My bedchamber had several doors. One to the hallway; one to the small chamber next door where Donagan slept within easy reach. A third door connected my chamber directly with Flidais's bedroom in the women's quarters. That door had remained firmly closed since her arrival at Winterfalls, and would do so until we were hand-fasted.

I'd had the women's quarters expanded and fitted out with all the comforts a highborn lady would expect, along with some additions of my own devising, such as a little chamber with a writing desk. When Flidais sat there she could look through a round window into a patch of garden planted with many of the flowers she had described in her letters. There was a strip of lawn for Bramble to roll on and a little door through which the dog could come in and out of the house unaided. I had seen nothing of Bramble since that first, awkward day.

I threw on some clothes and slipped out without waking Donagan. Folk were stirring. Sounds came to me from the kitchen, where they would be kindling cooking fires and preparing for the day's work. I went outside; a walk would clear my head.

The royal holding at Winterfalls was substantial and well maintained. While I was growing up, my family had usually stayed here over the summer, and I wondered, thinking back, whether my mother had enjoyed those respites from the formality of Cahercorcan as much as I had. The place had been in capable hands then, and it still was. My steward, Aedan, and his wife, Fíona, had been here as long as I could remember. Their children were of an age with me. My stable master, Eochu, could be abrasive when displeased but had such a remarkable touch with horses that nobody ever said a word against him. Eochu went everywhere accompanied by his dogs, a pair of brindled lurchers who were the loves of his life, though nobody else thought much of them. Then there was Niall, who tended to the Winterfalls acreage, its fine breeding cattle and its crops, with assistance from a small army of folk and a team of well-trained herding dogs.

My lands extended far beyond the walls of the home acreage, of course; several villages, the small farms around them, Dreamer's Wood and the wild lands beyond were all part of my holding, and under Dalriadan law there was a give and take requirement between my tenants and me. I provided assistance as required; I helped them in times of flood, fire or other hardship and I arbitrated over their disputes at a monthly open council. The people had been accustomed to my riding down from Cahercorcan for these councils, staying a day or two, then riding home again. Now that I was established here permanently, the whole thing was much easier, since folk could reach me quickly if they needed me.

In the presence of my father and his councillors I had always felt I was only playing at being a prince; that people regarded me as a pale shadow of my father. My visits to Winterfalls for the councils had felt like a sham, though I had done my best to find just and fair solutions to the problems my people brought before me, and they had generally seemed satisfied. Now I could be out among them, seeing the problems for myself, perhaps helping resolve them before there was any need for a formal hearing. I could meet folk as soon as they moved into the district, like that fellow Grim, the ill-tempered thatcher. I had yet to meet the healer, Blackthorn, who had opened her house to Flidais on the day of the unfortunate accident at Dreamer's Pool. That day, my mind had been all on bringing my beloved safely home. And, of course, arranging a burial for the girl who'd drowned. A sad arrival and a sadder farewell. Flidais had been too distraught to attend the ritual we'd held for her maid.

We had a burial ground beyond our grazing land, and we'd interred the girl there. It was in a quiet area near a copse of elders. I walked to the spot now, thinking to say a silent prayer or two. It was a sad thing to die so far from home and be laid to rest in a place your loved ones would likely never visit.

I sat awhile among the graves as the sun came up and the cows stirred themselves, moving at a leisurely pace toward the barn for the morning milking. I said a prayer for the departed—not only the girl who had drowned, but the others who lay nearby, folk who had lived and died at Winterfalls in the service of our family. I practiced a skill taught to me a year or two ago by a wandering druid: sitting with my eyes closed, concentrating on sounds, finding music in the way they fitted together. So many sounds. The lowing of the cattle, the singing of birds—chirping, calling, crying, warbling—and the whisper and rustle of their movement in the trees. The flowing of the stream, which was many voices in one. Eochu over by the stables calling his dogs, and one of them barking. And . . . something else, a whimpering, as of some creature in distress. Eyes still closed, I made myself concentrate as I'd been taught, and when I opened them there was Bramble, hunkered down on the other side of the girl's grave, her coat all stuck with whinnies and burrs. There was blood on the little dog's face.

I was careful not to make any sudden movement. "Bramble," I said in a murmur. "It's all right. Good dog." If I startled the creature now, she might bolt. Far from all she knew, on open ground, it would be near-impossible to find her. Flidais would be devastated. "Friend," I said. "I'm a friend. I hope your mistress explained that."

Bramble stayed where she was, big eyes on me. She was shivering with some violence. I kept talking, low-voiced, speaking of matters that might interest a dog, such as a warm fire to lie in front of, a meaty bone, a cozy basket. I mentioned Flidais, who would be missing her little companion. I kept this up awhile, all the time edging gradually closer and hoping nobody would come looking for me and frighten the little one away. And after a certain time, much to my astonishment, for I had been sure that I would eventually have to resort to a sudden snatch, Bramble crept forward, the ghost of a whimper emerging from her throat, until she was right beside me.

I found that I was smiling for the first time in days.

Slowly I reached out a hand, holding it where the dog could sniff, and she touched my fingers with her cold nose. She was exactly as portrayed in the painting, where she had been cradled in Flidais's arms: a delicately made thing, her eyes and ears rather too large for the rest of her, her body somewhat spindly. Her long whippy tail was cautiously wagging now. Her hair was as fine as thistledown and tangled with debris. I did not gather her up; not yet.

"You are very brave, Bramble," I said. "Calm girl, good girl. Let's sit and talk awhile before I take you home." Just as well I had come out alone. If I'd had Donagan with me, or a guard, I could not have coaxed my lady's dog this way without being viewed as ridiculous. My mother would certainly have thought me foolish to address a creature as if it could understand me. But this was not just any creature; it was Flidais's beloved pet. "Your mistress once told me she thought you were a fey dog, strayed into this world from another," I told Bramble, who had moved to sit right beside my leg, her tiny form warm against me. I stroked her back, gently teasing out the worst of the burrs, and she endured my ministrations with patience. "I do not think that can be true, or you would surely not get in so much trouble. Come, show me that front paw. Is it hurting?"

A slow process, but I got all the prickles out and ascertained that apart from a cut or two the dog was uninjured. When that was done she climbed onto my knee and settled there, curled up in a ball with one eye open. It was plain to me why Flidais loved her. I allowed myself to sit awhile, and eventually the eye closed, and I felt the small form relax into sleep. The sun rose higher; the cows conducted a lowing conversation as they went in and out from milking; the stream babbled and a small wind stirred the grasses. Contentment stole over me, and for a brief while I was at peace.

I could not stay here long; Flidais would be frantic with worry over her missing pet. Besides, it must be nearly breakfast time, and I had not told Donagan where I was going. I woke Bramble with gentle words, then wrapped her in my cloak and headed for the house.

"Of course," I said to her as I walked, "you have provided me with a perfect excuse to visit your mistress early without seeming overeager or intrusive. But I am a little ashamed that I thought of that, so please don't bring it to her attention."

What Bramble thought was a mystery, though as we approached the house she tensed in my arms, and I regretted that I had not troubled myself to contrive a leash of some kind. "Don't run off now, please," I told her. "Remember the warm fire, the bone, the kind words? We're nearly there." She did not seem convinced; I struggled to keep her still without hurting her, for every part of her was delicately made.

I went straight to the women's quarters, not through the house but across the garden I had created for Flidais. The door to the writing room was locked, but farther along there was another entry, and here I came face-to-face with one of my lady's waiting women.

"Oh! My lord!" Not unreasonably, she was taken aback to see me. Then she saw what I was carrying. "Oh, you found her!"

"Deirdre, isn't it?" I had made a point of learning their names on that first day. "Yes, I stumbled on Bramble while out walking. She was some distance from the house. Unhurt save for a few cuts, but frightened."

Deirdre reached out to take the dog, but Bramble shrank away, scrabbling against my chest, thrusting her nose under my arm as if to hide.

"Perhaps," I said, "I might give Bramble to Lady Flidais myself. I do wish to speak with her this morning. Out here, if she prefers, or indoors."

"My lady is still unwell, Prince Oran. I don't know if she can receive you . . ."

I would not be fobbed off again. I fixed my gaze on the hapless Deirdre and used my princely tone. "I wish to see Lady Flidais now. I will keep my visit brief. I will wait for her indoors." I wondered if perhaps Flidais had not been told her beloved pet was missing. I did not want to cause a rift between her and her waiting women. On the other hand, they should take more care.

"Of course, my lord." Deirdre stepped back to let me in. There was a small chamber immediately within the doorway, and I stationed myself there. As head of the household

I was perfectly entitled to enter the women's quarters, but it would be uncouth to go barging in on Flidais before breakfast. In my arms, Bramble hunkered down, shivering.

Time passed and I began to feel foolish. Donagan would be looking for me. I would be expected at breakfast. Guests would be starting to come in from everywhere. Why was I sitting at my beloved's doorstep like a supplicant?

"Prince Oran?"

The voice was sweet and soft. I rose to my feet, Bramble still in my arms, and there she was: Flidais, clad in a violet gown with a fine gray shawl over it, and her dark hair rippling down over her shoulders. My mouth went dry. I could not find any words at all. As for Bramble, she stiffened in my grasp and I almost dropped her.

"Oh, you have Bramble!" Flidais exclaimed. "Where was she?"

"Out on the farmland. A long way from the house." I made to detach Bramble from my person and pass her to her mistress, but the little dog started a shrill, panicky yapping that drowned any attempt at speech. In the end I stepped back, still holding her, and she quieted.

"I'm so sorry, my lord." Flidais's pale cheeks were flushed with embarrassment. "This is most unlike Bramble; she is always so well behaved. Since the . . . since that terrible day, the day we arrived, her behavior has been most odd."

"I suppose she needs time," I said. I could feel the pounding of Bramble's heart through her whole body. "Many changes. A long journey."

"Yes, but . . . I do not wish to inconvenience you, Prince Oran. I cannot imagine how Bramble got out." Flidais glanced at her maid, who had come in behind her. "Deirdre, please shut Bramble in the sewing room, and make sure this does not happen again. She's not to be let outside without the leash."

With some difficulty, I passed the dog to Deirdre. Bramble gave a piteous cry as she was borne away; I felt as if I had betrayed her. "Please don't worry about inconvenience," I said. "I am fond of dogs, as I told you in my letters. I'm glad to have been of service this morning. And please, not Prince Oran or my lord, just Oran."

"I am most grateful to you . . . Oran," said Flidais.

"Is your health improved?" I asked. "I was hoping you might be well enough to join the household for breakfast today."

"I—I am still rather tired. What happened—it upset me a great deal." "Come," I said, "let us walk around the garden; this little chamber is not the best place for a conversation. Were you pleased with the writing room I made for you?"

"The writing room? Oh, yes. That was very kind. Thank you."

We went down the step and into the garden; Flidais slipped her hand through the arm I offered, and her touch was pleasing to me. More than pleasing. I felt a flush rising to my cheeks, and hoped she would not notice.

"I drafted a letter to my mother last night," I said, "suggesting that we consider delaying the betrothal until you are feeling better. I don't want to rush you. We had planned to hold the ceremony in eight days' time, but I think that may be too soon." My doubts were returning, despite Flidais's willingness to talk with me this morning. She looked unwell and sounded uncertain. Perhaps she was too well-mannered to say she was not ready for the betrothal. "Much too soon," I went on. "We must wait until you are quite happy with the arrangements."

"Oh, but what will your mother think of me?" exclaimed Flidais, looking everywhere but at me. "Such inconvenience for everyone . . ."

"You've been greatly upset," I said. "And the journey itself must have been grueling. You must take all the time you need." I laid my free hand over hers, trying to ignore the stirring of my body, since it was entirely inappropriate to the current situation. "There will be a lot of folk here for the betrothal. Not as many as there will be for the hand-fasting at my father's court, but many all the same. When my mother descends on the household things can become somewhat overwhelming. She means well."

Flidais stopped walking, and turned to face me. She took both my hands in hers. "There's no need to wait, Oran. Truly. I do feel somewhat poorly at present, that is true. But I will be myself again soon, I'm certain of it." Her smile warmed me, and I found myself smiling back.

"Let us take a day or two to think about this," I said. She looked so frail, her eyes huge, her skin milky pale, that it was hard for me to imagine her fully restored to herself so soon. If I hurt her in any way, I would never forgive myself.

"But—"

"Shh," I said, and laid a finger on her lips. Ah, the softness of them! I snatched my finger away. "A day, at least. We will talk about this again tomorrow. Now I must let you go; you'll be wanting to greet poor Bramble, who was much shaken by her ordeal. I cannot understand how she got out. This garden is walled—I took particular care about it—and I do not imagine your little dog can jump very high."

"One of the women must have let her out. I will make sure it does not happen again, Oran." She glanced around the garden. "It is very pretty here. The flowers are lovely."

"I hope you liked my poem," I ventured.

"Thank you, yes."

"Perhaps, in time, you will write another for me."

Her face clouded. "In time, yes. Since Ciar's accident, I've been afflicted by headaches, bad ones. When I try to read, my head throbs and my eyes blur. I cannot even think of writing. One of my women read your poem to me. It was very sweet."

I swallowed a certain disappointment at her comment. "Headaches? That is troubling. We should seek the advice of a physician. There is a very capable man at Cahercorcan. Or you may prefer the services of the local healer, Blackthorn. Folk speak highly of her skills. You met her, of course."

"I don't need a physician or a wise woman. All I need is rest." She glanced toward the doorway. "I'm sorry to be such a nuisance, Oran."

"You are not a nuisance; don't ever think that. You are the lady of the house here, and you must ask me if you need anything at all. Now, I am keeping you from your rest, and I see Donagan over there at the gate, with a look on his face that tells me I am late for breakfast. Rest well, Flidais. I'm happy I was able to bring Bramble home for you. I must speak to my household this morning, but I hope later I may come and read to you awhile." I bent to kiss her on the cheek, hoping the simple gesture of affection would not offend her. I had not expected to be so unsure of myself.

Her proximity filled me with desire, yet I felt as awkward as a green lad of fourteen.

"Farewell, Oran," Flidais said, and for a moment she laid both her hands against my chest, over my heart, which must surely be beating as violently as poor Bramble's had done. "I will be better in time for the betrothal. I promise." She turned and headed up the path to the house.

"Do you wish me to dispatch that letter?" Donagan asked as he and I walked back to the main entry.

"To my mother?" He must have seen it lying on my desk. "I am not sure whether to send it. Lady Flidais is unwell; she assures me she will be recovered in time for the betrothal, but I am in some doubt. If the ritual is to be delayed a while, I need to advise my parents as soon as possible."

"A while. How long?"

"I don't know. A few days." My tone was less than courteous, and I made myself take a deep breath. "I'm sorry. Leave the letter for now. I'll think about it over breakfast."

He looked at me, and in his gaze I saw what he was not prepared to say: *For a man who's about to be married, you seem more than a little on edge, Oran.* What he did say was, "You want my advice? Take control. Tell everyone what's going to happen and stick to the plan, whatever it is."

"Like a prince?"

"Like the prince you are, my friend."

After breakfast I gathered my household together as Donagan had suggested. I congratulated my folk on their hard work and praised their forbearance in a time of significant change. Nobody was in any doubt as to the challenges presented by the royal visit—that the king and queen were my parents made no difference. Winterfalls would be crammed with folk, and they'd all need to be well looked after. It would, I suspected, be particularly trying for people who were used to running an establishment with minimal interference to find their house full of someone else's serving folk, who would inevitably bring their own ideas on how everything should be organized, and who might not take kindly to direction from, say, Aedan or Eochu.

"My lord," said Aedan, "what about the next open council? Will you be delaying that until everything returns to normal?"

"I don't think we need delay it," I said. The councils were held at full moon, which gave us nearly twenty days until the next one. The open gatherings were important; they gave all who lived on my land the opportunity to bring their problems to me and to be heard. We held them in the main hall at Winterfalls and they were always attended by a great number of folk, some of whom, I was fairly sure, came only to catch up on the latest gossip.

Attendances had increased markedly since we'd started serving refreshments when the formal part of the proceedings was over. The settlement of Silverlake had a baker of exceptional skill. Branoc, a man born and raised in Armorica, did not bother with everyday loaves, but specialized solely in cakes. His creations were small miracles of the pastry cook's art. In my mother's opinion, such masterpieces were wasted on the ordinary folk who attended my councils, and the provision of them was yet another example of my being too soft in my dealings with such people. I disagreed. The refreshments allowed time for everyone to mingle and chat, to discuss openly the issues that had arisen and to come to terms with my decisions. This helped maintain a healthy, happy community. The quality of Branoc's cakes ensured good attendances. I had tried to explain this to my mother, but she had simply thrown up her hands with a sigh, as if my ways were beyond understanding. "And we'll hold the following council as planned," I told Aedan, "even though that will be very close to the hand-fasting. When Flidais and I return from court, we could have a celebration for everyone, with a bonfire, feasting and dancing."

"The traveling folk may be camped in these parts by then," said Niall, my farmer. "There are some fine musicians among them; you could ask them to play, my lord."

"And buy a couple of fine yearlings while you're about it," put in Eochu.

"Can we send a message south to wherever the traveling folk are likely to be now, letting them know they're invited to the festivities? And yes, Eochu, I will most certainly consider the purchase of some horses, though you'd best take a look at what they have first and advise me."

Eochu gave a nod, pleased to be asked.

"We'll get word to them one way or another," Niall said. "When they come is up to them, of course. The travelers keep their own time."

The travelers were horse traders, musicians, makers of fine craftwork, storytellers. In the summers they camped in the south while their young horses fattened and grew strong. They'd head for the horse fairs in autumn, and most years they'd come far enough north to spend time at Winterfalls. My stable owed its best horseflesh to the traveling folk. Though, of course, Eochu's eye for a fine breeding animal also played its part.

"My lord," said my head cook, Brid, "how is Lady Flidais? We're very much hoping she'll be well enough to come out for her meals soon, and perhaps make herself known to us in the kitchens. I want to be sure everything we provide for the visitors is to her taste."

"Thank you for the good wishes, Brid. My lady is improving, yes." Flidais's responsibilities as my wife would include dealing with Brid and her helpers on matters of cookery and kitchen supplies. Brid would be wanting to get some idea of my lady's tastes and her manner of dealing with the household folk, since Winterfalls had been managing itself capably without a mistress since before my father became king. I hesitated. "I had thought perhaps to delay the betrothal by a few days in view of her current indisposition. But I will not make that decision until tomorrow morning. We should be ready for everything to go ahead as planned. I know I can rely on you all."

The letter to my mother lay on my writing table all day. I did not change the wording, and I did not dispatch it. There was no further sign of Flidais. I told myself that since Aunt Sochla had not yet arrived to carry out the duties of chaperone, it was more seemly that my lady remained closeted away, uncomfortable though her absence made me.

With Donagan by my side I spent the rest of the day inspecting everything: the kitchen, the sleeping quarters we had arranged for our visitors and for their army of serving people, the stables where extra stalls had been prepared for the influx of additional mounts. I met the young men from the district who had come in to work as assistant grooms or gardeners, and the young women who would be helping out in the kitchen or around the house.

I had a word with the men who had ridden north as guards to Flidais's party. Their situation was awkward. My father had a sizable complement of men-at-arms at Cahercorcan, which was appropriate to the monarch's court. As heir to the Dalriadan throne I was expected to maintain a substantial force of my own, but in practice I kept it to the minimum required. My guards were well trained and well led by Lochlan; there were enough of them to deal with most situations. I knew, as did my household, that if a major territorial dispute should arise, such as that currently faced by Flidais's father, the arrangements would have to change.

I faced a difficulty now. The men of Flidais's escort had expected to return to Cloud Hill when my lady no longer required their services. If Cadhan was under threat from Mathuin of Laois, he probably needed every fighting man he could get. But I could not send such a small body of fighters straight back into what might, by the time they got there, have developed into a full-scale conflict. On the other hand, there was no real work for them at Winterfalls. Our region was peaceful; we had allies to the south and west, and the sea to the north and east. My father's court with its established fighting force was only twenty miles away.

For now, I thanked the Cloud Hill men-at-arms once again for looking after my lady so well on the long journey north, and told them they should stay in Dalriada at least until the hand-fasting. After that they could make the choice to ride back to Cloud Hill or, if they wished, stay on over the winter in my household or my father's and add their strength to that of our forces. I told them I was sure it would make Lady Flidais happy to have some familiar faces among those protecting her and her new household. They should consider themselves off duty until the betrothal took place. After that they could report to Lochlan, who would assign them responsibilities as he did for our regular guards.

The long day came to an end. Flidais did not appear at suppertime. I sent a message with one of her women, wishing her good night and saying I had missed her. Then, with a heavy heart, I retired to my chamber, certain that my first task in the morning would be to postpone the betrothal.

I slept poorly; even with a tapestry hanging over the connecting door, I could hear Bramble barking in the women's quarters, and at a certain point there came a sound that might have been weeping. And my body, my treacherous body, was stirred by memories of those fleeting touches, her arm slipped through mine, her hands resting against my heart. How could I wait two whole months for her, how could I bear these exquisite, painful feelings? How did other men manage? There was nobody I could talk to; Donagan, close as he was to me, would surely laugh if I confided my difficulty. I could wait. Of course I could wait. I was a prince. Let that not be Flidais weeping through there; let her not be regretting ever agreeing to marry me. Oh, if only I could tap on that door, and be admitted, and fold her in my arms with words of comfort, with soft kisses and tenderness. It would be so easy. I ached to do it. Instead I lay restless and wakeful, my manly parts in a shameful state of arousal, and waited for the dawn.

13

BLACKTHORN

It was odd, the way folk wanted to tell me all their troubles. It wasn't as if I ever gave them the slightest encouragement. Mostly I answered with a grunt or an mm-hm. Sometimes, as with the lovesick lads and girls, I dispensed down-to-earth advice, not wanting to see them undone by their own foolishness. A girl—Becca, her name was—came to me one day asking for a potion that would make a certain young man adore her to the exclusion of all others. It was a ridiculous idea, and I told her so. Explained how silly it was to believe that a spell, even a good one, could conjure the sort of love that would last a lifetime. Added that a young woman of fifteen or sixteen should be making something of herself before she even started to think about finding a man.

Becca had brought a friend with her. Many of the girls came in pairs, being a little scared of dealing with me alone. As I explained the differences between friendship, desire and love, I noticed the friend casting her eye over my supply of herbs and spices, my equipment for making distillations and decoctions, oils and salves, without saying a word. It was only when Becca had had enough of my lecture and expressed a wish to leave that the other girl, Emer, started asking questions, and good questions they were, about my methods and my materials and how a person might learn to become a healer. To my surprise, I found myself inviting her to come back some time—I did not say *without Becca* but she understood. Not that one sensible girl would make up for a whole village of silly ones, but it would be a start.

After that, Emer would drop in to the cottage every now and then, when her duties at the weaver's workshop allowed it, and undertake such tasks as I had for her. She learned quickly and did not waste time in gossip, which suited me well. Indeed, sometimes she seemed a little too quiet, as if something might be preying on her mind. I did not ask what was wrong. Chances were that would lead to another request for help, and I'd had more than enough of those already.

Emer might be quiet by nature, but everyone else in these parts was the opposite. I'd never known such folk for talking. As the autumn drew on and the mornings became misty, as mushrooms sprang up under the oaks and the leaves began to fall, I could have kept Grim entertained for hours every night with what I learned about the residents of Winterfalls, though in fact I passed on only the most interesting snippets. In return he brought me his share of the local gossip, which wasn't much, Grim being a man of few words and all of them carefully chosen. We understood each other's need for silence. We knew that the tales we told served a purpose. They filled up the spaces in the mind that would otherwise be open to the bad things, the memories we wanted gone. But sometimes a body needed to sit quiet and simply listen to the wind and the rain and the birds.

The longer we stayed at Winterfalls, the harder it became to find those quiet times. A steady stream of folk visited the cottage for remedies or for treatment of one kind or another, and often enough I was called away, since some patients could not be brought to me. One day it was a heavily built farmer felled by a sprained ankle. Another day, a whole family afflicted by a vomiting and purging sickness. And, inevitably, I was called to bring new life into the world and see the old leave it.

I was summoned one afternoon to an old woman lying alone and helpless in her tiny dwelling. When I got to the house, to be ushered in by the neighbor who had sent for me, I found the old one lying on her pallet staring out the window, and I guessed she was hoping Black Crow would come soon and not drag things out. The crone was laboring to breathe, but she wanted to talk, and since there was little else I could do for her, I sat by her pallet and listened. She told me a story about a princess shut up in a tower by an evil mage. At least, that was how the story began, but it grew strange and complicated, and eventually she seemed to lose the thread of it, fixing me with her gaze and whispering, "We all take our own ways. We all make our own choices, for good or ill."

No kinsfolk had come to this bedside—perhaps she had none, or maybe they were scattered far and did not know she had seen her last sunrise. No druid had spoken final blessings; no friend was present to hold her hand as she passed through the gateway. Only me, a stranger. And although this was a duty wise women often performed, I wondered if I'd lost any fitness I'd ever had for such a task.

"I hope you are content with your choices," I said, thinking that if I lived so long—unlikely—I'd probably die just as lonely a death as hers, or maybe even lonelier, since at least she had me, even if I was a wretched thing eaten up by anger and bitterness.

The rheumy old eyes gazed into mine, and I wondered if what she saw there made her sad or shocked or merely tired. "Now you tell . . . story," she whispered.

I could hardly refuse, since this, too, was a duty wise women were expected to perform. As she struggled from one breath to the next, I felt the leaden weight of the past settle on my shoulders, and instead of a tale that would be comforting and uplifting, all I could think of was the story of a woman who was robbed of her treasure, the thing she loved more than life itself; a woman who'd once had some good in her, some gift for making folk's lives better, but who'd been turned into a twisted, furious weapon of vengeance. Right now, a blunted, useless weapon, thanks to wretched Conmael. "I can't," I told her. "The story that's in me is too sad. Too angry. Wrong for now."

The ghost of a chuckle came from the dry old lips, soon turning into a wheezing battle to catch her breath. I helped her into a sitting position, my arm supporting her back. She was a bag of bones with the foulest breath I'd ever smelled, though not the worst stink; that description was reserved for Mathuin's hellhole.

"Some use you are to the dying," the crone rasped. "Call yourself a wise woman, and you can't even tell a story to send me on my way? Holly, now, she knew a whole forest of tales. A whole fishing net of them. A whole starry sky of them."

"There's only one in my head right now," I said, "and it's not fit for sharing." And then I thought, no, there was another, not the kind she wanted, probably, but a tale all the same. "Ah; I have one. It's about a girl who was riding to her wedding and stopped for a swim in a spot where she shouldn't have."

The old woman settled against my arm, trapping me where I was and making me feel a bit like a mother telling her child a bedtime story. Which was wrong, all wrong.

"Her name was Lady Flidais from Cloud Hill, and she was riding north to marry the prince of Dalriada."

I embroidered the tale a bit, had to, since I knew very little about the personages involved in the true story. I made Flidais a less than kindly young woman, given to ordering her women about on a whim. I made the dead girl, Ciar, a simple soul, ready to obey the most ridiculous commands such as to strip off and join her mistress in the forest pool, even though they were almost at their destination after days and days of riding, and there was a crowd of men-at-arms with them, and . . . well, there were many reasons why this had not been the wisest of ideas. I told of the drowning and its aftermath: Flidais being tended to by the local wise woman, Ciar's body being conveyed away for burial, at least I assumed so, and Prince Oran riding up and whisking everyone off to his stronghold—as a prince in a story is expected to do—leaving behind bags of largesse for the underlings. It wasn't much of a story. It lacked the element of learning that exists in the most satisfying tales. And most likely it wasn't finished yet. Who knew what the ending might be?

"Pigs," the old woman said when at last I fell silent. "Something about pigs."

"What about them?"

"Old story, Holly used to tell it. About that pool. Pigs."

"Who is Holly?" It was a wise woman's name.

"Lived there once. Long time ago. Dead now. Dead and forgotten."

I eased the old woman back onto her pillows, then moved so I could see her face. But she had closed her eyes now, and I could not read her expression. The skin was sunken on the bone, making her face a pattern of white and gray, and her breath rasped like a stick run along wattles. "Was Holly the wise woman at Dreamer's Wood? Did she live in the cottage there?"

"Wise . . ." With a sighing exhalation she was gone. Whatever the story was about the pigs, I'd never hear it now.

I called the neighbor in, and between us we got the old woman laid out on the kitchen table of her meager dwelling, washed, dried and wrapped ready for burial. I had sweet herbs in my healer's bag, and a pair of flat stones to lay on her eyes, and the neighbor found cloth for the shroud.

I had thought this crone's burial might be as lonely as her death. But once the word got around that she was gone, a couple of the local boys came by and offered to dig a grave in the field set aside for the purpose, and another neighbor dropped in to tell us a few of the local folk would gather while the old woman was put in it. I asked the neighbor if she'd heard of Holly, and she gave me a blank look.

A druid was coming to Winterfalls for the betrothal of Prince Oran and Lady Flidais. Grim had passed on this information. But the druid had not arrived yet, and this old woman could not wait long for burial. That left me responsible for conducting a graveside rite, complete with prayers and blessings. I did my best, part of me thinking of my promise to Conmael, the other half thinking it would be good to die precisely when you were ready for it, not before and not after. By the time the ritual was finished, it was nearing dusk and I was as weary as if I'd done a full day's labor in the fields. The straggle of folk who'd been at the graveside thanked me; I nodded, gathered my cloak around me and headed for home.

I was almost there—close enough to see lamplight from

the window, where Grim had left the shutters open—when I realized I was not walking alone. I slowed my pace; my unseen companion did the same. I stood still; the presence behind me also halted. If I'd been hearing footsteps, I'd have been worried about being attacked and robbed, not that I had anything worth stealing. A wise woman did not request payment for attending a deathbed, and even if I had, in this case there would have been nobody to provide it. But there were no footsteps, only a sensation of being followed.

"What do you want, Conmael?" I asked, not turning.

"To see you safely home, Blackthorn." My fey benefactor came up beside me. "Why would you assume that I want anything more?"

"Let's just say I'm a natural doubter." I walked on, and he walked with me, a deeper shadow in the growing dusk. It was disturbing the way he moved without a sound. "Besides," I added, "I can see myself safely home. I've been doing so for years."

"In the past," Conmael said quietly, "there have been certain occasions when a protector might have been useful to you. That is not to deny your courage or your fighting spirit. But there is such a thing as too much independence."

"Bollocks," I said. "I don't need a protector. I'm best left to get on with things alone." Even as I spoke, I knew that at least part of what he'd said was true. I'd never be able to confront Mathuin of Laois on my own. I'd tried, and look where it had got me. "For now, at least," I felt obliged to say.

"Ah. But you're not alone anymore, are you?" Conmael's gaze went toward the cottage window, a bright square of lamplight against the gathering dark.

I made no reply.

"Planning to keep your guard dog long?" he asked, offhand.

"What business is that of yours?" I heard the snap in my voice; could not quite understand the sudden flare of anger. I had never intended Grim to stay, not even as long as he had. Every day I considered how I might put the suggestion to him that it was time he moved on. But it was not for Conmael to weigh in on the matter.

"Your welfare is my business. You brought the big man with you to Dalriada, I imagine, because he asked for your help. He's done a good enough job of making the cottage comfortable. But you don't need him anymore. In time he might prove a liability. His story is unsavory. If you heard it, you might have second thoughts."

"Stop right there." I halted and turned to look him in the eye. "It's up to him and me what we tell about the past. I don't want him knowing my story, and I surely don't want to hear his from you. Grim always said the fey were meddlers, and I'm starting to believe him."

"He would stay, no doubt, even if he knew the whole truth about you. The doglike devotion in his eyes makes that abundantly clear. You, on the other hand, might not be so quick to give him space in your house, indeed in your bedchamber, if you knew his background."

"There's one thing I did not think the fey could be, Conmael," I said, "and that was petty. I don't want to hear anything at all about Grim. If there's any question I want you to answer, it's why you decided to take an interest in my fortunes in the first place, since to the best of my knowledge you were a complete stranger to me. Your kind are not exactly known for doing favors to human folk, unless it's to play some kind of trick. As for my sleeping arrangements, they're nobody's concern but my own."

He lifted his brows. "Human memory is a strange thing," he observed. "How it comes and goes. How sometimes folk tuck the past away so deep they forget it's there at all. The human mind is full of byways, dead ends, locked chambers. Strongboxes guarding matters too painful to be brought into the light; dusty corners where items considered too trivial are tossed away. You'll remember one day. And if you do not, perhaps it is no matter."

He spoke with nonchalance, lightly, but the look on his face did not match his tone.

If there was anything that irked me, it was folk playing games of this kind. I could see no reason for him to withhold the truth, whatever it might be. "Why not just tell me?" I asked.

"I —" began Conmael.

Light flooded out from the cottage as Grim opened the

door. Almost immediately the light was blocked by his large form standing there, arms folded and legs apart. The moment was lost.

"Good night, Conmael." I hastened forward, praying that he would take himself off before Grim decided on some kind of confrontation.

"Good night, Blackthorn." Conmael's words were only a murmur, drifting away into the shadows even as they were spoken. As I came up the steps to the cottage door, I was on my own.

"What did *he* want?"

"Nothing."

"Mm-hm." Grim had the sense to leave it at that, though the way he clattered bowls and spoons around as he put the supper on the table spoke louder than words.

I went out the back, used the privy, washed my face and hands in the bucket of clean water. When I came back in the food was on the table. Grim was standing by the open window, looking out into the night. "All right?" I said to his back.

A grunt in response.

"I hope that's a yes, because I'm bone weary. I attended a deathbed today. And a burial. I didn't think I had it in me to speak prayers, seeing as I've more or less stopped believing in such things. But folk thanked me afterward so I suppose it was good enough."

"A deathbed? Whose?" He came over to the table and sat down.

"An old woman who used to be a seamstress. Glad to go, I think. She knew the last wise woman—at least I think that was who she meant."

Grim ladled out vegetable soup. There was bread as well, heavy with grains. We ate in silence. It occurred to me that although Conmael had departed, he was still here with us, an invisible presence constraining everything we said and did. And that made me angry.

"About Conmael," I said as I gathered the empty bowls. "He offered to tell me your past history. I said no, thank you. Interfering bastard." I made sure I did not look at him. "If he makes the same offer to you, I'd be pleased if you'd give him the same reply."

There was a long silence. When at last I turned in Grim's direction, he was still seated at the table but had his head in his hands.

"Grim?"

He lifted his head; his face was ashen. "How could he know?"

"I asked myself the same question the night he came to visit me in that place and spoke of things a stranger shouldn't have known about. Where you're concerned, he might just be making mischief. With me, he really does know. Enough of my story, at least, to offer me a compact I couldn't say no to."

"I don't like it," Grim muttered. "Not right. Playing games with folk as if they were a child's poppets. Why would he do that?"

I shrugged. "It's beyond me. But he did get me out. He did save my life. So I'm stuck with him for seven years, like it or not." Now was the time to add, *But you're not—you're free to go whenever you want.* The words got trapped somewhere between my thoughts and my lips. "Brew?" I asked.

"I'll make it. You sit down awhile."

His hands were shaking as he measured herbs, poured water from the kettle, passed a cup over to me. I pretended not to notice. Conmael had a lot to answer for.

14

Flidais surprised me. The day after Bramble's escape, my lady emerged from her quarters to take her place beside me at the breakfast table. Her appearance still gave me concern; though lovely as a spring flower in her deep blue gown and cream overdress, with her hair braided in a circlet, she was ghostly pale and had dark smudges under her eyes. I passed her the choicest morsels of food and ensured her ale cup was refilled. She sat quiet as a mouse, with Mhairi in attendance behind her. Her other women were seated with members of my household, and appeared to be enjoying their release from seclusion. Despite the very recent loss of one of their number, their table was lively with conversation.

"I hope you are feeling better, Lady Flidais," said Donagan, who sat on my other side. "Prince Oran mentioned headaches. The local wise woman is very good, so folk say."

Flidais managed a wan smile. "I am somewhat recovered, thank you. No need for the wise woman's services. Does she visit the household often?"

"Mistress Blackthorn is newly arrived in the district," I said. "I understand she mostly looks after the folk of the settlement and the farms. We'll need to put some arrangement in place for the future, now that we are living permanently at Winterfalls. A household physician, perhaps, if you are not comfortable with a wise woman."

Flidais made no comment.

"My mother will most likely insist on a physician," I added, then caught Donagan's look. I knew him well; he was warning me not to rush into the topic of childbirth and confinement. I turned a quelling look on him. My judgment was not quite as woefully askew as he believed. "But there is no need for a decision yet. I'm delighted that you are a little better, Flidais. It's a fine day. Perhaps we might go walking after breakfast? I would love to show you some of the places we spoke of in our letters." She flinched visibly, and I remembered too late that I had been eloquent in my praise of Dreamer's Wood. "Just around the farm for now. I know you enjoy a good walk, and Bramble's recent adventure suggests she would appreciate the exercise. On the leash, of course. There are farm dogs here that would frighten her."

"Whatever you prefer, Oran. You must be busy."

"I think the household can do without me for a little," I said with a smile. "You'll find my folk are very capable. If you prefer a quiet morning, I could show you my library. I have a small surprise for you there, which I'm hoping you will enjoy. But you must be the one to choose how we spend the day. I am at your service, my lady."

She looked almost alarmed, though I had spoken lightly. "Oh," she said. "But it's not for me—that is, a walk would be good. I should learn where everything is. And meet everyone. It seems quite a large household."

"Wait until you see Cahercorcan," I said with a grimace. "You will get a taste of it when my parents and their attendants arrive in a few days. My advice is, enjoy the quiet while you can."

In the endless time of waiting for Flidais's arrival at Winterfalls, I had often pictured us out walking, just the two of us, hand in hand or arm in arm, sharing our delight in the plants and creatures that were abundant around Winterfalls, exchanging tales and tender words as we went. That could not happen until we were husband and wife. I had no qualms about going out unattended, but with Flidais's reputation at stake, I had to be mindful of what was considered correct. I suggested that she bring Mhairi, who seemed to have taken Ciar's place as her personal maid. And I asked Donagan to come with us. While the women went off to fetch cloaks and change their shoes, he and I waited in the garden.

"But where is Bramble?" I asked as Flidais and Mhairi came out to join us.

"I thought it best not to bring her," said Flidais. "She seems to have taken against me; it's all snarling and snapping now."

I hesitated before speaking. If I challenged her handling of Bramble she might be offended. On the other hand, I was sure she was wrong. "My aunt, who is coming here to stay soon, is something of an expert on dogs. She's of the opinion that if a good dog starts behaving badly, the best remedy is to keep her—or him—busy. She would recommend exercise, I'm certain."

Flidais dropped her gaze as if I had chastised her. It seemed she was indeed offended.

"My lord," put in Mhairi, "Bramble will very likely snap and bite all the way, or bark and howl. She's been keeping Lady Flidais awake at night with her carry-on."

I recalled the terrified little creature I had found at the burial ground. How she had crept close, nestling against me. How she had fallen asleep in my arms. I thought of the portrait, with mistress and pet depicted in a pose of deepest trust and affection. Whatever had gone wrong between them, it was important to remedy it quickly. No wonder my lady was in poor spirits. "Let's try, shall we?" I suggested. "Bramble can be kept on the leash, and if we happen to encounter the farm dogs, I will carry her."

All three of them, Donagan included, stared at me as if I were out of my wits. Then Mhairi said, "Yes, my lord," and went back to fetch the dog. What ensued was a little awkward. When Mhairi reemerged from the women's quarters with Bramble on the leash, Flidais's pet was struggling against the restraint. We had heard her yelps of complaint well before she appeared. When she saw us, Bramble stiffened, falling abruptly silent. Then she ran toward me, hauling Mhairi along behind her. I crouched to greet the dog. She put her forefeet up on my knee and tried to lick my face. No greeting for her beloved mistress; Flidais might as well not have been there.

"You've made a friend," observed Donagan, who perhaps did not quite understand the subtleties of the situation.

"So it seems." I rose to my feet. "Go to your mistress, little one. There she is, see?"

"She won't walk with me." Flidais was looking at the ground. "Mhairi will take her."

"Which way would you like to go?" I asked, hoping the walk would lift her spirits as well as the dog's. "We should avoid the stables, which are over there. Bramble is certainly not ready for an encounter with Eochu's lurchers, though they're well trained." The mare my father had chosen as a wedding gift for Flidais had arrived and was being settled by our grooms; I would take my lady to see it some other time, without Bramble.

I had thought Flidais might ask to visit the place where Ciar had been buried, but all she said was, "You choose, Oran."

"Let's walk to the top of that rise, up past the farm cottages," I suggested. "See, where the hazel trees are? From there we can show you the lay of the land." As we set off, I added, "The folk of Winterfalls settlement will be anxious to get to know you. I visit them regularly, and they come here for my monthly open council, where we hear various matters of concern, arbitrate on disputes and so on. And chat over cakes and ale afterward. There's been much interest in my future bride, as you may imagine." Gods, I seemed capable of only the most stilted of utterances this morning. Where was the fluent poet of the letters? Perhaps I should have defied convention and left both Donagan and Mhairi behind. It was not as if my lady and I were likely to engage in any form of intimacy out here, with so many folk going along the paths or working in the fields.

"My lady," put in Donagan, "Prince Oran may have told you in his letters that his territory covers an area far wider than Winterfalls and its surrounding farmlands. There's another village, Silverlake, to the east, as well as various smaller settlements in the hills around. Folk come in from everywhere for the council. You'll have an opportunity to attend two such gatherings before your hand-fasting."

Flidais said nothing. Her eyes were on Bramble, who was doing her best to prove her mistress's misgivings well-founded. The dog pulled in one direction, then another, skittered underfoot, wound the leash around Mhairi's legs, whining.

"You see, my lord?" said Mhairi.

"Let me take her." I crouched down again and spoke to the dog in an undertone, words designed to soothe. I did not try to pat her; she was trembling in a way that was all too familiar.

"Mhairi should take her back to the house. I cannot imagine what has got into the creature. Like this, she is not fit company for anyone," said Flidais.

This felt wrong. It did not match the way I had expected things to be. Remembering Donagan's advice to take control, I picked Bramble up, took the leash from Mhairi and settled the dog in my arms. The yapping ceased. She stuck her nose under my arm, as if that might make her invisible.

"I'll carry her until she's calmer," I said. "Now, that cottage is Aedan and Fíona's. He is my very capable steward, and I imagine you have met his wife already—she supervises most of the indoor folk. The one next to it is Niall's . . ."

As our tour continued, Flidais grew even quieter. I realized it must be difficult to remember everything. I assured her that nobody expected her to do so overnight. We reached the hazel grove, and Donagan and I pointed out the barn, the stables, the boundaries, the way to the settlement. We explained what crops we grew, what animals we raised, how our trading was conducted with the folk of the community. Mhairi asked more questions than Flidais did, and I saw Flidais frown at her maidservant as if she thought this inappropriate. No doubt, back home at Cloud Hill, her parents ran their household along more conventional lines. I was immensely glad of the arrangement that had allowed me to make Winterfalls my home, for I could not put my own philosophies into practice at Cahercorcan. At least, not until I became king, and I hoped that was a long way off.

"I'm accustomed to allowing the community a role in making decisions," I told Flidais, "that is, decisions that affect their own lives and those of their neighbors. That is why I hold the councils; so I can listen to their concerns and take them into consideration. And I adopt the same approach within my own household. Everyone has a voice, from the most junior of stablehands to . . ."

"To the prince's body servant," said Donagan, poker-faced.

Mhairi laughed; Flidais did not.

"I don't consider Donagan a servant, though he'd tell you that is what he is," I said with a smile. "As I wrote in my letters, he and I have been companions and friends since we were boys. He's my wisest adviser; worth ten royal councillors."

"Now you jest," said Donagan. "But, my lady, you will most certainly find that Prince Oran believes in allowing his folk freedoms that some other leaders might not. Aedan, Fíona and Brid ensure every aspect of the household runs smoothly. Eochu and Niall look after the stables and the farm. The prince trusts his folk, and they return that trust by doing their work well, with minimal direction."

"I see," said Flidais. "You are saying, then, that the prince's wife will not have many responsibilities?"

"I don't believe that is what Donagan means, exactly." I bent to set Bramble down, taking care not to startle her. I was rewarded for my trust when she moved away to sniff something interesting in the long grass, trailing the leash. "True, you will not need to fill your days with constant supervision of our serving folk unless you choose to. You will not need to plan the work of the kitchens. You'll want to play your part, of course. But it is early days. There will be time for those activities we both enjoy so much. And I hope you will assist me with the councils; the women of the community, in particular, will welcome your views."

Bramble began to dig. Soil flew everywhere, making both women pull their skirts out of the way. "Oh, I'm so sorry," said Flidais. "Bramble, don't do that!"

"What's a little dirt? She's a dog, after all." I glanced at Donagan, who favored me with a grimace—the task of cleaning my clothing would fall to him. "It's good to see your little friend more confident," I told Flidais. "Your letters described so beautifully the outings you and she enjoyed at Cloud Hill. If we take her walking every day, she'll soon be herself again, I'm sure of it."

"Every day," echoed Flidais. "That is too much to ask of you, my lord. You must be so busy."

I would indeed be busy from now on, with the impending arrival of my father the king and my mother the queen, along with their councillors and various hangers-on. There was the betrothal ritual, two open councils, a celebration for the folk of the local community, and later the ride to Cahercorcan for the formal hand-fasting, to which an even grander array of guests would be traveling from many parts of Erin. Yes, I could be sure my household would handle the domestic arrangements perfectly, but I would need to smooth the way for our visitors, ensure the serving folk from court did not clash with my own people, keep my temper and maintain a princely demeanor no matter what happened. Of course, as the daughter of a chieftain, Flidais would understand this.

"I am not so busy that I cannot make time for a daily walk," I told her. "Indeed, walking helps me stay calm at such times." Curse Donagan, he had that little smile on his face again. I could read him like a book. *You, calm?* he was thinking. *You've been wound tight as a bowstring since the day you read her first letter.* But then, perhaps it was good that Donagan and I knew each other so well. Such a friend helped a man keep his feet on the ground.

"I'm feeling rather faint." Flidais swayed suddenly, and Mhairi darted forward to support her. "I'm sorry . . . my head . . ."

Donagan was quicker than I, whipping off his cloak and laying it on the ground. "Here, my lady, please sit down."

"We've exhausted you," I murmured as Mhairi eased her mistress onto the cloak. "This has been too much—I should have realized . . ."

"I'm all right. I need a few moments; then I can walk back." Flidais put her head in her hands.

Bramble chose this moment to run over and start a shrill barking. For such a tiny dog, she had a very loud voice.

"Stop it!" ordered Mhairi, but Bramble took no notice.

I reached down and picked up the dog, less gently than before. "Enough!" I told her, then tucked her under my arm. She fell mercifully quiet. "Flidais, we must get you home. I cannot say how sorry I am — we've talked too much and tired you out."

"I'm fine. I need a rest, that is all. Perhaps if I could hold your arm on the way back . . . Mhairi, you take Bramble."

That plan was unworkable, since Bramble refused to walk with anyone but me. When Mhairi or Donagan tried to take the leash she complained at the top of her voice. What was wrong, there was no telling, but since the noise was hurting my ears, I could imagine how poor Flidais must be feeling. In the end, my lady walked back with Mhairi on one side and Donagan on the other, and I came behind with Bramble, who trotted quietly at my heel as if she had never set a foot wrong in her life.

Back at the women's quarters, Flidais brushed off my concerns, assuring me she would be better soon. It was only after the door closed behind them that I realized she and Mhairi had forgotten Bramble, now seated at my feet, gazing up at me. Donagan went to knock.

"Leave it," I said. "Flidais needs quiet, and it seems Bramble is not allowing that. She can come with us for now."

He lifted his brows. "Better tell them, at least, or they'll assume she's run away again."

"Later. Let Mhairi settle Flidais to rest first. I'll send someone."

In my chamber, as I changed into my indoor shoes, I felt the weight of my friend's gaze and was uncomfortable. "What?" I snapped, not looking at him. Bramble had settled herself on the bed, curled into a ball, her eyes hardly open.

"You seem somewhat on edge," observed Donagan, who had moved over to the storage chest under my window and was rearranging something. "Your demeanor is not what I would have expected, my friend. I hesitate to say this, but you don't seem happy."

I lay down at full length on my bed, one hand stroking the small form of Bramble. She was not happy either and nor, I suspected, was Flidais.

"What is it?" Donagan closed the chest. "If it's simply the weight of having too much to do, coupled with the unsettling presence of the lady at Winterfalls, you must know you can depend on me, as on your whole household, to share the load. There is no requirement that you take so much on yourself." When I still said nothing, since I did not really know how to answer his question, he said, "I'm sure Lady Flidais will be fine, Oran. If you wish, I can send for Mistress Blackthorn."

Bramble wriggled closer, pressing herself up against me. "Flidais said she didn't want the services of either wise woman or physician," I said. "I've already upset her by insisting on taking Bramble walking with us. If I produce Mistress Blackthorn against her wishes, I'll only make matters worse."

"Mm-hm. Oran, I need to brush down those trousers. And your tunic, I suspect, if that creature is shedding. You might put on these clean things, and I will take those away."

Not a word of reproach for my moodiness. He was a good man. I rose from the bed and let him assist me with changing. Bramble lay low, watching every move.

"Better," said Donagan after he had examined me. "One more thing, if the creature's to stay in here." He fetched a folded blanket from atop the chest and laid it on the bed next to Bramble. "Fíona won't be impressed if there's dog hair all over the bedding. I suggest we sacrifice one blanket for the good of the others. You can move her onto it. At such a busy time, I'll be needing the use of all my fingers."

Bramble had not growled when he came close; she had not snapped. "No, you do it," I said, using my princely tone. "Consider it an experiment. Bramble, no biting."

Donagan gave me a look but reached to lift the little creature onto the blanket—a good one in gray wool, softened from laundering. My friend did know how to handle dogs. He had helped me with Grey when my beloved hound was old and sick; he'd had his own dog, which had died when Donagan was sixteen. He had sworn he'd never have another.

"There," I said as Bramble settled down again, snuggling in. "You have the touch."

"Or this one knows a good thing when she sees it. How long is she staying up here? Are you adding frequent trips outside to my duties, or will she be doing her business in a corner of your bedchamber?"

"How long? I don't know. Long enough to give Lady Flidais some respite at night."

"Not much respite if she does her barking in here, with the lady just through that door."

"If that occurs we'll take her somewhere else." I was almost certain Bramble would sleep peacefully, tucked in next to me. Her whole demeanor was different here. "Once my parents arrive, Aunt Sochla might take charge of her. She should quickly identify what is wrong. I hope so, anyway. I believe Bramble's apparent change of character must be responsible for Flidais's low spirits. At least in part. They were devoted companions."

"I'll make sure word gets to the lady that her dog is safe here and will be looked after. And I might speak to Fíona about the headaches, with your permission. We may not have a healer in the house, but very likely one of the women knows a remedy—we coped without Mistress Blackthorn's services until very recently."

"I suppose my parents may bring one of the court physicians with them. But I believe Flidais will refuse his services as well. She does seem to believe her malady is not serious."

Donagan was scrutinizing me again. "And no doubt she is right," he said. "Oran, what's really troubling you? Are you concerned that Lady Flidais may be too frail to serve as the wife of a future king? That she may not be fit to bear the required sons?"

I felt myself flush. "Of course not! That had not occurred to me for a moment!" The idea shocked me.

"Then what?"

"Nothing. I'm concerned for her health, that's all. Angry with myself for insisting we go walking when I should have known it would be too much for her. Troubled by Bramble's turning against her mistress for no reason, when they were so close. And . . . no, it's nothing."

Donagan waited. He had grown patient over the years.

"I was expecting . . . no, this is fanciful."

Donagan seated himself on a bench. Leaned forward with elbows on knees. Spoke not a word.

"Don't laugh at me. I had imagined the bond she and I shared, through our letters—the closeness that made my reluctance to wed vanish as if it had never been—would be apparent from the moment we met. We have so much in common. We love the same pastimes, we share the same philosophies, we were both so full of hope . . . Am I a fool, Donagan? Flidais is lovely. If anything, she's even more beautiful than her portrait. I find her desirable to a degree that is at times uncomfortable. I understand that she's exhausted from the journey and distressed by her maid's death. I know only a few days have passed. But . . . the Flidais of the letters would have let me comfort her. She would have wished to spend time with me, even if she was a little unwell. She would have . . . never mind. I should stop this. I despise myself."

"May I speak honestly?"

"I'm sure you will, whatever I say. But yes, please do."

"Lord Cadhan is only a district chieftain. It's possible that Lady Flidais's home is a far more modest establishment than Winterfalls. And you are a prince, if a somewhat unconventional one. You are a future king. Very possibly the lady feels overwhelmed. Shy. Not sure how to speak to you."

"Everything I say to her comes out labored and formal. I've lost the ability to share the words of my heart."

Donagan smiled; his expression was kindly. "No man would be comfortable doing that in the presence of chaperones. After the hand-fasting, when you are alone with your new wife, those words will come back to you, Oran."

"I wanted this to be perfect. I wanted her to be happy. Indeed, I expected it. In her letters she spoke so warmly of Winterfalls, of the things we would do together, of . . . of me, Donagan."

"Letters are not the most reliable guide to matters of the heart."

"You're wrong." I sat up, making Bramble start. "Letters tell the truths a person will not speak. They contain the deepest of feelings, the wisest of stories. Letters are powerful. They contain messages of hope, love, change."

Donagan raised his brows. "Oran," he said.

"What?"

"Have you considered that a scribe might have assisted the lady to write those letters? A household like Cadhan's would almost certainly have one."

"Of course not!" Now he had really shocked me. "Her letters were ... they were personal. Deeply personal. And utterly in tune with my own. Flidais would not have shared them with anyone else." He must be wrong. I could not bear to consider the alternative.

"If a letter can contain the truths that are too difficult to speak, why don't you write her one?" Donagan suggested. "I'll take it to her."

"Now? She'll be resting, probably asleep." For some reason my heart was racing.

"I'll leave it with one of the waiting women."

I did not answer. What I wanted to do was lie on the bed with Bramble beside me, and surrender to my dreams. I knew quite well that if I sat down at the writing desk, no words would come. There was a restlessness in me that would not allow them. "You can leave me now," I said. "If I need you I will call. You must have a great deal to do."

"Very well, my lord. Oh, you'll need a dish of water. For the dog."

"Go, Donagan. I'm fine, Bramble's fine, I just want to be left alone."

The door closed behind him, so quietly I barely heard it.

I wrote no letter. I lay on my bed awhile with Bramble quiet beside me, and imagined how horrified my mother would be if she could see me. *Have you forgotten that one day you will be king of Dalriada, Oran? Such self-indulgence is entirely inappropriate. I will remind you once, and once only, that this marriage is taking place thanks to your own dogged insistence. It is time you recognized that you live in the real world, with real responsibilities, and not in some fairy tale.* Then she would look at me, and perhaps the mother would for a moment overcome the queen, and she would say, *It's natural to feel a little nervous at such a time, son. Remind yourself that your life is one of privilege. You are young and healthy. You have a beautiful bride, suitable in every way. Your doubts do no service to Flidais or to you. Cast them aside and walk forward as the prince and the man you are.*

"Entirely true, Bramble," I murmured. "And very soon I will rise, and go out there, and do exactly that. This is all in my head. It's not real. Probably all Flidais needs is a good night's sleep."

The next morning Flidais was at breakfast again, with some color in her cheeks and a new brightness in her eyes. She thanked me for her undisturbed sleep and professed herself happy to walk to the stable with me and see her new horse. I had brought Bramble down early to run about outside awhile, then prevailed upon Brid to give her a meaty bone. The dog was even now devouring this in my bedchamber, not the tidiest of arrangements, perhaps, but it should keep her quiet for some time.

The morning gave me new heart. Donagan was busy, but Mhairi and the older maidservant, Nuala, came with us. Flidais was delighted with the gray mare, whom she named Apple. The creature was well bred and well schooled, which was no more than I expected. My father had a good eye for horseflesh; had he not been born into kingship, he might have made a name for himself as a breeder. Eochu led Apple around the yard, explaining her finer points to Flidais, and Flidais, more animated than I had seen her before, stroked Apple's neck and asked a number of questions.

"She'll need a bit more time to get over the journey from Cahercorcan, my lady," my stable master said. "But I'll have her ready for riding within a few days. Good country in these parts for a gallop, if you're so inclined."

Flidais glanced my way. "I will look forward to that. What a wonderful gift! More than I could possibly have hoped for. Which is your riding horse? Remind me, Oran."

I introduced her to Snow; the two horses would look very fine going side by side, which my father had perhaps thought of when selecting the gray for Flidais. "After the betrothal, we might ride to the settlement to speak with the folk there, and afterward go on to Silverlake. That's a fine ride."

"I'd like that, Oran." Flidais slipped her hand through my arm, and for a moment her whole body brushed against mine, setting my heart racing.

"It's settled, then." Gods, two whole turnings of the moon until the hand-fasting! How did other men cope with the ache of desire? Her closeness made my manhood stand to attention in a manner entirely inappropriate to the circumstances. Much more of this and I'd have to start wearing shapeless robes like an elderly scholar. "I have another gift for you, in my library. Perhaps after we walk back, if you are not too tired, I might show you my collection." Every word I spoke seemed heavy with double meaning. My cheeks were hot; I must be red as a ripe apple. And no doubt Eochu and his assistant, and the two waiting women, and possibly Flidais herself, were aware of the reason for my discomfort. "Let's go now, shall we?"

I longed to give Flidais my personal gift. But by the time we reached the house, her headache had returned.

"I'm so sorry, Oran. I need to rest awhile. I have enjoyed this morning; I look forward to riding out with you when Apple is ready." She laid her hand on my arm and favored me with a smile.

"Rest well, my dear," I said, and risked a formal kiss on her cheek. "Perhaps before supper, for the library."

"Perhaps." She turned away, and her maidservants ushered her indoors.

I was disappointed. But there was plenty to occupy my time. Our guests were starting to ride in: chieftains from Dalriada and Tirconnell and Ulaid, landholders and lawmen and their wives. And, of course, their guards and attendants. All would be accommodated in my household until some days after the betrothal ceremony, as Winterfalls was a considerable ride from any other major establishment. In the absence of Flidais, I greeted the new arrivals with Donagan by my side, and Aedan's helpers shepherded them away to their various quarters. We had sufficient private apartments to house the chieftains and their wives; others went to the men's or women's quarters, which we'd expanded considerably in preparation for Flidais's arrival. Some of my people had vacated their cottages to make room for visitors, and if needed, we'd use the grooms' quarters out by the stables for any overflow.

By the time everyone was settled, the afternoon was almost over. Donagan more or less ordered me to go to the

library and sit down awhile before the guests emerged
again, rested and ready for supper.

Library was perhaps too grand a name for the chamber
where I kept my treasured collection of books and manu-
scripts. The room opened off my council chamber. It had
deep storage shelves, an oak table and a number of carefully shielded lamps. Tapestries softened the walls; the floor
was of slate. Few other folk came here. In my library I
could lose myself in the world of a book, or simply sit and
dream. When the weather was too inclement to allow a
walk or a ride, I would retire here and let the beauty of
words and illuminations fill my mind.

Donagan had left me, but now he returned with a flask
of mead, two goblets and some little cakes on a tray.

"Thank you, my friend. It's been a long day for you too."

He poured the mead; only one goblet.

"What about you?" I asked.

"Oran . . . I took the liberty of sending a message to
Lady Flidais. I suggested you would like her to come here,
now. I know how much you want to give her the book, and
I understand you'll prefer to do so in private. With more
and more folk arriving, that's likely to prove ever more difficult. I can stay outside the door."

So much for sitting in peace—my heart was hammering
again. "Donagan, I believe I'm a little shocked. Won't she
bring one of her women with her?"

"Trust me, Oran."

So it was that I found myself alone with Flidais in the
library, with both Donagan and Mhairi outside. Mhairi had
wanted to protest, I had seen it, but she was not prepared
to challenge me. And Flidais, contrary to my expectations,
had come into the room quite willingly. She had changed
her gown, and now wore a fetching outfit in green and gold.

"You look like summer, Flidais," I said as she approached. "Come, sit down. I don't suppose we have long;
we do need to be mindful of what's appropriate." Gods, I
was doing it again, speaking like some doddery old councillor. I struggled to find the right words. "You seem happier today, and that makes me happy too. From the moment
I first saw your portrait . . . Well, you have read how I felt.
The time of waiting tried me hard. Your letters strength-

ened me. They were so beautiful, so deep and thoughtful." I took both her hands in mine, and there it was again—the powerful pull of bodily desire, awakened by the slightest touch.

Flidais dropped her gaze, blushing. "Thank you," she said.

"I'm sorry if I have disappointed you in any way." I drew a deep, steadying breath. "My—my appearance, my behavior—my woeful struggle to express what is in my heart . . ."

Flidais looked up. She smiled. Then she stood on tiptoes and kissed me full on the lips. Her kiss sent a shock through my whole body; if I had thought the touch of her hand potent, it was nothing to this. I wrapped my arms around her, returning the kiss a hundredfold. This, this was all we had needed to make things right again. To find each other again.

After a considerable time, Flidais drew away from my embrace, putting her palms against my chest. "Did you say you had a gift for me?"

"Ah. Yes, I do. I hope it is to your liking." The silk-wrapped book was on a low shelf, well away from the lamps—it was precious both in its rarity and in its link to our courtship. "Please accept this as my wedding gift to you, Flidais. And as a token of my love." There, I had spoken the word, if somewhat shakily.

Flidais unwrapped the length of silk and held the little book in her hands. The cover was of finest oxhide, with the corner pieces cast in a pattern suggesting oak leaves. The central medallion was inset with rubies and pearls. "Oh, how lovely!" she exclaimed.

"Look inside."

She opened the book. Turned the pages, where a master scribe had copied faithfully not only the fine hand of the original, but also the illuminations that had given that book its particular appeal for Flidais. Her father had had a copy in his personal library.

"What beautiful pictures," she said. "Look, a little dog. A strange creature that is part snake, part bird. And here, an owl. How charming, Oran. Thank you so much." She closed the little volume and turned her lovely smile on me.

This was not quite the response I had expected. "It is a near-exact copy of Lucian's *Bestiary*," I said, wondering if the upheaval of the journey could have made her forget a book she had described to me in such meticulous detail. "Ordered especially for you, long ago when we were first writing to each other. I was so full of hope, I arranged this even before we had agreed to wed. I knew you would find it hard to leave behind the treasure you so loved. I knew, also, that your father was unlikely to let such a valuable item travel with you halfway across Erin. It was copied for me in the monastic library where the original is held."

Flidais was looking a little flushed now. "Oh, how silly of me! Of course it is the same, how could I mistake it? Oran, that is very sweet of you, and very romantic, and I love you for it." She set the book down on the table and put her arms around my neck, pressing herself close. "Sadly, the headache prevents me from reading at present," she said against my chest, "but perhaps you would read something to me? Just a short passage?"

"Of course." I bent to bestow a kiss on her hair. She smelled of sweet herbs. In my arms she felt warm and pliant. How could I doubt her even for a moment?

Propriety suggested I should step back, and I did so, not without reluctance. It would be all too easy for the embrace to become something more, and something more again, and I could not allow that to happen. Not before we were hand-fasted. "Shall we sit down and take some of this mead? It's Brid's own brew. And Donagan has provided spice cakes." I was about to add that my body servant, usually such a stickler for correct behavior, had surprised me this afternoon, but I did not. Better if Flidais believed this private encounter had been my idea.

I read her the description of the unicorn, knowing it was one of her favorite parts of the bestiary. We had differed, in our letters, over the scholar Lucian's text, which he had rendered in both Latin and Irish, scribed on opposite pages. I had thought the parallel texts reasonably faithful to each other; Flidais had found passages in which she believed Lucian used the vernacular more creatively. We had enjoyed debating matters of this kind and would again, no doubt, when Flidais was feeling better.

"*The unicorn is fierce of temperament and wild in nature, finding its home in the dark recesses of ancient forests,*" read the last part of the description. "*When pursued by hunters, it will outpace the fleetest of horses. Only when cornered can it be taken. It will sacrifice its life rather than be captured. A unicorn driven toward a cliff will not veer one way or the other but leap, even should the precipice be sheer and high. When it falls, the creature will turn so that the horn is downmost. Thus the shock of the landing is absorbed by the hard material of that horn, and the unicorn may walk away unharmed.*

"The horn of the unicorn has remarkable curative properties. Powdered and made into a salve, it is effective in the treatment of many illnesses." Had Flidais just stifled a yawn? "I will not read the next passage," I said. What followed was a detailed description of the various salves, drafts, and other potions that could be prepared from alicorn, the substance that formed the horns of unicorns. Flidais knew the book as well as I did; no need for her to hear that somewhat less interesting section. "I hope that very soon you will be reading again—I know how much you enjoy it. Perhaps we should ask Mistress Blackthorn if she has a supply of powdered alicorn. It's said to be effective for headaches."

It was a joke, but Flidais did not look amused, and I regretted it. "I'm sorry, Flidais. I did not mean to make light of your malady. The last thing I want is to hurt you in any way. You must know that."

"I am the one who should say sorry," Flidais murmured. "The headaches are a nuisance to you. I have been indisposed when you've needed me to do things—greeting the guests, speaking to the household—and I do not like to displease you. I will be better soon, I promise. Already I feel much stronger."

"You don't displease me, Flidais." I set down my goblet and came to kneel beside her where she sat on the bench. I took her hands in mine. "Never think that. The situation was difficult, meeting face-to-face for the first time after our letters . . . And the terrible event at Dreamer's Pool . . . Little wonder that we both felt somewhat awkward. And what occurred with Bramble did not make it easier for you."

"Donagan told me Bramble spent last night in your bedchamber."

"She did, and slept soundly. But that cannot be a long-term arrangement, of course." I would have been happy to keep it thus; but if Bramble was likely to bark and bite in Flidais's presence, she clearly could not sleep on the bed once we were hand-fasted. "With your permission, when Aunt Sochla arrives I will ask her to take charge of your little friend."

"You don't need my permission," Flidais said. "You're a prince."

"I'm your future husband. I'm the man who loves you. And Bramble is your dog. I may be a prince, but I try to respect the wishes of others. That applies not only to the people close to me but to everyone I encounter."

She dropped her gaze. "Now I've made you cross."

"Not at all." I reached up to lay my hand against her cheek. "Sometimes I do get a little pompous; it's one of my failings. Now we'd best open the door, or Donagan and Mhairi will be imagining all manner of things."

"It seems a long time until the hand-fasting," Flidais said softly. "Don't you think so, Oran?" She was looking directly at me now, and what I saw in her eyes stirred me.

"A very long time," I said, tracing my finger across her lips. "I know it will try my patience to the limit."

"Mine too," said Flidais with a smile.

At that moment there was a discreet tapping on the door—Donagan, no doubt, warning me that it was time to bring this to a close. Which was perhaps just as well, since desire was threatening to overwhelm me yet again.

"Farewell for now, dearest," I said, rising to my feet.

"Farewell, Oran." She rose and went to the door. It was only after she was gone, and Mhairi with her, that I noticed she had left my gift behind.

15

BLACKTHORN

The entire neighborhood was swept up in preparations for the betrothal of Prince Oran and Lady Flidais. I was much relieved that I had not been invited to the celebrations, though in fact Grim had heard everyone was welcome. Folk from the village would be there, farmers and craftsmen and laborers—there'd been much excitement about it—but there'd be the prince and his kind too, and Grim and I had no reason to be wanting that sort of company. Let them enjoy their dancing and singing, their whistles and drums, their great bonfire. We'd sit by our own little fire, glad to be out of it all.

I could have done without the endless talk. Folk came to see me almost every day, and I had no choice but to listen as they chattered on about the ritual and the court visitors and what Lady Flidais would be wearing. They talked about Prince Oran and how much everyone liked him, because he took the time to listen to them, really listen, instead of nodding his head when they told him their concerns, then doing nothing. They told me how some Gaul who lived in Silverlake was baking a wedding cake, and how they hoped there'd be a share for the ordinary folk, not only the lords and ladies. Soon enough my head was so full of the betrothal that I wanted to scream. But generally while someone was prattling on about gowns and music and cake I was attending to their sore back or nasty rash, so I buttoned my lip and let them talk.

The only company I didn't mind, apart from Grim's, which I was stuck with whether I liked it or not, was Emer's. The girl didn't gossip the way other folk did. And she was genuinely useful around the place: a quick learner. I was surprised when, one morning as she was watching me prepare a salve, even she started talking about the upcoming celebrations. I handed her the mortar and pestle and a handful of seeds to grind so she could make herself useful at the same time.

"Are you sure you don't want to be there, Mistress Blackthorn?" Emer asked. "You're welcome to come along with my family, if you care to. There'll be music and dancing—court musicians for the formal part, my brother says, but later on just the village band. Fraoch plays the bodhran, and there are a couple of fellows on whistle and fiddle. That's for us, the ordinary folk. And stories. There's a druid coming to perform the ritual; I expect he'll tell some tales. I think you would like that." She paused, peering into the mortar, testing the mixture between her fingers.

"Not ready yet," I said. "You want a much finer powder. Almost like dust." My mind went off on a path of its own, thinking about families and how different they were. Emer's brother Fraoch was the local smith, the only man in Winterfalls who came anywhere near Grim's size. Emer was a tall girl, strongly built; that would stand her in good stead as a healer, since she'd likely be able to handle bonesetting without assistance. She had soft brown hair and a thoughtful look to her. I wondered if Grim had ever fathered children, and if so whether they had grown into giants like him. I could have asked him. But that would be breaking our rule, and besides, it would give him the right to put the same sort of question to me. And I wouldn't be able to answer, because the moment I started to talk about it I would break in pieces.

"I keep thinking of my friend," Emer said, continuing to grind the seeds. "She loves music and dancing; she'd enjoy the betrothal celebration so much."

I was glad of the diversion from my perilous thoughts.

"This is your friend who not so long ago believed she could slip a potion into a lad's ale and make him love her forever?"

"Oh, not Becca. She's already decided she doesn't like Cathan anymore. No, I mean Ness, my friend from Silver-lake."

There was a note of such sadness in her voice that I asked a question, though I really did not want to involve myself in these folk's business. "She won't be at the betrothal?"

"She's gone," Emer said, the pestle stilling in her hand. "Everyone says she ran away with her young man. He's a horse trader, one of the traveling folk. They say she slipped off secretly at night and took all her father's money. I thought you would have heard the story. Everyone tells it. Everyone blames her."

"For stealing the money, you mean?"

"Worse than that." Emer's voice was uneven; her cheeks had flushed red. "Her father died the same day she left. A terrible accident. Crushed under his own grindstone. People were all too quick to say it was Ness's fault. That she broke his heart, and that made him careless, so he wasn't watching what he was doing."

I set down my little pot of softened wax. "But you don't believe that?"

"Ness wouldn't leave her dad. She's devoted to him. Her mother died when Ness was only seven, and she's looked after him and the house ever since. She does love her fellow, no doubt of that. He wanted her to go away with him, to leave Dalriada and join the travelers—he'd never be able to settle down here, it isn't in those folk's nature. But Ness wouldn't just up and go; not while her dad still needed her. And she'd never take his money. Never."

"But she's gone."

Emer bowed her head. "Gone that same day, and never even told me she was leaving. I miss her."

I considered this sad tale for a while, and something Grim had told me came to mind. "Aren't the traveling folk due back in these parts sometime soon? You'll be able to find out for yourself if what people are saying about your friend is true."

"If it was true," said Emer, "and I don't believe it for an instant, then how could she show her face here again?"

"But if it isn't true," I said, "where is she?"

"I wish I knew."

The wax was ready. I waited while Emer finished the grinding, then I showed her how to mix the components to make the salve. The sad little story was at the back of my mind, a puzzle to which the solution was almost certainly the obvious one: Ness had indeed robbed her father and run away with her lover, and did not deserve such a loyal friend.

"Now scoop it carefully into the jar, and make sure the stopper is tight. Good work." Praising folk did not come naturally to me. Perhaps it never had. Helping people of my own accord was easier than helping them because of Conmael's agreement. That didn't stop me wishing for the life of a hermit. No Emer, no Grim, no local folk with their ailments, and most certainly no prince and his household of hangers-on. And no Conmael. I didn't think leaking thatch or muddy paths would trouble me much, if only I could live undisturbed. I wouldn't be lonely. There were the memories, mostly memories I didn't want, but a scattering of good ones too. And I could always get a dog. Not a silly little lap dog like Lady Flidais's creature. I'd have a big ugly hound that kept folk away from my door.

Nice dream. Pity that was all it was. There would be no getting away from Conmael and the promise he'd extracted from me. Besides, I'd last about a week on my own before the memories had me heading back to Laois with a knife in my hand. If my fey friend thought seven years were going to wipe Mathuin's sins out of my mind, he underestimated the wrong the man had done me.

Emer had finished the job. "You'd best be off home now," I said. "I'll see you out."

By now the girl could read the signs. She knew when I'd had enough of her company, and went to get her cloak from the peg. Still upset about her runaway friend; her eyes were red. I couldn't think of anything to say that would both comfort her and not be a lie, so I held my tongue.

"Thank you, Mistress Blackthorn," Emer said, and was away down the path.

When she was gone, I went back in and shut the door. Made a brew; sat down at the table to drink it. The salve was for the fellow at Silverlake, the one who made the special cakes. It seemed he often had problems with his shoulders and wrists, no surprise with all that mixing. The baker hadn't come to see me; he hadn't called me to come over there. I'd got a message, brought by a boy, asking for the remedy. It went against my better judgment to provide it without taking a look at the patient. Chances were he needed not only the salve itself but someone with strong and expert hands to massage it into his shoulders. And probably not just once, but often. Otherwise the pain would only keep getting worse. Men could be like that, thinking they were all better after one treatment and not bothering to keep it up. On the other hand, Silverlake was a fair way on foot, and I wasn't overeager to waste a day getting there and back. Especially when I hadn't been asked to go. I set the salve on a shelf. If the man wanted it, let him come and fetch it.

Emer's tale nagged at me as I made up the fire, swept the cottage floor, then went out into Dreamer's Wood with my basket over my arm, looking for mushrooms. It stuck in my head like one of those tunes you hear once and then can't forget even when you want to.

The wood had a restless feeling about it, as if unseen things were moving about in there. Maybe just the autumn wind; maybe creatures looking for shelter from the coming storm. Maybe Conmael and his kind moving between the leafless trees, hardly more visible than shadows. Grim didn't trust the place; never wanted to stay in there long. Dreamer's Wood didn't bother me. Perhaps that was down to Conmael, who seemed keen that I should survive. Maybe, if I followed his rules, I'd stay safe. For seven years, at least. Which was better, to break free of the promise, to be my own mistress for as long as it took for me to destroy myself, which mightn't be long at all, or to abide by the rules and live the next seven years—a bit less, now—doing what somebody else wanted? Was that really living, or was it being a coward?

16

ORAN

The day I gave her the book, Flidais was so quiet at supper that I thought the headache must be worse. When our guests spoke directly to her, she answered courteously enough but with as few words as possible. If this continued I would have to insist she seek expert help, however much she protested that she did not need it.

I did not tax her about the bestiary. The little book was probably safest in the library anyway, since the chamber was designed to keep such items in the best condition, though the reading room I had made for Flidais would do equally well provided the door was not left open in wet weather.

After supper we mingled in the hall awhile before the fire. The druid had not yet arrived, but one of the lawmen had some talent as a storyteller. He was prevailed upon to entertain us with a tale—an amusing account of warring *clurichauns*—and I told one of my own invention, in which lovers were parted by fate, sought each other across all Erin, and found each other only when they were old and gray. The point of the tale being that true love never dies. Folk seemed to enjoy it, though Flidais had as little to say about my effort as about anything else. I drew the evening to a close somewhat early, telling my guests that as the next few days would be so busy, it was best if we all retired to sleep. I would see them at breakfast.

Donagan helped me undress, then bade me good night and retired to the anteroom where he slept. Bramble was down in the kitchen for the night; Brid had taken a fancy to her and provided a basket by the fire, which Donagan had said was a much more appropriate arrangement. I missed her.

With so much going through my mind, I did not expect a good night's rest, but I slept soundly for an hour or two. I awoke with a start, in pitch darkness, to the knowledge that someone was in the room with me, standing in silence right beside my bed. I opened my mouth to call out—Donagan was not far away—and a soft, small hand came out to cover my lips. A moment later someone was lifting the covers, slipping into the bed beside me, whispering, "Hush, Oran. It's me, Flidais."

I struggled to sit up, my heart pounding, my mind reeling with shock. Still half-asleep, I was slow to understand, though my senses were wide-awake—beneath an enveloping cloak she had cast aside as she crept in, Flidais was wearing only a flimsy shiftlike garment.

"Lie down," she murmured. "I'm sorry if I startled you."

She must have come through the connecting door. "No, Flidais," I hissed, praying that Donagan had not woken up. "We can't do this!"

"Shh," she whispered. "We'll be wed soon, surely it's all right. And nobody needs to know."

It was wrong, all wrong. The prince of Dalriada did not anticipate his wedding night.

"Flidais, you must go back. Right now. This is—"

She tensed, drawing away from me. "I thought— When you held me close, before, I was sure—don't you want me, Oran?" Her voice was shaky now.

"Of course I want you." I wrapped my arms around her and drew her close. "I want you so badly it hurts. But . . ." Oh gods! The silken touch of her skin, the delicious shiver her hands sent through me as she stroked my back, the warmth of her body pressed against mine, all combined to kill my further protests. I forced a few words out. "Flidais, who knows you are here?"

"Only Mhairi. I will be gone before dawn."

Then I really did sit up, dislodging her. "This cannot happen," I said, and my voice came out as a strangled croak, for my manhood was making itself painfully evident, and I feared I would soon have no control of the situation at all. "Not before we are hand-fasted. It's—it's—unseemly." Gods, what would she think of me? Unseemly? But my mother's image was foremost in my mind, her eyes chilly with disapproval. Not of Flidais, who was young and inexperienced, and perhaps had little idea of the constraints faced by the only son of a king, but of me for not exercising princely self-control.

"Hush," my sweetheart said, and stopped my words with a kiss. It was a kiss that continued for a long time, and ended with the two of us lying down once more, she atop me in a position that must have left her in no doubt at all of my immediate physical dilemma. "Nobody need know," she said. "Mhairi won't tell."

I opened my mouth to protest again, but her lips and tongue silenced my words. Her hands and warm body erased rational thought from my mind. They wiped away the certainty that in the morning I would rue my lack of self-restraint. I surrendered, and let the morning take care of itself.

"Your sweetheart is charming," my mother said, watching Flidais glide away down the hall.

Two nights had passed since Flidais had first crept into my bed, and it was the eve of the betrothal ceremony. The house was full. Today had seen the last of the distinguished guests settled in. There had been a magnificent supper of several courses, and entertainment by the musicians my parents had brought with them from court. The wedding cake had been on display, though it would not be cut and eaten until tomorrow night, after the ritual. It was a confection of towering proportions decorated with delicate flowers and foliage, all edible. Aunt Sochla had declared that she had never seen anything so impressive; the baker, she had said, must have magic in his hands. Branoc was not present to accept the compliments of the assembly; the man was reluctant to venture beyond his home village of

Silverlake, or indeed to go much farther than the doors of his bakery, so folk said. He had never attended my open councils; carters conveyed his creations to Winterfalls for us to enjoy.

"Indeed," I said to Mother. My sweetheart looked every bit a princess tonight. She was wearing a violet gown and a deep pink overtunic, with her dark hair caught up in a cunning jeweled net, and as she moved about the hall, stopping to exchange a few words with one group of visitors after another, she was the picture of a happy young woman about to be wed. My father was speaking to her now; I saw her dip a graceful curtsy, then respond with a slight flush in her cheeks, as if she found the prospect of a real king becoming her father-in-law both thrilling and a little daunting. She was doing well. Who would have thought that demure young woman had spent the last two nights in my bed? Who would imagine that I, the only son of a king, had allowed such a thing to happen, not once, but twice? It seemed to me the truth must be written all over my guilty face.

When Flidais had left me, some time before today's dawn, I had told her it must not occur again. With Aunt Sochla here, not to speak of the large number of waiting women now accommodated in that part of the house, our behavior could not fail to be noticed. We could not afford to have it become common knowledge. After that first night, Donagan had packed up his things and moved to the men's quarters, telling me I could call for him if I needed him. He had offered no explanation, and I had not asked for one. That I deserved his disapproval did not make it hurt any less.

"I'm delighted that you are marrying at last, Oran," said Aunt Sochla. I was seated between her and my mother. This was a little unsettling, since both had a habit of asking penetrating questions without warning. They reminded me of a pair of bright-eyed, sharp-beaked birds. "She's a pretty girl, if rather slight in build," my aunt went on. "Nice manners. Happy?"

I opened my mouth and closed it again. Fortunately, my aunt was not looking at me, but across the crowd of chattering folk to Flidais, who was now speaking to my father's chief councillor. If my intended could charm Feabhal, she could charm anyone. "Of course," I said, hoping the general level of noise would conceal any doubt in my tone.

"No *of course* about it," said Aunt Sochla. "Arranged marriage, pair of strangers, a man would consider himself lucky if he found his bride tolerable in short doses, at least at such an early stage. What are her interests? Does she ride? Hunt? Hawk? Or is she the music and needlework kind of girl?"

I was again lost for words. Evidently, Mother had not shared the fact that Flidais and I had corresponded for some time before I'd agreed to marry her.

"Sochla," put in my mother, rescuing me, "you can't imagine Oran would choose a woman who loved blood sports. This is a softhearted young lady who enjoys music and poetry. Did you not see the portrait that so took my son's fancy?"

"Ah! The lap dog, how could I forget? And has Flidais brought her little treasure all the way from Laigin?"

My mother suppressed what might have been a snort of derision. Sisters they might be, and in agreement on many matters, but each was strong-willed and over the years of my growing up I had witnessed some monumental disputes.

"She brought her dog, yes." I hesitated. "But she's been having difficulties with Bramble since the unfortunate episode at Dreamer's Pool. Snarling, snapping, a refusal to obey. It's become intolerable for Flidais to have her close by."

Aunt Sochla's brows went up. "That does surprise me. I've never yet encountered a dog that could not be trained out of bad habits, even under the most challenging of circumstances. Where is the creature?"

"Sochla," murmured my mother, "now is not the time for this."

"Tomorrow," said my aunt. "Have the dog brought to me in the morning, Oran. I'll set it to rights."

"Thank you, Aunt," I said. "If you can spare the time, your help will be most welcome." I did not mention that, with me, Bramble was perfectly well behaved. Or that the little dog had become a favorite with all who worked in my kitchen. That would be to imply that the fault lay with Flidais.

"I don't suppose there'll be a great deal for me to do as a chaperone," Aunt Sochla said, "since you are surely old enough to know how to behave. So you may as well make use of my services with the dog. The terriers I breed are much sought after as companions for ladies, largely because of their sweet temperament."

"Thank you, Aunt." It was true, Aunt Sochla's residence was generally swarming with little dogs, and I could not remember any of them snapping, barking or leaving puddles in inconvenient spots. "Bramble is not to be taken outdoors without a leash. She's been lost on the farm once already, and of course there are bigger dogs—"

"Oran, don't fuss. I know what I am doing. Tomorrow, after breakfast."

"Yes, Aunt." I might have been ten years old again, and receiving a reprimand for daydreaming.

"Flidais is so like her portrait." Mother patted my hand, adding to my feelings of inadequacy. "I'm becoming convinced that you have made a wise choice, Oran."

That was the moment, I believe, when I first felt the pangs of true misgiving. Somehow, oddly, Flidais's perfect demeanor tonight, her grace and apparent confidence, only served to emphasize the times when her behavior had seemed odd. Words were on the tip of my tongue, words I could not speak: *She looks like her portrait, yes. But this is not the woman I thought I would be marrying.* That woman would have known Lucian's *Bestiary* the moment she opened the cover. That woman would have received Bramble's love and trust even in the most trying times. That woman would have loved and wanted me, yes. But she would never have crept into my bed before we were husband and wife. That I had allowed it to happen, that I had acquiesced to it, was my shame. Even as I had enjoyed what she'd offered so generously, I had wondered at a certain lack of . . . of tenderness. Of gentleness. Of sweet words to accompany the pleasures of the body. Our coupling had not been as I might have expected. That had only added to my confusion.

"Oran?"

I could not say it. It was already too late. I was complicit in what had taken place on those two nights; I was as guilty as Flidais. More so, in truth, because I was her senior, and I was a prince, and I should have known better. Now that I had lain with her, I must set my doubts aside. What basis had I for them, anyway, other than my disappointment that she was less than a perfect match for the woman of the letters? Maybe Donagan had been right; maybe a scribe had helped Flidais write them. Maybe half of Cloud Hill knew what a romantic fool I was.

"The portrait is indeed a true likeness," I said.

After a moment, Mother said, "You seem a little weary, Oran. You've done well today. The preparations were faultless; the house and garden look wonderful."

This was high praise indeed. A month or two earlier it would have pleased me greatly. Now I felt a cold weight inside me, made up of confusion and guilt and sheer exhaustion. I had not had much sleep for the last two nights. "Thank you, Mother. I will pass your kind remarks on to my people. Now, if you will excuse me, I'd best have a word with Master Oisin. He looks a little overwhelmed by so much company; I should rescue him."

Master Oisin was the druid, come to enact the ritual. I had met him before. While some of his kind lived in forest communities, Oisin was of the wandering variety of druid, and passed through Winterfalls from time to time on his travels, staying a few nights and telling tales as recompense for our hospitality. We always housed him away from the main dwelling, understanding that although he enjoyed sitting at table for a good supper and sharing a story afterward, he was most content in solitude. While the need to speak to him had been something of an excuse to escape the scrutiny of my female relatives, I had observed how tired the druid looked as he stood near the hearth, listening politely while my father's chief councillor held forth.

I made my way through the crowd, stopping as I went to nod and smile and accept the congratulations of a number of highborn folk who did not know me very well at all. My smiling face felt like a mask, tight and false.

"Master Oisin. Feabhal. More mead?"

"Your folk have not been slow to replenish our goblets, Prince Oran," Oisin said. He was a short, spare man with the look of a scholar. I knew, however, that he was accustomed to walking many miles a day, in all weathers. One would not think such a man, clad as he was in a plain gray robe, would stand out in tonight's brilliant assembly. But the eye was drawn to Oisin. It was something in the serenity of his gaze and the unusual repose of his features. I wished he could lend me some of that peace. I longed to unburden myself to him, not here in the hall but in private, just the two of us. But how could I? How could I talk to a druid about my pathetic failure to deny my bodily lusts? How stupid I would sound if I told him of the picture I had built for myself of Flidais, and of my unrealistic expectation that she would perfectly match it in every particular. This was an arranged marriage. My bride was young, healthy, comely, highborn and well-mannered. Oisin would think me a naïve young fool, and he would not be wrong.

Feabhal was saying something, congratulating me. I needed to pay attention. "Thank you for your kindness," I murmured with a distinct lack of sincerity. He and I had never been friends. "Master Oisin, you may wish to retire soon. I'll walk with you over to the cottage." The cottage lay across a meadow from the main dwelling; Niall and his wife had vacated it for the duration of the celebrations to allow the druid a modicum of peace and quiet.

"In person, Prince Oran?" Oisin smiled, while Feabhal frowned in disapproval—he would consider it more appropriate for one of the serving people to escort the druid, no doubt.

"I need some fresh air. It's been a long day." Bramble would have liked a walk, but I could not think of a plausible excuse to go and fetch her. Most likely Brid's helpers had taken her out earlier. Or Donagan might have done it. He and I had been almost like strangers today; he had laid out garments for me, brought warm water for washing, been at hand when I needed him. But we had not talked; not of the things that mattered.

The druid and I walked outside into the autumn chill. A man-at-arms offered to accompany us, and I told him his services would not be required, though I did ask him to fetch me a lantern. I should have asked for a cloak as well. I had never enjoyed dressing up in the kind of garments a prince is supposed to appear in on formal occasions, even though Donagan took great care with sponging, brushing and pressing. I probably owed it to him to wear my best attire with more pride. At least the rich blue tunic and trousers were of wool, though the weave was so fine there was little real warmth in them. And the embroidered silk shirt I had on underneath did not help much. Oisin was better off in his druidic robe.

"Cold, my lord?" He regarded me with a half smile. "Shall we walk briskly?"

We did. Oisin, whose legs were shorter than mine, kept up a pace that had me somewhat breathless by the time we reached the cottage door. Conversation had been out of the question.

"Well, now," said the druid, reaching to open the door. "I feel I should offer you a brew, the chance to sit by my fire awhile—if it is still burning—and to recover yourself from a day that I believe has left you exhausted. But this house is yours. It is not for me to invite you in. And you'll be wanting to get back to your guests."

The lantern light illuminated his plain features and glinted in his kindly, shrewd eyes. Here was a man who saw beneath the surface of things; the kind of man I should be able to confide in.

"Thank you for the offer, Master Oisin. I am indeed very tired; I have been sleeping badly. Another full day tomorrow, for you as well. Don't worry about the brew. You should get off to bed."

He examined me a few moments longer. "It is a time of profound change for you, my lord. And for Lady Flidais. Are you content with the arrangements for tomorrow's ritual? Still happy for me to entertain your guests with a tale or two afterward?"

Why did I feel he was not asking about rituals and tales, but something much closer to the bone?

"I'll be happy to see the ritual performed by such a trusted friend. I should get back to the hall, yes. Donagan will be wondering where I am." I had hardly seen Donagan all evening; today, my welfare seemed to be his last concern.

"My lord." Oisin spoke as I was turning away, his voice little more than a murmur. "Is all well with you?"

Sudden tears pricked my eyes; I was glad my back was to the lantern light. "As you said, it is a time of change."

"Do not lose sight of the wisdom that is all around you. The rising of the sun, each day's new hope; the moon gliding above, watchful and mysterious, reminding us of the tides within. The flight of birds; the quick grace of the running deer; the affection of a loyal hound. You have grown up in the understanding of these things. The wonder that resides in them also exists in a promise between husband and wife. A betrothal is the beginning of a new story; it is a compact of hope and possibility. All marriages have their difficulties, no doubt of that. But the bond between husband and wife is precious beyond jewels."

Before Flidais came to Winterfalls, I had believed this wholeheartedly. My vision of true love had been a little unrealistic, no doubt. As for married life . . . I had seen that it was sometimes difficult—my parents had had their fallings-out, though those were mostly short-lived and always well concealed from the public eye. Of course, my mother and father were past the age when physical passion might be expected to play much part in their lives—they often seemed more like old friends than husband and wife. Among common people, I had seen that marriage could be a fine thing. In my household there were several married couples, some with children; entire families had grown up at Winterfalls. I had seen trust, friendship and tenderness there, as well as an enjoyment in working side by side. It was not a grand passion like that of Diarmid and Grainne, or of Deirdre and Naoise, but that was just as well, since both tales ended tragically.

"Prince Oran?"

"Thank you for your wisdom, Master Oisin. I'd best be on my way; the night is chilly."

He opened the cottage door. "Ah. The fire still burns under its blanket of ash, and the house is warm. Sure you won't come in awhile?"

"Thank you, no." If I went in, if I sat down and he continued to coax answers from me in his gentle, understanding way, I would disgrace myself by shedding tears. A sorry specimen indeed. "I'll bid you good night."

"Good night, my lord. May the gods walk with you and your lady."

17

BLACKTHORN

The betrothal ritual was over, thank the gods, and most of the guests were gone from the prince's house, which meant folk had started talking about other things. Which was just as well, since I'd had a hard time not snapping at them. If I'd heard about that cake once, I'd heard a thousand times.

I came home from a visit to one of the farms—a fellow with a scythe wound to the leg; he'd been lucky not to bleed to death—to find Grim sitting at the table shelling beans into a pot. I hung up my cloak and set the basket down.

"Saw the prince riding out this morning," Grim said. "Lady Flidais too."

"Why would I be interested in that?"

He fell silent.

"I've heard nothing but Prince Oran this and Lady Flidais that ever since the betrothal. I'm sick of the two of them and their household."

Grim picked up the kettle; poured water onto the beans.

"Sorry," I made myself say. "It's the young girls who carry on about it, and their mothers aren't much better."

"Harmless enough," said Grim, stirring. "Dumplings?"

"Mm-hm." I sniffed. "Grim, what have you been doing this morning?"

"This and that. Helping a fellow with some pigs. Why?"

"You stink. Leave the cooking, I'll do it. You find some clean clothes and wash the ones you've got on. You can do those other things too; I'm sick of them lying in the corner. Bring in some more water and I'll heat it up. You're not going to get that smell out in cold."

It came to me, as he headed out to the well, that I was sounding like a nagging wife, which wasn't good. Still, there was only so much pig smell a person could tolerate at close quarters. I salved my conscience by picking up the small mountain of dirty clothing and taking it outside for him. It was mostly shirts and hose; autumn weather being what it was, our heavier garments were lucky to get a sponge and a brush around the hems to take the worst of the mud off.

That was odd; there was my red kerchief, the one Grim had bought me at a fair, crumpled and filthy at the bottom of the heap. I couldn't recall wearing it for a long while. What in the name of the gods was that all over it? It looked as if someone had used it to clean the floor. Never mind; it wasn't as if I'd ever liked the thing much.

The house went quiet, with only a bit of splashing from out there as Grim scrubbed and rinsed and wrung, and a bit of stirring inside as I made herb dumplings and thought about Emer and her disappearing friend, the miller's daughter. I wasn't sure why the story was bothering me, since there was an obvious conclusion to be reached, the one everyone but Emer seemed to believe. Perhaps it was that Emer was a good girl, a clever girl, and that she'd sounded so sure. Ah well, when the traveling folk came it would be sorted out one way or another.

18

I'm hanging up the wash when Blackthorn comes out. I expect her to say the food's ready, but she just stands there. She's got her red kerchief in her hands. Which is funny, because I've just put her red kerchief on the line after scrubbing all the flour out of it.

"Two of them," I say. And when she doesn't answer, I say, "What?"

"I don't like people giving me things."

She means she doesn't like *me* giving her things, though at least she hasn't thrown her kerchief away. Even wears it sometimes. I hang up a pair of stockings and a shirt. Blackthorn's still standing there, staring at me and the washing line. "You mean the kerchief?" I ask. "Which one?"

Blackthorn takes her time answering. "The one you didn't buy at the fair," she says, coming down the steps.

That day comes back to me, the trip over to Silverlake, the load of flour, the red kerchief under the sacks on the cart. Out of place. But it's out of place here, too. The one I got at the fair is in Blackthorn's hands right now, clean and folded. Last time I saw her wearing it was the day Prince Oran and his man Donagan dropped in, the day she made sure she wasn't home.

"Found it on Scannal's cart one day when I got back

from a delivery," I tell her. "He said it wasn't his. Thought it must be yours. Thought I must have had it in my pocket, from the last wash. Or snagged on my cloak." Sounds far-fetched to me, and her face tells me she thinks so too. Though if I was giving her another kerchief I'd pick one in a different color. Green would look nice on her.

"Mm-hm."

"All over flour, so I put it in the washing pile." I remember why I didn't tell her. That was the day the girl drowned in Dreamer's Pool. The day Blackthorn had to look after the prince's lady. She had enough of a tale to tell, without mine on top of it. "Would have said. Slipped my mind."

"Mm-hm." That's all she's got to say, so I hang up the rest of the wash, and after a bit she goes back inside. It's only when I'm all finished that I take a look at the kerchief on the line, and I see it's not the same as the other one after all.

19

ORAN

D onagan did not come back to sleep in the antechamber. Our old friendship, the easy way we had been with each other for so long, was entirely gone. He behaved exactly as a superior kind of serving man behaves, performing his duties to perfection, setting not a foot wrong. He said only what was required to ensure I was washed, brushed and where I was supposed to be. He was cool. Distant.

I should have taxed him with it. I should have challenged him. Even, perhaps, played him at his own game, assuming my most princely manner and ordering him to return to the old arrangement, so we could resume our late-night talks over a jug of mead. But I could not. Perhaps he was right. Perhaps, once a prince married, it was inappropriate for his body servant to sleep next door. And though Flidais and I were not yet wed, we had most certainly anticipated the event.

The arrival of Aunt Sochla had meant Flidais was no longer coming to my chamber at night. I lay awake nonetheless, wondering if she might take it into her head to pay me another secret visit, right under the nose of her chaperone. If she did, I would have to say no this time; I would have to bundle her physically back through the connecting door, awkward though that would be. What had occurred could not be allowed to occur again. And yet my treacherous body wanted it; even now, the memory of those two nights was stirring me to readiness. I despised my weakness.

What if my father should die soon? I would become king of Dalriada. How fit was a man to rule a kingdom if he could not even rule himself?

I had not imagined, back in the time of the letters, that I would be sorry to see my mother leave Winterfalls. But I watched her ride away with deep regret, knowing in my heart that I owed her the truth. The next time I saw my parents would be at Cahercorcan for the hand-fasting.

The royal party left behind Aunt Sochla and a contingent of the Cahercorcan serving folk. My mother believed Winterfalls required additional retainers now that Flidais was in residence. I left the domestic arrangements to Aedan and Fíona, and since Flidais was now the lady of the house, I asked them to report direct to her. I was aware of a certain unrest in the household, unsurprising at a time of such change, but I trusted my steward to deal with it.

Flidais's headaches were still troubling her, and she took to spending most of the day in the women's quarters. I wondered if she was avoiding me. I tried to think what I had done wrong, what I might have said to offend her. I suggested, once again, that we summon Mistress Blackthorn to the house, and Flidais answered as before. It was nothing. I was not to worry. She would be better soon.

One lady of the household, at least, did not care to spend her days shut away indoors. Aunt Sochla, breeder of sturdy terriers, was in the habit of striding out energetically come rain or shine, and she plainly had no intention of letting her duties as chaperone alter this. I was accustomed to rising early—my sleep was still fitful—but she was generally up before me. I often glimpsed her heading out along the farm tracks with no companion other than Bramble, who trotted obediently at her heels. Should I be out walking myself and encounter the two of them at close quarters, Bramble would run to me, whimpering with excitement, wanting kind words and caresses. I observed with interest how well she responded to my aunt's commands, which

were delivered with gentle authority, and was glad the little
dog was calmer.

Sadly, all Aunt Sochla's good work had not improved
Bramble's behavior when Flidais was nearby. The dog's
fear of her former mistress remained. In Flidais's company
Bramble cowered. She growled. She panicked, leaving pud-
dles on the floor and biting people at random. It seemed
Flidais had lost the devotion of her little pet forever.

I pulled myself together. Told myself to stop worrying and
get on with things. With the next open council drawing ever
closer, I must ride out to visit my people again, and this
time I must take Flidais with me. On the night of the betrothal folk had come to Winterfalls for the bonfire and
merriment, but she'd had scant opportunity to talk to them.
She would be their lady, and that meant taking an interest
in their affairs, keeping an eye on their welfare, ensuring
small difficulties were noted and dealt with before they
grew into major problems. Far easier for Flidais to play her
part at the approaching council if she had made herself
known in the district beforehand.

I called Donagan to my chamber.

"The weather seems good for riding today," I said. He was
looking pale; was he unwell? "I plan to go to Winterfalls village and speak to a few folk. Perhaps also ride over Silverlake way. Will you convey a message to Lady Flidais, please,
letting her know I require her company for the day? The
fresh air and exercise can only do her good. You may tell her
I said so."

Donagan looked me in the eye. "Will that be all, my lord?"

"I doubt if Aunt Sochla will be wanting a long ride, so
Lady Flidais should bring one of her attendants. And you
will come too, of course. Please put the usual arrangements
in place." Gods, this was hard! What was the man doing,
that he stood there gazing at me as if I were a stranger, and
one that he did not especially care for at that? I swallowed
the urge to blurt out what was in my heart—that he was the
nearest thing I had ever had to a brother, and that a man
needed the support of his brother when he was lonely and
confused.

"Yes, my lord." A pause. "My lord, Lady Flidais may prefer that I stay behind."

That sent a strange chill down my spine. "What do you mean?"

"That is for Lady Flidais to say, my lord." Donagan's tone was oddly flat.

"Donagan. You always come with me. What possible reason could Lady Flidais have to object to that?" Even if a reason existed, it was not up to Flidais to make the decision.

"As you say, my lord. I will deliver the message."

I had expected him to return with Flidais's reply, but he did not. I changed into my riding clothes unassisted, waited awhile for Donagan, then from my window spotted Eochu bringing a string of horses down from the stable: Snow for me, Apple for Flidais, a mare for her maidservant and a couple of mounts for men-at-arms. No Star and no Donagan, though as I watched, Flidais came out of the house clad for riding, with Mhairi by her side.

I went down, and we waited, and still Donagan did not appear. Eventually I sent one of the men to look for him. The fellow returned alone.

"My lord, Donagan sends his apologies. Some kind of crisis in the house that requires his immediate attention."

"What crisis? Should I be concerned?"

"He said not, my lord. Only asked if you wanted someone else to accompany you in his place."

It sounded like a trumped-up excuse not to come. As for taking a substitute, there was nobody else who could do what Donagan did for me. The duties of a body servant, maybe, but not the wise counsel, the honest talk, the friendship. What had got into him? Could he really have been so shocked by what had occurred between Flidais and me—I had little doubt he had heard us, that first night—that I had lost his trust entirely?

"Never mind that. We'll ride on as we are."

We headed out, Flidais and I side by side, Mhairi a length behind, the guards flanking us.

"The weather seems set fair, at least until late afternoon," I observed, thinking that Flidais looked charming in her fur-trimmed cloak, deep blue to match her eyes, with her hair in a complicated sort of plait. Like something from an old tale. My spirits lifted in anticipation of the ride. Autumn colors were everywhere; the trees wore brilliant capes of scarlet and gold, and the recent rain had left miniature lakes here and there on the fields, silver sheets under the sun. On such a day, in my imaginings, Flidais and I had walked out together, just the two of us with Bramble, to enjoy the beauty of growing things and muse on the passing of the seasons. Perhaps to invent a poem or two, trying with words to capture the enchantment that we saw. After her response to my gift, I hesitated to suggest anything of the kind.

"We might ride over to Silverlake and see the folk there as well," I suggested. "I try to visit both villages in between the open councils, in case folk have any concerns they wish to raise. Sometimes I can resolve a problem without the need for it to be aired in the more formal setting of the council. The women will welcome your presence; I imagine there are some issues they will find easier to bring to your attention than to mine."

"If that is what you wish, of course," Flidais said. "I do wonder why your steward cannot do this for you."

We rode on in silence for a little, while I considered and discarded various replies. Surely I had already made my philosophy on a leader's responsibilities clear to her, not only in my letters but in our discussions since. "As I've told you before," I said eventually, "I believe it's important that we make these visits in person. Yes, it's unconventional. But it's the way I prefer to do things." I recalled somewhat belatedly the circumstances under which she had left home. "It is a time of peace here, of course," I said. "Riding out like this, with only a small escort, is perfectly safe."

"I understand, Oran," she murmured. "Though I would have thought you might have other matters on your mind." She glanced at me sideways as we rode, and the look in her eyes made the heat rise to my cheeks. I turned my gaze forward, hoping the men-at-arms had not noticed.

"Bramble seems happier under Aunt Sochla's eye," I said, changing the subject. "The two of them have quickly become good companions."

A silence, as we rode down a gentle hill toward the village of Winterfalls, where the dry weather had brought folk out of doors to tend to gardens, hang up washing and chat with their neighbors. Then Flidais said, "Your aunt is a formidable woman. I suppose any dog would obey rather than earn her anger."

Had she not noticed what Aunt Sochla was doing with Bramble? "I've seen no evidence of anger; my aunt's training is always conducted with kindness. A dog responds best to a firm but gentle approach, I've found, whether it is a pet like Bramble or a working dog like Niall's herders."

Flidais looked at me under her lashes. "Now I've offended you," she said.

"Offended, no," I said, taken aback. "You have misread my aunt, that's all. When I was growing up I did find her somewhat alarming, that is true—she is very definite in her opinions and always has been. But she is a good-hearted person. I liked to visit her; her house was full of little dogs and she was happy for me to play with them, feed them, take them out walking. At Aunt Sochla's I could forget, for a brief while, that I was a prince. That gift did not come often." We were almost at the village; folk were walking up the track to meet us. "Donagan's friendship allowed me the same opportunity," I said. "There are times when it still does."

"I have wondered, sometimes," said Flidais, "what kind of life it is to be body servant to a prince or princess. Take Donagan, for instance. He sorts out your clothing, he wakes you in the morning and sees you into bed at night, he hovers by your side all day, at your constant beck and call. What if such a man wanted to marry? To father children? What woman would want a husband whose life was not his own?"

I was spared the need to respond to this extraordinary speech, for the welcoming party had reached us. We reined in our mounts.

"Welcome, my lord!" Iobhar the brewer was there with his wife, Eibhlin; by them stood Scannal the miller and Luach the weaver with her daughter.

I swung down from Snow's back, helped Flidais dismount, then greeted each of the villagers by name. There was a pattern to my visits, and although Flidais was new to that pattern, it was clear she'd been expected. I was soon swept away to Iobhar's brewery and ale house with the men, while Flidais and Mhairi were shepherded to the weaver's by the women. A boy came to lead our horses into the yard behind the ale house. On my orders, our guards split up, Garalt coming with me, Fergal going with Flidais.

"Garalt will relieve you in due course," I told Fergal. "There'll be time for you to partake of some ale before we ride on." Iobhar's brewing was almost as legendary as Branoc's cakes. Not that I expected to be eating any of those today, even if we did go all the way to Silverlake. Everyone knew Branoc was averse to company, and I would not subject him to a surprise visit, especially not with Flidais present. What in the name of the gods had possessed her to say what she had about body servants? Could it be true that my reliance on my old friend had blighted his whole future? Was I not so much a friend as a millstone around his neck?

The ale was good, the company good also, though with Donagan absent the men of the village were more reticent than usual. If I had not already known what an asset my friend was in smoothing the way for me, I would have realized it today. As my companion and personal servant, Donagan fell somewhere between me and these villagers, and in his presence they generally spoke out with confidence. Today they seemed anxious not to offend me. When they asked where my friend was, I told them he was indisposed.

I talked to some of the farmers about a troublesome patch of boggy ground and the need to dig a drainage ditch. They could not agree on its position. I suggested they consider a compromise that would not encroach too severely on either man's farm, and told them to bring it to the council if they had not reached agreement by then. Scannal had a complaint about Branoc, the baker from Silverlake. For now, the miller said, he could supply the special types of flour Branoc required. But the Gaul was very particular, soon finding fault if what he received was not up to his exacting standards. And transporting the stuff over to Silverlake was becoming a nuisance; it meant a whole day's use of the cart, more or less, and the services of a man to do the driving and the lifting.

"He won't send a carter from his end," Scannal said. "There are fellows in the village there who wouldn't mind the work, but Branoc won't give it to them. Very particular about who comes in and out. Mind you, he pays well, I'll admit that."

"Isn't there someone who would take over the job of miller at Silverlake?" I asked, remembering that there was a story attached to that mill; a tragic one, the miller killed in some gruesome way and the place more or less abandoned. It had happened not long before I moved to Winterfalls in preparation for my marriage. "Couldn't one of your assistants get everything working again, Scannal, while you keep your own place going? I understand there are living quarters at the old mill that could be refurbished." The land on which the Silverlake mill stood was in my gift. If the previous miller—what was his name, Ernan?—had died and the place had been allowed to run down, it was for me to determine its future. "Did Ernan not have sons?" I remembered, then, something about a daughter.

"He had no boys, only the girl. Ness. Turned to the bad. We'll see no more of her."

I was not quite sure what *turned to the bad* meant. "She's no longer in the district?"

"Gone off with the traveling folk, that was the story put about at the time," said Iobhar. "Though it was the wrong season for them to be here. But she had a fellow that was sweet on her, one of the travelers. Maybe he came on his own and fetched her away, who knows?"

"She helped herself to her dad's life savings before she went," put in someone sourly. "A traveler boy would come a long way for that."

"So it appears there's no claimant to the mill," I said. "But generally, folk would agree that we do need a mill in Silverlake as well as Scannal's place here, yes? There is enough work for both?"

"That's how it's always been, my lord," Scannal said. "Two mills and two bakers. Until Ernan died, that is. Branoc's fussy about his flour; too fussy for me, to tell you the truth. I could do without having to grind his special blends when I've got a big order for oaten flour or barley meal on hand. Problem is, nobody will take Ernan's mill on. Not after what happened."

"Crushed to blood and splinters," said Deaman the baker. "Who'd want to be using that grindstone again?"

As a man, I found myself in perfect agreement. As a prince, I understood the wastefulness of leaving a perfectly good mill to rot away in disuse. "We'll discuss this further at the council, when folk from Silverlake are present. Meanwhile, think about how we might remedy the situation. For instance, we might call Master Oisin or the local wise woman to conduct a cleansing ritual at the mill and set poor Ernan's spirit to rest. Or, in the shorter term, we might find a way to persuade Branoc to hire his own carter. That would go some way toward ameliorating your problem, Scannal."

"Thank you, my lord. I've been using that new fellow, Grim, from the healer's place. Good worker, but he's not always available to help. Gets a lot of jobs around the district. Strong as an ox."

"I have met Grim briefly." A man of intimidating proportions and few words. A man of considerable skill. "Now, is there anything else you want to discuss before the council?"

Iobhar reached over to top up my ale cup. "Nothing serious, my lord. We wouldn't want to be troubling you with too much just now. We all wish you the best for the future. You and Lady Flidais. Good to see her here. The women will like that."

"I hope they will, Iobhar. I imagine it is good for them to be able to raise their concerns with Lady Flidais in relative privacy."

"Keep her talking all morning, that'd be my guess, my lord."

"As to that," I said, "I'm hoping to ride to Silverlake, so if you're sure that's everything, we'd best be off shortly. Thank you for your hospitality. Iobhar, I think you brew the finest ale in all Dalriada."

Iobhar grinned broadly. "Thank you, my lord. I won't argue with that."

I sent Garalt to relieve Fergal and to tell Flidais that we would be riding on soon. Then I excused myself to visit the privy, which was out the back of the ale house, near the stable where travelers' horses were tended to while their riders partook of Iobhar's fine brew. The meeting had gone well; my mood was much improved.

I was stepping out from the privy, still adjusting my trousers, when someone grabbed my arm and pulled me into a dark corner of the stables. I drew breath to shout, and a small hand placed itself firmly over my mouth.

"Hush, Oran, it's me!" Flidais, pressing herself up against me, her hands now moving down to undo the fastenings I had just tied up, to slip inside my clothing and attach themselves firmly to my manhood. What in the name of the gods was she doing? This, here, in Iobhar's stables, in the middle of the day with several folk no farther away than the other side of the courtyard, and our own guards likely to be looking for us in moments?

"Flidais, no!" I tried to extricate myself, but my back was hard up against the wall, and she was hard up against me. It seemed desire would always overcome common sense; even as I saw the folly in the situation, my manhood made a liar of me. "Flidais, stop it! Let go!"

Her agile fingers released their grip. I had barely time to snatch one quick, relieved breath when she fell to her knees and I realized she had a weapon in her armory that was new to me, if not in understanding, then most certainly in practice.

"Stop it!" My voice was a strangled gasp. "Now, Flidais! Quickly, get up before someone sees us!" But oh, how clever she was with her mouth; clever enough to stir me to boiling point even at a moment of such high risk. *"Flidais!"*

She drew me right to the brink, unwilling as I was. There was, perhaps, a count of ten in it, from the moment she took her mouth away to the moment when Garalt came back into the courtyard to get the horses ready. In that count of ten I remedied the disorder of my clothing, and Flidais stepped out into the light, smoothing down her skirt, her manner relaxed and confident. "Apple has been a joy to ride," she observed, walking over to give the mare's nose a stroke. "So gentle and calm. She was an excellent choice."

I gave a kind of grunt in response; I was still in some

physical discomfort, though sheer horror was quickly re-
ducing my problem. In truth, I could not believe Flidais
had done this. Why take such a foolish risk? It went beyond
stupidity. I could hardly think of a less appropriate occasion on which to engage in such an activity. These folk
looked to us as their leaders. We were their protectors,
their arbiters, their exemplars. How much respect would
we have, how much indeed would we merit, if we rutted
like animals where anyone might walk past and see us?
Worse than that; we were on Iobhar's premises, as his
guests.

I could not say anything with Garalt close by. And now
there was Mhairi coming in through a side gate—where
had she been?—and Iobhar's stable lad emerging from the
other end of the place. My belly tightened at the possibility
that he had been there all along; that he had seen everything. Should this unsavory tale be spread about, it would
cause untold damage to my reputation in the community.

"I've changed my mind," I said, not quite looking at
Flidais. "We won't ride to Silverlake after all; it will be too
much for you."

"Oh, I can—"

"Straight home," I said to Garalt. "We'll give Fergal time
for his ale; then we'll be off. Silverlake can wait until Donagan is available; we may even beard Branoc in his den."

"Yes, my lord. I'll go in and let Fergal know."

"Flidais," I said in a murmur, as soon as he was out of
earshot, "that was entirely unacceptable."

"Were you not enjoying it, Oran? You gave every sign
that you were." Her voice was warm honey, conjuring images of the nights we had shared. "You seemed a little out
of sorts earlier. Displeased with me. I thought only to make
it up to you."

"We will discuss this in private," I said. "At home."

"Ah." It was a sigh of anticipation; clearly she had not
picked up my mood.

I cleared my throat. "Were any matters of significance
raised by the women? Do they need answers from me before we leave?"

"Nothing important. Oran, I can ride on to Silverlake—"

"Don't argue with me, Flidais. We're going home, and

when we get there I must be quite plain with you, even if what I have to say is not to your liking."

She hung her head. "I'm sorry. I keep getting it wrong." She looked up, her big blue eyes suspiciously bright. "I only wanted to please you."

I could have let those melting eyes, that contrite stance, that sweet voice win me over; not so long ago, I would have been swayed by them. But my mind was on the years ahead, all the years of our life together. The life I had wished on myself through my stubborn belief that dreams come true, if only a man waits long enough. "As I said, we'll discuss this later. If you want the truth, Flidais, after this I cannot trust you to visit Silverlake with me. Or indeed anywhere."

But by the time we reached home again, Flidais had been stricken by one of her headaches and told me she must retire to rest.

"I'll send for the wise woman," I said. "These headaches have gone on too long. Mistress Blackthorn will surely have a remedy. Everyone speaks well of her skills."

"No!" Flidais spoke sharply, then put a hand to her brow as if the effort had made the pain worse. "I don't want her. All I need is to lie down for a while."

"But—"

"Really, Oran. I should be well by supper time. There is no need to trouble the wise woman, or indeed anyone."

I let her go, wishing I had taken Mother's advice and allowed one of the court physicians to stay on here when the rest of the royal party returned to Cahercorcan. Had Flidais been beset by these headaches before she came to Winterfalls? I should ask her women, perhaps; but that might convey the message that I doubted her.

"Is all well, Oran?"

I was started out of my reverie by the dry voice of Aunt Sochla, who had come into the entry hall with a panting Bramble at her heels. The little dog greeted me with whimpers of delight, and I had no choice but to gather her up and hold her close. She quivered with joy, stretching up to plant kisses on my cheek.

"Oran?" My aunt was regarding me with an expression

very like one of my mother's: it suggested an uncomfortable level of understanding. "I thought you were riding to Silverlake this morning. That was what Flidais told me earlier."

"We came back early. Flidais has a headache; she has gone off to rest."

Aunt Sochla did not reply, simply continued to stare at me. "Unfortunate," she observed.

I glanced around the entry hall and found it empty for now of listening ears. "Aunt," I said, "may I ask you a favor?"

"You can always ask, Oran. I may not say yes, of course."

Bramble was settling now, warm in my arms. Her fur was silky smooth under my fingers. "Could you have a quiet word with Flidais's women about these headaches, without disturbing Flidais herself? It would be useful to know how long she's been afflicted by them, and whether a physician was attending her back at Cloud Hill."

Aunt Sochla gave a crooked smile. It made her into a witch from an old story, a person neither good nor bad, but certainly dangerous. "Are not those questions you could ask her yourself?"

"Flidais is reluctant to discuss the matter with me. She brushes off my concerns."

"Mm-hm. Very well, I can try, though your lady keeps her women on a tight rein. One thing I do know. Until the day of the drowning, Lady Flidais was devoted to Bramble, and Bramble to her. Deirdre told me, and she's the most reliable of the handmaids. And that really does surprise me. I've never seen a dog change its allegiance in such a way. Even those that have been quite cruelly treated retain their loyalty. A dog's devotion to its owner goes deep; they are far more forgiving than we are. Anything else I should be asking, while I'm at it?"

I had no answer for her. My mind was full of questions, but all of them were impossible. Why did the Flidais of the letters not match the Flidais who had come to Winterfalls? What my aunt had just said about Bramble only emphasized that. Flidais *had* loved her little dog. In that, at least, the letters had been true. I had put the differences in my lady's character down to a scribe penning the missives in her name. But the more I considered that, the less likely it seemed. Such a blatant pretense would surely not have been sanctioned by a chieftain of Cadhan's status. And even if he had not known, the letters had rung so true—what scribe could have responded so perfectly to my own missives? Besides, that last letter had been written not at Cloud Hill but at Muadan's stronghold in Ulaid, when Flidais's party broke their journey there. It stretched credibility that Muadan's scribe, too, was able to capture that delicate tone.

I had heard an old tale once in which a serving woman tricked her mistress into changing places with her, and kept the lady from telling the truth by threatening those she loved. But that could not have happened here, for Flidais had brought her own entourage with her, folk who had known her a long time, and besides, the portrait her father had sent to mine was the perfect image of the woman who had come to Winterfalls to be my bride. And yet, something was wrong. I knew it in my heart.

"Nothing, Aunt Sochla," I said. "Just ask about the headaches. Oh, and another favor."

She waited.

"Might Bramble stay with me for a little while? I won't allow her to get on the bed or do anything else you'd disapprove of, naturally."

"If I am strict, Oran, it is for the dog's own good. Of course, take her awhile. Send your man to bring her back when you've had enough. That's if he's still here." She turned to go.

"Wait! What do you mean, if he's still here?"

"The word was, he was packing up ready to leave. So I was told not long after you headed off this morning."

"Leave? Leave for where?"

She lifted her brows at me, her eyes shrewd. "How would I know, Oran? Perhaps to visit his parents. Perhaps elsewhere. I'm not privy to the business of your entire household." After a moment, as I gazed at her in shocked incomprehension, she added more gently, "A good friend, young Donagan; he has been since the two of you were lads. You'd best go and find him. Here, give me the dog."

"I'll take her with me." Still carrying Bramble, I headed

for the men's quarters, hoping beyond hope that my aunt was wrong. I could see, at least, if Donagan's belongings were still there.

The men's quarters were deserted, save for a lone figure with a pack on his back, heading out the far door.

"Donagan! Wait!"

For a moment I thought my friend was going to ignore me. I thought he would walk away without a word. But he turned and stood there in the open doorway. He held his quiet as I walked down the long chamber to halt a few paces from him.

I could order him to stay, of course. Put on the princely voice and demand that he remain where he was needed. Keep playing whatever the unfortunate game was that had made us enemies so quickly. Probably lose my best friend in all the world as a result.

I set Bramble down on the floor. "Donagan," I said, "if I've offended you, I'm sorry. Aunt Sochla told me you were going away, and I see that may be true. Please don't leave. I need you."

"I don't see how I can stay." Donagan's tone was odd; he bent down to scratch Bramble behind the ears, perhaps so he need not meet my eye.

"Tell me why. Speak honestly, as you used to."

He did look at me then, and I knew him well enough to see that he was as deeply unhappy as I was. "Best if I don't, Oran."

I grasped for an explanation. "Is it because you see no future for yourself if you stay with me? No wife and children of your own, because you will always be at my beck and call?"

"Of course not, Oran, that's ridiculous! Have you forgotten that my mother and father both serve in your parents' household, and have done since before I was born? Half your retainers here are married folk with families."

"What, then?" If he brought up the subject of my nocturnal activities with Flidais, I was not sure what I would say. I had asked my friend to be honest. To be completely honest myself would be to expose Flidais's behavior, and that felt . . . dishonorable. If I had said no to her from the first, I would have been on stronger ground.

"I can't talk about it. Not here." Donagan glanced around the chamber. Nobody else was there, but he was right, this was not the ideal place for a private conversation.

My instincts told me not to suggest we talk in my bedchamber. "Then put down your bag, to reassure me that you're not going to bolt until we've talked about this, and come out walking with me. We'll find somewhere far from prying eyes and listening ears, and you can explain yourself. I can't just let you go."

He didn't want to come with me, I could see it. But he put down his bag and we went outside. Bramble danced around us, and I wished I could experience the same uncomplicated joy a dog feels at something as simple as a walk with a friend. If I managed to persuade Donagan to stay, I would never, ever take him for granted again.

Neither of us said a word until we reached the burial ground, the spot where I had found Bramble on the day she ran away. There we sat down on a bench, side by side, and the little dog hunkered down by my feet, content to rest after her second long walk for the morning.

"I thought you were riding to Silverlake today," Donagan said.

"Flidais has a headache." I drew a deep breath. "The visit to Winterfalls village did not go entirely to plan. I won't take her with me again until . . ." Until what? Until she turned into a different woman, the one I'd once imagined I would be marrying? "It is much easier when you are with me," I said. "If I have perhaps forgotten to thank you for all you do, that does not mean . . ."

"Oran," said my friend, "I will not lie to you. I was disturbed when you made the decision to move me to the men's quarters. More than disturbed. Perplexed. Hurt. I had perhaps come to expect too much, since you have always treated me more as friend than servant. But—"

"Wait a moment. I made the decision that you were not to sleep in the antechamber any longer? No such thing— you moved of your own volition. One day there, the next day gone. And suddenly not a friend anymore. Suddenly as cool as if you despised me."

No response from Donagan; he had his elbows on his

knees and was looking with apparent fascination at a beetle crawling across a leaf.

"Donagan? I gave no order for you to move out of the antechamber."

He gave me a sideways look. "An order came from Lady Flidais, through one of her women. Saying that I was to remove myself and my belongings to the men's quarters and leave the antechamber empty. I did question it. I was told the arrangement would provide better privacy, in view of your impending marriage."

"You should have spoken to me," I said, stunned. She'd got him out of the way so she could continue to steal into my bedchamber. I could think of no other reason. And she must have known I wouldn't like it, or surely she would have consulted me first. "Why didn't you tell me straight-away? Surely you know me well enough to realize I would never do this." Gods, Donagan probably imagined we were still disporting together on a nightly basis.

"Before Lady Flidais came here," Donagan said quietly, "I thought I knew you very well indeed. Now I'm not sure I know you at all."

His words were like a blow. I looked down at my hands, unable to speak. Bramble leaned against my leg, and at her touch I felt tears start in my eyes.

"You're betrothed, Oran," Donagan said. "As good as hand-fasted. I can't do my job with Lady Flidais here. I want to help you. I don't want to leave you. But I can't stand by and watch her destroy the man I knew; the man who was my friend. And now"—he rose to his feet—"I've said it, and I should go."

"Wait," I said, struggling for calm. "Please."

He stood there, not looking at me but gazing out over the fields of Winterfalls. I saw in his expression that he did not truly wish to go away. I fought for words to convey what I was feeling.

"You must think me very weak," I said, "if you believe that. You must think me unfit to be the prince of Dalriada; unfit to lead."

Donagan sighed. "I think your nature has caused you to make an error. Unfortunately that error has led you into a situation that will be with you for the rest of your life. Believe me, Oran, if I could think of any way out of this, if I believed I could help you, I would stay. But you're betrothed to the lady. More than that, you . . ." He did not say it: *You have bedded her already, more than once.* "Your actions have not always met the standards I know you set for yourself," he said instead. "I cannot remain in your service."

"Where were you planning to go?"

He shrugged. "Does that matter? Away from here. To visit my parents, perhaps. But I will not stay at Cahercorcan, since you and Lady Flidais will be often there."

No way out. A shiver ran through me; I gathered up Bramble and held her close. "I know this is my fault," I said, failing to keep my voice steady. "I believed in a dream; I have learned that doing so is foolish. I would say to you, perhaps she can change, perhaps we can reach a compromise, perhaps, given time, this will not seem so difficult." I drew an uneven breath. "But . . . Donagan, don't dismiss this as another fancy, please . . . I think there's something wrong. Something about Flidais. I cannot say what, exactly, but . . . if she had not come here with her own folk, if she did not so closely resemble her portrait, I would have said the woman who put her hand in mine and promised to marry me is not Flidais of Cloud Hill at all. She seems reluctant to engage in real conversation with me. She shows little interest in the pastimes we discussed in our letters. Bramble, whom she described with such tenderness, is frightened of her. And . . . when we are in each other's company, her speech and her actions are sometimes . . . odd. Inappropriate. Something is amiss. I feel it in my bones."

"A prince does not wed for love, Oran. You know that quite well. Yes, you made an error in believing the woman of the portrait was some perfect ideal, the one true love you had waited for. But you knew, surely, that such a marriage is essentially a pairing of strangers, a man and woman suited to each other only by birth and breeding. Such marriages are made because leaders need to form strategic alliances, not because they want their sons and daughters to be happy. You might consider yourself fortunate that Lady Flidais is young, comely, and apparently healthy, despite the headaches."

"And yet you say you cannot live in the same household as my future wife."

"She and I would be enemies. We would be constantly at odds over your welfare. I am a servant; Lady Flidais will one day be queen. That means I must go."

Even he did not understand. Even my closest friend dismissed the idea that there was something deeply wrong, something that went far beyond a lack of compatibility between my betrothed and me.

"I'm not the only member of your household to experience difficulties," Donagan said. "Your mind has been otherwise occupied, I believe. I understand you gave Lady Flidais free rein to order the household. Folk have found her manner . . . a little difficult."

"Folk. What folk? And what do you mean, difficult?"

"Aedan. Brid. Fíona. Lady Flidais can be somewhat abrupt. Her approach to domestic matters is not in tune with what we have all come to expect from you."

"But why didn't anyone tell me this? None of them has said a word."

"Of course not. The lady is your newly betrothed; to complain about her would be to offend you deeply, and your trusted retainers view you not only with respect but with a certain fondness, having known you since you were a child."

How had I missed this? Had I indeed been so wrapped up in my own concerns that I had not noticed such a degree of unrest? It seemed so. I had been blinded, not only by confusion and disappointment but also, I was forced to admit, by the raging desire my lady was able to arouse in me. Yes, even under such appallingly risky conditions as this morning's.

"Donagan," I said, "I have two open councils to conduct before the hand-fasting. Will you stay until the second of those, at least? I would greatly appreciate your support and advice, even if you believe you can no longer be my friend. If you choose to walk away once the second council has taken place, then I will accept your decision."

He smiled. "Oran," he said, "I will always be your friend. Whatever happens. Even if I leave and we never see each other again."

"Please, Donagan. Sleep in the antechamber or in the men's quarters, whichever you prefer. Keep your distance from Lady Flidais if that makes it easier. But please stay to see me through the councils. And . . ."

He waited while I struggled to find the right words.

"I believe I'm right. This goes deeper than the obvious. It must. There must be a way out."

"Unless you mean to accuse the lady publicly of not meeting up to your expectations, I can't think what that way out could be. Oran, you would show strength by accepting this and making the best you can of it. You were born to kingship. You cannot let this disappointment prevent you from being the leader you should be. Then you would indeed be seen as weak, not only by me, but by your household, your community and, in time, your kingdom."

What was there to say? I had asked him to be honest.

"If you believe it will help," Donagan said more gently, "then I will stay until the second council is over. I'll give you what support I can. And then I'll go."

I rose to my feet. "Thank you," I said, but my heart was heavy. I could be strong. I could be a leader. In time, I could be a king. It seemed I could not also be happy.

And yet, as we walked back to the house, my old friend and I, with the little dog stopping here and there to investigate an exciting smell or an enticing rustle in the undergrowth, I found I had not lost my belief that something more was at play here, something beyond the obvious explanation. *You are a fool, Oran*, I told myself. *Even after this, even after everything, still you are ruled by your dreams. But your dreams cannot help you.*

20

BLACKTHORN

Grim came in with the second kerchief in his hands, still wet from the wash.

"You know your letters," he said. "What does this say?"

He spread the square of red linen out on the table, and I saw that, unlike mine, this kerchief was a lovers' token. Within the trailing leaf-and-flower border, the maker had embroidered a little heart, and on either side of it a letter. *A loves N.*

"This is the letter A," I told Grim, putting my finger on it to show him. "That stands for someone's name—Aine, for instance, or Aedan. And this is N for Niall, or Niamh, or Ness." I felt suddenly cold, though I was not sure why. "The heart means love. This is something a man might give his sweetheart. Who makes these kerchiefs, Grim? Do lots of folk have them?" Apart from the heart and the letters, this one was twin to my own; the same hand might have embroidered both.

"Bought the other one from the travelers. Their women make a lot of pretty things. I haven't seen anyone around here wearing one. Except for you." He narrowed his eyes at me. "You all right? You're looking a bit peaky. Gone white all of a sudden."

"You said you found this on the cart when you returned

it to Scannal's. Can you remember where you'd been that day?"

Grim got up to put the kettle on. "Hard to forget. Funny sort of day. Took a load of flour over to Silverlake. That baker, you'll have heard of him. Branoc. Fellow couldn't wait to see the last of me. Why?"

"Could this kerchief have got on the cart in Silverlake?"

"Things don't get on carts by themselves." Grim set two cups on the table, beside the red kerchief. "I stopped in the village for directions, talked to a woman. Couple of children had a ride on the horse."

"So any of them might have dropped it?"

"Think I'd have seen, if they did. Anyway, it wasn't on top of the load, it was underneath."

"You're saying it was on the cart before you loaded up? It could belong to someone at Scannal's?"

Grim dropped a generous pinch of dried peppermint leaves into each cup. "Nah. I'd have seen it." He poured hot water onto the herbs, releasing a sweet, healing smell. He found the honey jar and set it on the table, with a spoon. "Why are you asking?"

"Because I prefer my stories to have an ending, and this one doesn't. Not yet, anyway. Something's bothering me about this kerchief and how you came by it."

Grim straightened. After a moment he said, "You saying I stole it?"

"Would I be shocked by that? I've stolen before when I had to, and worse than a kerchief from a traveler's market. I'm not saying that at all. It's more a . . . a feeling. Something out of place. Tell me everything you did that day, Grim. From picking up the cart at Scannal's to bringing it back again."

He gave me the story: how he'd harnessed up the two big horses, loaded on his bags of flour, driven the cart to Silverlake village. The woman who'd given him directions had invited him to drop in on the way home. Then he'd gone up the hill to the baker's, which had a house and a barn with big doors and a loft.

"I backed the cart in, so the load was just outside the doors. You sure you want to hear all this? Can't think why."

"Go on. Where was Branoc while you were doing this?"

"Standing there in the yard with his eye on me. I offered to carry the bags up, thinking he'd want them high and dry in the loft, and he said he'd do that himself later. I was glad enough; saved me the extra work. Looked narrow, not easy to get the load up there. Branoc took the ladder away to make more room down below. Then I—"

"Wait. He took the ladder away?"

"Mm-hm. Here, drink your tea, you look like you're seeing ghosts. I unloaded the sacks, stacked them on the floor."

"With Branoc still watching?"

"He'd gone off by then. When I finished I went back out. Most folk give me a bite to eat after a long trip, but I didn't like the feel of the place. Decided to take the cart down by the lake to have my bread and cheese. Branoc came back over, I asked him for Scannal's payment, he went off to get it. He paid me, I left." He stared into his cup for a moment. "One more thing. Rats."

"Rats?"

"Up in the loft. Heard them scuttling around. Mentioned it to Branoc, joking-like, and he took offense."

Rats. Black Crow save me. "Grim," I asked carefully, "this loft, the one Branoc didn't want you to climb up to—did it have any kind of opening? I don't mean where the ladder came down, but toward the front of the barn. A window, a trapdoor, a crack in the boards."

Grim stared at me. "You mean up above where the cart was? But . . ."

"Was there anything?"

He frowned in concentration. "Might've been a window at the front. It's a high barn, there'd be quite a bit of room up there. You saying . . . ?"

"That the kerchief might have come down from that window onto the cart, and you might not have seen it until you got back to Scannal's. That's possible, isn't it?"

Grim frowned into his brew. "Could be. But why? Who'd be up there, and why would they drop a kerchief? If they wanted me to look up, why not just call out?"

"Perhaps they were afraid Branoc might hear." The chill sensation was being replaced by a terrible anger. A miller, a miller's daughter, a baker. By all the gods, I hoped I was wrong about this. "When folk are truly frightened, when

they're cowed and beaten down, asking for help can be almost impossible. You and I know that, Grim."

"You're saying the rats weren't rats at all," Grim said in a
shocked whisper. "The fellow's got something else up there."

"Some*one*." I wished I had asked Emer what the traveler boy's name was. Aedan. Art. Aillil. "Grim, there's a girl
missing from Silverlake. The miller's daughter, Ness, a
friend of young Emer's. It's commonly believed she ran
away with her sweetheart, one of the travelers, and took
her father's life savings with her. That same night the miller
was killed in a nasty accident, which folk put down to him
being upset and careless. Emer swears her friend wouldn't
do what they say she did. But nobody will believe her."

"Except you."

"I wish I didn't, Grim. But I think N is for Ness, and A is
for whatever the traveler lad's name is, and Branoc may
have someone in his loft who needs rescuing fast. Tell me,
how quickly could you fetch us a horse and cart?"

He gave a shocked whistle. "Not today. And maybe not
tomorrow. Couple of horses, I could manage. Why would
you need a cart?"

"If that girl's been up there all this time, who knows
what state she'll be in? Possibly unable to walk, almost certainly not up to riding, even as far as Silverlake village."

"We can't go in with a cart," Grim said. "That'd be sure
to make Branoc suspicious. Be different if I had a delivery
to make, but he's got all the flour he needs for a while."

"Ah. You may not have an excuse to go up there, but I
do." I pointed to the pot of salve Emer and I had made.
"Branoc sent a message asking for a remedy, something for
strained arms and shoulders. I could just send it with a boy.
Or I could deliver it myself, along with an offer to massage
away the pain."

"Too risky. Let me take it."

"This needs the two of us, Grim. And I want to do it today. If I'm right, and Branoc has got the girl, I don't want
her to spend another night as his prisoner. Let's get her out
of there."

"We could tell the prince or that man of his," Grim said.
"Ask him if he'll send folk to see if it's true. They could get

the girl back home quicker than we could, and they could send men-at-arms to deal with Branoc."

"Only one problem there, apart from the fact that I've good cause not to trust princes and the like, especially where women in trouble are concerned. Emer said every-one refused to believe her when she told them Ness wouldn't have run away, and that was despite her being Ness's closest friend and a sensible girl. Our tale sounds far-fetched; it sounds like we've put together bits and pieces that might mean nothing at all. I can't see Prince Oran being in a hurry to send folk storming over to Silver-lake on the evidence we've got. If there was time, I'd walk over to Winterfalls and ask Emer if Ness's sweetheart has a name beginning with A; I'd ask if the lad ever gave Ness a red kerchief. I'd ask if Branoc the baker wanted Ness for himself, and if she turned him down. But that would take time. It would mean leaving this until tomorrow, and I'm not going to do that; I can't. Anyway, what if I'm wrong? What if we gather a whole army of folk and descend on Branoc's barn, and it turns out what's up there is rats after all?"

"Mm. And if he heard folk coming and guessed why, he might panic and hurt the girl. He might do anything. It's an odd story, miller crushing himself with his own grindstone. Sounds too freakish to be true. Maybe it never was true. Maybe the miller was murdered."

"Not so much of a bonehead after all, are you? So, if you can get the horses and get them quickly, here's what we'll do."

21

Turns out she can ride, even with a blanket saddle and not much of a halter. Just as well. The two horses I borrow from a fellow who owes me a favor. Fixed his roof a while ago, knew he was struggling, told him to forget paying. While I fetch the horses Blackthorn puts together what we need: her healer's things, a bag of oats, a couple of blankets, a coil of rope. I've got a knife on me, and so has Blackthorn. That part of the plan bothers me. Knife or no knife, while I'm getting the girl out Blackthorn's going to be on her own with Branoc. If he sees what's up, she'll be in trouble.

I tell her this when we're on the road. She says not to worry, she's faced up to worse before. If she needs me she'll yell for help. All very good, but what if I'm halfway down the ladder with this girl when she does? What am I going to do, drop the girl and rush in to save Blackthorn? Maybe we should have gone to the prince after all, I tell her. She says nonsense, who needs men-at-arms? She's looking at me when she says it, and I feel funny. Someone like her trusting me to do the right thing, that's new to me. Could take some getting used to.

We ride fast. The day's nearly half gone, and what we have to do needs doing in daylight. I start wondering if we've made a stupid mistake, but Blackthorn's got her jaw set and her eyes angry, as if she might burst if she doesn't save this girl before dark, so I just keep on riding and hope for the best. Stick to the plan, she's told me, and we can do this. Oh, and make sure you don't frighten the girl. Hah! Big lump like me crashing through the door of a loft, when someone's been locked up in there for who knows how long — anyone in their right mind would be scared. And this is a little girl. I say why not change places, she rescues the girl, I deal with Branoc, and she tells me again why that won't work.

We keep on riding. In the middle of the afternoon we go through Silverlake settlement without stopping, and here we are, down the hill a bit from Branoc's barn, in a spot where the trees hide us.

We follow the plan. Horses tied up under the trees, healer's bag in her hand, other supplies on my back, the two of us walking up quiet-like. I stop a bit short of the barn, keeping in cover. Blackthorn goes on. She looks as if she's never been scared of anything in her life. This is the bit of the plan I hate — seeing her go off where I can't protect her. Makes my gut ache. Stupid.

I sneak around to a spot where I can see the courtyard. Branoc comes out before Blackthorn can knock on his door; it's like he's been watching. They talk a bit, then the two of them go into the house and the door shuts behind them. Don't like that. But it's the way the plan works.

I wait a bit, because that's what she said to do. Give her time to get Branoc sitting down and having his aches and pains tended to. Then I go up to the barn. Problem: the doors are bolted. Hard to slide the bolts open without making a racket. I do it slowly, inch by inch, and my heart's doing a bit of a dance, a fast reel it'd be. I swing the doors open and I'm in. Seems a good idea to close them over behind me, so I do, but not all the way. Might need to get out fast.

Problem: the ladder's not there. I think of calling out, but no, Branoc might hear, and even if he doesn't, there's what Blackthorn said about folk sometimes being too scared to ask for help, maybe too scared even to squeak. I go back outside, look around, find the ladder lying down against the wall. Fetch it in, put it in place. Think of Blackthorn in there with that man. Hope she'll use the knife quick and hard if she has to.

I climb up. Creak, creak, every step loud enough to wake the dead. Hope the thing doesn't break under me. In my head are the fellows from Mathuin's lockup, the ones I couldn't get out and the ones I did get out who ended up dead anyway. Poxy. Dribbles. Strangler, poor bastard. Frog Spawn. The other fellows down the end. Life's cruel sometimes. I'm at the top, on a flat bit, and in front of me there's a wall with a door in it, like there's a storage room up here. At the front. Over the spot where the cart was, that day. Shit. Looks like Blackthorn may have been right.

This door's bolted too, on the outside. Bastard. I stop to take a couple of breaths, not wanting to go in there with my face all hate and anger. Then I slip the bolts and pull the door open.

It's darkish and for a bit I don't see her. Then there's a shaky gasping noise, and she bursts out crying. Shutters on the window; I throw them open and light comes in. There she is, just a young thing, all bruises and big eyes, and she can't come out of the shadowy corner because around one wrist and one ankle she's got shackles, and there are chains joining them to rings in the wall. She's sort of crouching. Looks like she's too tired or hurt to stand up, but the wrist chain's too short for her to lie down. An oath bursts out of me, a bad one, then I get ahold of myself.

"It's all right," I say. "You're safe now. I've come to get you out."

Didn't bring any tools; didn't think I'd need them. Might be some down below, but I don't want to leave her on her own. Her gown's all ragged and dirty, and there's a stink from the bucket in the corner. A filthy mattress against the wall, with a blanket. Guess he undoes the shackles at night. A cup, empty. Nothing else.

"Picked up your kerchief," I say, moving closer, trying not to scare her. "Sorry we didn't come sooner; took a while to work out."

"I'm Ness," she sobs. "Daughter of Ernan the miller. My dad—where's my dad?"

Black Crow save me. She doesn't even know. "It's just me and my friend today," I tell her. "Got to get these shackles off you; hold still for a bit."

Fellow's done a thorough job, curse his poxy hide. Hard

to get the things off without hurting her. And I'm worried
about how long it's taking, since Blackthorn's down there
with him. If he comes out before I get Ness away this could
turn even nastier than it already is. I try to prize the leg
shackle open with my knife, but it's going to be too slow. In
the end I take hold of the chains and haul until the rings
break off the wall. They come crashing down and a shower
of rubble comes with them, and it's loud, too loud. Ness
sort of falls against me, then clutches onto me, sobbing
against my chest.

"Right, let's get you out of here quick," I say, wanting to
cry right along with her. I don't even bother with the blanket I've brought, I just pick Ness up and carry her down the
ladder, rings, chains and shackles dangling and dragging.
Which is awkward, but I don't trip myself up and I don't
drop her. Inside I'm cursing Branoc with every foul word I
know, and that's more than a few.

"He'll come," Ness whispers. "Branoc. He'll hear us and
come."

Just what I'm thinking, but I want to get these chains
off her before we go anywhere. Feels wrong to leave them
on, and anyway they'll slow us. I put Ness down on her
feet but she can't stand up, so I sit her on a bench. I find a
crowbar and a hammer. See her flinch when I bring them
over. My heart's going fast, not a dance now, more of a
charge into battle. I try to take deep breaths, to slow myself down. Need steady hands for this. Girl's been hurt
enough already, got to do it right the first time.

"Put your arm along here, like this." I show her, laying my
forearm along the bench. "And hold as still as you can. Just a
little tap with the hammer and this'll be off. Promise."

She's scared but she does it. I break open the shackles,
first the wrist, then the ankle, and she's free. Arm must hurt
a lot after being held up like that. Leg can't take her weight.
Who knows what else he's done to her? But she smiles at
me with tears dripping down her face and her nose running, and it's the best thing I've seen in a while.

"What's your name?" she asks.

"Grim. Hop up, we'll get you straight home." I pick her
up again, thinking I shouldn't have said that, seeing as her
dad's dead and the mill's a ruin, but too late now. "Down to

the village first. My friend's a healer, she'll fix you up. Hush now."

I kick the shackles and chains out of the way. Go over to the door, open it a bit. She squeezes her eyes shut when the light comes in though it's not a bright day. Next part of the plan's tricky. Need to get her to the horses, wait for Blackthorn to walk down, then put Ness up in the saddle and take her to the settlement without Branoc noticing that someone's been in the barn or that his prisoner's not there anymore. He's hardly going to come racing after us once we're down there telling the story of what he's done, with the girl to prove it's not lies.

I'm holding Ness up with one arm and closing the barn door with the other when I hear him. "You! What are you doing?"

There's a warmth against my leg, a smell I recognize. Ness is so terrified she's wet herself. Branoc's striding out his front door, red in the face, and there's Blackthorn coming after him with her bag in her hand.

"Done you a favor," I call out. "Cleared those rats out of your barn."

"You bastard!" He's heading straight for me, rolling up his sleeves. "You thieving bastard, you can't take her! She's mine! She's my wife, you bonehead!"

I take a step forward and he stops walking. "You scum," I say. "You filth. I'm taking her away. Now. Unless you fancy a fight."

Branoc looks me up and down, then he turns real quick, and before I can do anything he's got Blackthorn pinned in front of him with her back to his chest and her arm twisted up behind her. She hasn't had time to grab her knife.

"Try anything and I break your woman's arm," Branoc says. "Now let my wife go and back off slowly."

"Wife, hah!" Under my breath I say to Ness, "You're safe. Trust me." I look over and there's Blackthorn looking back at me, not nodding or anything, but I know what she wants me to do. "There," I say, letting go of Ness, who staggers and collapses on the ground. "Now you let *her* go."

"One, two, three," mouths Blackthorn without a sound, and as I charge forward with a big roar bursting out of me, she throws herself backward, her head cracks into Branoc's shoulder and he drops her with a curse. He bolts. I go after him, but he's quick, and before I get to the end of the house he's out of sight in the woods behind. And though I want to rip him apart with my bare hands for what he's done to the girl, I stop running and come back. Blackthorn needs me here. Last bit of the plan, she can't do on her own. Anyway, what matters is getting Ness to safety. And telling the story. The story Ness's friend tried to tell, and nobody would believe.

22

ORAN

"My lord?"

Aedan was at the door of my small council chamber,
where I had been attempting to sort out a pile of neglected
correspondence. I had no scribe at Winterfalls; up until
now there had been no need for one. As the mistress of the
house, Flidais should have been dealing with most of these
letters—congratulations from distant family connections,
invitations to hand-fastings or other celebrations, suggestions that she and I might visit one or another chieftain's
household. At present, her headaches prevented this. If she
was not better soon, I would need to seek assistance elsewhere. I hardly liked to ask Donagan to do it. "What is it,
Aedan?"

"My lord, the wise woman, Blackthorn, is here, with that
fellow Grim and a young woman from the village."

"Can't you deal with them?" Seeing the look on the face
of my loyal steward, I set down my pen and stood up, realizing as I did so how long I had been sitting hunched over
the letters; my back and shoulders ached. "I'm sorry, Aedan. I know you would not have disturbed me without
good cause. What do they want?"

"The wise woman says it's urgent, my lord, and she's

asked to see you in person. Something about Branoc the baker and a missing girl. And a murder at Silverlake."

"A murder! Very well, I'll see them now. Bring them in here, will you? And call Donagan for me." Accusations of unlawful killing would be best heard before a witness, and Donagan was the most reliable witness I could think of. "And make sure there's a man-at-arms out in the hallway, please."

"Yes, my lord."

Donagan arrived just as the three of them were being ushered in, and suddenly my council chamber—not, in fact, used for formal councils, but for writing, thinking and occasionally meeting with visitors—was quite full. That was very much down to Grim, who seemed to take up the space of at least three ordinary men. Blackthorn, a woman with oddly cropped hair of a startling red, had an intensity about her like that of a wild creature caged. I had never encountered a person with such blazing eyes or such a tightly held body. She was thin as a lath and not especially tall, with a tooth missing and a face that wore its years hard. But from the moment she walked in she filled the place with her presence. Between the two of them was the girl Aedan had mentioned. I recognized her as the young sister of Fraoch the smith, but I could not recall her name. She looked as if she had been crying.

"Sit down, please." I motioned to the bench opposite me, but none of them sat. "You are Mistress Blackthorn, I presume. Grim I have already met. And . . ."

"Emer," Blackthorn said. "She helps me in my work sometimes. My lord." There was a criticism in her tone; she expected the prince of Dalriada to know his people's names. I did, mostly.

"Thank you, Mistress Blackthorn. I understand there's been some trouble at Silverlake. What has happened?"

"Trouble," growled Grim. "You could call it trouble. I might have another word for it, a stronger one."

"It's all right, Grim," Blackthorn said. "We'd best tell the story."

The three of them told it together, and a terrible and violent tale it was. The baker, Branoc, abducting the miller's daughter and keeping her locked up for his pleasure over several turnings of the moon; the strange death of the miller on the same night his daughter was taken, perhaps not the accident everyone believed after all; Emer, the loyal friend, pleading with folk to believe her when she refused to accept that Ness must have run away with her traveler boy and her father's savings. The truth made a bizarre and unlikely story, and it was easy to understand why so many folk had long accepted the most plausible explanation. But Emer had never believed the loyal daughter would have abandoned her widowed father.

It had been Blackthorn and Grim who'd worked out the truth, by piecing together a collection of clues nobody else had understood. And yesterday, the two of them had gone up to the baker's loft and found the girl abused, half-starved and filthy, but alive. Too scared to call for help; chained up so she could not escape. With a whole village of folk only a short ride away, blind to the shocking truth. No wonder Blackthorn was angry.

"Where is the young woman now?" I asked, finding it somewhat confronting to hold the wise woman's gaze. I was the prince of Dalriada and leader of this district; that made this appalling incident my responsibility.

"Being tended to in Silverlake," Blackthorn said. "She can't be moved yet. There's a kindly couple there who are happy to house her for now." Her lip curled, and again I heard the unspoken message: *Now they know she's a good girl, not a runaway.* "Ness has some injuries. I'll deal with those. And she needs rest, quiet." She glanced at Emer. "She won't be her old self again anytime soon. Perhaps never."

"Ness will come to us when she's well enough to be moved," said the girl. "My mam says it's all right for her to stay. When we're done here I'm going over to Silverlake to help look after her."

"Good," I said. "You've done well, all of you. What I cannot understand is why you tackled this yourselves, just the two of you." It seemed Blackthorn and Grim had ridden up there to confront Branoc without any backup at all, knowing the girl might be a prisoner in his barn, and suspecting the baker might have killed her father. According to Emer, Branoc had had an eye for Ness long before this happened, but Ernan had refused to consider him as a suitor for his daughter. Ness had never thought of Branoc as a possible husband; her affections were all for her traveler lad, Abhan. Who was now very likely on the road with the rest of his folk and heading our way, knowing nothing at all of this. "Why didn't you bring it to me, ask for my help? We could have sent men-at-arms. We could have apprehended Branoc instead of letting him escape. Why didn't you raise it at the council, or when I came to the village?"

The look in Blackthorn's eyes might have withered me where I stood. "Grim and I didn't put the pieces together until yesterday," she said, not bothering with *my lord* or *Prince Oran* at all. "And we didn't know if we were right until we got there and Grim found Ness hidden in the barn. As for Emer, she's young, and speaking up before a lot of men can take courage. You wouldn't understand that, perhaps. As it was, Emer didn't know what had happened until Grim and I rode back to Winterfalls this morning. I spent the night in Silverlake getting Ness settled, patching up her injuries, talking to the local folk. Grim spent it on guard up at Branoc's place in case he came back to fetch anything. We've come straight here; we only stopped to pick up Emer and let her know her friend's safe. But don't forget, Emer's been trying to convince folk there was something wrong ever since Ness disappeared. Over and over. Nobody believed her. Everyone dismissed her concerns. Easier for them to believe Ness had gone to the bad. Meant they could simply forget her, put her out of their minds. Emer was hardly going to come knocking on your door and demand to be heard, was she?"

"Emer," I said, addressing myself to the girl and keeping my voice gentle, "you are a good and loyal friend. If you found it difficult to bring this to my attention, you could have raised it with Lady Flidais. That is why she and I visit the village from time to time; to make it easier for people to speak out, if the councils are too overwhelming."

Emer looked me in the eye, and I saw on her young face an echo of Blackthorn's fury. "I did tell Lady Flidais about Ness going missing, my lord. Yesterday morning when she came to the weaver's to talk to us. I told her the same story I told everyone, that Ness was a good daughter and wouldn't run away or thieve from her dad; she loved him. Lady Flidais said that when I got a bit older I wouldn't be so trusting, and that girls like Ness made their own beds. And the others laughed."

Donagan had folded his arms and was staring out the window. I struggled for the right words; there was enough anger in this room already without my adding to it.

"Then I owe you an apology, Emer," I said. "And to Blackthorn and Grim we all owe a great debt. The two of you took quite a risk."

"Sorry we let Branoc go." Grim spoke, not looking at me but down at the floor. "Would have liked to wring his neck, the bastard. Too quick for me. Be miles away by now. Took a rope, never used it. Girl had to come first."

"I understand that, Grim. You have all done your best, and a remarkable best it was. Yes, I suppose we will never apprehend Branoc now, though I will send men out to look for him."

"He'll be off to the nearest anchorage and taking ship for Armorica, that's my guess," said Donagan. "Leaving Silverlake with neither miller nor baker. Though that is hardly of importance, beside this. You believe Ernan's death might be Branoc's doing too? And the theft of his savings?"

"I can't see how a miller crushes himself with his own grindstone," Blackthorn said. "No matter how upset he is. No matter how much his wits aren't on the job. His work would be so familiar he'd be able to do it in his sleep. And who was the likeliest to guess where his daughter might really have gone? He knew Branoc fancied Ness and had been told he couldn't have her."

"This is a matter for the next open council," I said. "I'll ensure Ernan's death is investigated further before then. If Branoc is apprehended, he will be called to account for his treatment of Ness, and he will be questioned on the matter of the miller's demise. Even if he cannot be tracked down, there's the future of the mill and bakery to be considered, and compensation for the young lady."

"You won't expect Ness to come to the council, will you, my lord?" asked Emer. "Mistress Blackthorn says she didn't even know her father was dead; they had to tell her last night."

"I understand that, and of course she must be given time to recover. I offer you all my personal thanks. I'll arrange a search for Branoc immediately, and guards at the bakery. Blackthorn, if any further assistance is needed, don't hesitate to ask—Donagan will help you, or speak to Aedan, my steward. It seems the young lady may now be without any family support. We must ensure that she is properly provided for."

Blackthorn said nothing, but I saw a question in her eyes: *We?*

"This is an illustration to all of us, to the whole community, that we should take responsibility for each other. And it begins with me." *And with Flidais,* I thought, but I did not say it. "Now I'll let you go to some well-earned rest. Emer, you are going over to Silverlake this morning, you said? How will you get there?"

"My brother's taking me over on his cart, my lord."

"Good. I hope Ness is improving."

"Long road ahead," Grim said, surprising me. "When you're hurt as bad as that. Wish we'd worked it out sooner."

"You saved her," I said. "Don't lose sight of that."

Donagan ushered them out. I sent for Lochlan, my head guard, and set the situation before him, knowing he could be trusted to arrange protection for Branoc's premises and men to conduct an orderly search of the district. I sent for Aedan and asked him to ensure those who cared for Ness had the wherewithal to provide for her through what might be a lengthy recovery. I had not asked Blackthorn if the abused girl was with child; I hoped very much that she was not. I called Brid and asked her to spread word that the Silverlake bakery would not be in business for the foreseeable future. There would be more work for Deaman and his assistants.

When that was done, all I wanted was to escape out of doors, stride around the farm and work off the confusion of feelings that had come over me when Blackthorn told the story. At first, disbelief. Then horror. Then fury that any man would do so base a thing. Then guilt, that I had not known; that of my whole community, the folk whose leader and exemplar I was supposed to be, only Emer, a girl of

fifteen or so, had stood up for her friend and refused to be
silenced. Even Flidais had dismissed her concerns. Flidais,
who would one day be queen.

And because I would one day be king, I did not head
out across the fields, but went to find her.

"Flidais. A word with you in private."

I had broken a household rule and come right into the
women's quarters to find my betrothed. The attendants laid
aside their embroidery and vanished away like mist under
morning sun, leaving the two of us alone in the chamber
where they had been gathered. Aunt Sochla hesitated in
the doorway; Bramble waited by her skirts. I'd have liked
my aunt to stay. With her present, Flidais would not be able
to end an awkward conversation by twining herself around
me and inviting me to intimacy. That did often seem to be
her solution to a disagreement. But what I had to say was
best not shared with anyone else.

"Thank you, Aunt," I said. "I'm sure Bramble would like
a stroll in the garden."

"As would I. My eyes are getting too old for fine work.
Come, dog!"

I waited until the door closed behind her before moving
over to the table where Flidais was standing. She had her
embroidery clutched against her breast as if she were a
child expecting a reprimand; did I really look so angry?
The sun through the tall windows bathed my betrothed in
soft autumn light. Her gown was red, her lips redder; her
skin was smooth and perfect. Her long-lashed eyes regarded me with such trepidation that a small part of me
was tempted to enfold her in an embrace and suggest the
two of us might start again, forgetting what was past. I
hardened my heart.

"Sit down, please," I said, indicating the bench near her.
"I have a serious matter to discuss with you."

"Oh dear, Oran." She sat, still holding her handiwork.
"You look so solemn. Not the tiniest smile for me today?"

I ignored this blatant attempt to placate me. "Flidais, at
your parents' home, did you assist your mother with resolv-
ing difficulties in the household, or in the settlements
within your father's territory? Did she explain to you the

purpose of audiences and councils? Did she teach you how important it is for us, as leaders, to be open to the problems faced by our people?"

Flidais drew her needle from the fabric and applied herself to stitchery. Her hands were shaking visibly.

"Flidais?"

"That is a lot of questions, Oran. Have I done something wrong again? Please say I haven't." She looked up, turning the full power of her beautiful eyes on me.

"When we rode into Winterfalls you went to the weaver's workshop with the village women and spent some time talking to them. Did a young woman named Emer speak to you about her friend who had gone missing? The miller's daughter from Silverlake?"

A delicate frown creased Flidais's brow. "A miller's daughter? I don't believe so, Oran. I recall nothing of that kind. Why do you ask?"

I had thought she might have a ready reason for dismissing Emer's plea. I had thought she might be apologetic and promise to do better next time. I had not expected her to deny this outright.

"I've just had a visit from the healer, Mistress Blackthorn, along with her man and the young woman I mentioned." I gave her the story as a straightforward account, taking care not to sound accusatory, for after all, it was not she who had abducted Ness, nor had she been alone in discounting Emer's concerns.

"I don't remember anything like that," Flidais said when I was done. "She must have made a mistake; forgotten to tell me. What a terrible story, Oran! We must make sure this girl, the one who was imprisoned, is well looked after now. I suppose, after what has happened, her traveler sweetheart will no longer want her. She will be viewed as spoiled goods."

I swallowed a fresh surge of anger, though quite possibly this was true. "You say Emer did not seek your counsel on this matter. I don't believe you."

"Oran!" The big blue eyes were full of reproach, the delicate lips pouting. "How can you say such a thing?"

"More easily than I expected," I said. "It can be put to the test; all I need do is ask some of the other women who

were present at the time. It seems many folk in both Winterfalls and Silverlake disregarded Emer's plea, as you did,
and because of that Ness was chained and beaten and
abused for far longer than she would have been had her
friend's arguments been taken seriously from the first."

Flidais stabbed the needle into the linen, then cursed
under her breath. A drop of blood stained the cloth.

"If you are to be my wife, if you are one day to be queen,
you must learn what is expected of you. You must learn
that such a life is not only one of privilege but also one of
service and responsibility. We must be open to those under
our governance, Flidais; we must be ready to help when
they need us. I am certain your mother and father do that
for the folk of Cloud Hill, and did so as you were growing
up." I noticed that she had gone very pale. Had she understood the seriousness of her oversight at last?

"You said *if*. If you are to be my wife. What do you
mean?"

I longed to speak honestly. I was becoming ever surer
that I had made a mistake; that if she and I had to live out
our lives together we would both be utterly miserable. I
could feel the words on the tip of my tongue.

But we were already betrothed; the ceremony had taken
place. And we had lain together, she and I. Flidais might
even now be with child. What we had done, there was no
undoing. And now there could be no going back.

"I meant nothing by it," I said. "I want you to try a little
harder, that is all. Try to take an interest in the affairs of the
local people; make sure you give them due respect when
they bring their problems to you. Listen with intelligence."

Now she was really insulted. "Are you telling me I am
not only a liar but also a fool?"

"In this matter, it seems you have, at the very least, been
guilty of prejudice." I struggled to keep my tone even.

Flidais had hunched her shoulders; her head was bent
over her embroidery. A man would need a heart of stone
not to want to say, *Sorry, of course I did not mean it*, and to
comfort her with an embrace. It seemed that although my
mother thought me soft, I was developing just such a heart.

"That is all I have to say to you. You might consider visiting the women of both villages before the open council, and in Emer's case I think an apology would be in order."

"An apology? To a village girl? You cannot be serious."

"Oh, I am. I have apologized to her already, on my own behalf and on behalf of the community." I got up and went to the door. "Ask Donagan to arrange a visit for you," I added. "You might take Aunt Sochla next time; as the queen's sister, she has a very sound idea of what is expected."

"Donagan?" Flidais's tone was so furious that against my better judgment I turned. Her cheeks were stained with angry red. "I suppose this is all his doing! He didn't care for me from the first, and now someone's been spying on me and reported it back to him, otherwise you'd never accuse me in this way. How dare you treat me like some sort of— of serving woman? I am to be your wife!"

"This is nothing to do with Donagan, Flidais. But since you mention him, I will tell you this: he is my friend and companion, far more than a body servant, and he answers only to me. Managing a household seems as new to you as dealing with a community. As my future wife, it is indeed your responsibility to govern the serving folk in this house. I will expect you to do so with the blend of kindness, trust and common sense that they have long been accustomed to. If any decisions cause you difficulty, bring them to me. I am willing to help you, indeed eager to do so. Of course you will make errors; we all do. But you must learn from your mistakes. Learn quickly, and when you get something wrong, admit it and apologize."

She burst into tears, and through the sobbing I could hear a catalogue of wrongs: the long ride from the south, the drowning of her maid, wretched Bramble turning against her, Aunt Sochla who had stolen the dog's affections, Donagan eaten up by jealousy and always getting in the way. Why was I being so harsh with her? She had been doing her best.

I stood there while she raved and wept. I kept my counsel. She expected me to bend and bow, to give in to her. She thought me the kind of man who would surrender, every time, to her tears. And if not tears, then to her other weapon, the one she liked to surprise me with. But not this time.

"You'd best compose yourself before your women return," I said. "Unless, that is, you plan to regale them with our personal business. You do know, I hope, how inappropriate that would be. Speak to Aunt Sochla about a women's meeting. She'll help you arrange it. Now I'll leave you; I have work to attend to."

She muttered something as I went out, but I did not catch it. I did not go to my council chamber to finish dealing with the correspondence. I went, instead, to my own quarters, where I sat down at my desk and contemplated the ribbon-bound bundle that was Flidais's letters. My heart was racing; my palms were sweaty. I carried the letters to the small fire that burned on the hearth, keeping the chamber warm for me all day. A luxury; the privilege of a prince. But privilege was balanced, always, by responsibility. I considered the long years of my future, and wondered if I would feel like this every single day: as if my heart had been shredded. Or would the pain subside as I grew older and my dreams faded to nothing?

I slipped the letters from the ribbon and, one by one, consigned them to the flames.

23

GRIM

Long night on guard up at the bakery. Not on my own, at least. Couple of the fellows from Silverlake keep me company. Feeling a bit guilty, most likely, since the girl was right there in the village and nobody spotted anything wrong. We make a little fire to keep out the ghosts. Long, long night. Plenty of time to think about what I could have done, run a bit faster, yelled a bit louder, tried a bit harder to get to Branoc before he lost himself in the woods. Bad that he's still out there somewhere. Means he could do the same thing to some other girl.

Next day, we keep going, Blackthorn and me, though she hasn't slept either. She's been sitting up with Ness. Girl's wrung out as thin as an old rag by everything that's happened to her. We leave the village women looking after her and head on back to Winterfalls. We drop the horses off, pick up Emer from the smith's, give her the good news—good and bad, to tell the truth, but at least Ness is alive, and she's safe now—and go on to the prince's place.

Blackthorn's angry and it shows. Think she expects Prince Oran to do the sort of thing Mathuin would do, say it's only a village girl and she got what was coming to her, then send us packing. So, when he listens and takes it all in and says sorry, she's on the back foot. Not for long; she makes it plain she'll be watching, making sure he keeps on doing the right thing. Fellow strikes me as trustworthy. Reckon I can tell pretty quick. Seems to me he's trying to do good, and sometimes struggling with it. Got a sad look about him.

After that we walk Emer to the smithy and Fraoch gives us a slap-up meal, ale and all. By the time we're heading home, Blackthorn and me are just about asleep on our feet. Which is why we don't think too much about the smell of smoke or where it might be coming from until we're over the rise. That's when we see our house is on fire.

Then there's the drumbeat of my running feet, the wheezy bellows of my breath. And the smoke rising, the smell of burning thatch, burning wood, everything going up in flames. Blackthorn somewhere behind me.

A long run, chest hurting, heart going crazy, and I'm there. Hard to get in close, it's so hot. I reach the well, drop the bucket down, haul it up. Can't see Blackthorn for the smoke. I run and throw the water on, run back to pull up another bucketful. Fire's got too much of a hold but I keep on anyway. The place is all flickering light, flying sparks and straw from the roof. Another bucket, another one, another . . . Can't breathe. Bend over, hands on my knees.

Lot of noise, flames roaring, things falling down. And screaming. A woman screaming. Blackthorn. Didn't think my heart could go any quicker but it does. Gallops like a spooked horse.

I'm nearly blind in the smoke. I stumble around, shouting out her name, thinking she's in there and burning. The screaming goes on, and there are words in it but I can't catch them. One thing I can see is the path under my feet, so I follow that and nearly crash into her. She doesn't even see me. She's beating at the flames with her cloak, making embers jump all around her, onto her hair, onto her clothes, and what she's calling out is two names, over and over. Her voice is a deep-down rasping sob. Puts a pain in my chest to hear it.

"Cass! Brennan! No, no! Cass! Brennan!"

She's not here, she's in some other place, some other time, and if I don't do something it won't only be the house that goes up, it'll be her with it. I grab hold of her and haul her out of harm's way. For a bit she fights me, still shouting,

"Cass! Brennan!" Then all of a sudden she crumples down onto the path with her hands over her face. Her voice goes to a whisper. "Cass. Brennan."

I kneel down and wrap my arms around her. She's shaking like she's got a palsy, rocking to and fro, clutching at her hair, fighting something that's all in her own head. With the house ablaze in front of us, I hold on to her as she sobs. I tell her it's all right, it's over now. We're alive and we can go on. We've got through worse, I say, wondering if that's really true for her. She's crying and I'm crying with her. Our house is gone. All gone.

What makes me look up I don't know. Blackthorn's quieter now, but the fire's still roaring away, so I can't have heard him. But I lift my head, with her still in my arms, and I spot him under the trees, the bastard, watching us with an evil look on his face. Thought before that this couldn't be an accident. Now I know it's not.

"Got something to do," I murmur, and I unhook Blackthorn's hands, which are clutching on to my shirt as if she's drowning. I stand up. This time he's not getting away. "Won't be long."

Branoc backs off into Dreamer's Wood, and I go after him, not roaring and charging this time, but moving fast all the same. My head fills up with red thoughts. What he did to that little girl. What he's done to our house. What he's just done to my strong, fearless lady. I'll wrench the sorry baker in half. I'll smash his poxy head in. I'll hold him under the water, let him up for a breath, hold him down again. Keep it up until the last little spark's snuffed out.

I stalk him through the wood. I'm big, but I know how to walk quiet. The baker's not running. Gone to ground somewhere. Knows if he moves out from cover I'll take him. I don't like leaving Blackthorn on her own, not when she's in that state. But Branoc's got my mark on him.

Funny thing is, the wood doesn't scare me right now, though it's eerie with the smoke drifting past and the light from the burning house moving over everything, red, gold, yellow. I stay on the path where I can be quieter. I check for good hiding spots. Waiting for him to panic and move out. I remember how I felt the first time I came in here and wonder if he's feeling the same. Decide to find out.

"Branoc!" I call out in the deepest, scariest voice I can find. "I'm coming to get you! I'm coming to rip off your arms and then your legs and then your head, and feed what's left of you to the monster of Dreamer's Pool!"

There's a little movement out there that might be only a squirrel or might be him. I look in that direction but it's all shadows. Then the fire lends a hand. There's a big crash behind me as if a roof beam's come down, and there's a bright flare-up, and I spot him huddled in some bushes under a spreading elder tree.

The roar comes out of me then, and I charge, and he's got no hope of getting away. I grab him by the neck, lift him off the ground, scream right into his poxy, good-for-nothing face. "You godforsaken mongrel cur! You worm-ridden, woman-hating apology for a man! I'm going to peel off your skin inch by inch and watch you squirm! I'm going to bash your head against this tree until your brains turn to porridge!"

He answers by soiling himself, making a stink that's not at all to my liking. I tighten my grip, his face goes purple, I shake him a bit, and through the red haze that's filling me up I hear Blackthorn's voice, hoarse as a bullfrog's. She must be standing right behind me.

"Grim. No. Justice, remember? You've got to give him justice."

I make some kind of sound, sort of a growl. Can't seem to slacken my grip on the fellow.

"Rope," says Blackthorn, and here she is beside me with the coil in her hands. It's been in my bag since we went off to Silverlake yesterday. "Tie him up, take him in. If you kill him now, he can't answer at the council. He can't be questioned about the miller's death. He can't be punished under the law."

"Bastard doesn't deserve to live one moment longer," I say, but I'm shifting my hold to Branoc's arms, and Blackthorn's reaching in with the rope. We tie his wrists behind his back. The rope's long enough to do his ankles too. No running away this time. Anyway, the fight's gone out of him. I pick him up and sling him over my shoulder, and we walk back out to our house, which is four stone walls with a heap of burning rubble inside.

We're not on our own anymore. Me and Blackthorn and that evildoer Branoc have been joined by what looks like half of Winterfalls village. People are hauling up water, passing buckets along, dousing the last of the fire. That fellow Donagan is there, and some guards, and horses. I don't need to say much at all. The guards take Branoc from me, throw him over a horse and lead him away.

Blackthorn's sitting on the drystone wall with everyone moving around her, and a look in her eyes that says Cass and Brennan are only a finger's-breadth away. Folk are speaking to her and she's taking no heed at all. It's like she's blind and deaf. I find Donagan, tap him on the shoulder, make sure he's listening.

"Branoc. What happens to him?"

Donagan doesn't take offense, which is just as well since I'm not in the kindest mood. "He'll be kept in confinement. Within the prince's residence. There are many guards; he won't escape, I promise you. At the next open council he'll be called to account for his actions. Prince Oran will hear everyone's story of what happened. He'll arbitrate. That includes deciding on an appropriate punishment."

I make some kind of noise meaning *all right*, and glance over at Blackthorn, who hasn't moved. I can tell her, at least, that the bastard will face justice. Donagan's looking at me, and I think he's got some understanding of what's going through my head, so I say, quiet-like, "Wanted to kill him, that's the truth. Came close to it. She said no. Justice, she said, you've got to give him justice."

"She was right."

"Thing is, her and me, we haven't always seen justice done. Being a chieftain, being a prince, that doesn't always mean a man's wise or fair."

"On matters of this kind, Prince Oran is both," Donagan says, sounding as if he believes it. "Be assured that he will make a just decision."

"Mm-hm."

"Your house," Donagan goes on. "You'll need somewhere to live while it's rebuilt. If nobody can accommodate you in Winterfalls village, I am certain Prince Oran will wish to offer you a place within his own residence for as long as you need it. He was impressed by what you did yesterday, the two of you. Am I right in thinking Branoc may be responsible for this fire as well as the girl's abduction and her father's death? It seems improbable, otherwise, that he would have come so close to your house. Common sense would have seen him putting as many miles between himself and the scene of his offenses as he could."

"Vengeance," I say, nodding. "We take his woman, as he sees it, and he torches our house. Lucky we weren't in it at the time."

"Lucky indeed." Donagan takes a look at the broken and charred thing that was our home. "But unlucky too; I know how hard you worked on the place."

"I'll fix it up." In the back of my head is wretched Conmael—where was he while the house he sent us to was burning to the ground? I bet he could have used his magic to make it rain, or to turn the flames into butterflies or falling leaves. But he didn't. And I bet he could make the house new again, the way it was before, with all our things in it, even. If he popped up right now and offered, I'd say, *Bit late, aren't you? Forget helping, I'll do it myself.*

"A lot of work," says Donagan. "Prince Oran will provide building supplies. The season won't be on your side."

"Thank you. Won't refuse supplies if you can spare them. I can do the work." Seems to me a good idea to accept what's offered before Blackthorn gets the chance to say no.

That's when Fraoch comes up and says there's room for Blackthorn and me to sleep at the smithy because Emer's staying over at Silverlake to look after her friend. Then Scannal's here offering to bring his horses and cart in the morning to help clear the rubble, and Iobhar says he can send a couple of the lads from the brewery to do some of the heavy jobs, and Deaman tells me he's got some lengths of good oak that I can have in return for some work later on. The woman from the weaving workshop—Luach, that's her name—says she'll look out some blankets and clothing from her stores, and we're not to think about paying for them. At some point Blackthorn gets up and comes over, quiet as a mouse, to stand beside me listening, or I think she's listening, but she's so still it feels as if she's not really there.

What I want, and what I know she'd want, is for the two of us to stay here by Dreamer's Wood. We could sleep in the outhouse. Cook over a campfire, wash in cold water, live the way we did on the road. Staying in Winterfalls, among folk, that's going to be hard for both of us, her more than me. But I see the sense in it. Season's well into the dark now, sure to be storms, gales, bucketing rain. And there's lots of folk wanting to help us. Doesn't feel right to say no to them. Besides, how can Blackthorn go on being a healer if she's out here with nothing but the clothes on her back?

I don't ask her and she doesn't say what she thinks either way. When everyone heads off to the village, we just go with them. Fraoch feeds us again; then he has to get back to his work. His mother gives us blankets and clothing and shows us where everything is. We settle into a little chamber off the yard. It's where Emer sleeps when she's home, with another sister who's been moved out to make room for us.

Blackthorn's worrying me. She's hardly said a word. Got that faraway look about her, as if the smallest thing might break her in pieces. I put the blankets on the two pallets, smooth them out, sit down on mine. Remember that it's a long time since we got any sleep. She sits down on the other bed. Looks over at me. Her face is white, her eyes are red, her hair's straggling all over the place. Reminds me of when we were locked up together. Outside, people are moving around, doing things, and it's still afternoon. Feels like a hundred years since we went over to Branoc's bakery and found the girl, and it's only been one day.

"Look at us," she says.

"Way I see it, we've got a roof over our heads. Folk wanting to help. And that bastard's shut up where he can't hurt anyone else."

She's got her hands twisted up together, tight as tight. "Grim. I was shouting, wasn't I? When . . ."

"Mm-hm."

"What was I saying?"

I wonder if I should say, *Nothing much.* Kinder, maybe. But what she wants is the truth. "You were calling out, *Cass, Brennan, no!* Over and over. Right next to me, only you weren't seeing me." I don't ask who Cass and Brennan are, or were. I don't ask anything at all.

"Sleep," she mutters, and lies down on her pallet, pulling the blanket up over her.

I'm all aches and pains, and sleep sounds good, so I do the same. Might not drop off for a while, though. Head's got a lot churning around in it. Old stuff, new stuff. Good stuff, bad stuff. Wish I was better at forgetting.

Blackthorn's lying still and quiet. Be good if she slept through till tomorrow. Hurts to see her looking that way, as if she's lost a fight. As if she's . . . lost.

The light fades; it's evening outside. I'm falling asleep when Blackthorn starts talking.

"Are you still awake, Grim?"

"Mm-hm."

"I can't do it. The seven years. I can't let Mathuin go on doing what he does. It's all very well to catch Branoc and bring him to justice. Mathuin's crimes are ten times worse than Branoc's. A hundred times worse. Who's going to bring *him* to justice, unless I do?"

I've got nothing to say to this. Nothing that'll comfort her, nothing that's any use. Hate it when she's sad. Hate it when I can't help.

"Cass," she says, just over a whisper. "My man. Brennan, my baby. Burned, burned to ashes. Nothing in all the world can pay for what Mathuin did to them. Nothing."

I roll over and see she's sitting up now, with the blanket hugged around her. "A fire," I say.

"His men torched the house. I was down the other end of the settlement, tending to an old woman. I ran back, but I was too slow. By the time I got there it was well alight. I could hear them inside, oh gods, they were still alive, I could have saved them, I could . . . But Mathuin's guards had blocked the doors. They were stopping people from putting water on the fire. I tried to get in, I tried, but folk pulled me back. They didn't understand."

I wait a bit, then say, "You didn't want to go on without them. Better to die than live with the pain." Makes perfect sense to me.

"After a while the screaming stopped, and all I could hear was the fire. And Mathuin's guards laughing together, watching it burn."

"Why? Why would he do that?"

She grimaces. "Cass was a scribe. A scholar, but not the quiet kind. Outspoken. Someone wrote a letter listing a few of the injustices of Mathuin's rule. Suggesting it was time for a challenge. It went out to judges, lawmen, village elders, influential neighbors. Even to the High King. Word came to Mathuin that Cass had made the copies. This was his punishment."

Black Crow save us. "How old was your little boy?"

"Brennan was nearly two. He wanted to come with me that day, and I said no, stay home with your father, because the old woman had a wound full of ill humors and I didn't want my baby near it. If I'd taken him with me he'd still be alive. He'd be fourteen by now. Almost a man." Her voice is shaky. As for me, I've got tears in my eyes, big fellow that I am.

"He's with his dad," I say. "Waiting for you. Watching you, seeing how brave you are, what a fighter. Feeling proud."

"Don't tell me you believe that, Grim. That the dead live on, somehow."

I can't lie to her; I know she can see right through me. "I do sometimes. It helps. Hope, you know? Something to hold on to. What did you do, after?"

"There wasn't much left to bury," she says. "When it was done I picked up my healer's bag and walked away. Out of the village, out of Laois, as far as I could get. I was small fry to Mathuin. I doubt he even knew the troublesome scholar had a family. I went south. Had some dark years. Dreamed of them every night, my gentle Cass, my sweet Brennan, screaming in the flames. My baby calling out for his mama and wondering why she didn't come."

No point in saying it wasn't her doing. No point in telling her she couldn't have helped them any more than she could have put out today's fire all on her own. This is a burden she's carried a long time, and she won't ever be putting it down. "But you went back," I say. "Back to Laois and back to Mathuin."

"Fool that I am, yes, I went back. Heard from some travelers that he was still chieftain, the challenge hadn't happened, or hadn't succeeded. Heard he was still hurting folk, women in particular, and nobody was brave enough to stand up to him. You know what happened after that. I ended up in that place, with you to stare at through the bars. Hungry for justice. Eaten up with wanting that man to pay for what he did."

There's quiet for a bit, and then she says, "He didn't know. That I was Cass's wife. I came back to Laois with a different name, a different look, older, worn down. And I never went back to my home village. Never will. I can be brave sometimes, but I'm not brave enough for that." Another silence. "Makes me wonder if Mathuin had found out who I was. That day, I mean, when Slammer came to tell me I wasn't going to the council after all."

"Mm. Be risky to go back, then."

"Are you trying to tell me Conmael's in the right?"

"Nah. Don't care for the fellow. But he's not wrong either. If you went, you'd be a marked woman. Not much point in rushing back just to get yourself killed."

"I can't do it!" This bursts out of her; she's got her fists clenched and it sounds as if she's got her teeth clenched too. "Seven poxy years! I can't wait that long, I can't!" She bends forward and beats at her head with her fists, rocking back and forward.

"Blackthorn." I keep it quiet, low, like I'm talking to a creature that's had a fright. "You can. You can wait. You can be brave. I know you can." I can hear her breathing, quick and raspy, like she might cry again. "If he says seven years, maybe that's how long it needs to take. To put things right. To get things straight. What do you think?"

"I think I tell a rotten bedtime story," she says. "Your turn tomorrow night, and I'll be expecting a good one."

"Do my best." It's over, I hear it in her voice; she won't be talking about it anymore.

"Grim."

"Mm?"

"Never told anyone. Only you. Keep it to yourself, right?"

I'm stunned. Me. She told *me*. "Wouldn't tell a soul."

24

BLACKTHORN

Living in the smith's house drove me to distraction. If it hadn't been well into autumn I would have packed up and gone back out to the wood. The outhouse was still standing; Grim had slept in there when we first came, and I could have done the same. On the other hand, Grim found it hard to sleep if I wasn't close by, and the outhouse didn't have room for two.

I could have gone south, of course. Abandoned my promise to Conmael and headed off in pursuit of Mathuin. If I'd thought for a moment that the rage inside me was lessening with time, the fire at the cottage had proved me wrong. Telling my story had sharpened the pain and whipped up my urge for vengeance. But I wasn't entirely devoid of common sense. Soon it would be winter. It was a long way to Laois. Try it now and if I didn't end up dead, I'd probably find myself locked up in that cesspit again, and this time Conmael wouldn't come tapping on the door offering me a reprieve.

Besides, I wanted to be here when Branoc faced justice. And, like it or not, I was wise woman and healer to both Winterfalls and Silverlake. Ness would need me at least until she recovered from her physical injuries, and perhaps far longer, for the time of darkness and terror had marked her deep. Emer could help with that part of it. There was no doubting the healing power of a loyal friend. Whether that would be enough, only time would tell.

So I put up with living cheek by jowl with Fraoch's family. It was easier for Grim. If he wasn't over at the cottage rebuilding, which he was whenever the weather was dry enough, he was helping folk with other jobs, paying them back for the supplies they'd given us or the work they were doing at our place. Because this time he wasn't doing the fixing up all by himself. Folk wouldn't let him. Seemed we'd won respect for ourselves, goodwill, which was funny seeing as we were only at Winterfalls because of Conmael and his poxy agreement. We only saw Grim at the smith's to eat and sleep. As for the sleeping arrangements themselves, I cared little for what folk might think he and I were to each other. I told Fraoch's mother, Ornait, that one chamber was fine for the two of us, provided we had a bed each.

Instead of waiting for folk to come to me, I went out to tend to them. All the remedies I'd prepared since we came to the cottage, all the herbs I'd dried and ground and stored, all my equipment and materials had been destroyed in the fire. I walked out to the wood to gather what was in season. Ornait gave me a corner to work in and I made a small store of salves, lotions and tinctures. I tried to keep busy all day so I wouldn't have to talk to folk. Grim was a lot better at mingling with people than I was.

One person I could not avoid talking to was the king's man, Donagan. He rode down to Fraoch's one morning and asked for me. Ornait brought him into the kitchen, where I was wrist deep in the preparation of a poultice, and I had no choice but to be civil, especially as Ornait seemed to think his visit was an honor—she fetched a jug of her best mead, two cups, and a platter of barley bread, then took herself off and left me to it.

"I can't leave this in the middle," I said, glancing at Donagan, who had seated himself at the table as if quite at home. "If I stop mixing, I'll have to start again with fresh herbs, and supplies are limited right now."

"Go on, please." Donagan poured mead into the cups and pushed one in my general direction. "You seem to be managing well despite the setback, Mistress Blackthorn. In fact, that is why I've come to talk to you. There must have been a great deal of equipment lost in the fire, as well as all your personal things. If you can give me a list, Prince Oran will arrange to have the tools of your trade replaced at his expense. He considers your presence at Winterfalls an asset to the community. He believes the fire occurred because of a failing by that community. Therefore he will take responsibility for making good your losses."

I stared at him, fighting the urge to tell him no thanks, I didn't want help from princes and their like, and as for my losses, there would be no making those good, ever. I held back the words. "Sharp knives in different sizes. A bone saw. Some strong fine cord. A set of surgical instruments." I wondered where on earth they'd get those, then remembered there would be court physicians at Cahercorcan. "Everything else can be improvised without too much difficulty, though if there's a stillroom at court with a good store of dried herbs and spices, a few bags of the most essential items wouldn't go amiss. The healers there will know what they are. Some things, I won't be able to gather until spring or summer."

"I'll see to it," Donagan said. He drank his mead and watched me. "What about your personal belongings? Clothing, household goods and the like?"

"We didn't have much. Later on, when the cottage is fixed, we might need some bits and pieces." It was hard to think which would be more uncomfortable, being obliged to Prince Oran or to Conmael. Fey folk being what they were, quite likely a snap of the fingers would bring Conmael here; a second snap might furnish our little house with every comfort. A third might restore the garden Grim had made with such painstaking care. "We'll work to earn those things," I said.

A few days later a box came containing every item on my list. Nothing left out. And a few extra things put in: bags of herbs and powders, bottled oils and neatly labeled spice vials. I was forced to concede that Prince Oran might be a better man than others of his kind. Of course, this might be largely Donagan's doing.

The open council drew closer. We were expecting Emer back from Silverlake in time for it. She needed to stand up and tell her story, and so did I. When the prospect of being in the prince's hall among a big crowd of folk set my belly churning with unease, I reminded myself that Emer was fifteen years old, and that the very least I could do was stand by her and show her an example. We would see how just and fair Prince Oran was when really put to the test. I knew one thing: if he failed to dispense true justice where Branoc was concerned, Grim and I would be doing it for him.

The day of the council came. We joined a long line of people waiting to go into the prince's house. The main dwelling was a sprawling stone structure with a strange little tower. A spread of wattle-and-mud buildings surrounded it, and around all of this the wall was high; too high to admit casual entry. There were guards on the gate. We gave our names, then walked through with Emer between us. She was pale, I felt sick, and as for Grim, he was exchanging smiles and nods with one villager after another, almost as if he was enjoying himself. How could he be so calm? Didn't every single thing about this remind him of Laois, of Mathuin, of that place? I could smell the stink of it now, feel the cruel hands on my body, hear the screams of pain and the silence of utter humiliation.

"All right?" murmured Grim.

"No. But I'll cope." I had to, for Emer. And for Ness, whose voice we were today.

We were ushered into a grand hall, where benches were set ready for the hearing. The place filled up fast. Some folk I knew quite well—those who had made use of my services for themselves or their close kin—and some I knew a little. But many were complete strangers, for the council drew in people not only from Winterfalls and Silverlake, but from a much wider area that apparently lay under the prince's jurisdiction.

The place was so crowded, it looked as if some folk would need to stand at the back. I was about to suggest to Grim that we do so when Donagan called out from the dais at the front.

"Anyone who's going to get up and speak, down here in the front row! Let them through, please."

We moved forward—Grim was big enough to make a path through any crowd—and sat on the front bench. The place was full of chattering people. I tried to unclench my jaw, to relax my tight body, to turn my angry fists into polite, folded hands. Emer had her arms hugged around her under her shawl.

Close by us sat a group of well-dressed women, and among them I recognized some faces from that day at Dreamer's Wood, when the maid had drowned. Two of these had been among Lady Flidais's attendants who had come with her to my cottage: the kindly spoken one with dark hair, who nodded and smiled at me now, and beside her the gray-haired one. And there was the little dog that had bitten its mistress's hand. Not with Lady Flidais now, but curled up on the knee of a formidable-looking older woman in a fur-trimmed cape. This personage subjected me to a thorough scrutiny; I met her gaze with as much calm as I could summon. I wanted to go home. Not to Fraoch's, but to the cottage as it had been before the fire. Or, failing that, out into the woods to wander again. In this grand establishment I was like a crow among songbirds, shut in, out of place, dangerous.

There was a long table set crosswise on the dais, with a bench behind it. Donagan motioned to a serving man, who opened a door to one side. No trumpet fanfare, no bowing and scraping. Only a fellow with a loud voice, walking in and calling out, "Prince Oran of Dalriada, and Lady Flidais!"

Everyone stood up, so we did too, and Prince Oran and his modest entourage came in to take their places at the table. The official party consisted of the prince, the lady, who was clad in a flowing garment of soft blue with her hair covered by a veil, two men in long robes, and a stocky fellow of middle years, wearing a tunic that matched those of the prince's guards, deep green with an oak tree embroidered on the breast. Donagan placed himself at the far end of the table. An attendant trailed Lady Flidais: the tall waiting woman from that day at Dreamer's Wood. She stood behind her mistress. More guards had entered with them, but not as many as I would have expected. If I had things right, Oran was primary heir to the Dalriadan throne. It surprised me that he was prepared to let a crowd of folk like us come so close. I could have picked him off with a well-thrown knife before any of those guards could stop me.

"Welcome, all." Prince Oran spoke with firm authority, but there was a warmth in his tone as he looked out over the packed hall. Either he was well practiced at putting folk at ease, or he actually enjoyed mingling with his subjects. Of course, folk would know that the case against Branoc was to be heard at today's council; no wonder they'd come here in droves. "I am pleased to see so many of you here today. We have one particularly serious matter to deal with at this council, as I'm sure most of you know. And there are various other disputes to settle. I'm sure you will join me in welcoming Lady Flidais to her first open council." He glanced at his betrothed; she kept her eyes down. The lady didn't look comfortable. Perhaps they had argued. Perhaps she was missing home; regretting that she had agreed to wed sight unseen. Though she might have done worse. At least the prince was young and healthy. And some women liked that fine-boned, soft-mouthed type.

"Today we have with us two distinguished visitors," the prince went on, "men of the law who will provide expert advice. They will ensure that all parties are given adequate opportunity to present their arguments. Master Cael, Master Tassach, we welcome you." He nodded toward the robed men, who inclined their heads gravely. Sharp-featured Master Cael had something of the same look as that woman with the dog on her knee; both he and she, I suspected, were folk of acute intelligence. The other lawman, Master Tassach, was more portly in build, with a jovial manner. I wondered if he was one of those people who put folk off their guard by looking harmless, then pounced when they least expected. Lawmen could be like that.

"Aedan, we're ready to begin," the prince said, and seated himself. The chamber rustled as the rest of us did the same.

"Might be a long day," murmured Grim. "Sure you're all right?"

"Why wouldn't I be?" Stupid answer; there were a hundred reasons. "Emer, are you all right?"

"Mm."

The green-clad man—Aedan—called the crowd to order, and the noise died down. He called forward a pair of farmers; the prince spoke about a dispute over the placement of a drystone wall. It surprised me that he was able to outline the issue in such detail; I would have expected one of his underlings, Donagan or perhaps the steward, to perform that task. And the prince wasn't reading; he was speaking without reference to any documentation, though a scribe sat at a smaller table, making a record of the proceedings. The lawmen listened without comment.

There was some discussion. The two fellows set out their arguments, which had to do with rights-of-way and wandering cattle. My mind was wandering too, away from a matter that was of little interest to me and back to the past, where I didn't want it to go. A hearing in front of Mathuin, chieftain of Laois. My hands bound behind my back, as if they believed I might leap forward and strangle the man even with guards on either side of me. My gut churning with hate as I looked my enemy in the face and thought, *How can he not see the truth in my eyes? How can he not know that the day he killed my dear ones, he ripped out my heart?*

The prince was saying something about putting in another gate. Grim leaned forward, looking at me across Emer. His brows went up as if to ask again if I was all right. I managed a stiff nod. He may once have been known as Bonehead, but Grim was remarkably quick to notice things. It was a wisdom that had nothing to do with book learning, but came from much deeper down. It made me uncomfortable. It made me wish I hadn't told him my story.

The two farmers had agreed to what the prince proposed. They clasped hands, clapped each other on the shoulder, then returned to their seats. Aedan called up the next pair to be heard.

Another farmer—Brocc—gave an account of how three of his best breeding ewes had been attacked and mauled at dusk, only two days ago. He accused a neighbor—Cliona—of letting her dogs stray onto his fields. Cliona swore that her dogs were always kenneled before dusk, and that they could not have been responsible for the losses. It seemed nobody had actually seen the attack take place. Brocc had stumbled upon the dead and injured animals later.

"At what time did you find them?" asked the prince. "Later that night, or in the morning?"

"Same night, my lord. Heard barking, but by the time I got out there with a lantern, the dogs were gone. Had to slit one ewe's throat, put her out of her agony. Another was already dead. The third I've got in the barn, with a nasty wound to the foreleg." He glared at Cliona, who scowled back at him.

"Could not this attack have been carried out by animals from farther afield?" asked Master Tassach. "By wild dogs, perhaps, or even wolves?"

"It's her dogs," said Brocc, hands on hips. "Must be."

"Why are you so certain?" asked the prince.

"She's got those long-legged herding hounds. Sprinters. Jumpers. Over the wall in the blink of an eye. Besides, woman trying to farm on her own, stands to reason."

Prince Oran's eyes narrowed just a little. If I'd been Brocc I would have been starting to feel uneasy at this point. "What exactly stands to reason, Brocc?"

"Bound to be slipups, errors, things going wrong. Too much for a woman, keeping up a big place like that."

"That is opinion, not fact," said the prince, "and irrelevant to the matter in hand, though I know Niall thinks highly of Cliona's breeding stock; we've acquired some of her young ewes for our home farm, I believe." He glanced over at a tall man clad in the household colors, and the man gave a nod and a half smile. "Brocc, unfortunate as your losses are, without further evidence this cannot be proven one way or the other. I assume you are seeking compensation. On the basis of what we know to be fact, there are insufficient grounds for me to rule that Cliona should pay it."

I agreed with him. But I could see how a failure to resolve this type of petty dispute might lead to unrest in the district, with a continuing series of challenges and counterchallenges setting neighbor against neighbor.

"May I speak, Prince Oran?"

It was the richly dressed lady with the lap dog. She put the creature down and rose to her feet. Murmurs from the assembled crowd; this was as much of a surprise to them as it was to me.

"Please do, Lady Sochla." The prince looked toward the crowd. "My aunt is a renowned breeder of terriers, and something of an expert on canine behavior."

"You say this can't be proven one way or the other," said Lady Sochla. The prince's aunt; that made her a sister to the king or queen, and went a long way to explaining her authoritative manner. "But if the attack took place such a short time ago, and if you have the surviving ewe in your barn, Brocc, I believe it can be. Were the dead ewes butchered for the pot? What became of the skins?"

"I've got the skins, my lady," Brocc said. "But a bite's a bite. One big dog's the same as another. Makes no difference if it's a wolf or a herding dog."

"To you, perhaps not." Lady Sochla managed to convey that she thought him something of a fool. "Show me the skins, show me the injured ewe, and show me this lady's farm dogs, and I'll tell you if they did it. I can't help you any further if they didn't; I'm not planning to examine the teeth of every dog in the district and then start on the wolves." A ripple of laughter from the crowd. "But if her animals were responsible for the attack, I can confirm it. I've done this many times before."

A short silence. Cliona looked at Brocc; Brocc looked at Cliona.

"Haven't got time to mess about with all that," Brocc said. "I need compensation now. She should be made to pay up."

"Let's get this quite clear," said the prince. "Cliona, are you prepared to have Lady Sochla attend your farm and examine your dogs' teeth?"

"None of us has got spare time," said Cliona. "But if that's what it takes to prove this fool wrong, then yes." She hesitated. "Nobody likes to lose their stock; nobody likes to see a sheep mauled. It's a cruel way for them to go." She glanced at Lady Sochla. "Pity you can't find out whose dogs really did this," she said. "Seems to me, my lord, that what matters is making sure it doesn't happen again."

"Wisely spoken," said the prince. "I believe we have a choice. We can accept Lady Sochla's offer to examine the evidence and give us an answer. That would mean the matter could not be resolved today and any compensation would be determined at a later date, probably at the next council. It would also mean that, should Lady Sochla find that Cliona's dogs were not responsible, there would be no compensation payable unless the true culprits were discovered, and then only if their ownership was known." He drew breath; looked gravely at one party, then the other. "Or we can compromise in the interests of maintaining goodwill in the community. Cliona sells Brocc his first choice of her ewe lambs next season, at a fair price. Niall compensates him for the second sheep with one from our home farm, with no payment required. Brocc, in his turn, ensures his fine breeding animals are not left out overnight in a pasture with walls low enough to admit dogs, wolves or other predators. If you do not attend to that, Brocc, then you'll have no justification for bringing any further complaints of this kind to the council. I'll allow you a little time to think about this."

Lady Sochla resumed her seat. She picked up the lap dog and settled it on her knee again. I found myself impressed by her forthright manner; it seemed that in her case, at least, power and privilege had not got in the way of common sense. As for the prince's judgment, it was not at all what I had expected, and made me wonder if he knew something about this case that he was not making public. Had that last part meant Brocc had a history of bringing complaints? Perhaps an ongoing resentment toward this female neighbor who, for all his derogatory remarks, sounded to be doing quite well as a sheep farmer?

I imagined Mathuin of Laois confronted with the same issue. He'd have found Cliona guilty at the drop of a hat, made her pay, and laughed her out of the council while he was doing so. Or done to her what he had done to me.

The parties had conferred; the buzz in the hall died down as the steward gestured for quiet.

"Cliona?" asked the prince.

"I'm happy to go either way, my lord," she said. "But I'm busy. We all are. Easier to sell him a lamb than check the skins and the teeth and all. And save the lady a lot of bother. Though I wouldn't mind seeing how she does it."

"Brocc?"

"The ewe from your home farm, my lord—you talking about a breeder for this season, or a spring lamb?"

"Whichever you prefer, Brocc. It is a generous offer; do not undervalue it."

"No, my lord." Brocc scratched his head; shuffled his feet a little. "I'll accept the compromise, my lord." He shot a glance at Cliona. "But I want her dogs kept in. I don't want them coming onto—"

"Enough." The prince's tone, quiet as it was, silenced the complaint instantly. "You accept the compromise, and with that you cease this kind of talk. Cliona has told us her dogs are kenneled by dusk, and she'll make sure that is so. You've agreed to improve your sheepfold, and you will do it as soon as possible. You're being compensated to an extent. And we've saved my aunt some work, though I, too, confess that I would have found it interesting to observe your method, Lady Sochla." He smiled at the lady. "Very well, this matter is concluded; Niall will speak to you about the ewe, Brocc. Aedan, what's next?"

More disputes were heard, grievances aired, points of law clarified by the visiting experts. And then, at last, Aedan directed the guards to bring out Branoc the baker.

The prisoner was haggard, with a stubbly growth of dark beard. There were colorful bruises on his neck, legacy of his not-so-gentle capture in the woods. If I had not managed to drag myself out of my nightmare that day and go after Grim, he would have killed Branoc with his bare hands. He'd wanted to, that was plain. The irony of it was, I'd run after him thinking to support and protect him. I hadn't thought I'd need to stop him from committing murder.

Branoc cast the three of us a glance; his eyes lingered on Emer, and I heard her draw in a breath. The baker had a burly guard on either side, and his wrists were shackled. He wouldn't be going far.

"This is a very serious matter," Prince Oran said, "and already well-known to the communities of both Silverlake and Winterfalls, I'm told. I remind all parties that today's hearing is of the facts, not the gossip and rumor surrounding them. I have studied all the information to hand, and so have our two learned friends, Master Tassach and Master

Cael. Master Cael's role will be to interpret this in terms of the law and to ensure our proceedings and our judgment comply with that law in every respect. Master Tassach has discussed the matter in question with Branoc and has advised the accused of his rights. He will, as required by law, speak in Branoc's defense."

A rumble of protest from the crowd indicated what they thought of this. Donagan lifted a hand and the noise died down.

"I will judge with fairness and impartiality, taking all the facts into consideration," Prince Oran said. "This is a complex case, and if any element of it cannot be resolved today, it will be held over to the next council."

Get on with it, I thought, though in fact this kind of preamble was usual in a council; even Mathuin had expressed worthy intentions before he condemned both the guilty and the innocent to his wretched piss hole of a lockup. Emer was shivering. I took her hand again.

"Master Cael, will you read out the charges against Branoc?"

Master Cael stood up. He was not a tall man, but he had an air of calm authority that told me he had been presiding over proceedings like this for years. "Branoc, you are charged with the following: That on or around the day on which Ernan, the miller from Silverlake, died of a head injury at his mill, you abducted Ernan's daughter Ness, aged sixteen, and imprisoned her in your barn. There you subjected her to various indignities, including beatings and worse, while concealing her presence from the entire community. In addition, you are charged with setting fire to a cottage at Dreamer's Wood, the residence of Mistress Blackthorn, the healer."

Branoc attempted a toss of the head, as if to say, *rubbish*. One of the guards cuffed him on the ear.

"And further, you are under suspicion for the murder of Ernan the miller, whose death was assumed at the time to be accidental. The circumstances of Ernan's demise are still under investigation, and that matter will be not be heard today." Master Cael looked up from the document. His gaze was level; his expression was expertly guarded. "Branoc, if you are guilty of these crimes, you should admit it now and spare witnesses the need to revisit these disturbing events."

Did I detect a sigh of disappointment from the crowd? To folk who did not know Ness well, or who did not realize what it would cost Emer to speak up today, this might seem like good entertainment. A story full of drama, and none of it quite real.

"Admit to crimes I did not commit? Why would I do such a thing? It is lies. Nothing but lies." Branoc was all defiance. He squared his shoulders, and a grimace of pain passed over his features. That day at his house I had felt the knotted muscles, tightened by repeated kneading and stirring. When he'd had me in his grip, I'd aimed my head right for the spot where it would hurt him most.

"Branoc does not wish to make a confession," said Master Tassach calmly. "The evidence, such as it is, should be heard in full. It is possible, otherwise, that statements may be accepted that are mere hearsay or outright untruths."

"Very well," said Master Cael, "we will proceed with statements from the witnesses. Branoc, be seated."

The guards took Branoc to a bench and he sat, with a man on either side. Master Cael looked toward the three of us.

"Mistress Blackthorn, we will hear your account first. Step forward, please."

You are not in Laois now. This is not Mathuin. Do this for Ness. Do it for all those women who had no voice.

"Mistress Blackthorn?"

I stood up. Stepped forward. Cleared my throat and found my voice. "Some time ago, Emer here told me a story that may be familiar to you. Her friend Ness had disappeared, and it was generally believed that she had run away to be with her sweetheart, one of the travelers. Folk also said Ness had stolen her father's life savings.

"The night Ness vanished, her father, the miller Ernan from Silverlake, was killed in what appeared to be a freak accident, crushed by his own grindstone. Folk said he was careless because of his grief over what his daughter had done. Emer told me she couldn't believe that version of events. She knew her friend well. She said Ness was loyal to her father and would never leave home without his blessing."

Emer, snow-pale, gave me an encouraging nod. Grim had his gaze fixed on me; he managed a little smile.

"Some time later, Grim found a kerchief on the cart he had used to deliver a load of flour to Branoc's premises. He thought it was mine—it is very similar to one I own—and made nothing of it. But eventually we noticed there were two kerchiefs in our house where there had been only one, and that one of them bore an embroidered inscription: *A loves N*. It was a lover's token. Such items can be purchased at the travelers' markets."

I took the two red kerchiefs out of my pouch and walked over to the table to lay them before the prince.

"It came out, then," I said, "that on the day when Grim had delivered the load of flour, he had heard noises from Branoc's barn, from up in the loft. Perhaps Grim should tell the next part of this story."

"Lies!" shouted Branoc, struggling to rise. His guards shoved him back down. "It's all lies! These folk are nothing but meddlers!"

"Be silent," said Prince Oran. "In due course you will be given an opportunity to respond to these statements, or Master Tassach will do so on your behalf. Any further interruptions, and you will be removed immediately from this hall. If that occurs, you will lose your chance to hear the evidence against you. Do I make myself clear?"

Branoc grumbled something that might have been, "Yes, my lord."

"Grim, we'll hear from you," said Master Cael. "Tell us what happened that day at Branoc's barn."

Grim rose to his feet. He had his hands clasped together in front of him; perhaps only I knew that this was to prevent the shaking from being visible. He, too, had had his day in front of Mathuin; his time of humiliation and despair. "Heard a sort of shuffling up in the loft," he said. "Made a joke about rats, saying I'd bring Branoc a cat along with his flour next time. He didn't like that at all, got snappy with me. And he didn't want me carrying the bags up there, though it would have saved him a lot of work.

Loft looked the right place to store the flour; downstairs
was a bit damp."

"It wasn't until much later that we put the pieces together,"
I said. "It seemed possible the kerchief might have been
dropped down onto the cart from Branoc's loft, through a
crack in the floor or between the shutters. Once we thought of
that, it all seemed to fit, in a way that troubled me. The kerchief, very likely a gift from a traveler boy to his sweetheart. *A
loves N.* Then there were the noises up in the loft and Branoc
getting annoyed with Grim for mentioning them. Branoc not
wanting Grim to go up there. He even took the ladder away."

"This pointed to a possible abduction," Prince Oran
said. "But you chose not to bring it to me."

I wanted to tell him I had no cause to trust princes and the
like, especially where the plight of abused women was concerned. But that argument wasn't going to help anyone. "I suspected Branoc might have a prisoner up there," I said, keeping
my gaze on the calm features of the prince and the wise ones
of the two lawmen, and telling myself that perhaps not all
men in positions of authority were like Mathuin. "But there
was not enough evidence to bring it to your attention, my
lord, or to anyone's. I believed, rightly or wrongly, that you
might dismiss my concerns as being without foundation.
Emer had told folk in both Winterfalls and Silverlake that
Ness wouldn't have run away, and nobody had believed her.
The evidence was flimsy; there was no proof the kerchief
came from Branoc's. Nor did I know, then, the name of Ness's
sweetheart. We might have made a big fuss, all for nothing.

"But we knew that if we were right, that young girl must
be suffering unspeakable misery. We weren't going to leave
her in that loft any longer than we had to. So we went
straight over there to find out for ourselves."

The audience was hanging on our words now; I felt a
hunger in the hall that was quite disturbing. I wanted to
elbow my way out and take my companions with me, leaving the community to deal with Branoc. But I could not do
that. I hadn't had much justice in the past. At least today I
could help deliver justice for Ness.

"Grim?" said the prince.

Grim gave an account of our visit to the bakery and how

he had found Ness in the loft and rescued her. I told my side of that day's story—how I'd used Branoc's sore shoulders as an excuse to keep him out of the way while Grim rescued Ness; Branoc's fury when he realized his captive had been freed; his assault on me and his escape.

"Ness's injuries are very serious," I said. Just how serious, most of these folk could scarcely imagine; Ness had been lucky to survive. She would never be as she had been: a good daughter who had kept house for her widowed father, a lively young woman who had loved to go dancing. "I can provide you with further details, my lord, but I will not do so publicly. I am a healer. I confirm that Ness was beaten, abused and robbed of her innocence while kept prisoner. Denied the basic comforts of life. Kept compliant with threats. Ness's physical wounds will mend in time. But there are deeper hurts that may never heal. I remind you that she is just sixteen years old."

There, I had said what had to be said. And the crowd was utterly silent.

"Thank you, Mistress Blackthorn," said the prince. "This is indeed a disturbing matter, and one for which the entire community bears some responsibility. Regarding Ness's injuries, I accept your word. I agree that the details should not be made public. Master Cael? Master Tassach?"

Master Tassach gave a nod. "If the information comes under dispute," he said, "I will speak to Mistress Blackthorn in private."

"Acceptable," said Master Cael, giving his colleague a sideways glance, "though unlikely to be required, I believe. To return to the day of the rescue, Grim—you attempted to apprehend Branoc?"

"Too quick for me," Grim said. "Bolted into the woods. Couldn't go after him. Needed two of us to get the girl safely down to Silverlake. She couldn't walk."

"I stayed with Ness overnight," I said. "I tended to her as best I could and made sure she'd be properly looked after. As you know, she is still too frail to be moved. But she told us her story: that Branoc abducted her, and that he kept her in the loft for the whole time she was missing. His acts of violence were the cause of all her injuries. On the rare occasions when there were visitors to Branoc's premises, Ness was too frightened to call for help; he'd threatened to harm her father if she did. She did not know Ernan was already dead. She hardly dared do what she did with the kerchief. She knew her captor would punish her if he found out."

I saw Branoc gathering himself to leap up and protest again, but Master Tassach gave him a long, steady look and he seemed to think better of it. Just as well. If justice was to be served here, that included letting him hear the proceedings in full.

"Came back here the next morning, told Emer what had happened, then reported to you, my lord," said Grim.

"And went home to find your house on fire."

It came flooding back, robbing me of words, stealing even the ability to think. Filling my mind with images of death. Filling my ears with my baby's screams and the roar of the flames.

Grim moved past Emer to put an arm around my shoulders. He was talking, telling the rest of the story. Holding me up. Doing the job for me. I tried to breathe. I fought to get out of the fire.

"Managed to grab him this time," Grim said. "Then folk came to help. That's about it. Didn't see Branoc start the blaze. But it couldn't have started on its own. We'd been gone overnight. Hearth fire would have been cold long before then."

Dimly, I was aware that a lot of folk were looking at me, the prince, Lady Flidais and the two lawmen included. The prince said something, but the crackling of the flames drowned his words. Then Grim was steering me back to the bench, sitting me down. Someone brought me a cup of water. I took a gulp, wiped my mouth, felt tears rolling down my cheeks.

"It's all right," whispered Emer, putting a handkerchief in my hand. "It's all right, Mistress Blackthorn."

A pox on it! I wanted to stand strong. I wanted to be a voice for truth, not some weeping, wilting apology for a woman. "I'm fine," I said, dashing away the tears. "Nothing wrong with me."

"Mistress Blackthorn, I don't believe we need trouble you any further." It was Prince Oran speaking. "We accept your word and Grim's. We understand that Ness cannot speak for herself at this council, but there can be no doubt that Branoc is responsible for what happened to her. The fire is a different matter, with responsibility not yet proven. However, grave suspicion rests on Branoc, whom we would have expected to leave the district after Ness was freed. Why would he be close by your cottage only one day after his captive was rescued, when Grim had made it quite clear he meant to apprehend him and bring him to justice? That is a question we will shortly put to Branoc himself."

The prince smiled at me; Master Cael gave me a nod. Master Tassach was making notes on his parchment. "Before we move on to Branoc's account," said Master Cael, "does anyone wish to provide further information, particularly in the matter of the fire at Blackthorn's cottage? Are there any questions in relation to the statements we have heard? Keep your comments relevant. As the prince said earlier, we cannot take heed of opinion, only fact."

The crowd murmured and whispered among themselves. But it was Lady Flidais who spoke out, startling me. I had not expected her to contribute to the council; I'd assumed she was present only because of custom. "My lord, what happened to the young woman is quite shocking. It seems she has indeed been wronged. But every case has two sides to it. Surely we must give some weight to the girl's character; to what she was before she caught the baker's eye. Was she a young woman of high morals, pure and untouched? Or was the reluctance of the community to believe her friend's story based, at least partly, on folk's knowledge that Ness already had a sweetheart, and that he was one of the traveling folk? A girl who favors that feckless sort of man is surely setting herself up for trouble."

I was on my feet in an instant. "That's offensive! And it's completely irrelevant! Are you saying that if a woman has lain with her sweetheart before they are wed, that makes her fair game for any oaf who decides to lock her up in his barn and use her as a toy for his pleasure?"

Lady Flidais turned a chilly gaze on me. "The baker is entitled to a defense," she said. "Perhaps the girl encouraged him. Flirted a little; made suggestions. Women do."

Master Tassach was about to say something, but I got in

first, whirling to face the crowd. "This community has already done Ness a gross injustice! Is her character now to be questioned in a public forum when she is not present to defend herself? There's no excuse for what Branoc did to her! It makes no difference what kind of girl she is, or what she may or may not have done before. He hurt her. He imprisoned her. He terrified her. She's sixteen years old." I gazed across the sea of faces, dimly aware that I must be breaking all sorts of rules, but not caring in the least. "Ness is not the accused here," I said. "She's the victim."

I faltered. Had I lost control so badly that I was seeing things now? Down at the back of the hall, a pale man in a cloak was standing very still, watching me with a little half smile on his aristocratic features. Conmael. A man of the fey right here in Prince Oran's house, among all these human folk. Why weren't the people around him looking more surprised? The fey appeared so rarely these days that most folk believed them creatures of story, something from the ancient past. It was only in certain pockets of the land that they were sometimes seen; and even then, folk invented tales to explain them away, as if the truth was too hard. I could make no sense of Conmael's being here.

"I'll answer your question, Lady Flidais."

A firm young voice spoke from beside me; Emer was on her feet. I turned and seated myself again, wishing I could slow my heart.

"I am Ness's closest friend," she went on. "If anyone can speak for her, I can."

"Thank you, Emer," said Prince Oran. "Please proceed." His cheeks were flushed, as if he were in danger of losing the calm control with which he had thus far handled the proceedings. But his tone was warm and reassuring.

"It's true that Ness had—has—a sweetheart. Abhan, a horse trader, one of the traveling folk. They see each other when the travelers come north, once a year. They've been fond of each other since Ness was only thirteen, but because her father needed her at home, she told Abhan she couldn't marry him, at least not for a few years. There was nobody else to look after the house, to make sure her father ate properly, to keep him company. Abhan said he'd wait for her. My lord, Ness is a good girl. She and Abhan have never . . .

they've never lain together." Emer's face had gone fiery red, but her voice was steady. She should not have been required to say this; I hoped wretched Lady Flidais was satisfied now.

It seemed she was not. "Forgive me," the lady said, raising her brows at Emer, "but would a girl of sixteen confide such a matter even to her dearest friend? Especially if her father believed her a good and dutiful daughter?"

I opened my mouth to protest, but Emer went on steadily. "I know my friend better than anyone, Lady Flidais. She would not lie to me. She would not lie to her father. She would not run away from home, and she would not steal her father's savings. Ness is a good girl, a loyal daughter. And her sweetheart, Abhan, is a good man. He wouldn't have risked getting Ness with child before they were wed. Ernan liked him; he'd told Ness that when she was eighteen he'd give her permission to marry Abhan and go off with the travelers. Branoc knew that. Ness's father had told him she was promised to another man."

"Ernan told Branoc this?" Master Tassach's gaze had sharpened. It seemed that in their discussions prior to the council Branoc had neglected to share this significant detail.

"She's lying!" the baker shouted. "He said no such thing! The girl was always meant for me!"

"Be silent!" ordered the prince, startling me with the strength of his voice. He turned to the lawmen. "Master Cael, Master Tassach, do we need to hear anything further from the young lady?"

"I think not," said Master Cael. "Emer, please be seated. Thank you for speaking with courage and clarity. I, for one, am in no doubt as to the veracity of your statement."

"This council allows every man the opportunity to speak for himself," Prince Oran said. "Even those accused of the basest acts, the most abhorrent crimes. Branoc, you have heard the testimony of these three folk in the matter of the abduction and imprisonment of Ness, daughter of Ernan. The evidence is damning; Grim found her shackled and hurt on your premises, and Ness has told Mistress Blackthorn that you were responsible. Unless you can give a convincing explanation for your presence at Mistress Blackthorn's cottage at the time of the fire, it seems almost certain you carried out that burning in retaliation for the rescue of your captive. You are also under grave suspicion in the matter of Ernan's death. When you were apprehended after the fire, you had on your person one hundred silver pieces." A gasp from the crowd. It was a sum beyond most folk's wildest dreams, mine included. He must have slipped back to the bakery and retrieved it while Grim and I were taking Ness down to the village. Or perhaps he'd had it hidden out in the woods. "That suggests, at the very least, that you planned a rapid departure from the district. It adds weight to the possibility that you stole Ernan's savings. Now is your opportunity to speak in your own defense on all these matters. Or you may prefer Master Tassach to speak on your behalf. What have you to say?"

"What does it matter?" growled the baker. "I speak, the lawman speaks, there is no difference. No point in it. You already determine me guilty, all of you! You make up your minds on the word of a crazed witch, a half-witted thug and a child!"

Master Tassach opened his mouth to speak, then closed it again. He looked deeply uncomfortable. I felt Grim's tension even though Emer sat between us. He was on the edge of the bench, like a weapon drawn and ready to strike.

"A child the same age as the one you abducted and abused," said Master Cael in a voice no less terrible for its softness.

"So they say." Branoc glared at the three of us. "That woman, the witch, she is full of anger at men. Bitter in her rage, since she is shriveled and plain, and the only man she can get for herself is that addle-brained lump! Does it surprise you that she accuses me of these crimes? A woman like this, she is eaten up with jealousy!"

Donagan was on his feet, and so was Aedan; there was a rumble of protest from the crowd. But Prince Oran motioned to the other men to sit, and gestured to the guards to let Branoc continue. Which was odd, I thought, considering that not so long ago he had threatened to have the baker thrown out of the hall. Unease gripped me, something that went beyond the sting of Branoc's insults. I had heard worse before; I had suffered blows far deeper. What troubled me was the prince's choice to let this man spew forth his hatred for all to hear. Had I been foolish to believe, even for a moment, that this hearing would result in justice? Had Ness's voice after all not been heard?

". . . always meant for me," Branoc's rant continued. "Ernan gave me his word. He told me I could have her. And Ness, she wanted me from the first. It was there in the way she looked at me. A blind man could have seen it. This talk of a sweetheart, a lover to whom she was promised, it is all lies. When this oaf came to my house, when he laid his clumsy hands on her, I told him, *She is my wife*. But he took no heed. He stole her away."

"Explain to this gathering," Prince Oran said, "why it is that a young woman whom you say returned your affections found herself shackled and imprisoned in your barn. If her father promised her to you, as you say, and if she was willing to marry you, why were the two of you not hand-fasted? Why was not this relationship known to everyone in Silverlake?"

"He broke his word." There was a darkness in Branoc's face, as if he carried a storm within him, a consuming fury. I knew how that felt.

"You're referring to Ernan?" The prince was maintaining his calm composure.

"The wretched miller, yes. He told me I had misunderstood. He told me his daughter would not wed until she was eighteen years old. Eighteen! Two whole years. Why should any man have to wait so long? Ness was a grown woman. She was more than ready for the marriage bed."

The hush was profound. It was full of things not quite spoken, perilous things that could unbalance this entirely. Emer had her teeth sunk in her lip. Grim's hands were furious fists; his cheeks wore spots of angry red.

"Branoc," said Prince Oran softly, and I was put in mind of a creature stalking its prey, step by careful step. It seemed there was method in his decision to let the baker speak freely. "Am I right in thinking Ernan promised you could marry his daughter in two years' time? And that Ness herself agreed to that arrangement?"

"Of course she didn't—" burst out Emer, to be hushed by the prince's raised hand.

"She was mine," Branoc repeated. "My wife."

"You told her so, I imagine," said Prince Oran. The scribe was writing furiously. I hoped he was keeping a true record of the conversation. I hoped the facts would not be twisted and turned to suit a particular purpose, as was common in Mathuin's hearings. "When her father was gone, I mean."

"She knew what was to be," Branoc said. "She knew what was right."

"Then why the shackles? Why had Ness been beaten?"

Branoc's gaze went one way, the other way. He was wondering, perhaps, if there was any point in denying responsibility outright. "Ah, women," he said with a shrug. "There is no understanding them. Ness and I, we liked to play games. She would make a pretense of resisting. I would be forceful; women enjoy that. Perhaps, once or twice, our play went a little far, but I did not beat Ness, my lord. Why would I do such a thing? I love her. She is my wife. A bruise or two, that is all part of learning. Besides, she is a creature of volatile moods, like many young women of her age. Time and experience will calm her."

I thought I might be sick on the floor of Prince Oran's hall.

"You vile scum!" shouted Grim, and before I could stop him he had charged across the chamber and put his big hands around the baker's throat. It was the fire again, and the nightmare, and the way he had gone into the wood with death in his eyes. Only this time there were guards everywhere, and they pulled him away before he could kill the wretch. It took five of them, and by the time they hauled him off everyone was shouting. And above all the hubbub, now, came Branoc's voice as he was released from Grim's grip.

"You pox-ridden cur, you stinking mongrel! More pity that you were not in the house when I burned it, you and the witch! Until you came here all was as it should be! I should have fried the two of you to cinders and rid the place of your accursed presence!"

Everyone heard it, and the noise died down in an instant. But Grim was still fighting; the guards had his arms pinioned behind his back. The look on his face told me only part of him was there, and the rest was somewhere else, perhaps in Mathuin's hall, perhaps in a time before that, when something had set scars on him as deep as Ness's.

"Take him out," the steward said to the men who were holding him.

Out where? Was he to be charged with unruly behavior, attempted assault? Locked up in some dank cell? It would destroy him.

"My lord," I said, "we are here to see justice done. I know Grim regrets his loss of self-control. If you will ask your guards to release him, I will give my word that such an outburst will not happen again. It has not been easy for either of us to be here today. We came for Ness's sake, and for Emer's. My lord, we need to witness the proceedings right to the end." I swallowed, then added, "Please, Prince Oran."

The prince looked somewhat startled, as well he might be. "It is not your word I require, Mistress Blackthorn," he said, "but Grim's. Grim, I understand the desire to take things into your own hands; to dispense summary justice. But that is not the way we conduct matters at Winterfalls. The open council provides a forum for grievances to be heard and settled; it provides everyone with the opportunity to express an opinion. Everyone. That extends even to a person accused of a heinous crime. Do you understand?"

Grim drew a ragged breath. "Yes, my lord." His voice was the growl of a hunting hound straining against the leash.

"Curb your anger; it does not serve you well. Guards, release him. Grim, this is your only warning. Next time you will be removed from the hall."

Grim did not look in the least contrite, but the guards let him go, and he came back to sit by me. He put his elbows on his knees and turned his gaze on the floor. I did not think he was ashamed of his outburst. I guessed he was keeping his eyes off Branoc, lest the desire to throttle the man became too much for him.

"Branoc, I believe we just heard you confess to lighting the fire," said the prince levelly. "Is this so?"

"You call it lighting a fire, my lord." Branoc spread his hands and shrugged. "I call it ridding the community of a danger. This man, you see his anger, you see how he charges like a mad bull, heedless of the damage he does. This woman is a witch, a meddler, a bringer of trouble. If they can steal my wife, they can steal yours. If they can enter my home uninvited and trick me, they can do the same to each of you. They are a blight, a pox, a constant danger. Better that they had burned."

There was a silence. Prince Oran gazed at Branoc, his expression one of stunned disbelief. Master Cael's sharp features were tight with offense. Master Tassach looked as if he'd swallowed something unpleasant. My own belly churned with disgust; my gorge rose. I willed myself to be calm. I had pleaded that we be allowed to stay until the end, and stay we would.

"Is that the end of your statement?" the prince asked. "You wish, perhaps, to speak on the matter of Ernan's death as well?"

But Branoc was done. "No, my lord," he muttered. Perhaps he had realized at last that Oran was not some jumped-up princeling but a person of real authority.

"Master Tassach, do you have anything to add in Branoc's defense?"

"No, my lord. I believe Branoc has been offered a fair hearing. It was his choice to speak on his own behalf. You might consider, on determining what is to unfold, that this is a highly skilled craftsman with a great deal to offer the community, and that prior to the events in question his abilities were much valued."

"Thank you, Master Tassach," said Oran, rising to his feet. The crowd rose with him. "I will retire to consider the matter. Aedan?"

Aedan addressed the assembled folk. "Refreshments are served in the courtyard. Please leave the hall in an orderly manner and return promptly when we ring the bell."

The prince and his party filed out. The hall emptied quickly; there was nothing like the prospect of food and drink to get folk moving. I turned my head to see if Conmael was still there but could catch no sight of him.

Fraoch came over to fetch Emer. "Coming?" he asked Grim and me.

Standing in the middle of that throng, with everyone talking nonstop about Branoc and Ness and the fire, would be a kind of torture.

"In a while," Grim said. "Need a bit of quiet first."

The smith nodded; he was getting used to us, since we

had been staying in his house. He put his arm around his sister and shepherded her out of the hall. I heard him say, "I'm proud of you."

The place was empty but for a guard on each door, and the two of us.

"You know what I want more than anything?" I said.

"I could guess."

"I'd like to be out in the woods somewhere, sitting by a little fire, with the moon shining down and only the night birds for company. Somewhere far, far away from folk. Somewhere I can forget what wretched, flawed creatures men and women can be."

Grim nodded. "Not all of them, though," he said.

"Enough of them to make me want to turn my back on Winterfalls and any other poxy village Conmael thinks I should live in." Grim was right, of course; there was Emer. There was that lady, the prince's aunt, who had intervened so wisely in the matter of the mauled sheep. I might even add Prince Oran to the list, provided he brought this to the right conclusion.

"Living at Fraoch's getting to you, is it?"

"You know it is."

"Soon as I've got the thatch on we can move back."

"And how long will that take? It'll soon be winter; you can't thatch in the rain. We might find ourselves at the smith's until next spring." Impossible. I would go mad. Even madder than I'd been just now when I'd jumped up and shouted at the lot of them.

"Outhouse is still standing. I could plug a few cracks, make it cozier." A long pause. "Bit small, though. For the two of us."

I attempted a smile. "Don't think I haven't already considered that. Make it cozy? That'd be a miracle beyond even you. Sorry I sent you out there to sleep, back then. I was selfish."

"Nah," said Grim. "Just prickly, like a hedgehog. You want a drink? A bite to eat? I'll fetch it."

I shook my head. "You go, get yourself something. I'm best on my own."

"He was here, you know," Grim said. "Conmael. Up the

back, sticking out like a snaggly tooth. Thought I was seeing things."

"I saw him. But I'm wondering if we were the only ones
who could. Otherwise people would have been pointing
and whispering. The fey don't wander about as if they were
just like everyone else. I'd guess most of these folk have
never seen Conmael's kind."

"Funny. Why would the fellow be here?"

I did not get the chance to answer, because a door
opened and the prince's man, Donagan, came back into the
hall.

"Blackthorn, Grim, come with me, please. Prince Oran
needs to speak with you."

What was this? We got up and followed him out of the
hall, down a passageway and into the chamber where we'd
told the prince the story of Ness's rescue. Inside, Prince
Oran and the two lawmen were seated at the table. No sign
of Lady Flidais or the steward. The prince bade Grim and
me sit down. Donagan took a place on the bench beside us.
He poured us each a cup of ale and passed along a platter
of oatcakes. A guard closed the door. I fought back memories of Mathuin's council, Mathuin's judgment, Mathuin's
punishment.

"Thank you," the prince said. "We find ourselves with
something of a dilemma, Mistress Blackthorn. The three of
us are in agreement as to Branoc's guilt in the matter of
Ness's abduction and abuse, and also in the matter of the
fire at your cottage, since we heard him confess to that act
of destruction. But we're having some difficulty in determining an appropriate penalty for his offenses."

"I do not know how far your understanding of the law
stretches," Master Cael said, looking from me to Grim and
back again.

"Not far," I said, though that was not entirely true. One
way or another, over the years I had picked up a fair bit of
knowledge.

"There are various penalties Prince Oran could impose," said Master Cael. "A fine, payable by the perpetrator
to the blood kin of the victim. The level of fine to be determined in part by the severity of the offense and in part by

the capacity of the offender's family to pay. A period of exile. A period of incarceration."

"Too good for him," said Grim. "A fellow who'd do that to a girl—he doesn't deserve to live."

The prince spoke with a certain sympathy. "I understand your anger, Grim. In some places, such a matter might be left to the kin of the two families to settle between them, whether by payment of a fine such as those I mentioned, or by some kind of physical punishment. Or, indeed, where the offender cannot or will not pay, by summary execution. I don't refer to an execution carried out by the local authority, you understand, but something . . . unofficial." His eyes were on Grim.

"But you can't do that," I said, "because Ness has no family. Nobody to make sure the man who wronged her cannot go out and do the same to another young woman, and another after her." Mathuin all over again.

"I'm not in favor of the community taking the law into its own hands," said the prince. "In the long run, that does not serve justice well. It can give rise to feuds that last for generations; festering resentment that lies on a place like a sickness. But yes, there is a certain difficulty here, and it is the lack of family support for Ness who, I understand, had only her father."

"You sure you don't want it dealt with quietly, my lord?" Grim's voice was dark. "Blackthorn and me and young Emer, we came here for Ness, to speak up for her, since there was nobody else. What kinsfolk would do for her, we'll do. Just say the word."

The prince gave a crooked smile. "Let Branoc out, and you'll make sure that before he gets farther than Dreamer's Wood he'll be dead and buried? I think not. That would rest ill on my conscience, and perhaps on yours, in time. We must make a wiser choice."

The two of us sat there staring at him, not saying a word. What was he getting at? How could there be a wiser choice than making sure that vile creature never set his hands on another innocent young girl again?

Master Tassach spoke up. "In the matter of the fire, it is for you to recommend the penalty, since that offense was against the two of you. If you stand in place of Ness's kinsfolk, then you also have a part to play in deciding the punishment for Branoc's crimes against her."

"Execution," said Grim. "Official execution."

"Reparations," I said, my mind on the hundred silver pieces that had been mentioned. "A fine, large enough to allow Ness to build her life again. I do not know if Branoc owned the bakery, but if he did, it could be sold. The mill too. And ..."

"And her father's money should be given back to her," said Prince Oran. "I agree on all those points, save for execution. Cannot even a man capable of such base acts learn to mend his ways?"

He meant he'd throw the offender into the lockup and leave him there to muse over his crimes as he moldered away and went half crazy. Like Strangler and Frog Spawn and the others. Like us.

I must have turned white, for suddenly all eyes were on me, and everyone looked concerned. Donagan put a hand on my arm.

"Mistress Blackthorn, are you unwell?"

Gods! This was a choice to make anyone sick. It was a dilemma to test the wisest of sages. Branoc had performed acts of great evil—all the more heinous because he did not seem to understand they were wrong. He had shown himself to be without a conscience. But how could I condemn him—how could I condemn anyone—to incarceration in a place like Mathuin's lockup? Yet if I did not agree to imprisonment, and Prince Oran would not countenance execution, did that mean Branoc's only punishment would be the payment of a fine? That would leave him free to molest more young women, to wreck more innocent lives. He'd head away to another region, establish his bakery anew, and go straight back to his hideous ways. We could not let that happen.

"Mistress Blackthorn?"

"Give her some time!" snarled Grim, who was doubtless having the same problem I was. It was a pity Prince Oran did not fancy the idea of unofficial execution. In Branoc's case, that solution seemed to me both tidy and just.

I must pull myself together; I must not become that woman who had collapsed and wept out there in front of the whole community. I straightened my shoulders and took a few deep breaths. "Master Cael, Master Tassach," I said, "under the law, are those the only options? Incarceration or a fine, or perhaps both?"

"And if it's incarceration," said Grim, "where would you be locking him up?"

"Not here at Winterfalls," Prince Oran said. "I don't have the facilities to hold a prisoner securely for longer than a few days, and I don't plan to change that. He'd have to go to Cahercorcan."

He didn't say whether the prison there was dank and filthy and cruel, and we didn't ask.

"As for the other question," said Master Cael, "if there were kinsfolk, and if they were not satisfied with the payment of the fine, they could demand that the offender serve a period as a bondsman. He would not be a prisoner, but he would be required to remain at a certain place, in the household of one of those kin, and work for the good of the family and community."

"Branoc's skills as a baker would allow him to make a worthwhile contribution," put in Master Tassach. "But as Ness is without surviving kin, an arrangement of that kind could not be put in place."

In the delicate silence that followed, it came to me that they were going to ask *us* to take responsibility for Branoc—hadn't we just said we were acting in place of Ness's kin? If they asked me to do it, my vow to Conmael meant I'd have to say yes. And things would fall apart, because I'd be obliged to keep Branoc alive while Grim would want to kill him.

"Master Cael," said Donagan, "after what has happened—a series of events that has shocked the whole community—Branoc has become a target for folk's wrath. His continuing presence in the Winterfalls area, even after the payment of a substantial fine, would be a thorn in the flesh, a constant disturbance."

"My lord," I said, glancing at Grim, "we don't favor a long period of incarceration."

"But you can't set him free," said Grim. "Doesn't matter if you make him pay a king's ransom. Let him go anywhere in these parts and if I don't kill the wretch someone else will."

"I'll pretend I didn't hear that," said the prince. "Master Cael, Master Tassach, I wonder if there is another solution available to us under the law. Ness is one of my people. I am responsible for this region and all the folk who live and work in it. Is it not within my authority to make Branoc a bondsman to my own family, and send him to Cahercorcan to work out his time in my father's household? Not in incarceration," he added, looking at Grim and me, "but under the very strict supervision that is possible at my father's court. Branoc is an expert baker; his creations are in high demand. He could most certainly be put to work there. I would, of course, provide the king with full details of his offenses, and appropriate measures would be put in place to ensure he could not repeat them."

"And he would be far enough away to deter anyone here from taking the law into their own hands," put in Donagan.

A silence, while all of us looked at the lawmen. It was a good solution, a just one. A clever one. I hoped it was possible.

"Very astute of you, my lord," said Master Tassach. "In cases of debt-bondage such an arrangement is common, and it is within the accepted interpretation of the law for a wrongdoer to work out the time required in the service of a king or chieftain in lieu of the victim's kin, most certainly. But that would not apply in this case. Branoc has the resources to pay even a heavy fine—not only the hundred silver pieces he had on his person when captured but the value of the bakery buildings and equipment. Those assets, along with the mill, would be sufficient to provide quite handsomely for Ness's future; they would more than meet the law's requirement for sick-maintenance even if her recovery is slow."

We sat in silence, looking at one another.

"Thing is," put in Grim, "the hundred silver pieces aren't his. They're the miller's life savings, that Ness was supposed to have stolen."

"And the mill doesn't come into it," I said. "That was Ernan's too. And now Ness's."

Master Cael gave a slow smile. He would, I thought, make a formidable enemy. "Indeed. Branoc might argue that the silver was his, of course. But I doubt he could make a convincing case, under the circumstances."

"So, if I understand you correctly, Master Tassach," said Prince Oran, "should I wish to place this man in debt-bondage, I would need to impose a fine that was higher than the value of his current assets. Significantly higher, if we wish him to serve a lengthy period." He lifted his brows at me as if to seek my approval. *My* approval. That of a . . . what was it Branoc had called me? A witch, a meddler, a bringer of trouble. Other things too, insults that had stung more than they should have.

"It's not up to me to determine the penalty, my lord," I said. "But Branoc has shown himself to have no regard for women, and scant respect for the community that sustains him. Such a man would take a long time to mend his ways. Years, I would think." Could this be true? Was the prince of Dalriada really taking heed of our arguments, mine and Grim's, in dispensing justice on such a serious matter?

It seemed he was. "Very well. With your agreement, Master Tassach, Master Cael, I will set the fine at five hundred silver pieces. The sale of the bakery might realize perhaps a quarter of that amount. In addition, I will set a condition on Branoc's release when he has worked off the remainder of the debt. An expert assessment will be conducted to determine whether he has learned his lesson; I will not allow his release into the community unless I am sure he will not reoffend."

"Had Branoc not taken it into his head to confess to the offense of burning the cottage," said Master Tassach with a grimace, "I'd have been in a position to argue for a lower fine or a shorter period of service. As it is, I have no alternative but to agree to your terms. They seem perfectly appropriate."

"I'm satisfied with the decision," said Master Cael.

We sat in silence for a few moments. Then the prince said, "Donagan, will you call in the scribe? Let's have this in writing before we return to open council."

I wanted to congratulate Prince Oran on not being like other men of power; to thank all of them for seeing the truth of this matter and reaching a just resolution. They did not realize, perhaps, how unusual that was. It was hard to find the words. He was the future king of Dalriada. I was a witch and a meddler. And not so long ago, I had been that wretched creature in Mathuin's lockup.

"Should we leave now, my lord?" I asked.

The prince took an assessing look at me. "Sit here awhile if you will; have something to eat and drink. It will take a little time to prepare the document. That's a big crowd of folk out there, all of them doubtless talking at once, and I imagine you'd rather not be in the middle of it. Where is young Emer?"

"Her brother's looking after her. Thank you, my lord." Right now, it wasn't so difficult to speak politely. "And thank you for your wise judgment."

"Ah, well," said the prince, and for some reason he sounded sad. "We all played a part in that."

25

It was nearly dusk, and the household was quiet at last. The council was over and the folk of the district had headed home. Tomorrow the lawmen would ride back to Cahercorcan. With them would go a message to my father on the matter of Branoc. Within a few days I would send the prisoner himself, appropriately guarded. Having that man in my house was like harboring vermin; I could not wait to see him gone.

I made my way up the track toward the burial ground. There was time to get there and back before nightfall, though if Bramble kept stopping to investigate interesting smells under bushes, we might be running all the way home.

"Come, Bramble!"

She trotted after me, tail held high, eyes bright: a different dog from the frightened, aggressive creature Flidais had brought into my house. Perhaps, when it was time for Aunt Sochla to go home, I should suggest she take Bramble with her. That would be kinder. And my aunt's household always had room for one more.

"But I would miss you," I said as the two of us climbed the rise, heading toward the little copse. "Who else would listen to my ramblings with such forbearance?" Donagan could no longer be asked to do so. I felt very much alone.

Today should have been a triumph. The matter of Branoc had been troubling me; I had doubted my own ability to deal with it wisely and fairly. But everyone except Branoc himself had seemed well satisfied with both judgment and sentence. "Perhaps," I said to the little dog, "it's the nature of his crime. In such a terrible matter, there can be no real resolution. Yes, he was found guilty, and he will pay a penalty. But what payment could truly compensate for what he did? He's blighted the life of that young woman. All very well to haul a man up before a council and sentence him to debt-bondage. Tidy him away, as it were. But the young woman he wronged can't be tidied away. She shouldn't be, Bramble. The whole community should be brought to account for the way they misjudged her."

Bramble had nothing to say on the matter, but as she looked up at me I imagined I saw understanding in her eyes.

I had said this, of course. I had made a statement at the council about the way we had all failed Ness, and how we needed to make sure such a thing never happened again. And folk had nodded and murmured and apparently agreed. "But the truth is," I told Bramble, "time passes, and people forget. And before we know it, another innocent is wronged, and another brave person steps up to tell folk something has gone awry, and we don't listen. We don't act until it's almost too late. Humankind can be sorely lacking in wisdom and compassion, Bramble. Indeed, we can be blind fools."

We reached the burial ground. Dusk was near and the air was bitterly cold. When I sat down on the bench, Bramble pressed close to my ankles, shivering. I scooped her up and held her in my arms, under my cloak.

The day had wearied me, and I found myself dreading the prospect of supper and the need to pretend before the guests that there was nothing amiss between Flidais and me. Her comments at the council, on the matter of Ness's character, had only served to deepen my unease about the future. "She'll be queen one day, Bramble. These folk look up to her. Or should. But I'm starting to wonder if she'll ever be worthy of that. I don't know if she has it in her to change."

You are a coward, some part of me said. *If that is what you truly believe, go and tell Flidais so. Tell her outright that her statements disturb you, that they are not in tune with the way you want to rule your people. Tell her that if she cannot change, you will not wed her. If you go ahead without taking any action, what follows will be on your own head.*

"I can't," I murmured. "You know all the arguments, Bramble. Haven't I been over them a hundred times? I should never have trusted in my dreams. Come, we'd best be going back while we can still see the path before our feet."

But when I looked down, I saw that Bramble had fallen asleep on my knee, quickly and completely, as if she had not a care in the world. I did not want to rise and disturb her. She looked so perfect, her small form curled neatly save for one paw that was up against my chest as if to ensure I would not go away and leave her. As I sat holding her, with the light fading around me, I was reminded of the portrait. I remembered how I had felt on the day my mother had first shown it to me; it had been as if all my hopes for the future were contained in that one scrap of painted wood. At first glance I had been transported into a world of ancient story, a world where true love won out against all odds, a realm in which dreams and magic were as real as growing crops or settling disputes over drains. What had made it so remarkable? What had touched me to the core?

Flidais's beauty had certainly played a part. But Flidais in the flesh was every bit as lovely as her painted image. The portrait was an excellent likeness. I desired my betrothed; that had been well and truly proven. But I could never love her as I had loved the woman in the portrait. I recalled the curve of her wrist as she supported the little dog; the graceful, tender position of her fingers against Bramble's neck. The look of devotion in the dog's eyes as she gazed up at her mistress. Most of all, the expression on Flidais's face. I had seen sweetness, honesty, perhaps a little shyness. I had seen a dreamer like myself; I had seen a young woman who understood hope and magic and beauty. Surely no painter was clever enough to build so many lies into a portrait. When the image was created, neither the artist nor the subject had known anything about my character. There could have been no reason to work into that depiction everything that would most touch my heart.

The letters were a different matter, since Flidais had not written to me until she had received the first of my own missives. It was possible they had been crafted especially to please me. A skillful scribe might have conjured them from the excess of tender feelings I had been all too ready to pour out onto the page. But there had been that last missive, sent from a different household, with a different scribe. Besides, there was such poetic truth in the letters that they were hard to disbelieve. Or had been, before I consigned them to the fire.

The clouds parted to reveal the full moon, pale and perfect in the darkening sky. A shiver went through me, far deeper than simple cold. At such a moment, sitting by the graves of the departed, I found it easy to believe in spirits, in ghosts, in the magical and wondrous. It was easy to become, again, the man who had set such trust in ancient tales of love. *I wish . . . I wish . . .*

In my arms, Bramble stirred and the spell was broken. I got up and walked toward home. How dared I spend even a moment feeling sorry for myself? My misfortune was nothing alongside what had happened to young Ness. What sort of leader was I, to be so wrapped up in my own concerns? I remembered, somewhat to my shame, the time of waiting for Flidais to arrive. I had fussed about all manner of things. I could recall pressing Donagan on the matter of a woman's confinement and what manner of assistance Flidais might prefer should we be blessed with a child. A child! The thought of her bearing my children, raising them and teaching them to think as she did made me feel sick. But she would. If I let matters take their natural course, she most certainly would.

I made my way down toward the house, cradling Bramble in my arms. Moonlight lay across the roof; lantern light shone out between the shutters. A pair of torches burned outside the entry. It must be close to supper time. I was glad the two lawmen had not yet departed; they and Aunt

Sochla would be able to maintain a reasonable conversation while we ate.

I headed for the women's quarters, thinking to pass Bramble over to one of the attendants. Against the odds, the little dog was still sleeping. I wandered into the garden I had made for Flidais, beyond the door of her reading room. I had chosen each plant with care, using what I had learned from my lady's letters. I had supervised everything from the curve of the path to the shape of the pond to the choice of stones for the wall, a barrier designed to make the place safe for Bramble. I stood there quietly for a little, knowing I must go indoors before folk came looking for me, yet finding myself unable to move on. In this tranquil spot the dream still lived. It was present in the warmth of the dog in my arms; in the perfection of the garden; in the aching of my wounded heart.

Deep down, I knew something was wrong. Something more than a woman whose letters had not given a true picture of her character. Something more than an arranged marriage whose parties had proved to be ill-matched. Something a great deal stranger. And if I did not examine it, if I did not search as hard as I could for answers, how could I expect a future based on truth, honesty and courage? If I gave up now, I had surely never been worthy of the dream.

I could not deal with this myself. But how could I expect anyone else to investigate a matter that was so private? Besides, the problem was . . . nebulous. When I'd tried to explain it to Donagan, even he had expressed the view that I was imagining things.

But . . . after today, after the council, it seemed maybe there was someone who could help. Someone good at solving puzzles, someone brave enough to tackle the most baffling mystery. Someone wise enough not to dismiss the truth of old tales.

"She might refuse, of course," I murmured to Bramble. "She might think me a complete fool, and I suspect she would not hesitate to say so to my face. But I can ask." Somewhere inside me there awoke a tiny, flickering flame of hope.

26

GRIM

Day after the council, it's cold but dry. Got no jobs on hand for anyone. I'm thinking I can put in a good day on the cottage, maybe find someone to help me get the roof beams up. Blackthorn's not saying much. Spent the night muttering and cursing in her dreams. Sooner I can get the house weatherproof, sooner we can move back in. Fraoch's place is comfortable enough and they're good people. But Blackthorn can't live long among folk.

We haven't talked about the council much. Big day. Lot to take in. Too much to get my head around. Full of surprises. Hard to believe, but the judgment was fair. Didn't think that happened anywhere. Didn't think they'd listen to us, but they did.

I'm putting together a few things before I head off for the day, and Blackthorn says she's coming with me. So I wait while she gets her basket and a knife, and Ornait packs up some food for us. Fraoch's taking Emer back over to Silverlake to give Ness the news. He offers us a lift on the cart and we say no, we'll walk.

We get as far as Iobhar's brewery, where I'm planning to stop in and see if the lads are free to help. But before I can do that, up rides the prince's man, Donagan. He says good morning and tells us Prince Oran wants to talk to us, now.

What about, he doesn't say. That's a worry. Did we get something wrong without knowing? I don't want to go, and I'm sure Blackthorn doesn't. But you don't say no to a prince. Not even one who seems like he might be a good man.

Blackthorn says what I'm not saying. "Can't this wait? We need to put in a day at the cottage while the weather's dry."

Donagan gives her a look, and she stares right back at him.

"Roof won't mend itself," I say. "Want to be back in there as soon as we can."

"If it'll help," Donagan says, "Niall can send a couple of our fellows across to give you a hand. But later, after you've spoken with the prince." And even though he's the serving man, he's got enough of that princely way about him to stop me from arguing. Maybe this won't take too long. Whatever it is.

Blackthorn's hugging her shawl around herself. She's worried. After the council, seemed things might be good for a while. But if we've learned anything from the past, her and me, it's this: good things don't last. Soon as you think they might be here to stay, someone takes them away again. Freedom. Trust. Family. Love. All those and more.

"I've got work to do," Blackthorn says. "Herbs to gather. Cures to prepare. Folk to tend to." Though I know she was planning to spend the whole day at the cottage, where she can gather the herbs but not do the other things. What she wants is not to have to talk to anyone for a while.

"When the prince summons you to a meeting," says Donagan, and he's trying hard not to snap, I hear it, "it's usual to attend without question."

"Ah," says Blackthorn. "But we're new to these parts. What's usual for your folk doesn't come naturally to us." He's made her angry. "I don't like doing things without question. Why does Prince Oran want to see us?"

"In part, to thank you for your contribution yesterday."

"No need to do that twice over."

Donagan's holding on to his temper by a thread. "Prince Oran also has a private matter to discuss with you. It is you in particular, Blackthorn, whom he wishes to talk to. It's not essential that Grim comes with you."

A private matter. That'd be some kind of sickness, like poxy Branoc and his sore shoulders. Compared with the council, it should be easy. And Donagan's right, Blackthorn doesn't need me trailing along getting in the way. I open my mouth to say, *I'll be heading off, then.*

"Grim comes with me," Blackthorn says. "And since we've got a day's work to do afterward, we'd best go now."

It's not like yesterday, when we went in the big gates with the crowd and there were guards everywhere. This time Donagan takes us down a long side path and in through a farm gate. There's a few folk working in the fields, over the far side. Some cows turn their heads and have a look at us. Donagan leads his horse and we walk alongside. We're headed away from the prince's house, up a hill toward some birch trees. They look spindly and cold without their leaves. Puts me on edge a bit. Keep expecting Slammer and his cronies to jump out of the bushes and slap us in shackles. Fact that Slammer's dead makes no difference; there's plenty more like him around.

"What is this?" I ask. "Where are you taking us?"

Before Donagan can answer, there's the prince himself, coming out from under the trees and walking down the track to meet us with that little dog at his heels. He thanks Donagan, and Donagan gets on his horse and rides off back the way we came. Really is a private meeting; as private as it can be, just Prince Oran and the two of us, if you don't count the dog. Must've decided he can trust us. That was quick.

"Thank you for coming," the prince says. "I know you both have work to do, not only your daily work but rebuilding the cottage as well."

I give him a nod. Blackthorn makes a sound meaning, *Yes, we're busy, so get on with it.*

"Your help at the council, and your courage and wisdom in the matter of Branoc's crimes, were invaluable," he says. "Please know that I appreciate your contribution deeply."

One thing I do know. You don't take folk to an out-of-the-way spot like this just to say thank you. Especially when you've already thanked them the day before. For a bit nobody says anything, then the prince clears his throat. He's looking down, scuffing his shoe on the path. Nervous. Can't think why.

"I have a favor to ask," he says.

"Ask it, then," says Blackthorn. Sounding edgy now.

"It's a little difficult," says the prince. "You may think it sounds foolish."

We wait.

"I need your help to solve a mystery. Something that has been troubling me for some time; something whose answer I cannot work out for myself. A dilemma I cannot take to anyone else."

"Why not?" I ask. Blackthorn's got enough to worry about without some prince dumping his problems on her shoulders.

"Because anyone else would tell me I'm imagining things."

From the way he says this, I guess he's told someone the story already and got the answer that it's rubbish. Though who says that to a prince, when he could lock them up if he wanted and throw away the key?

"And you think I wouldn't?" says Blackthorn.

"You seem . . . open to possibilities," the prince says. "You are a wise woman. That means—I understand it to mean that you see things differently from other folk. That you believe in the power of stories. That perhaps you do not dismiss the existence of . . . of the Other."

He means the fey. Or maybe magic. I think of Conmael, but I don't say the fellow's been wandering around in Dreamer's Wood. I don't tell the prince one of the fey was at his council. Chances are Blackthorn and me were the only folk who could see him anyway.

"Perhaps we could sit down somewhere." Blackthorn looks around. There's a bench under the birches, beside the path. She sits at one end and the prince sits at the other. The dog jumps up on his knee. I lean on a tree trunk, close enough to hear but not too close. The prince is all knotted up with worry. Might be easier for him to talk if he can pretend it's just him and her.

"This is ... private. Absolutely confidential. You understand?"

"Mm-hm," says Blackthorn.

Maybe the prince has done something he shouldn't and picked up a nasty ailment. Doesn't want to pass it on to his new bride once they're wed. Awkward for him to come out with. Still, it would take a lot to make Blackthorn blush.

"It concerns Lady Flidais," the prince says, lowering his voice, though there are only the three of us here. "This is indeed difficult ... I hardly ..."

"I know how to keep secrets," says Blackthorn. "Even the most sensitive ones. If you want someone who can hold her counsel, you could do worse than choose a wise woman."

Oran takes in a big breath and lets it out again like a sigh. "The lady ... she is afflicted by severe headaches. Crippling headaches that come without warning. They prevent her from pursuing many activities she formerly enjoyed such as ... such as reading and writing."

Blackthorn's looking at him, waiting for more. After a while she says, "You didn't bring the two of us up here to talk about your lady's headaches. I don't need to be clever at solving puzzles to work that out. If the problem concerned Lady Flidais's health, you'd have invited me into your house to talk to her."

"Lady Flidais does not ..."

"Before I can offer a solution, a remedy, I must first examine a patient. Speak with her in person," Blackthorn says. "If Lady Flidais doesn't care to make use of my services, why don't you send for one of the royal physicians? Cahercorcan is not so very far away."

You'd think they'd have called someone already, with the headaches so bad and all. But I'm not the healer, so I keep quiet. And so does the prince. He's stroking the dog and looking as if he wants to be somewhere else. Which makes three of us, I'm guessing.

"This is more than the headaches, isn't it, my lord?" Blackthorn's sounding almost kindly, which is a surprise. "In my experience, sometimes it's easier to get these things out if you make them into a tale. We'll hold our counsel until you're done."

That's what he needed, seems like. Out comes the story, and it's nothing we would have expected. A tale like one of those old ones, true love, magic, tears and sorrow, everything. Seems Prince Oran fell in love with Lady Flidais's picture. Then they wrote letters. Love letters. Only when he met the real lady she wasn't what he expected. Or, she was in looks, but not in much else. One thing's plain: the prince is deep-down unhappy.

"You know what I'll say," says Blackthorn when the story's finished.

"That it is all in my mind. That such disappointments are common in arranged marriages, which are made for reasons of strategy, not love. That I should be glad my betrothed is young, healthy and pleasant to look upon. I understand those arguments. I know I was foolish to expect more. But . . . her letters . . . I cannot believe they were not heartfelt. And I cannot believe that Flidais, as she is now, could have written them."

"Your lady is a chieftain's daughter," Blackthorn says. I hear in her voice that she's being careful. It's awkward to talk about this without seeming to insult the lady, and folk get punished for a lot less than that. "Chieftains have scribes. Skillful ones."

"The letters were . . . poetic. And personal. Very personal."

"How long did you say it was until the hand-fasting?"

Oran holds the dog against his chest; it stretches up and gives him a lick on the chin. "Just over one turning of the moon."

"And what exactly are you hoping we can do? Are you suggesting the lady is here under false pretenses? That this is an imposter?"

"She cannot be." His voice is flat. "She is the image of her portrait, and that came from her father to mine. Besides, she traveled here with her own folk and none of them has mentioned anything amiss. The only oddity is . . ." His face goes red.

"What?" If Blackthorn has noticed he's embarrassed, she's not showing it.

"Bramble," says the prince, looking at the dog. I'm sure he was going to say something else and changed his mind.

"In the portrait, and in the letters, Flidais was devoted to her little dog. Bramble went everywhere with her. Slept on her bed; loved to go for long walks in the woods. But Bramble's behavior changed from the day they arrived here. She seems in great fear of Flidais. She has bitten her more than once. And Flidais wants nothing to do with her. My aunt, Lady Sochla, has been caring for the dog."

"Bramble seems to like you well enough," Blackthorn says.

The prince doesn't answer for a bit. He's fondling the dog's ears, looking at her, not at us. Then he says, "She reminds me of the dream. The dream that Flidais and I would be happy together. In the portrait, Flidais was holding Bramble so tenderly. It touched my heart from the first glance."

I'm thinking, this man's far too soft to be a prince. But then I remember the council and how he spoke to Branoc, and I think, it takes a brave man to admit he's got a weak spot.

"My mother has been urging me to wed for several years now," he says. "I refused a number of suitable women who were suggested. I insisted on waiting for the right one; for someone I could love, someone I could be truly happy with. I loved the portrait, but I did exercise some caution. Hence the correspondence. Flidais's letters won me over completely. So the marriage was agreed, and she came here. And from our first encounter I found myself . . . confused. Surprised. As time has passed, that confusion has become a deep and unsettling doubt. The hand-fasting is drawing ever closer. Lady Flidais's parents are in a difficult situation, with a powerful neighbor threatening their holdings; she cannot be dispatched home, and even if she could, I have no real grounds for taking such drastic action. I remind myself, daily, that if I had not been so insistent on marrying this particular woman, I would not be in such difficulty now. And neither would she."

"Have you spoken to Lady Flidais about your doubts?" Blackthorn asks.

"What could I possibly say?"

There's a silence, then she says, "Prince Oran, are you asking me to spy on your betrothed?"

"I don't know," says the prince. "I don't know what it will take to find the truth."

"The truth might be that you made a mistake." Blackthorn says it straight, not trying to sweeten things. "That your hopes and dreams didn't match up with the reality."

Prince Oran's looking like a ghost. He's looking like the saddest man in the world. Seems to me he'd be better off without the lady. From what I've seen of her, I'd be guessing they're not much of a match.

"Yes, that is possible," he says. "I almost believe it. But not quite. Something is wrong, Mistress Blackthorn. Deeply wrong. Lady Flidais . . . She does not behave at all like the woman I was expecting. Not at all."

"In what respects?" Blackthorn asks.

The prince doesn't answer. The silence goes on, and I'm wondering what the lady might be doing that isn't very ladylike. Things her own folk must be keeping quiet about. Because he said they hadn't mentioned anything being out of the usual.

"If you want me to investigate this," says Blackthorn, "you need to give me all the relevant information, my lord." And when he still doesn't, she says, "I'm not asking these questions to embarrass or shame you or Lady Flidais. I have no reason to do that. Let's start with something easy. You said the headaches are stopping her from reading and writing. But not all ladies enjoy scholarship."

"Flidais does. Did. The letters . . . She wrote poems, beautiful poems. And we shared a love of old tales. She has completely lost her interest in such things. I understand about the headaches. But the Flidais of the letters would still have wanted to talk about poetry and tales, and perhaps to have me read to her. And . . . there was a certain book, Lucian's *Bestiary*, which we discussed at some length in our correspondence. A book held in her father's library; a volume she particularly loved. I had a perfect copy made as her wedding gift. When I gave it to her, she did not know what it was."

"Odd," observed Blackthorn. "You're convinced a scribe did not pen those letters for Lady Flidais, my lord?"

"I'm not sure of anything. Her last letter was written when she was far from home, and far from her father's scribe, and it was in the same mode and the same hand as

the others. You may think I am clutching at straws." This
fellow's lost his dreams, and it's broken his heart. Doesn't
know how lucky he's been to keep them until he was a man
grown. "But something's wrong," he goes on. "I feel it in
my bones. Something strange has happened. So strange it
seems almost . . . uncanny. I owe it to . . . I owe it to what
might have been, to seek out the truth."

"May I look at Lady Flidais's letters?" Blackthorn asks,
straight out.

"I burned them."

That's a surprise. Blackthorn gives him a look, as if she
thinks he's a silly boy, and he says, "All but one." And fishes
it out of the pouch at his belt, which is not so easy with the
dog lying on his knee. "Don't ask me to read it," Prince
Oran says. He sounds as if he might cry, but he doesn't. He's
a prince, after all. Letter looks a bit the worse for wear. He
passes it over.

"Why did you burn the others?" Blackthorn asks.

"There was a time . . . a moment . . . when I . . ."

"Never mind that." She's reading the letter. The look on
her face says she's interested now.

"Long walk for a little dog," I say to the prince, to fill in
the silence.

He manages a smile. "Bramble loves her walks. My aunt
says that is typical of terriers." Bramble lifts her head and
takes a good look at me. Pretty little thing. I go over and squat
down beside the prince. Could be useful to find out if Bramble's a biter, or if the only person she snaps at is Lady Flidais.
When the dog doesn't growl, I reach out a hand, slowly, and
she gives my fingers a good sniff. I tickle her behind the ears.
She pushes her head against my hand, almost like a cat.

"Seems friendly enough."

Prince Oran nods. "To those whom she trusts, yes."

"My lord," says Blackthorn, with the letter in her
hands, "you know I'll have to talk to Lady Flidais. And to
her women. And to many other folk in your household.
Any reasonable person will be asking questions about
why I'm in and out of your house every day, even if I say
I'm trying to find a cure for the lady's headaches. Besides,
that's not going to work if Lady Flidais doesn't want me
tending to her."

"Ah," said the prince. "But won't the two of you be looking for somewhere to stay while your cottage is being rebuilt? I understand the arrangement with Fraoch is only for the short term. I can accommodate you here; it would be an appropriate gesture of thanks. And if you are here, in the house, you'll be perfectly placed to . . ."

"Spy?" Blackthorn sounds the way I feel, very uncomfortable with this idea. Though it makes sense.

"To talk, in a natural way, with those others you mentioned, Flidais's waiting women, my own folk. That should give you time to win Flidais's trust."

"Just over a turning of the moon, I think you said." Blackthorn's frowning. "You expect a lot of us."

"It would not be necessary for Grim to be here all the time; he could continue his work on the cottage. Even stay elsewhere, if you prefer." Prince Oran gives me a glance, and looks a bit surprised. What I'm thinking must be written all over my face. If I'm not with her, I won't sleep. If I can't sleep how can I do a good job on the cottage? Anyway, I'd worry about her, is she all right, who's looking out for her and so on. Not that I want to stay here either. But it's not for me to say yes or no.

"No," says Blackthorn. "If you want answers in one turning of the moon, you need both of us. I didn't solve the puzzle of Ness's disappearance on my own. Besides, we need to talk to the men of the household too, in particular the guards who rode here with Lady Flidais. That's best done in casual conversation, and they're more likely to talk to Grim than to me." She looks at me. "You can still go and work on the cottage some of the time. And it's not as if we've had no offers of help."

"Niall has one of the farm cottages vacant," the prince says. "That would allow you some privacy."

That's good. A cottage to ourselves means we can shut the door on the prince's folk when we've had enough.

"I must clarify," he goes on. "Flidais and I will be expected to travel to court at least seven days before the hand-fasting, perhaps earlier. So we have something less than a full turning of the moon. After that it would be too late to . . . to change the plan."

"Just as long as you understand," says Blackthorn, "that the answers we give you might not be the ones you want."

"I accept that," he says, getting to his feet. "I know you'll do your best."

"About the offer of a cottage to stay in," Blackthorn says. "That won't do. With so little time to solve the problem, I'll need to be sleeping in the women's quarters. And Grim will have to be somewhere he can talk to the guards when they're off duty."

Wish she wasn't right, but she is. If we want to hear secrets we have to get in there next to the prince's folk. Make friends of them. Blackthorn's going to love that. It's Fraoch's place all over again, only with ten times more people and no getting away.

"Of course," says the prince, putting Bramble down. "You can be accommodated; I'll have a word with Aedan. It's understood, is it not, that what we have just discussed will not be aired before anyone else? That includes not only my household but the wider community. And my family."

"It's understood," Blackthorn says. "Though I might come close once or twice. To get answers, sometimes you have to take risks. Especially when time's short, my lord."

"Very well. I appreciate your discretion. You'll be wanting to go and collect your belongings from the smithy. Let me know if you need assistance. When you return, ask for Aedan."

There's been no more sign of Donagan. Seems his job was to go and fetch us, then make himself scarce. Wonder if he's been let into the secret, and if not, why not?

Blackthorn looks at me. "Grim needs to work on the cottage today, to take advantage of the weather. And I must gather herbs in the wood. We'll move here after supper. There's nothing much to bring."

"We can find our own way out," I say. Got a heavy feeling in my chest.

"I'll bid you good morning, then. And I will speak with you again soon. Mistress Blackthorn, I understand that your work will sometimes take you out into the community during this period. Of course you must continue that. But I believe that once you are in residence here, the folk of my household will consult you more regularly. Opportunities to talk to them in confidence may be quite easy to find."

"Maybe so, maybe not," she says. "Best if you leave us to get on with the job, my lord, and if we have questions, or something to report, we'll find a way to let you know. You might need to develop a mysterious ailment."

It's a joke, but the prince doesn't smile. "Thank you," he says. "For believing in this enough to try."

"Just one question," I say.

"Yes, Grim?"

"Does anyone else know about this? Your problem, I mean, and why we'll be here?"

Now he does smile, but it's the sad smile of a man who's all alone with his troubles.

"Only Bramble," Prince Oran says. "And she can be relied upon not to tell."

27

BLACKTHORN

I cursed Conmael for the seven years of obedience he'd bound me to, and I cursed the prince for seeking my help. The mystery of Lady Flidais was all very well; I'd do my best to solve it, even if the whole thing ended with me telling the prince what he didn't want to hear. I was even somewhat interested. The letter wasn't the kind of thing any scribe would pen with ease; whoever had written it was at least half a poet. And if anything was sure, it was that the young woman I'd encountered that first day in Dreamer's Wood, the woman I'd heard at the council suggesting Ness might have lied to Emer, could not have written such a letter. There was no pretense in it, no contrivance. It was sweet, romantic and a little tentative, the outpouring of a young girl who loved her dog and old tales and walks in the woods, a girl who was not yet quite sure whether to trust the man who seemed to be offering her not only a marriage that would one day make her a queen but his heart along with it. If I were asked to say what sort of woman had written that letter, I'd have said a woman who believed in dreams; a woman who was very like Prince Oran himself. I had to admit that the whole thing was intriguing.

It was the way I'd have to go about it that I hated. Too

many folk, too close, too loud. Prince Oran's residence was swarming with them. I cursed myself for not accepting the farm cottage, even as I knew that if I wanted people to drop their guard with me—or with Grim—this was the only way. Especially with time so short. Pity I wasn't a different person, one who liked mending and embroidery and wasting half the day gossiping. Pity I didn't enjoy the company of fools.

The women's quarters had a degree of comfort that was little short of ridiculous. The place was vast, almost another house in itself, with a long sleeping chamber for serving folk and attendants—this was where I had been allocated a bed—and a separate, private area for Lady Flidais and Lady Sochla. Flidais had her personal maid, Mhairi, sleeping in an alcove near her. Lady Sochla had brought a number of maidservants with her from court, including her own attendant, Sinead. Sinead slept in the communal area with the rest of us. Sometimes she walked, fed or brushed the dog, Bramble. Sometimes she helped Lady Sochla to dress, but the prince's aunt was an early riser and fiercely independent. Like her mistress, Sinead seemed a sensible person, someone who might answer questions without leaping to all manner of conclusions. But since she and Lady Sochla had only known Flidais since her arrival at Winterfalls, they would not be much help to me.

It seemed sensible to start with the three handmaids Flidais had brought with her from Cloud Hill, if I could get them to talk. Mhairi had evidently become Flidais's personal attendant after the other one, Ciar, drowned in Dreamer's Pool. She and Flidais seemed very close. The other two were Deirdre, the woman who had spoken kindly to me on the day of the drowning, and the older Nuala. Between them they looked after the lady's wardrobe, ran to fetch things when she asked for them, made conversation to keep her entertained during the long hours spent over handiwork and generally made sure her day ran as smoothly as it could.

Nuala's husband, Domnall, was leader of the men-at-arms who had traveled in Flidais's party, but for now the two of them were sleeping apart. That was apparently quite usual in households such as the prince's; you took your op-

portunities where you could, and hoped that in time a cottage or other married quarters might become available.
The prince's offer of private accommodation for me and
Grim had been more generous than I'd realized. If we'd accepted, we'd no doubt have put a few folk's noses out of
joint.

There were levels of authority in the prince's household,
and they took me a while to work out. Him at the top, of
course, though he didn't go around giving orders—things
ran smoothly without any need for that. Lady Flidais and
Lady Sochla were family, folk of noble birth. Then came
Donagan—both servant and friend, only a step away from
the prince himself. Aedan the steward had responsibility
for the smooth daily running of the entire household, and
was assisted by his wife, Fíona. Brid ruled the kitchen; Niall
was in charge of a great body of farm workers; the grooms
and stable hands answered to the cantankerous Eochu. The
guards were led by a big man called Lochlan, Prince Oran's
master-at-arms. At the bottom of the heap were ordinary
servants such as kitchen workers, seamstresses, folk who
scrubbed floors or dug the garden or looked after the cows.
Lady Flidais's waiting women seemed to believe themselves on much the same level as Donagan, superior to all
but the prince's blood kin. That made approaching them
tricky.

I did not fit anywhere. A wise woman might have many
folk coming in and out of her house, bringing gifts or bribes
or payment, taking away herbs and drafts and good advice.
But our kind generally lived alone. If I'd been attached
permanently to a noble household—unlikely—I'd perhaps
have been afforded the respect owed to, say, a druid. Perhaps. But at Winterfalls I was an oddity, and it was clear
folk did not quite know what to make of me.

For all its smooth and seamless organization, this was
not a household in harmony. There was tension between
the household guards and those who had come to Winterfalls in Lady Flidais's escort. Nobody could fail to pick up
on the unease when they were all gathered together at
mealtimes. Maybe Grim could find the reason for this ani-
mosity, and whether it was important to us.

Something was going on between the prince and Donagan. If anyone had asked me, I'd have said the two of them were avoiding speaking to each other. Maybe they'd had a falling-out. And while I hadn't been asked to investigate that, I was learning that the slightest oddity could prove important in hindsight.

The women's days followed a pattern. First to rise was Lady Sochla, who would head out early for a walk with Bramble. Only a storm of the sleeting, tempestuous kind would keep the prince's aunt indoors. If the day was inclement she would leave the dog behind and have Sinead take it into the garden instead. A pretty little garden. I heard from Brid the cook that Prince Oran had created it especially for Lady Flidais, but I didn't once see her spend time in it. Nor did I ever see her walk her own dog. But in that first letter, the one the prince had let me read, Flidais had given a charming description of the woodland near her home; she had implied that she enjoyed walking in it with her maid and Bramble. I wondered which maid she meant: Ciar, who had drowned, or one of the others? I'd have to talk to all three of them: Deirdre, Nuala and Mhairi.

After breakfast, Lady Flidais and her attendants generally went to the sewing room, a long chamber with windows placed to let in morning light, and a hearth where a crackling fire would already be burning. That was unless Lady Flidais had some reason to ride out—a visit to the settlement, for instance. This did not occur often. At this time of year, I'd have expected the prince to be off hunting stag or boar, as princes and chieftains commonly did in autumn. But I already knew Oran was not like other princes, and it seemed he was more likely to be writing letters, inspecting his cattle or holding councils than engaging in blood sport. When I asked Brid about this, she told me Niall's men took what game was necessary to sustain the household, and the cottagers had permission to provide for their own needs in the same manner. Meat and fish were salted away for the winter months. But the prince had declared there would be no wanton slaughter of wild creatures on his land, and since his folk held him in high respect, despite his unusual attitudes, they abided by his rules.

The headaches afflicted Lady Flidais severely. More often than not she retired to her bedchamber rather than at-

tend the midday meal in the hall. This malady was surely
the key to winning her trust. At eighteen years old she was
living the life of an invalid. I could not understand why she
had not asked me for help before, unless she was one of
those folk who feared wise women, suspecting us of dark
magic. The day I'd first met her, the day of the drowning, I
could not recall doing or saying anything to earn her distrust. The headaches were alarming. If the story of Oran's
courtship was accurate, this young woman had been in
good health at the time she left home.

I did not want to believe she was lying. An imposter
would have an obvious reason for pretending to be indisposed. But Flidais was no imposter; not unless her entire
escort was telling lies along with her. An imposter could
have used the headaches to conceal the fact that she could
not read and write. She might have been conveniently indisposed so she need not respond to questions she could
not easily answer; so she need not make conversation with
her future husband until they were safely hand-fasted.
Oran was not a simple kind of man. He would not be content with a wife who looked decorative, said little and kept
out of his way. No, Oran had expected a wife who was his
equal. A wife who could converse on his own level. A wife
who loved the things he loved, a wife who was in every respect the Lady Flidais of the letters. Whoever had written
those letters had done Flidais no favors at all. If they were
a trick, the perpetrator had vastly underestimated the
prince of Dalriada.

I'd have to tread carefully, despite the short time we had
left. No leaping right in with probing questions, no tests of
the lady's skill with the pen or her knowledge of strategy or
scholarship. I was in this household as a guest, and I must
keep the real reason for my presence among these women
secret.

On one point at least, Prince Oran had been right. I was
good at my craft, and I'd been in Winterfalls long enough
for the local people to know they could trust me. Within
three days of our arrival, the prince's serving people started
bringing their aches and pains to me in the little storeroom
off the kitchen where, at Brid's invitation, I had set up my
healer's equipment. A day or two later I strapped up a

training injury suffered by a man-at-arms and gave a groom a curative wash for a nasty case of nettle rash. I went out to the village to attend to one or two folk with chronic complaints, people who were used to seeing me every few days. In the past I'd undertaken those visits grudgingly. Now they made me feel like a captive creature set free.

I made sure I was in the sewing room with Flidais and her attendants for a good part of each morning. It was necessary to find some sort of task for myself so my presence there did not draw suspicion. The choice was limited. Me, sewing? Hah! If anything at the cottage needed mending, Grim did it. I could sew up a wound just fine, but the hem of a garment was another matter. Once, in that long-ago life, I must have managed. But the skills were lost. They were part of what I had left behind.

The solution was to write. I had long maintained a record of my work. The healer's craft was not static in nature. Each salve, each solution, each remedy changed and progressed and improved each time it was prepared and applied. It was like a story told and retold over the years, passed from grandmother to mother to daughter. A wise woman would not be worthy of that name if she could not learn from her mistakes, if she did not keep on striving to find new and better ways. It might be a matter of gathering an herb just a little later in the season, or taking only the leaves from the very tip of each branch. It might be a decision to bruise a root before chopping it, or to make the slightest change in the proportions of a salve. Small variations, small risks, could lead to significant improvements.

Since Grim and I had taken up residence in the cottage I had been keeping a record of the preparations I made, the folk I tended to and the results. My notebook had survived the fire; it had been in the bag I'd carried over to Silverlake that day. My writing materials had burned with the house, but the prince had replaced them.

The other women did not know how much I loathed company. They were ignorant of the truth: that if I'd had a real choice in the matter, I'd have been out in the woods on my own, not shut within four walls listening to their silly chatter. No, that was not quite true. Given a real choice, I'd

be back in Laois seeing justice done. Seven years. Seven in-
terminable, suffocating years. Where would I get the
strength?

I took pains to tell the women the place was ideal for
writing. The same light that enabled them to do their fine
embroidery, their weaving and spinning, would allow me to
complete my day's record neatly and read over my previous notes. It seemed to be convincing, for nobody challenged my presence there. That did not mean they went out
of their way to welcome me, but I had not expected that.
Seeking a wise woman's advice over an ailment was one
thing; making her your friend was quite another.

Alongside Flidais's ladies and the prince's formidable
aunt, there was a pair of girls from the household whose
job was plain sewing and an older woman who did fine
mending, including work on what looked like Prince Oran's
clothing. Others came in and out. The household linen was
stored in this chamber, in chests set against the walls, and
this seemed to require daily attention by a number of serving women. There were always folk putting items away,
taking others out, slipping lavender between the folds of
aired sheets, rearranging the chests' contents, debating
whether something could be mended or was to be torn up
for cleaning cloths. I could almost understand why Lady
Flidais spent so much time in her bedchamber.

Fíona, wife of Aedan the steward, was a solidly built
woman of middle years who wore her hair pulled back under a neat veil. She was generally present in the chamber at
some point of the morning, instructing the other serving
folk or inquiring courteously as to whether any of the ladies wanted refreshments. At my request she'd cleared a
small table of various objects so I could sit there to work. I
liked the way she did her job without fuss, and the way she
spoke to those under her authority—kindly but firmly, so
they wanted to do well for her. I saw, too, that Lady Flidais
did not care for her, finding fault with any number of little
things, while Fíona listened without interrupting, and answered politely that of course the problem would be remedied right away. If I'd been her, I'd have told Lady Flidais
she was a lazy, selfish cow who should make an effort to do
things for herself. Which would, no doubt, have led to my

being instantly dismissed from the prince's service. Aedan
and Fíona had been at Winterfalls since Prince Oran was a
child. They'd had plenty of time to learn tolerance. I'd have
to do so a lot more quickly.

"Tell me, Mistress Blackthorn," said Lady Sochla, giving
me a shrewd look across the roomful of women as I sat at
my little desk trying to look busy and listen at the same
time, "what are the questions folk most often ask you?
What are the most common ailments they bring to you?"

I guessed she was asking out of genuine interest, not in
an attempt to make me feel welcome. Though if the prince's
aunt was as astute as I suspected, she'd have noticed the
sideways looks some of the other women were still giving
me, days after I had first joined them, as if they thought me
as out of place as a fox in a rabbit warren.

"It depends on the circumstances, Lady Sochla. A wise
woman tends to all manner of injuries and ailments. There
can be combat wounds; limbs broken in farm accidents;
burns. Heads cracked in foolish brawls over nothing in particular. Agues, fevers, ill humors, complications in childbirth. We see new life into the world; we hold the hands of
the dying and lay out the dead."

Lady Sochla seemed to be waiting for more, and now all
the others were listening too.

"Then there are the chronic ailments, such as persistent
rashes or weakness of the stomach or maladies of the mind.
For those who suffer in that way, we have a range of preparations that can be made up regularly." I would not mention
headaches; it was too soon. "For instance, on the day the
young woman, Ness, was rescued—you'll have heard the tale
at the last council—I was at Branoc's bakery tending to his
sore neck and shoulders. That was a genuine ailment, and I
had taken a salve with me, prepared for the purpose."

A buzz of talk broke out among them, in lowered voices.
I applied myself to a drawing of the various parts of thyme:
root, stem, leaves, flowers.

Someone was breathing down my neck.

"Oh, that is pretty!" exclaimed Deirdre. "You are clever,
Mistress Blackthorn."

"It's not meant to be pretty. The drawings provide a record. Each is an accurate depiction of the herb—or as accurate as I can manage, not being a skilled artist—with notes to illustrate how it is used and for what purpose." I reminded myself that of them all, Deirdre had been most civil to me on the day of the drowning. "But yes," I made myself say, "some of the herbs are very decorative. Though at this time of year, only a few are in flower."

"I'd say you are something of an artist, Blackthorn," put in Lady Sochla's maid, Sinead, who had wandered over to have a look. With two of them crowding me, I gave up the attempt to draw. "You have a fine hand with the pen."

Lady Flidais whispered in Mhairi's ear, and they both smiled.

"One cannot perform tasks such as sewing up wounds or extracting foreign bodies from folk's ears or noses without a certain delicacy of touch," I observed, suppressing the urge to kick someone. "Just as one cannot set a broken limb to rights or pull out a diseased tooth without a certain brute strength. A wise woman needs both."

"Does your man help you?" inquired Mhairi, lifting her brows.

I did not like her tone. Nor did I like the look on her face, which was mirrored on Lady Flidais's. They were ready to mock me, the two of them, at the first opportunity. Never mind that. I had endured far worse in my time. *Don't snap. Don't bite. Remember why you are here.*

"You mean Grim?" I said lightly. "It is sometimes useful to have the assistance of a person who is physically stronger, yes. To restrain a patient who is thrashing about in pain, for instance, or to hold a severely broken limb straight while I splint and bandage it. Grim has helped me once or twice."

"Only once or twice?" Mhairi was not letting this go. "Surely you've needed help more than that."

"Grim and I have not been traveling together long." I turned my attention back to my notebook. It was hard to work with Deirdre and Sinead standing right beside me; they were still too close, and it set my teeth on edge. "What are you working on?" I asked, with a glance intended to take in both of them.

They did as I'd hoped, retreating to fetch their work so I could admire it. Sinead was embroidering a border of ivy around the hem of a skirt. It seemed a waste of time to me—wouldn't it soon get muddy?—but the result was pleasing enough. Deirdre was making a little gown for a baby, with birds on it. I muttered a comment, finding it impossible to be kind. She could not know what images had flooded my mind when I saw the garment. My baby in a gown almost twin to this. Brennan in my arms, his slight, sleeping weight, the sweetness of his breath, his mouth hungry on the breast. My baby gone. Gone to the flames.

"Mistress Blackthorn?"

Someone had been talking and I had not heard a word. "I'm sorry, what was that?" *Pull yourself together. Listen. Learn.* If only I hadn't told Grim the story. I'd had it well locked away before. Now it was close again, a darkness on the edge of everything.

"It was a foolish question." Lady Sochla sounded repressive. "Teafa asked whether folk come to you for spells. Magical potions and cures."

Teafa was one of the young seamstresses. She was blushing now, her head bent over her work. Had I seen her before, perhaps asking for something to make a certain youth notice her? I couldn't remember; one silly girl tended to fade into another after a while. "They ask, yes. Cures for broken hearts. Love potions. Sometimes they want curses to be cast on an enemy, or spells to make them beautiful or to help them please their wives better."

Now I really had everyone's attention.

"And do you give them what they want?" asked Fíona.

"I give them what they need."

Sinead's eyes had gone wide. "You can do magic?" she breathed. "Real magic?"

"I didn't say that. These matters are not as simple as they may sound. If by magic you mean the right gathering of plants, the thoughtful preparation of drafts and suchlike, and the wise dispensing of the same, then yes. If you refer to a person waving a hand and conjuring colored lights or heaps of gold coins, then no."

"But a love potion," said Sinead, "or what you said, a curse on an enemy, have you given folk those things? They are magic, surely, or any one of us could find the ingredients and make up the mixture ourselves."

"That way lies disaster. Get the smallest component wrong, or make a slight error with the proportions, and you might find yourself charged with unlawful killing. That's if the draft was for someone other than yourself."

"And if it was for yourself," put in Lady Sochla, "you might be dead. I think that is what Mistress Blackthorn is telling us."

"Indeed so. That is why the details of potions and charms are kept secret. Always."

They looked suitably impressed, and for a little while there was silence. Then Lady Flidais spoke up. "Don't you have them written in your little book, Blackthorn? You're always scribbling in there."

Count to five before you speak. "This is a record of my daily work, my lady. My book does include some cures and remedies, but it is by no means a comprehensive guide. It contains nothing of a magical nature." Not strictly true; but only a person of some wisdom and skill would recognize that.

"Isn't one of the village girls learning from you?" one of the women asked. "I'm sure I heard someone say you were training a girl up to be a healer."

"Emer. Yes, she is learning the skills." This was starting to feel a little like an interrogation.

"But if they're secret," said Deirdre, "how can she learn them?"

"Some are secret. Those, a wise woman learns only when she is ready. That may take many years of study, many years of practical work. Not every student achieves the wisdom and good judgment that allow her to be trusted with the most arcane learning. But some do, or there would be no wise women to teach the next generation, and the one after that. From what I have been told, I believe the last one at Winterfalls—Holly, was that her name?—died without leaving a successor." This might turn the conversation away from me and onto more general lines.

"By successor you mean a student, not a son or daughter, I imagine," said Nuala. "Can wise women marry?"

Seems my attempt had failed. "We usually don't. Best if our whole energy is devoted to our craft. Besides, the work of a healer requires her to be often away from home, and calls for our help can come at any time of the day or night. Babies are born in their own time; old folk often pass away at dawn. Accidents happen when they happen. We must be able to drop everything and go."

"Not easy for a mother, then."

"As you say."

"But aren't you and Grim . . . ?" This was Mhairi.

I turned a level gaze on her. "Aren't we what?" I asked coolly, taking a certain pleasure in her surprise. She had expected me to blush, perhaps, and mumble an awkward response.

"Perhaps I am wrong," Mhairi said, "but as you both live in the cottage, and as you've moved in here together, I assumed . . ."

I lifted my brows in query and waited for her to finish.

"*Mhairi,*" murmured Deirdre, frowning.

"Assumptions can be dangerous," put in Lady Sochla, looking up from her handiwork. "They can lead us down pathways we'd be better to avoid. I'm sure Mistress Blackthorn has better things to do than answer a lot of personal questions."

"Blackthorn is a stranger among us, Aunt." Flidais's tone was sweet. "We know little about her. Mhairi wants to fill in the gaps, that is all."

Lady Sochla had provided me with time to gather my wits. "Why don't we do it this way?" I asked. "I answer your question, and then you answer one for me."

"I?" Lady Flidais sounded shocked; clearly she thought this most inappropriate. Or she was afraid.

"You, my lady, or Mhairi—whomever wishes to reply."

"Go on, then," said Mhairi.

"Very well. The answer is, Grim and I met on the road here. We are traveling companions."

"But you're not traveling now."

"Is that another question?"

The whole chamber had gone silent.

"If I answer two," I went on, "then you must answer two as well."

Mhairi tossed her head. "This is silly."

"It sounds perfectly fair to me," said Lady Sochla. "I would most certainly count that as a second question."

"I have stayed in Winterfalls because there's a need for my services here," I said. "It helped that there was also a place to live: the old cottage. Grim stayed on to help make the cottage habitable. It turned out there was work for him in the district as well. There's your answer, and now it's my turn to ask. Mhairi, what does the work of a lady's personal attendant involve? See, I am only asking you the same question you asked me. Absolutely fair."

"Surely you can guess the answer."

"Maybe so. But it's for you to tell me."

"I look after Lady Flidais's clothing. I help her dress and bathe. I'm on hand whenever she needs me."

"Mhairi took over all of Ciar's duties," said Nuala. "She's with Lady Flidais night and day."

"Thank you," I said, giving her a smile. "My second question is for Lady Flidais. My lady, I have noticed you are often indisposed with headaches. I am expert in dealing with such maladies. It is very likely I could help you. But your personal attendant has not sought me out on your behalf. I will not risk offending anyone by asking why not. I will simply say that I am well qualified to help, and that my services are at your disposal if you wish to use them. I believe I could cure the headaches quite quickly, allowing you to live your life to the full, as before. Would you allow me to try?"

Lady Flidais turned her wide blue gaze on me. "I have no faith in old wives' remedies," she said.

There were a few gasps around the chamber—the barb in this comment was hardly subtle. Lady Sochla opened her mouth, then closed it again. She might have reprimanded one of the waiting women if she'd spoken with such discourtesy, but she would not do so to the lady of the house. And, hard as it was to believe, Flidais was that lady.

I held my tongue. In this girl's opinion I was a crone. I could have protested. I could have told her that despite appearances, I was still of child-bearing years. I could have said that under the worn-out, beaten-down exterior, the woman I might have been still lingered. An old wife would not have cared about Mathuin's crimes. An old wife could not have contained such a burning will for justice. But what was the point? Flidais and her kind would care nothing for that. She would still see me as the shriveled, desperate hag of Branoc's unsavory speech. If I argued the point, I'd be letting her know that her comment had struck home. And while I might be physically capable of it, I had no intention of ever lying with a man or bearing a child again. There was only so much heartbreak a person could carry.

"That is your choice, of course, my lady." With some difficulty I kept my tone coolly courteous. "If you change your mind, please let me know. It seems I will be staying here until the cottage is fully rebuilt, and since Brid has so kindly allowed me to set up my stillroom near the kitchen, it's now easy for anyone in the household to consult me. It would be sad if you were still afflicted in this way at the time of your hand-fasting."

"It's not for you to express an opinion on the matter." Flidais rose abruptly to her feet; Mhairi caught the embroidery as it fell from her lap. "Tend to the grooms and kitchen folk and gardeners, of course, if they want you. As for the headaches, I need no remedy. They will pass."

For a moment, looking at her, I wondered if she could possibly be with child. Some women did suffer headaches in the early stages; could that be the cause? But no. A highborn lady, young, unwed and always surrounded by serving women—it could hardly be so. I could not for the life of me imagine Prince Oran, that poetic dreamer, anticipating his wedding night. And if Flidais had been dispatched from home already pregnant, which would have provided the prince with the perfect justification for canceling his wedding, she would by now have been showing.

"If my offer of help offended you in some way, Lady Flidais, I am sorry." The words stuck in my craw, but I got them out. There was indeed something very odd going on here. Why would she refuse the only help on offer? Maybe, many years ago, her old nurse had been poisoned by a wise woman's remedy gone wrong. I looked around the chamber, where most of the women were again industriously bent over their work, no doubt wishing the awkward conversation was over. "Of course, anyone in the household is welcome to consult me if they wish, or not to do so. I do not pretend to have the answer to every question, or to be able to effect a complete cure for every ailment. But folk will tell you I do a good enough job."

"That is indeed so," said Fíona, after a nervous glance at Lady Flidais. "I've heard nothing but praise for your efforts in the district, Mistress Blackthorn. Folk are very pleased you've come to settle at Winterfalls."

"Thank you. That is most kind. And while we're speaking of efforts, I have a visit to make this morning to an old man with a wheezy chest. So I will excuse myself, Lady Sochla, Lady Flidais." I capped my ink pot, wiped my pen, closed my book. As I left the chamber, I thought that if matters progressed at this snail-like pace, I had no chance at all of solving the prince's mystery before he was wed. Maybe Grim was having better luck.

28

GRIM

Isn't so bad when I can put in a good day's work on the house. Easier to get through supper and the time after. I can think, job well done, things moving along all right. Doesn't help much with the nights. One thing I know, Prince Oran won't be wanting me in his men's quarters babbling away half the night and keeping them all awake.

Season doesn't help. Rain, wind, sometimes snow. Have to grab the bits in between, when it's dryish. Need to work in a hurry. Not the way I like doing things. Plenty of helpers, but it's hard to get them when I need them. The other jobs, the ones for Scannal or Deaman or one of the farmers, mostly need doing in dry weather too. Doesn't leave much time for spying. By the time I'm sitting with the fellows of an evening, I'm not at my best.

There's sleeping quarters with pallets against the walls, and there's another place with a long table and benches, where they go after supper. Guards clean their weapons, fletch arrows, sharpen knives and so on. The fellows from the house talk, sit around, drink ale. Grooms and farmhands have got their own quarters out near the barn. Sometimes they drop in for a drink with this lot. Don't see much of Donagan. He'll come and sit with us for a bit, then he's off to bed. Odd that he sleeps in here. Would've thought he'd have a bedchamber of his own. Not something I can ask about.

First few days I'm trying to sort them all out. Who knew Lady Flidais before she came here, who didn't. Who's likely to talk to me and who isn't. It's not like the village in here, not at all. Folk who belong in the house are friendly enough. Grooms aren't bad either. But the men-at-arms . . . something wrong there, can't quite put my finger on it. Even when they're all drinking and laughing, nobody's at ease.

Doesn't help that I'm awake all night. Wishing I'd never agreed to this, knowing I have to do it, for Blackthorn. Be easier if there was a light in the sleeping quarters, a lamp that could burn till dawn. But no. Aedan comes around, same time every night, and puts the lamps out, then goes off with his candle. He's married, got private quarters. And once he's left, it's pitch dark.

First few nights I get through all right. But each night it's harder. Comes a time when it's too much. I hold the blanket over my mouth and whisper the words into it. I make myself hold still though I've got aches and pains all over. But the whisper's building up, getting louder and louder. I have to move. I have to get outside before it grows into a scream. I stand up, quiet as I can, and head for the door. Or where I guess the door is. Blunder into one or two things on the way. Fellows grumble and swear. I manage to slip the bolt and go out into the yard, and it's not black dark anymore. There are lights by the main entry.

It's raining. I'll soon be soaked through. But I'm not going back in there, not before dawn. I find a spot behind some barrels and hunker down. Should've brought a blanket. Though that would get wet soon enough. I put my head on my knees and start the words again. No Slammer here, no prison walls. But I still need the words. Seems like I've brought Mathuin's lockup all the way to Winterfalls with me, in my head. Not only that, the old stuff, the hidden-away stuff, is still in there. Just waiting for the dark. And no Blackthorn to keep me brave.

Didn't want to disturb anyone, hoped they'd drop off again once I was out. But not long after I've settled in my damp corner, someone comes out after me. He's got a cloak on with the hood up. Comes over and squats down beside me.

"Grim?"

Donagan. A pox on it. Sure to report to the prince in the morning, tell him I'm too crazy to be allowed here. I've ruined Blackthorn's mission already.

"Grim? Are you ill?"

"Can't sleep, that's all. Go back in, no need for you to get wet."

"You're soaked through. Come with me, let's find you some dry clothes—"

"I said leave it!" This bursts out of me.

He goes quiet. But he doesn't get up and head off. The rain keeps on falling, and the two of us get wetter.

"Didn't mean to snap," I say after a bit. "Can't sleep in there. Don't want to keep the rest of them awake. Best out here."

"Soaked through and shivering? Nonsense. If you're worried about waking the men up, we can go in through the kitchen. The night guard will open up for us."

I want to explain, but I can't. The thing's too big, too dark, and in his eyes too stupid. I shake my head. Wish I could shake all the bad stuff out and have it gone forever.

Donagan sits down on the ground next to me with his back against the wall. "Sleepless nights, that's not so good," he says. "Is something troubling you? Or is it only the need to share the quarters with so many others?"

I wish he would go away and leave me alone. But I want him to stay too. Since he came out the bad stuff's faded a bit and I don't need to keep saying the words. "Sleep better in our own place," I say. "Be all right when we can move back in."

"Didn't Prince Oran offer you and Blackthorn the empty cottage here? That would give you some privacy."

"No!" I say, too sharply by half. "That is, he did, but we said no. Need to be here, with the others." Now I've said too much. A pox on night, and the dark things, and the way they mix up my head.

Donagan keeps quiet for a while. Then he says, "Why don't the two of us go in and sit by the kitchen fire awhile? We could share some mead. You're right, the fellows won't appreciate being woken. If you want to sleep, you can roll up in a blanket on one of the benches there. If you want company, I'll stay with you until morning. Brid's usually in pretty early, and no doubt she'll sweep the two of us out the door." And when I don't say anything, because I'm wondering why he'd bother doing this, he goes on, "You've got a job to do, haven't you? Spend the night out here, and you'll be too sick to do it."

I'm shocked. He knows about the spying job? The prince said he hadn't told anyone.

"Your house, I mean," Donagan says. "You want to be back in as soon as you can, don't you?"

I let out my breath in a rush. "Fair point," I say. "But why should you miss your sleep?"

The torchlight's not the best, but I see the flash of Donagan's teeth; he's smiling. "Never mind that," he says, and I wonder if, after all, he does know the real reason we're here. I wonder if he's giving me a good excuse for bolting out of the sleeping quarters in the middle of the night. Because if he's with me, the prince's right-hand man and all, nobody's going to ask awkward questions. Could be Prince Oran summons Donagan whenever he likes. Could be there was some reason he needed me to go with him. "Are you coming, or are you set on dying of cold?" he says.

I don't answer, but I get up, and we head for the kitchen. Fact is, the company will be welcome. Never thought, that day when I was thatching and Donagan came riding by our place with the prince, that I'd be sitting up at night drinking mead with the fellow. And feeling like he'd saved me from something.

The fire's warm, the mead's good and the company suits me. Donagan's not asking questions and neither am I. He finds me a blanket, I hang my wet shirt and trousers up to dry. Might look a bit odd if anyone walked in, but they don't.

We sit there for a while; then I say, because I know I should, "You don't have to wait up. You must need your sleep. Calls you pretty early, doesn't he? Prince Oran, I mean."

He smiles, and this time it's a sad sort of smile. "I won't sleep now. Don't let it concern you. After the next council, I suppose I'll have time to sleep all I want."

No idea what the fellow's talking about. "Mm-hm?" I say. Then I remember that the prince is heading to Caher-corcan to be hand-fasted right after the next council. "Be busy, won't you? Wedding and all?" Wouldn't that be the sort of time a nobleman needed his body servant most?

He waits so long I think he's not going to answer. Then he says, quiet-like, "I won't be there for the wedding. I'm planning to move on."

From the way he speaks, I know he's sad about this. Which makes two of them, him and the prince both. Sad old place. "That's a change," I say. Hasn't he been with Prince Oran since the two of them were lads? Where would a fellow like him go? Only done the one job all his life, and you wouldn't think there'd be much call for body servants. But what would I know? "Got plans?"

Seems to me nighttime and firelight bring out things folk wouldn't be sharing in the day. In here, with the rest of the house asleep, could be we're the only two people in the world. "In fact, no," Donagan says, stretching out his legs and folding his arms. "Just an empty road ahead, Grim. But it happens sometimes. When you least expect it, everything changes."

They've had a falling-out, that's plain as the eyes on your face. But it wasn't Donagan the prince asked us to spy on. "Learned that early," I say. "Soon as you think every-thing's going right, soon as you get content, something hap-pens to take it all away."

Donagan stares at me in the firelight. "That's very bleak," he says.

I shrug. "Story of my life."

"You mean the cottage burning? That must have been a hard loss after all the work you put into it."

"Can't say I was happy to see it go up. Though if Branoc hadn't come back to do his dirty work, we wouldn't have caught the bastard. And a house can be mended easy enough. There's some things you can't mend." And some things buried too deep to share, even in the quiet of night-time by the fire.

"Mm," murmurs Donagan. After a while he says, out of the blue, "Did he ask you to question me?"

That wakes me up quick smart. "What?"

"Oran. Did he ask you to talk to me?"

Stick to the story. "Don't know what you mean. We're here, Blackthorn and me, because our house burned down and the prince was kind enough to offer us room. You know that."

"I know it's the official story, yes."

So he's not being friendly after all. He's done this because he's suspicious. Gives me a bad feeling in my gut, one I should be used to by now. Could be disappointment. "What other story would there be?" I ask.

"You tell me, Grim."

I just look at him.

"He asked me to fetch you that day. If all he was planning to do was offer you accommodation here in the house, why did he tell me to bring you in the back way, so folk wouldn't see you? Why not speak to you in the council chamber, or have Aedan do it?"

Time for some straight talking. "Tell me something," I say. "You're the prince's man. Have been for years, from what I understand. If he told you to keep something secret, would you go blurting it out to the first person to ask you?"

He flinches as if I've struck him. Then he says, in a tight sort of voice, "If you'd asked me that last spring, I'd have said no, never."

"What about now?" Don't like to press it. What I've said has hit the man hard. Didn't expect that. But I want an answer. Isn't that what this is all about, getting answers?

"I would do what was best for him," Donagan says, looking wretched.

What in Black Crow's name is going on with those one-time friends? I know nothing about this kind of folk, but I know a man in pain when I see one. "Thing is," I say, "you want me to tell you what the prince said to me and Blackthorn that day up on the hill. But if it was private, it was private."

"Fair enough," Donagan says. "But if he's asked you to help him . . . to find answers to something he sees as a puzzle . . . I have to warn you that you're probably wasting your time. There's no puzzle there, just a . . . a mistake, an error. Look for answers all you want, but you won't find any."

This feels like wandering into a swamp with a blindfold on. Take a step the wrong way and you're in over your head. Is Donagan guessing? Or does he know all about the prince's problem? Could be Oran wants it kept from everyone, even this trusted friend. That's what he said, more or less. I keep my trap shut. Seems safest.

"If I could help him," says the prince's man after a long, long time, "I would. Believe me."

I'm remembering, then, something Prince Oran said to Blackthorn, after he'd told us the story. He said if he told anyone they'd say it was a fancy. *Only in my mind*, that was what he said. And I'm doing some guessing myself. He's told his friend, and his friend doesn't like what he hears, and now that friend has decided to take himself off after years and years of loyal service. Can't be just the prince getting married; everyone must have known that would happen someday. What could be big enough to turn them cold toward each other? Could Donagan be one of those fellows that likes other men? Is he jealous of Lady Flidais?

I'm staring at him with my mouth open like a half-wit. I turn it into a yawn.

"Do you have bad dreams every night?" Donagan asks.

"Been restless, have I? Sorry. Don't want to disturb anyone." It's not dreams. Doubt if I've dropped off more than a moment or two at a time, these last three nights.

"You do thrash around and talk in your sleep."

Thought I'd been doing a good job of keeping the words in. And lying as still as I could. Seems not. Have I been falling asleep without knowing? Maybe I can't tell the difference anymore, sleep, wake, in between. Morrigan's curse. Don't know what to say to him.

"I could arrange for you to sleep somewhere else," he goes on. "If you prefer. Close by, but not in with all of them."

Yes fights to get out. I shove it back. "I need to be with the others."

Donagan gives me a sharp look. "Not by night, surely."

He knows why we're here. Must do. "Well, no, but . . ." How can I say I need Blackthorn, or at least a lamp or a fire? How can I tell him I'd be better out of doors than in the men's quarters, even when it's pouring wet and cold

enough to freeze a man's bollocks off? "More used to life
on the road," I say. "Sorry."

"No need for apologies. And certainly not to me. Let me
think about this, talk to a couple of people. I might have an
answer for you before tomorrow night."

This bothers me. Any sort of special treatment's going
to get folk talking, and that's just what Blackthorn doesn't
want. "Might be best to leave it," I say, hearing the growl in
my voice that's not for Donagan, only for stupid Bonehead
who can't keep himself under control.

"Why's that?"

I shrug. "I can get by."

Look on his face says he knows that's a lie. Truth is, if we
leave it I'll be in trouble very soon. "Don't want the whole
place knowing about this," I tell him.

"Understood," says Donagan. "Don't trouble yourself,
I'll be discreet. I think I can do this without saying anything
about tonight. Trust me."

Funny how things sometimes come clear all of a sudden.
I guessed already that he doesn't want to leave Winterfalls,
doesn't want to leave the prince, but for some reason he's
going to anyway. Now I see that he wants to help his friend
but doesn't know how. Maybe, deep down, he's hoping he's
wrong and we can find answers. "Seems a good fellow," I
say. "Prince Oran."

Donagan nods. He picks up the poker and stirs the fire.
Throws on a bit more wood. "The best," he says. "You
heard him at the council. A fine man. A worthy leader. His
modest demeanor makes some folk underestimate him."
He falls silent a bit, and I wonder if there's a *but* coming. I
don't say anything.

"If he has a failing," Donagan says, still not looking at
me, "it's that he is not very . . . worldly-wise."

"Mm-hm." Not sure what he means, and not going to
ask. Is he talking about women? Wouldn't a prince be able
to bed whatever woman he fancied?

"That's in confidence," says Donagan.

"Wouldn't breathe a word." *Except to Blackthorn*, I'm
thinking, but I don't say it. Wonder how she's getting on
among the ladies of the house. Hardly seen her since we got

here. Big crowd at mealtimes, both of us listening hard to who's saying what, no time to have more than a word or two. The way it's going, it'll be full moon before we know it and Prince Oran will be off to his hand-fasting with no way out.

"Big step, going away," I say. "Leaving your position and all. Any chance you'd change your mind?"

He's holding a bit of firewood in his hands, looking at it as if he doesn't remember why he picked it up. "If I thought you and Blackthorn could turn back time," he says, "or work magic, I'd say yes."

I've always thought wise women *could* work magic. Seems he's got no faith in that.

"If anyone can fix this," I say, "Blackthorn can."

29

ORAN

It was harder than I would have dreamed possible to maintain an air of calm. How could I go about my daily business as usual when the days seemed to be slipping by ever more quickly? The moon became a waxing crescent. It swelled toward half-full. Blackthorn did not report to me. I had done as she requested, and neither called her to see me nor sought her out. Evidently she had as yet uncovered nothing.

Grim had been put on night watch. I did not understand this, but under Blackthorn's rules I did not question Lochlan as to why a man who was in my house as a guest would be allocated guard duty. Perhaps Grim fancied a future in my service and had asked for a trial. Or, more likely, working alongside my guards gave him a better opportunity to talk to them in confidence. I did wonder how much sleep he was getting. Had he given up rebuilding his burned cottage? That made me uncomfortable. It had been clear to me how badly the two of them wanted that job done, and done quickly.

When barely fourteen days remained until full moon and my next open council, Winterfalls had visitors. They sent a messenger to let us know when they were a half-day's ride away: the chieftain of southern Ulaid, Muadan;

his wife, Breda; and two councillors, traveling to Cahercor-can early for the hand-fasting so Muadan could spend time consulting with my father. With them came an escort of men-at-arms.

My household was accustomed to coping with unex-pected arrivals. Aedan and Fíona had quarters prepared for all of them. Savory smells from the kitchen told me Brid and her helpers were preparing a special supper. The stables stood ready to accommodate the tired horses.

I had become something of a coward where Flidais was concerned, for with Blackthorn and Grim in the house I did not trust myself to act as if nothing were wrong. I was terri-fied of giving the secret away, alerting my betrothed to the fact that she and her circle were being watched. So I had ceased trying to coax her out of the women's quarters to go for a walk or a ride, or to spend time with me in the council chamber or the library. Instead, I left her to her own devices. At mealtimes I exchanged the necessary pleasantries with her, no more. But with Muadan's party present she would have to sit at table and be the lady of the house, and I would have to put on a convincing show that everything was fine. More than that, indeed, with our hand-fasting so close. If I seemed unduly cool toward my soon-to-be-wife, word might get to my parents that something was amiss.

When the visitors were spotted a mile or so from Win-terfalls, I sent Donagan to fetch Flidais and my aunt. They came to join me in the courtyard: Aunt Sochla accompa-nied by Bramble, Flidais pale but lovely in one of her blue gowns, with her hair covered by a light veil. Mhairi hovered close behind.

As the visitors rode in, I saw that among them was one I had not expected. Riding along with Muadan's party was a familiar, gray-robed figure.

"Master Oisin!" It was unusual for the druid to visit twice in such quick succession; I wondered what had brought him back to Winterfalls. "Welcome! Muadan, greetings. I hope you had a comfortable journey, Lady Breda." Once my grooms had helped everyone down, I led Flidais for-ward by the hand. "You have met Lady Flidais, I believe, on her journey from the south, when you were kind enough to accommodate her party. And of course you know my aunt, Lady Sochla."

"And the dog," observed Lady Breda with a wry smile. "Though I would have expected that creature to be in your arms, Lady Flidais. If there's one thing I remember about your visit, it's that the animal—what is its name, Bundle?— refused to leave your side for a moment. I see it's settled in well here. I hope it's been as easy for you, Lady Flidais. Many changes for you."

Flidais smiled and nodded.

"Please, come indoors," I said, wishing my betrothed could manage *welcome*, if nothing else. "You'll be wanting to rest before supper, I'm sure. Master Oisin, my steward will make sleeping arrangements for you."

"Thank you, my lord. Any corner will do. I trust you are well? And you, Lady Flidais?" The druid's was not the quick glance that went with a casual inquiry, but a deep, shrewd gaze that examined each of us in turn.

"Well enough, thank you," I said.

Our visitors dispersed, led by Aedan's helpers to their various bedchambers or, in the case of the escort, to the sleeping quarters in the stables. Men-at-arms generally weren't happy to have strangers look after their horses for long, even if those strangers were capable grooms. Besides, we had more room there. Muadan and his attendant were still in the entrance hall with me.

"Some mead?" I asked Muadan. Clearly he wanted to speak to me in private, or he would have gone with his wife.

"And a word, Prince Oran, if I may."

We made our way to the small council chamber. After refreshments had been provided, I had the attendants close the door, leaving the two of us on our own. Muadan's expression told me this was a weighty matter. Not too weighty, I hoped, with time passing and the question of Flidais still unresolved.

"I have some news from the south," Muadan said.

I was suddenly cold. "From Cloud Hill?"

"Mm-hm. I didn't want to upset Lady Flidais; best for you to tell her in private, my lord."

What was coming? Her father killed? His lands overrun? A wave of shame ran through me, for my first feeling, when Muadan spoke, had not been shock and sympathy for Flidais's family but the realization that if either guess was true, I was trapped. If her father had lost his battle, Flidais's entire future would hang on her marriage to me. Her home, as it had been, would no longer exist. "Tell me what has happened," I said, setting down the cup around which my hands had fastened themselves tightly.

"I got word through a man of mine who was in the south on unrelated business. As far as I know, Cadhan and his family are safe, but I heard that Mathuin of Laois tried to make a bargain. He wanted Cadhan to cede a large parcel of grazing land in return for Mathuin's promise to cease these border attacks. As any leader worth his salt would do, Cadhan refused him outright. And that should be the end of it, but . . ."

"But Mathuin seldom takes no for an answer."

"So I've heard." Muadan frowned into his goblet. "I don't like Cadhan's chances of dealing with this on his own. But the chieftains of the region won't want it developing into outright territorial war."

"Is this fact, Muadan, or only rumor?"

"The source was reliable," Muadan said. "It's common knowledge that Mathuin is both ambitious and ruthless. And his personal army is sizable; he could seize not only the stretch of land in question but Cadhan's entire holdings, I suspect. Probably thought he was being magnanimous in offering the so-called bargain. But now Cadhan's refused, Mathuin may feel justified in taking what he wants by force. I did hear he'd had hopes of marrying Lady Flidais, and was mightily put out when her father promised her to you."

"Mathuin? He's fifty if he's a day. And . . ." What I had heard of the fellow suggested he would not be a fit husband for any woman.

"Mm-hm. I think your lady may have had a lucky escape, my lord. But the betrothal can't have sweetened Mathuin's temper. You may have made an enemy."

I did not especially care if Mathuin of Laois loathed and despised me. Should we ever meet in the flesh, I was fairly sure the feeling would be mutual. His lands lay far from my father's, and the likelihood of our ever being at war was

slight. On the other hand, one day I would be king of Dalriada and a senior member of the High King's council.

"Thank you for bringing this to me, Muadan. Please
pass all the information on to my father when you reach
Cahercorcan. You'll be there before me, and so, possibly,
will Lorcan of Mide. Flidais and I won't be at court until a
few days before the hand-fasting."

"Nobody's going to make any moves before spring,"
Muadan said. "Not the kind of moves that involve men-at-
arms, anyway. What goes on behind closed doors is a different matter. This marriage may bring you some challenging
times in the future, my lord."

I could almost have laughed at that. "So it seems. Now
I'll let you go and rest, and I'd better break the news to
Flidais." Would this give her an excuse to develop another
headache and be absent from supper? "Again, thank you.
Are your councillors aware of the situation?"

"Not fully. I thought it best to bring the news to you and
your father first."

"I appreciate your discretion, Muadan."

When he was gone, I called Flidais into the council chamber. I asked Mhairi to wait outside.

"Please sit down, Flidais," I said when the door had
closed behind her maidservant.

"This is very formal, Oran," said my betrothed, seating
herself as instructed. She was indeed pale today; had the
headache come even before the bad news?

I poured mead for her and waited until she had taken a
sip before I told her. I kept it simple: her parents were apparently well, but the threat from Mathuin had increased,
making it unsafe for any of her party to return to Cloud
Hill until we knew more. It could be that they must all stay
permanently in the north.

She heard me out in silence, not responding with gasps
or tears or questions. When I was finished she said, "I see."
And then, "Thank you for telling me, Oran. It all sounds
rather serious."

This was so inadequate a response that for a few moments I could think of nothing to say to her. We sat in awkward silence, not looking at each other.

"Oran?"

"Yes?"

"I was thinking we might travel to court a little earlier. Perhaps even ride on with Lord Muadan's party. Your plan . . . arriving there only a few days before the handfasting . . . that will be difficult for me, as I have never been at Cahercorcan, or indeed any king's court, before."

"It is not necessary to go any earlier. We will have sufficient time."

"But, Oran . . ." She looked at me now, with her head on one side and her lashes half lowered over her eyes.

"You know I must be at Winterfalls for the open council. My people need me. I explained that to you, Flidais."

"You think a mob of muddy-booted farmers and whining village folk more important than your own wedding?" She was suddenly, inexplicably furious. "Anyone could preside over your council! Ask Donagan to do it, or Aedan! Or, if you really must be there in person, why not put it off until we return from Cahercorcan? It's only squabbles over a patch of land or a cow or two. You are a prince, Oran." And, as I made to answer, she added, "If this is all you care about me, I might as well pack my bags and head straight back home." She drew a deep, shuddering breath. A tear ran down her flawless cheek.

I was a hairbreadth from telling her I'd be most happy if she'd do just that, and the sooner the better. But she could not go. Muadan's news had only confirmed what I already knew. If Blackthorn did not uncover something truly remarkable—a proven plot to defraud me, or worse—I would have no choice but to go ahead with the marriage.

"Were you not listening when I explained what Muadan told me?" I used the kind of tone I employed in meeting with my father's councillors, calm, firm, a little detached, though my heart was a mad jumble of emotions. "Even if the season allowed such a journey, you could not go. Your father is in serious trouble, Flidais. The last thing he would want was for his daughter to ride into the middle of it." I drew breath. "Why wasn't I told that Mathuin of Laois had offered for your hand?"

She stared at me, big-eyed and silent.

"Muadan mentioned it in passing," I said. "I would have

thought you, or your father, would have included that fact in a letter."

"I . . ." She dropped her gaze. Her hands were knotted together, tight with nerves. Was I so intimidating? "I don't know. I didn't think. Perhaps he—my father—perhaps he forgot."

I did not believe that for a moment. "Your father showed good sense in refusing the offer. And considerable courage. The match would have been most unsuitable. But this means Lord Cadhan has angered Mathuin, and Mathuin is a man no leader would want as an enemy. The situation has implications for me and for my father. Our marriage will not please the chieftain of Laois, who has powerful friends."

There was a silence, then Flidais said, "I don't understand why you are so angry with me, Oran. I know nothing of such matters. Why would I be wanting to think about them so close to our hand-fasting? You are making my head ache."

"Not so badly, I hope, that you will be unable to attend supper this evening with our guests."

She gazed at me, mute with reproach.

"Ask Mistress Blackthorn to give you a draft for the pain," I said. "Since she is in residence here, that should be easy, provided you can overcome your reluctance to let her help you. I want you present at table tonight. We have guests." Would a woman afflicted by a severe headache be wanting to get on a horse and ride to court within a day or so, as Muadan's party planned to do?

"I will be there." Her voice was a small girl's now, soft and apologetic. She had as many moods as an autumn day. The way she changed from one to the next, quick as a heartbeat, was deeply disconcerting. As I got up from the table she came around to me and, rising on tiptoes, put her hands on my shoulders and kissed my cheek. "I'm sorry if I offended you," she said. "I am trying my best." She did not step back, but stayed close, almost leaning on me. Her breath was sweet; her eyes were bright with unshed tears. She was waiting, perhaps, for a kiss in return, an embrace, a tender word or two. How little she knew me, despite those nights of intimacy.

I stepped away from her, letting her hands drop. "I'm glad to hear that," I said, wondering that I could be so cold. "You might make an effort to engage our guests in conversation this evening. Since you've met Mistress Breda before, that should not be too much of a challenge for you."

It was as if I had struck her. Already pale, she became still paler, save for a spot of red in each cheek. Her lips tightened. "You speak to me as if I were not your promised wife, but a serving woman."

"I hope I speak to all women with courtesy," I said.

"I had hoped for a little more than that," said Flidais. As she turned to leave the chamber, she put a hand up to brush away the tears, and for a moment I wavered, seeing a trace of the woman whose image had captured my heart, wondering if I was terribly wrong, thinking I might be destroying what little hope remained of a marriage that, if not the perfect one I had dreamed of, might in time become at least acceptable. Then the door closed behind her, and I realized that for the first time the brush of her body against mine had entirely failed to stir my manhood.

I sat down, thinking of what we had shared, she and I, and how little it had meant. Why had I acquiesced that night when she slipped into my bed? Why had I let her lead the way with barely a word of protest? Desire was a perilous thing; on those two fevered nights, I had allowed my body to overrule my mind. Oh, yes, I had put up arguments to justify my weakness to myself, but one ugly truth remained: I could have refused her. I could have pushed her back into her own quarters and bolted the door after her. Flidais would hardly have chosen to make a fuss, knowing that if she did so the whole household would be alerted to her behavior. Responsibility for what had happened rested squarely on my shoulders.

I poured mead from the jug but did not drink. I did not like the man who had done that. He was weak, foolish, short-sighted. And I did not like the man I was today: cold, heartless, a bully. Donagan's words had been a scourge to my heart, that day when he had told me he was leaving. *I can't stand by and watch her destroy the man I knew; the man who was my friend.* But it wasn't Flidais who was destroying that man; I was doing a fine job of that all by myself.

30

BLACKTHORN

Somewhat to my horror, I was informed by Donagan that I would be sitting at Prince Oran's table for supper while the visiting druid, Master Oisin, was at Winterfalls. The prince thought, perhaps, that I would keep this druid entertained with conversation on arcane topics. Or maybe this was Oran's way of reminding me that time was passing, and that thus far I had reported nothing to him. As if I needed reminding—getting the information I needed from Flidais's women felt like trying to prise a particularly obstinate winkle from its shell. The conversations in the sewing room told me little, save that Lady Flidais had no respect for those below her own station. Even with her handmaids, she was often snappish and out of sorts. Mhairi was the only one she seemed to trust; they were a tight pair. I tried to be unobtrusive, but among the Winterfalls women I stuck out like a nettle in a patch of wildflowers. Me with my flame red hair, as short as a man's, and my workaday clothing, not to speak of my demeanour—it was no wonder I made no friends. I could not hide how much being in their presence irked me. And even when I was trying to be pleasant Flidais's women were wary of me.

It was, perhaps, not all personal. Consulting a wise woman when you needed a remedy of some kind was all very well—the local folk seemed to have no difficulty in approaching me at such times. They knew they should be courteous, ask politely, offer something in return even if it was only an apple or help to bring in a basket of firewood. But having a wise woman staying in your house, sleeping in a bed close to your own, sitting across the room, perhaps listening as you chatted to your friends over needlework, that was another matter. It was all about power. And fear. My power to ease a painful death, to bring new life safely into the world, to cure an illness or mend an injury; my ability—hah! They did not know how rusty it was—to change things by means of spellcraft. Their fear that I might take it into my head to do just that. Render them as lumpy as toads, perhaps, to punish their pride. Make them suddenly old and withered. Turn golden hair white, rosy cheeks sunken, fair skin shriveled parchment-dry. It was a long time since I had ventured down the deeper pathways of my craft, and I was not sure I wanted to visit them again. But I was fairly sure most of the women of the house believed I would, and could, do so whenever I chose. No wonder they were reluctant to talk.

It was a surprise, then, when on the afternoon of the day the druid arrived there was a tapping on the door of my makeshift stillroom, and when I called out "Come in!" the person who entered was not Brid or Fíona or one of the men wanting a remedy, but Nuala, the oldest of Flidais's three personal attendants.

I had been stringing up herbs to dry; I was standing on a bench with my arms stretched high. "I'll just finish this," I said, keeping my tone coolly courteous. "Can I help you with something, Nuala?"

"It's not for me. It's for Lady Flidais." She stood awkwardly, hands clasped before her, feet shifting on the rush-strewn floor. "Her headache is bad today."

I concentrated on knotting the twine firmly, wondering if this was an opportunity or some kind of trick. I had given up any hope that Flidais would ask for my assistance as a healer. "I thought Lady Flidais did not trust my kind," I said, securing the ends of the twine, then climbing down. "What was it she said—*I have no faith in old wives' remedies*?"

Nuala had the grace to look discomforted. "She was in

pain that day, not watching her words," she said. "I'm sorry if you were offended."

I took a good look at her, noticing that she seemed tired, almost worn out. She appeared older than she had that day at Dreamer's Pool. Those red eyes suggested she had been weeping. "Are you quite well yourself?" I asked. "This must have been difficult for you, having to travel so far from home, and not being altogether sure of the future. For Lady Flidais too, of course."

Nuala nodded. She looked over her shoulder, through the open door of my temporary stillroom and out into the kitchen, as if someone might be hanging on every word.

"It will take a little time to make up a draft for the headache," I said, moving to close the door. "Why don't you sit down, and I'll brew a restorative tea first? I could do with a cup, and it's good to have the company." Which was a lie, at least the bit about company, but she looked as if she needed a brew.

"Thank you, Mistress Blackthorn." Nuala sat, hands in her lap, her shoulders bowed as if she were too tired to sit up straight. Or perhaps not so much tired as sad. Disappointed?

I held back from asking questions until the brew—a safe chamomile and peppermint—was made, and a steaming cup set on the worktable beside her. "There. Now, I do have to ask you something. You know, I'm sure, that I should see Lady Flidais in person so I can determine the cause of the headaches. It's best to do that before providing any kind of remedy."

"But you said you would do it—"

"Yes, I did; and I will. I can make up a draft to ease the lady's pain. But only for the short term: a night or two at most. For a more lasting remedy, I would most certainly need to examine her. From what I've seen and heard, Lady Flidais's malady is severe and ongoing. Preventing her from many pursuits she has enjoyed in the past, such as reading." I forbore to mention that this seemed particularly odd in view of the lady's continuing ability to work embroidery.

Nuala took a sip of her drink. She closed her eyes.

"I will brew sufficient for two days only," I said, beginning to assemble the ingredients. "If Lady Flidais wants more, she must allow me to examine her and to ask a few questions."

"That smells good, Mistress Blackthorn."

"Wild thyme; dried, but still effective. Certain mushrooms, powdered. A few leaves of rosemary. Though if the headaches continue once the lady is married, I would cease to include that. It is not recommended if a woman might be with child." I glanced at her. "You'll perhaps remember what I said when Mhairi quizzed me about my work. It's that kind of detail that makes it unwise for folk to attempt making up these cures themselves."

"I hope you were not upset that day, Mistress Blackthorn. We were discourteous to you."

That was a surprise. "It takes more than a few ill-judged words to upset me," I said. "Besides, I seem to recall those comments did not come from you, Nuala. I bear no grudges. I have more important matters to occupy me." I tipped my dry ingredients into a bowl. "I suppose you and your husband will be off to court soon for the hand-fasting," I ventured. "Will you be staying on at Cahercorcan afterward or returning here?"

To my surprise she began to cry, helpless tears streaming down her face. She fished out a handkerchief and wiped her eyes. "So sorry, please forgive me. I'm just so . . ."

I wiped my hands and moved to sit beside her, setting aside my preparations. "What is it?" I asked. "What's wrong?"

"I can't . . . Lady Flidais . . ."

"If it helps, anything a person tells me within this chamber is confidential. I will not pass it on to anyone. As for Lady Flidais's draft, if she chides you for taking too long to fetch it, feel free to lay all the blame on me. Her opinion of me can hardly sink much lower."

"I'm sorry," Nuala said again, drawing a deep breath and squaring her shoulders. I judged she was not the kind of woman generally subject to floods of tears or admissions of defeat. Losing control made her uncomfortable. "I'm fine. Really."

I waited, saying nothing.

"There was some bad news. From Cloud Hill. Lord Muadan brought it. The prince passed it on to the men, and

Domnall just told me. We can't go back there in spring. And perhaps not at all."

A number of questions came to me; I juggled them quickly. "You mean you were thinking of leaving Lady Flidais?"

She nodded, clearly miserable. "Most of the men have been feeling they should go home and fight alongside Lord Cadhan. Besides . . ." She hesitated. "Some of us are not entirely happy here. Lady Flidais seems restless, discontent. Not herself since we came to Winterfalls."

I must tread gently. Not push too hard. "Not herself? The headaches, of course . . ."

"I should not speak of this. She would be very angry if she thought I had mentioned it to you."

"And that in itself is surprising?" I murmured, taking a risk.

A ghost of a smile appeared on Nuala's face. "Yes, that is exactly it, Mistress Blackthorn. Lady Flidais was always such a model of kindness. Not a conventional girl, but a pleasure to serve, just like her mother. She never forgot to thank us for our work or to ask after our families. Bright, busy, sweet-tempered; a lovely girl."

So she had been the Flidais of the letters after all. When had she changed? "Did Lady Flidais have these headaches when she lived at Cloud Hill?" I asked.

Nuala shook her head. "If she did, she never mentioned them. You will keep this to yourself, won't you?" She sounded genuinely frightened.

"You have my word." A lie. But I would, at least, not tell Flidais, and Flidais was the one this woman was afraid of. Had she threatened her handmaids with punishment if they spoke out?

"It has been difficult," Nuala said. "For Deirdre and me in particular. Mhairi seems happy enough. Pleased to have the position of senior handmaid, though both Deirdre and I have been in Lord Cadhan's household longer. But I don't resent that. It means—it meant—it would be easier for us to leave. Domnall and me. But now . . ."

"What was the news from Cloud Hill?"

"A challenge. From Mathuin of Laois."

I rose abruptly, turning away before she could see my face.

"Lord Cadhan's enemy," Nuala went on. "A very dangerous man. They share a border, and when we left there was a threat of war. Now Mathuin has told Lord Cadhan that if he does not give up a certain parcel of land, he will attack. Domnall says that won't happen before the spring, but in any case, it means it is too dangerous for us to go home."

"I wondered where I had heard of Cloud Hill before," I said, working on keeping my voice level. "Grim and I must have passed quite close to it on our way to Dalriada. Yes, that is bad news. Lady Flidais must be terribly worried about her family."

Nuala said nothing.

"Difficult for all of you." I took the kettle from the brazier and poured hot water over my mixture.

"We talked about leaving now, straightaway." Nuala's voice was a whisper. "Domnall and I. If we had an opportunity to work in another household we would take it. It may be possible to stay at Cahercorcan; Lady Sochla said it's a huge establishment. I think most of the men-at-arms will choose to stay there, and Domnall has a good chance of securing a position. This house . . . it's not a happy place."

"Mm-hm." I stirred the mixture. "We'll have to wait until this cools a little. Let me refill your cup."

"Thank you. It won't take too long, will it?"

"Not long. May I ask you a question, Nuala?"

"Of course."

"When you set out from Cloud Hill with Lady Flidais, you did mean to stay with her, didn't you? You and your husband, here at Winterfalls?"

"That's right, yes. It was harder for Domnall than for me, with Lord Cadhan in such strife. But Lady Flidais is so young, and not the most worldly-wise of girls, and we knew—we thought—it would be good for her to have folk from home around her in her new household. We did not expect . . . we did not imagine it would be so difficult for her to settle. That she would . . ."

"Change so much?"

"I shouldn't talk about this. I shouldn't discuss Lady Flidais behind her back."

"Well," I said briskly, "this may be cool enough for you to carry safely now. If you wrap this cloth around it, it should be easier to handle. Lady Flidais should drink a small cupful before breakfast and another at bedtime; it can be warmed up to make it more palatable. And if she wants more, she must come to see me herself."

"She won't be happy about that."

I shrugged. "I won't set aside the rules of my craft because someone's taken a dislike to me. You may tell her I said that." In fact, I could tell her myself, since I would be sitting at the high table for supper tonight. An unwelcome thought came to me. "Oh, no," I muttered.

"What is it, Mistress Blackthorn?" Nuala had picked up the jug and was ready to leave.

"Nothing. Only . . . I have been asked to sit at the prince's table tonight; I believe I'm to make conversation with a druid. And it has occurred to me that I have no suitable clothing." I would have been quite happy to wear my somewhat tired-looking everyday gown, but since Prince Oran had guests, I should probably try not to embarrass him. Druids, with their robes, had a distinct advantage.

"You're so thin," Nuala said, looking at me with the critical eye of the lady's maid she was, "you'd be swamped in anything of mine, and Deirdre's would be too long on you. But you can't wear that. Oh, I know! Sinead, Lady Sochla's maid—she's a slip of a thing. I'll ask her, shall I?"

"I'd better ask her myself," I said, thinking Nuala had done enough of other folk's bidding for one day. "But if you could mention it to Sinead when you go back, that would smooth the way for me. Thank you. And, Nuala . . ."

"Mm?"

"Please come and talk to me any time you want. Sometimes it does help."

A wan smile. "Thank you, Mistress Blackthorn. You are kind."

Kind? Me? Hah! Still, she seemed a good person, better than I'd been ready to believe earlier. Deserving of a listening ear, at the very least. As for supper and the need to don apparel fitting the guest of a prince, both would try me hard. Especially if the talk turned to Mathuin of Laois. That man cast a long shadow.

31

Suppertime, I'm looking around, trying to spot Blackthorn. Long time since I spoke to her. Can't see her with
the waiting women. I'm thinking maybe she's been called
away to do healer's work. Then I see her at Prince Oran's
table, sitting down like a fine lady. She's got a druid on one
side and the prince's auntie on the other.

My jaw drops. She's all dressed up, fine gown in gray-
green like willow leaves, and her hair's pushed back under
a sort of band with embroidery on it. She looks ... she
looks good. But not like herself. I know what she's thinking. It's in her eyes, on her face, in the way she's sitting, tight
as a creature in a cage. *Let me out of here.*

I'm staring. I make myself look away, sit down with the
fellows, keep myself to myself. Just as well if I don't get to
talk to her tonight. I'd have to tell the truth; tell her how I
nearly got myself thrown out of the prince's house. Could
have wrecked the mission for her. Me being still here tonight, that's only luck.

It happened like this. Some of the fellows weren't happy
with me taking night watch. Not the prince's men. The ones
from the south, Lady Flidais's guards. Seems there's not
enough work to go around, and since I don't belong here, they

think they should come first. Which is funny, since they grumble all the time about night watch. No pleasing folk sometimes.

I'd done quite a few nights before trouble happened. Thought it was working well: stand guard at night, work on the cottage in the morning, sleep in the afternoon up by the wood, where it's quiet. Outhouse is weather-tight now. Back to Winterfalls in time for supper. Couldn't see why anyone would object.

But the fellows, the ones from Cloud Hill, weren't happy. Took their time letting me know, but when they did it all blew up fast. First one of them making a remark, then another one saying his bit, an insult, another insult, a knock that wasn't quite an accident. A push. A harder push.

Told them I wasn't interested in a fight. Told them they should save their blows for a proper battle, like the one Lord Cadhan might be fighting back in Cloud Hill. Shouldn't have said that. Quick sharp there were six of them around me in the men's quarters, voices coming at me like knives, saying I was a half-wit, an ignorant oaf, a numbskull, and what would a dolt like me know about Lord Cadhan's business anyway? I should stick to the work the villagers were kind enough to give me and stop robbing trained men of their livelihood. Where was I from, anyway? I was a wanderer, a nobody, not to be trusted. And so on.

Thing is, those years in Mathuin's lockup gave me a thick hide, and a lot bounces off it. Sometimes something'll get through. But I've got big shoulders. Sat there quiet, that night, and let them say what they wanted to say.

If Domnall had been in the men's quarters they wouldn't have dared say those things, and they wouldn't have done what came next. Good man, Domnall; keeps the fellows in line as well as he can. But he was off talking to someone, so they grabbed their chance.

Didn't see it coming. Thought they were finished with me. They sat down at the table and started talking among themselves. Acted as if I wasn't there, which suited me fine. They were talking about women, the way men sometimes do, unseemly talk that I didn't like, but I stayed there anyway. The mood they were in, if I'd walked out they'd have taken it as an insult.

"Another thing," said one fellow. All of them had had too much ale, and it was showing. "Too many rules here. Stay in the men's quarters overnight, no fraternizing, don't speak the wrong way to the ladies and so on."

"And no bothering the village girls," said one of the others. "Back home, the girls didn't call it bothering, they called it fun."

"Fun?" said a third man. "Not much of that around here. What's a man to do? No work, no amusements, house full of tight-arsed maids and fat serving women . . ."

"Oh, I don't know," said someone else. "I reckon that Sinead might be up for something, if you asked the right way."

"That skinny bitch? Not her. Isn't she Lady Sochla's maid? You wouldn't want to fall foul of the prince's aunt."

"Why would the old woman need to know? Quickie up against the wall, that's all I'm after, not a night in the girl's bed."

Someone laughed. "Since she sleeps in the old lady's room, you'd hardly be wanting that, lad. What if you got the two of them mixed up? The shock would turn your hair white."

"Nice surprise for the old woman, though," one of them said. "Probably invite you back the next night."

General guffawing at this. I was feeling pretty bad by this stage. Wanted to tell them to shut up, but didn't want to draw attention by speaking out. Wished I was somewhere else. Common enough feeling these days.

"Pity about Ciar. Now she was a real firebrand of a girl. Always ready, always willing, hundred different ways to please a man. What a waste."

"Come on, Niall, the girl's dead. Show some respect."

"Just saying. If any of them had to go, shame it was her. Real woman. Juicy as a ripe plum. Should be more like her, then we'd all be satisfied."

Then it came. "Hey, Grim! How about that woman of yours? Is she juicy? Lonely old bed, now you're on night watch."

Felt the red rising inside me. Shoved it down. Told myself not to answer. Knew they were trying to goad me, get me angry, the fools.

"Cat got your tongue, bonehead? Speak up when you're spoken to, can't you? Tell us about the witch. Dried-up old thing, isn't she? Skinny as a mangy cur and evil-eyed with it. Big man like you can't be getting much satisfaction from—"

The red was in my head, filling it up, blocking out everything. I was roaring, grabbing, squeezing, pounding. And then someone shouted, "Stop it!" and the red faded and there I was with a man in my grip, ready to thump his head down on the table one more time. "Stop!" yelled Domnall again, and I let the man go. Looked around. Saw five of them white as ghosts, staring at me, and Domnall striding over from the doorway. The fellow I'd been holding was making a moaning sound. Not dead, then. Nobody was rushing to help him.

I stepped back. Black Crow's curse! I'd just undone all Blackthorn's good work. I'd just wrecked the mission. I'd get thrown out of Winterfalls or worse. Couldn't bring myself to say sorry, though.

"He called Blackthorn bad names," I said.

Domnall came up, gave the fellow a quick check. "You could have killed him," he said, looking at me. Truth was, if he hadn't come in, I wouldn't have stopped. I could see he knew that. "You're due on watch," he said, though it was early. "Go now. Report to me first thing in the morning."

That meant my time at Winterfalls was over. Would be over by morning. Even if Domnall gave me another chance, unlikely as that was, the men-at-arms wouldn't accept what I'd done. I'd just made enemies of the lot of them.

Life's full of surprises. Mostly bad ones—had plenty of those. Disappointments. Reversals. Nasty accidents. But sometimes there are good surprises, like Blackthorn letting me come with her to Dalriada, and then letting me stay. Or the folk from the village helping me rebuild our place after the fire. The morning after I nearly beat one of his men to a pulp, I reported to Domnall as ordered. Lochlan was with him, the prince's master-at-arms, which made it even worse than I'd expected. I stood there in the guard room with my bag on my back, ready to leave as soon as they'd said what they had to say. One good thing, I was thinking. If they'd been going to lock me up they'd have done it already, not waited until I'd stood watch another night.

"Well, Grim," Lochlan said. "How do you account for your violent outburst last night?"

"What I said to Domnall, Master Lochlan. The men insulted Blackthorn. The lady is my friend. Just standing up for my friend."

"Could you not have used words rather than blows?"

"Not good with words. They'd have laughed."

"Perhaps that is true," Lochlan said. "But Domnall tells me you looked as if you would kill Seanan. I know you are taking a turn as night guard, and I recognize your ability to do a good job at that. But you are not trained as our men are, to curb your anger and to know when to stop. That can be dangerous. Especially when a man is as big and strong as you are. An insult to a lady, however disrespectful, surely does not merit death."

"Wouldn't have killed him." But maybe that was a lie. When the red came, sometimes I didn't know what I was doing until it was over.

Neither of them said anything for a bit. "You want me to leave now?" I made myself say. Nothing worse than bad news being dragged out.

Lochlan looked at Domnall; Domnall looked back at him.

"Leave?" Domnall said. "We won't ask you to leave, Grim. Unless you find yourself unable to comply with the penalty we've determined."

My head filled up with all kinds of penalties, most of which I wouldn't like at all. I wished they'd get on with it. I'd spent the whole night thinking I'd ruined Blackthorn's mission, and now this. Whatever it was.

"I want you to make amends with the men," Domnall said. "Continue with your duties, but ensure this kind of thing does not happen again."

"If you decide you wish to stay with us longer," said Lochlan, "we'll provide you with the same training as all the men get. That includes learning to control your temper and not to take to your fellow guards with your fists, no matter how much they provoke you."

This was a surprise. I didn't tell him I had no intention of joining Prince Oran's guards, even if the prince wanted me, which I was sure he wouldn't. *Make amends.* That didn't sit well with me, but there was no choice, not if I wanted to help Blackthorn.

"I see," I said. "One thing, though."

"And that is?"

"The fellows. The way they were talking. Not just about Blackthorn, but the other women too. Disrespectful. Making amends, that could be hard. I'll do my best. But I won't sit there and listen to that sort of thing. Training in keeping their tempers, that's all very well. But why not training in holding their tongues, if all they can say is that rubbish?"

There was a proper smile on Domnall's face now. "You may find making amends isn't so difficult," he said. "As for the other, I think your presence among them may go some way to moderating their speech. Just keep your fists out of it."

It's funny. Me belting that fellow Seanan's head on the table hasn't made the men-at-arms hate me more. It's earned me respect. Overnight, like magic. Since that morning I've tried harder to be friendly, but not overfriendly. Had no trouble with the men. I've joined in their talk when I could. I've done my share of the work. The one time they got onto the subject of women, I glared and bunched up my fists and they went quiet. Nobody's even mentioned Blackthorn. Which is just as well, because if they speak ill of her I'll do it again, and this time I won't be so quick to stop.

So here I am at the supper table, glad they didn't send me packing but worried too. Time's running out and between night watch and mending the cottage I've hardly had a chance to say a word to Blackthorn. Looks like tonight will be no different. If she's up at the high table with Lady Flidais, she'll most likely have to stay in the hall after they finish supper, and I'm on duty.

Seanan passes me the salt. I make myself say thanks. Domnall has his eye on us, and I see him nod. So far, so good. Be glad when we get out of here, though. The thatching's all done now, thanks to those two lads from the brewery, and there's only inside work to finish, jobs we can work on even in bad weather. Want to tell Blackthorn we might be in there before winter after all. That'll make her happy. Be good to see a smile on her face. Even bigger smile, of course, if we solve Prince Oran's mystery first. Have to say I don't like our chances.

32

At this table I was a figure of fun, a scarecrow in a group of beautifully embroidered dolls. It was a relief to find that Master Oisin was of the friendly variety of druid. He began a conversation about the terrain around Winterfalls and what kind of herbs I had been able to gather. Over the soup I found myself discussing teas brewed from holly leaves and how best to render them palatable without losing their efficacy.

Supper progressed through various courses. Lady Flidais, who was seated on the other side of Master Oisin, seemed uncomfortable. She was beautifully dressed, with her hair elaborately plaited and her head held proudly high. But she looked ill at ease, as if those who shared her table were not only strangers, but strangers whom she did not particularly trust. If my draft had eased her headache — it should have done — there was no sign of it in her demeanour. She exchanged a word or two with the visiting chieftain and his wife; she responded to innocuous questions from Lady Sochla and Oisin. But mostly she sat in silence, toying with her food.

How could I get her to talk to me? How could I persuade her to trust me enough to tell the truth, whatever it was? It was a pity I wasn't more like Master Oisin, whose very manner inspired trust. I was pondering this and trying to catch what Lord Muadan was saying to the prince — were they speaking of Mathuin of Laois? — when Lady Sochla leaned forward and addressed the druid.

"Master Oisin, I'm hoping you will favor us with a tale or two after supper."

"Of course, Lady Sochla. What manner of tale would the company prefer? A story of true love, perhaps? A tale of transformation? An epic adventure — journeys and battles and quests?"

"I enjoy a tale of magic and mystery," I said. "But, of course, the choice is not up to me."

Master Oisin smiled. "I expect you are something of a storyteller yourself, Mistress Blackthorn. We could perhaps share the duty."

Flidais spoke, suddenly sharp as broken glass. "Since Blackthorn sits with us every morning in the sewing room, we've heard more than enough of her tales. I'm sure you have something more interesting, Master Oisin."

There was a frozen silence; even the weighty discussion between Prince Oran and Lord Muadan ceased. Then the prince spoke. "That was uncalled-for, Flidais. Mistress Blackthorn sits at this table as my guest." He made no attempt to hide his displeasure.

Flidais flushed scarlet. She looked down at her platter. Mhairi, standing behind, laid a comforting hand on her mistress's shoulder, and the lady shook it off.

"A tale of transformation would suit very well," said Lady Sochla, smoothing over the difficult moment. "The dream of Aengus; the wooing of Etain. Or there's that strange old story about the brothers being turned into swans."

"Not so very old, and close enough to home, that one," said Master Oisin. "But perhaps Lady Flidais fancies the tale of true love instead."

"You must tell whatever tale you please," muttered Flidais. She was deeply unsettled, as well she might be. It must be almost unheard-of for a prince to reprimand his lady before a table full of guests. With the hand-fasting so close, was Oran starting to panic? I'd have to speak to him in the morning, if the opportunity arose, and warn him to keep up the pretense that nothing was amiss, or I'd never get Flidais to talk.

The promise of a tale kept most of the household in the hall once supper was over. Men moved tables aside and benches were set by the hearth. Oisin had a little harp and one of the fellows had a whistle, so there was music first. Then the druid told his tale, one I had never heard before, about a sad creature that could live neither entirely in the water nor entirely on the land; a being that dwelled all alone in a seaside cavern and cried by night for a companion in its solitude. But there was no companion, for it was the only one of its kind in all Erin.

Some eyebrows went up as the druid's tale unfolded, for it was indeed sorrowful, and after Oisin's earlier suggestion of a story suited to a hand-fasting, this one seemed an unlikely choice.

But Master Oisin struck me as a subtle man even by druidic standards. This odd tale might turn out to be exactly right for the occasion.

"The local people, fishermen and the like," went on the druid, "were becoming weary of the creature's moaning and wailing. They were losing sleep, and fisherfolk keep early hours. They spoke of creeping up with spears and ridding the cave of its occupant forever. But the wise woman of the settlement warned them that such violent action would put a curse on the place, and the noise would likely continue, night after night, even when the cave was empty. One of the women said maybe there was another creature like this one somewhere, and shouldn't someone go out and look for it, for who could say with certainty that it did not exist on some lonely island or in the bottom of a well or in some other mysterious place where earth and water met? Not in Erin, maybe, but in a realm close by? And one or two of the men liked this idea, and said they might put out in their boat and go on a quest to find it, but their wives pointed out that they could be looking for a long time, and who was going to catch the fish they would have caught if they'd stayed at home as sensible folk should?

"So they were in something of a dilemma, as you can understand. Perhaps you can help me here, Mistress Blackthorn."

Already on edge in this chamber packed with folk, I felt my body tighten still further. "Of course," I said in a tone I hoped was not too strangled.

"Had you been present that day, what course of action would you have suggested, as a wise woman?"

Ah. This was not difficult. "I'd have said, consult the oldest person in the neighborhood. Ask that person if they can remember a story about this kind of creature, something they heard from their grandmother or grandfather. Search in that story for clues. The lore holds all the wisdom we need; it's just a matter of looking." And it came to me that I had done this myself, not so very long ago. That crone whose deathbed I had attended—she'd spoken of a wise woman named Holly, and Dreamer's Pool, and pigs. A shiver passed through me. *The lore holds all the wisdom we need.* Had Grim and I been looking for solutions in the wrong place?

"A good answer," said Lady Sochla. The little dog, absent during supper, had come back in; she had it on her knee.

"Indeed, and I thank you for it, Mistress Blackthorn. Of course, they had already consulted their own wise woman, who had advised them against killing the creature. But although she was wise, she was not the oldest among them. That honor went to an ancient man who once, many years ago, had caught a gigantic salmon and let it go again. He'd sworn at the time that the fish had whispered a secret in his ear, but he'd never said what it was.

"This old fellow lived on a rocky promontory up above the creature's cave, in a hut he'd built himself, carrying stones from the fields. He was gnarled and crabbed, shriveled and bowed, and over the years his life had become as solitary as the creature's, since any time folk went up to check how he was faring, he'd greet them with a snarl or a curse. A lad took fish up each morning so the old fellow wouldn't starve, and that lad learned so many oaths he could have used a different one every day, if his mother had let him."

Some laughter at this. A pity Grim had left the hall straight after supper; he'd have liked the story.

"The folk of the settlement discussed who would go up and ask the old fellow about the creature," Master Oisin went on, "and the wise woman was chosen. She took a flask of mead, a loaf of bread, a basket of pears and a fillet of fresh codfish, as well as a warm woolen blanket and a pair of boots. The lad carried this offering for her as far as the stone wall that marked off the old man's land, and she took it the rest of the way on her own. Although it was daytime, she could hear the creature crying in the cave down below. It was a sound fit to freeze your heart, such was the sorrow in it.

"It took a while for her to be let in the door, and even longer to get the old man talking, but a wise woman is nothing if not determined"—here, Master Oisin cast a glance at me—"and it did help that she offered to cook the fish for him right away, though that proved a challenge, since the hearth was cold and the only cook pot thick with grime. And if she used an uncanny trick or two to get the pot clean, and to bring in wood, and to start the fire burning, that was reasonable enough, since she was a wise woman, not a village wife. She bullied the old fellow into washing his face and changing his shirt, though the other one was as filthy as the first, then she sat him down with a platter of bread and fish and a cup of mead in front of him, and let him enjoy his meal in peace.

"When he was done, she cut up a pear for him with her little knife and set it out prettily on the platter, in the shape of a petaled flower. And she asked him if he knew any old stories that might shed light on the creature below, bellowing in its sadness."

Master Oisin looked around the circle of listeners. All of us were rapt with attention. This time he did not pick me. "Prince Oran, although you are no druid, I know you are well versed in ancient tales. Have you a suggestion for me?"

Oran looked as startled as I had been when the druid had asked me for a contribution. But he gathered his composure quickly. "An existing tale, Master Oisin? Or may I devise one to suit?"

"Devise all you wish, my lord. Is not a tale a living thing that grows and changes with every telling?"

The prince cleared his throat. This was a far more challenging task than mine. To come up with an appropriate story out of the blue before a waiting crowd required quick thinking. "The old man said, 'I was telling tales before you were born, young woman. I was telling tales when I was two years old, and mighty fine ones they were, too.'"

The crowd chuckled. It seemed Master Oisin was not the only one with a talent for storytelling.

"'But can you remember them?' challenged the wise woman.

"The old fellow looked at her. 'Maybe,' he said. 'If I've a mind to. The time I caught the salmon and threw it back in. That's a tale.'

"It was indeed; all the folk of the settlement knew it, and the size of the salmon had grown a little with each telling. But every coastal village has its story of an unrivaled catch, be it the full net of herring or the one gigantic fish. The old man's tale could surely have nothing to do with the sad creature in the cave.

"On the other hand," Prince Oran went on, looking around his audience, "a wise woman's instincts are usually sound. And this wise woman knew, in her heart, that if the old fisherman had brought up that story first, it was the one she needed. 'I'd like to hear it,' she said.

"'What'll you give me if I tell it?' said the old man, quick as a wink.

"'A hot dinner tomorrow, cooked by my own hand.' If he was quick, she was his match.

"The old man laughed. The sound was like the creaking of a rusty old cartwheel. Then he told the tale of the mysterious salmon and of the magic pool where it swam. It was a creature of legend, so long had it been living there. Nobody had ever seen it, not properly; only the whisk of its graceful tail or the gleam of its great eyes from the shadows under the bank. The folk of that village—the place of the old man's youth—gave the pool a wide berth, feeling the tinge of the uncanny on it. It was said the fey lived nearby, and the fey were not to be trusted.

"By now the wise woman was fascinated," the prince continued. "In truth, she had thought the old fellow so hostile that even if he still had stories in his mind, he would refuse to tell them. This one, he both remembered and told well. 'But you went to the pool,' she ventured.

"'Ah, well,' the ancient said, 'I was young and foolish in

those days. Took no heed of my elders and betters. Yes, I went there, every day I went, when I should by rights have been helping with the nets or digging the garden. Went and watched. Waited for that big old fish to come out and show himself.'"

The shiver came again, a chill breath passing through me. This, like the tale mentioned by a dying woman, was a story about a creature. And a pool, a place of magic and mystery. I looked at Lady Flidais. She had seemed uncomfortable before. She was more so now, her hands clutched together on her lap, her gaze anywhere but on her betrothed as he told the story. I was not the only one watching her; the druid, too, had noticed her demeanor.

"The old fellow had been patient; remarkably patient for a young lad, as he was then," said Prince Oran. "And after many turnings of the moon, as the trees around the mysterious pool grew to summer splendor, then to the golds and yellows of autumn, and then to the bare-branched austerity of winter, he found himself on the bank in a season of soft light and fresh new leaves, and at last he saw the great fish emerge from hiding to show itself beneath the water, graceful and strong, swift and beautiful. And, being a young lad, he baited a hook and dangled his line into the pool. To his amazement, in a trice the fish was caught and fighting hard.

"It was only when he had hauled the monster out onto the bank, where it lay thrashing and gasping, that the young man heard its voice. For this, of course, was no ordinary fish. It was not only far bigger than others of its kind, but its home was a place of deep magic, and the creature possessed a wisdom far beyond the usual. 'Spare me,' the fish pleaded, and the sound was the strangest thing the lad had ever heard, 'and I will grant you a wish.' Not three wishes, you note, only the one; the lad would have to think carefully.

"Now that fish could have fed the entire village for a week or two, so this was not an easy choice. Not only that, but folk had been teasing the boy about the long days he'd been wasting up at the pool, for nobody had believed he would ever catch the thing. He'd have liked to carry it back and show them. Tell them, *There, see?* But he'd heard a few old tales of magic and mystery, and with the knife in his hand, ready to strike the blow that would end the creature's life, he paused. 'A wish? Why would I want a wish?'

"'Riches,' croaked the dying salmon. 'A sweetheart. Admiration. Nobility. Happiness. A new cottage for your old mother. How would I know what you might want? I'm a fish.'

"Something odd came over the lad then. For the rest of his life, he was never able to explain it. He saw how the bright eyes were fading, and the shining scales losing their luster, and the gasps becoming more desperate. Then he eased the hook gently from the creature's mouth. 'Don't bother about the wish,' he said, and with a certain amount of difficulty, since it was a very big fish and he was only an ordinary-sized lad, he threw the salmon back in the water, where it swam with surprising speed into the shadows and out of sight. Then he ran home with his story. And if there hadn't happened to be a fellow taking his pigs into the wood that day to forage, who'd looked down between the trees at precisely the right moment and seen the whole thing unfold, nobody would ever have believed a word of it."

There was a ripple of appreciation from the audience. Prince Oran glanced at the druid. "That was the tale the old man told the wise woman. And though she'd heard the story of the giant salmon before, more than once, she was surprised. This was the first time the old man had said anything about a wish."

"Thank you, my lord," Master Oisin said. "You have given us not only a fine story, but the clue to solving the dilemma of the sad creature in the cave. For the wise woman knew that a wish once offered, and refused with kindness for the right reasons, is a wish still waiting to be granted. She regarded the old fellow, and he looked back at her with his rheumy eyes. 'That thing in the cave down below,' she said. 'It needs your help. You've got a wish. Why not use it?'

"'To put the creature out of its misery?' the old man asked. 'Are you saying that I spared that fish's life as a young man so I can kill now? You want me to go to my deathbed with the weight of that on me?'"

Don't call on me to solve this for you, I willed the druid.

"Lady Flidais," said Master Oisin, "how would you choose to end this tale?"

She started with some violence. Despite my dislike of the girl, for a moment I felt something akin to pity. "To tell you the truth, Master Oisin," she said, "I do not much care for the story; I do not really see the point of it. If you need so much help to tell it, why not choose another, one with which you are more familiar?"

Several people made to speak, the prince among them, but Master Oisin got in first. "Indeed, indeed, my lady." He sketched a little bow in Flidais's direction and spread his hands out as if in apology. "Let me bring this tale swiftly to its conclusion.

"'I am not sure exactly what you should do,' said the wise woman, 'only that a wish is a chance, an opportunity, and now seems the right time to use it. Not to kill; a wish born out of a generous impulse should surely not be used in such a way. Use it to heal what is wounded. To mend what is broken.' And as she said this she looked not in the direction of the cave with its forlorn inhabitant but straight at the old man.

"Worn and crooked and ill-tempered as he was, he was no fool. 'Best on my own,' he growled. 'Don't need company. Can't abide folk.'

"'Truly?' the wise woman asked. 'For a solitary man, you tell a fine story. Shame if there's nobody to listen. And it seems a waste for that lad who had the courage to go to the uncanny pool, and the patience to wait through the seasons, and the compassion to set the salmon free, to end up living on his own in a place like this, getting older and wearier every day, without even the will to scrub his own cook pot.'

"'Who cares about a cook pot?' the old man snarled, but the wise woman could see she'd got him thinking. 'Anyway, that's no selkie down there, to be turned into a beautiful girl as soon as a man makes a wish. It's a grumly thing. A monster. And it can't live on the land, not all the time. Nor in the sea.'

"'Men and women have it in them to be far more monstrous than this creature,' said the wise woman. 'It's lonely. Like you. As for the sea or the land, you'll need to make your wish carefully. Now I'm off, since you don't care for company. I'll be back tomorrow with that hot dinner.'

"But when she did come back, with a stew in a covered pot, she heard voices from inside the old man's hut, so she left the pot on the doorstep and went away, not before noticing that there was a trail of watery slime stretching all the way from that very doorstep down to the cave, or as near as she could see. And there was a cloak dripping on the line outside the back door, a lovely thing that seemed fashioned of seaweed, in every shade of blue and green and brown a person could ever dream of and a few more besides.

"There was no more moaning and crying from the cave. Not ever again. The folk of the settlement were wary for a while, knowing the old man had someone staying in his cottage with him, not sure exactly who or what that someone might be. But when, after quite a long time and a lot of dinners left on the doorstep, his guest allowed herself to be seen, she turned out to be nothing remarkable at all, only an old woman with raggedy white hair and steady eyes, who bade folk good day in a voice as soothing as the wash of wavelets on a summer shore. As for the old man, he stayed the same, bent and worn, crabbed and argumentative. Mostly. But he did open his door to some: the wise woman, the lad who used to bring fish, one or two others, and when supper was over he'd tell tales, and the old woman would sing songs, and those tales and those songs were the most wondrous and enchanting ever heard, from one end of Erin to the other. And that is the end of the story." The druid turned toward Lady Flidais. "As for the point of it, my lady, that's likely to be different for every listener. But it is, in the end, both tale of magic and mystery and tale of transformation."

Flidais seemed about to speak but evidently thought better of it. She was looking pale and pinched, as if the headache had returned tenfold. Now, as various folk congratulated the druid and Prince Oran for the odd but satisfying story, the lady rose to her feet, swayed, then collapsed into a dead faint.

I reached her quickly and knelt by her side. Mhairi, on the other side, was rolling up a shawl to put under Flidais's head, while Lady Sochla shooed people out of the way. And now Master Oisin was there, crouching down beside me, taking the lady's wrist between his fingers.

"She'll be all right, it's only a faint," I said. "Mhairi, did she take the draft I prepared for her? The one she sent Nuala to fetch?"

Mhairi scowled at me. "Maybe. I don't know."

"You are her maidservant. You must know."

"Yes, then. She took it because she was told to take it. And look at all the good it's done."

With admirable speed, Aedan organized a pair of men with a stretcher to carry the lady to the women's quarters. It was notable that Prince Oran was not among those clustered around his unconscious betrothed. He came over belatedly, as the bearers were about to take her away, and regarded her with an expression that told me he thought she was pretending.

"No need for concern, my lord," I said, wishing I could warn him to dissemble better. "The heat from the fire, the crowd . . . Lady Flidais should be herself again by morning." Hah! I could have expressed that better. "A good rest, a sleeping draft, that should be all she needs."

"I concur," said Master Oisin. "The lady is exhausted. We should leave her to Mistress Blackthorn's excellent care."

"Thank you, Mistress Blackthorn," said the prince. "I know you will tend her well."

I followed the stretcher out of the hall, feeling the temptation, while Flidais lay unconscious, to work a little spell that would make her tell the truth when she woke. That should lead to quick answers for the prince, and we surely needed those. But magic was perilous. It had a habit of coming back and biting you, especially if the reason for using it was selfish, destructive or otherwise flawed. Besides, hadn't I promised Conmael I'd use my gifts only for good? While saving Prince Oran from a loveless marriage might be viewed as beneficial, robbing Lady Flidais of her secure future was less admirable, and the two went hand in hand. The fact that I thought the prince a good man and Lady Flidais ill-mannered and ignorant made no difference to that.

So, no spellcraft. Chances were I'd lost the knack anyway. I'd try kindness instead, if the lady would let me. She'd been disturbed tonight, not only by the prince's public reprimand at the table but also, badly, by Master Oisin's story. A tale about a pool, and magic, and a transformation. Everything pointed to that day at Dreamer's Pool when they'd gone bathing. That, surely, was the time when the sweet, scholarly Flidais of the letters became the abrasive, unhappy creature who would soon be marrying the prince. Wasn't Dreamer's Pool exactly the kind of mysterious fey spot—like that cave in the druid's story—where transformations took place?

This couldn't be a simple impersonation. This woman *was* Flidais. Or, at least, she was Flidais in the flesh. What had apparently changed was her character. Seeing someone close to her drown would have been shocking, distressing. But it would not have been enough to change her entirely. Could this really be a magical transformation? The notion was enough to make my head spin. A spell that somehow switched the two women's bodies, leaving their spirits and their awareness behind? That would be a most powerful enchantment. I did not doubt that there still existed in Erin certain places of deep magic; wells, caverns, waterfalls, crags whose power sang in the bones and beat in the blood. Could Dreamer's Pool be such a place? I had felt the strangeness there, and I knew Grim had too.

Or might what had befallen Flidais have a different cause? Conmael's folk were in the wood, or so he had suggested. Conmael had come to Prince Oran's council. Conmael had caused the roof of Mathuin's lockup to cave in on a calm, sunny summer day. He had worked a spell to ensure my future took the course he wanted, not the one I would have chosen. He knew how angry that made me. Could he be meddling with these folk's lives for the sole purpose of testing my resolve?

If this really was a magical transformation, hard though that was to believe, it was bad news for Prince Oran. If the woman now being carried into her bedchamber was the maid in her mistress's body, it meant the true Flidais had drowned that day in Dreamer's Pool. There was no revers-

ing this; not even the fey could bring the dead back to life.
And I could not think of a way this would extricate the
prince from his betrothal. Most folk wouldn't believe the
story, not even if the maid confessed. How could it ever be
proved?

I'd have to ask Conmael outright if this was his doing.
And since Conmael was hardly going to come when I
called him, like a well-trained dog, I'd have to go to Dreamer's Wood and look for him. The prospect of a walk over
there and a day spent in the quiet was pleasing, though
time was short. The cottage was as close to being home as
anything ever was, and Grim made undemanding company.
I could try my theory out on him first, and find out if he'd
discovered anything useful. I would go in the morning.

Flidais came out of her faint soon after we reached the
bedchamber. Mhairi seemed uncomfortable with my presence. But her lady was unwell, and the prince had said he
wished me to look after her, so the maidservant could
hardly ask me to leave. She helped her mistress undress
and put on a night-robe. Flidais's monthly courses had
started, which went some way to explaining both her discomfort and the faint, so while Mhairi cleaned her up and
fetched a supply of rags, I checked the level in the jug I had
given Nuala earlier and judged that Flidais had taken at
most half a cup of the headache draft before supper.

Now was not the time to bully her about that, or indeed
about anything. She was as white as the linen of her pillows, with shadows under her eyes. Exhausted, in pain and,
I thought, frightened. Whatever was going on, it had become too big for her and she seemed lost.

"Mistress Blackthorn?" Nuala was in the doorway with
Deirdre behind her. "How can I help?"

"Go to the kitchen and ask for warm milk with honey.
That may help Lady Flidais sleep better." I should make up
a sleeping draft. But that meant going to my stillroom, and
I did not want to leave Flidais's side. It was at times like
this, when folk were at their lowest, that they were inclined
to let slip their secrets.

Mhairi had gathered Flidais's clothing and taken it away

to be laundered. Nuala headed off to the kitchen, and Deirdre went with her. For now, Flidais and I were alone.

"Where does it hurt?" I asked. "Your head? Your belly?
Both?"

Flidais put a hand on her stomach; tears welled in her
eyes.

"You have this pain every month? I can make up a simple remedy for you, a tea, not at all bad tasting if you add
honey. I know you don't trust me, my lady, but believe me, I
do know my craft."

She shook her head. "It's not that," she whispered. "It's . . .
never mind. I only have cramps the first day, then it passes."

I sat down on the stool beside her bed. The chamber was
beautiful; the walls were hung with embroidered scenes of
women sitting in a garden, playing with a ball by a fountain,
walking with small dogs, picking flowers. I suspected every
ornately carved chair, every delicate little table, every fine
detail had been chosen by Prince Oran especially for his
sweetheart. And here she was, utterly miserable.

"Something is troubling you, Lady Flidais," I said, deciding on a direct approach. "Not just a headache or a bel-
lyache, but something worse. I do know my herb lore. I do
know how to ease pain. And they say I am good at solving
puzzles. If there's anything I can do, please ask." I hesitated, glancing toward the open doorway. Soon the household would be settling for sleep. "I am very discreet," I
added.

Flidais's gaze went to the door again, and back to me.
"Later," she said. "When Mhairi is here. I can't—it's difficult—"

"Then lie quiet until she comes back." I put my hand to
her brow; it did not feel unduly warm. Did she mean she
would tell me the truth once her maid was by her side?
Would I finally have the answer? This felt almost too easy.

"Mistress Blackthorn," Flidais whispered.

"Mm?"

"Did Oran bring you into the house to spy on me?"

Morrigan's britches! She knew? "Why would you imagine that, my lady?" I had no trouble sounding shocked. "I
assure you, Grim and I are here only because the prince was

kind enough to offer us shelter while our cottage is being rebuilt. Prince Oran was grateful, I think, for the action we took over Branoc's abduction of the miller's daughter. That is the only reason we came." Flidais was staring at me, her eyes full of distrust. I decided to take a risk; to treat her as maid, not mistress. "To tell you the truth, Lady Flidais, although I am grateful for Prince Oran's generosity, I am very uncomfortable staying in a grand establishment like this, and so is Grim. We are both used to a far simpler life, with less company. That has been obvious in my manner, I imagine." And when she said nothing, I added, "I cannot think why the prince would send anyone to spy on you. You must be imagining things, surely. Have you spoken to him about this?"

She shook her head. "I can't," she said.

I did not ask why. For now, I would take advantage of this surprising thaw in her attitude to me. "With your handfasting coming so soon, you'll want to be at your best, my lady. I'm speaking not only of headaches and the cramps that come with your moon cycle but also of anything that might be troubling you."

"What do you mean, Mistress Blackthorn?"

"A young woman who believes her betrothed may be spying on her is not likely to be looking forward to her wedding with undimmed pleasure."

"Forget it. Forget what I said." She closed her eyes. When I did not answer, she spoke again. "I don't think you can help. You won't believe me; nobody will. You all think he's perfect."

Before I could begin to grasp this, Mhairi was back, with various garments draped over one arm. She laid the clothing across a bench.

"Mistress Blackthorn," said Flidais, "will you leave the room for a while? I need to talk to Mhairi in private."

Wonderful. The two of them would decide, no doubt, that my questions and I had no place in a lady's bedchamber and ban me from returning. "If that's what you wish," I said. "I can go to the stillroom and make you a sleeping draft. It won't take long. Since you don't trust old wives' remedies, I'll make sure Master Oisin checks the ingredients."

"That won't be necessary," said Flidais, and managed a watery smile. "Your mixture will do very well."

What had got into Flidais? She was being quite civil. Had she finally realized she needed help, or was this all some elaborate game? I went out, closing the door behind me. As I made my way to the kitchen, where a few of Brid's helpers were doing the last of the after-supper cleaning, I found myself wishing Grim was at hand so I could ask him for his opinion before I spoke to Flidais again. Was I crazy to think it possible that swimming in Dreamer's Pool had somehow switched maid and mistress into each other's bodies? Should I press this with Flidais if she gave me the chance, or was it best to wait and speak to Conmael first? If I put my theory to her and it turned out to be wrong, she'd have good cause to throw me out of the prince's household for suggesting she had lied, and there'd be no way of solving the mystery before the hand-fasting.

Unfortunately, Grim was on night watch. There'd be no going out looking for him without attracting a lot of attention and wasting too much time. I'd have to leave it until tomorrow.

I made up the sleeping draft, taking particular care with the measurements. If Flidais took this on top of the other potion, she should enjoy a good night's rest, no matter what demons beset her. By the time I got back to the women's quarters most folk were abed, though lamps were still burning in the hallway outside Flidais's bedchamber. I tapped on the door and, somewhat to my surprise, was quickly admitted by Mhairi.

Flidais was sitting up in bed, drinking the warm milk I had requested, and there was more color in her cheeks.

Perhaps it had helped when I'd imagined she was the maid, Ciar, out of her depth in this odd situation. Of course, if that was true, she had been telling lies since the moment she came out of Dreamer's Pool. Enough lies to weigh a woman down until her dying day, if she had a conscience at all. She'd have been terrified when the changeover happened; she would still be frightened.

"Here is your sleeping draft. It's quite safe to take this along with the headache remedy." I poured a measure into the cup I had brought and set it on the chest beside her bed. "Lady Flidais," I ventured, "I can see that you are up-set, and I don't want to tax you further. But something you said earlier is troubling me. About Prince Oran."

Neither of them offered a comment. Flidais sipped her milk; Mhairi stood looking at me.

"This is awkward," I said. "I don't wish to offend you by speaking out of turn about the prince or indeed about any-thing. But . . . it seemed to me you were implying that Prince Oran was not the man he seemed to be, and that this was the cause of your distress. I do not know him well. I do know he is respected by the people of the district and by many in this household. Perfect? Few of us are. But most folk believe him to be a good man."

"I . . . I don't know how to say it." Flidais passed the cup to Mhairi; Mhairi set it on the bench and took Flidais's hand. "If my bleeding hadn't come . . . If I'd thought there might be a chance . . ."

A number of ideas passed rapidly through my mind, to be dismissed each in turn as impossible. Could she be say-ing she'd thought she might be with child? That she had wanted it to be so?

"A chance of what, my lady?"

"You are a wise woman, Blackthorn, can't you guess?" Flidais put her hands up over her face. "Mhairi, you tell her."

"Prince Oran might seem the most kindly and consider-ate of men," Mhairi said. "And perhaps he is, when it suits him. He was less than considerate of my lady when we first came to Winterfalls. Helped himself as soon as he got the chance, and never mind that she had never lain with a man before. Over and over, in the dead of night, with her too frightened to call out or tell anyone except me, and what could a lowly maidservant do? It was only when Lady Sochla arrived that he stopped. That's what Lady Flidais is trying to tell you. She's afraid of the man."

And suddenly, just like that, I was back in Laois, with a woman sobbing on my shoulder, telling me how Mathuin had taken her by force, casually, as if he had the right to; and how her husband, when he discovered that the child she was carrying was not his own, had thrown her out of the house to fend for herself. I saw her face, red with weep-ing; felt her body shaking with grief; heard her voice, harsh

with weeping: *I can't bear that man's child! It will surely be
a monster! I've nobody else to turn to, Mistress Blackthorn!
Help me!* And later, when I started asking questions, when
the women of the district heard that I was prepared to listen, there was another story about Mathuin, and another
and another, all along the same lines. Men! They were liars,
takers, hurters, selfish bastards who cared nothing for the
harm they caused. Men of power and privilege were the
worst of all.

I drew a ragged breath, forcing myself back from the
past. Prince Oran. The wretch! He'd had me completely
fooled. For a brief time, I'd let myself believe that there
were good men out there. But it seemed the prince of Dalriada, for all his pretty manners, was as bad as any of them.
My heart was pounding fit to burst from my chest. I had to
do something, act on this, now, straightaway.

"He gets so angry with me," Flidais said, sounding like a
miserable child. "Every day it's worse. I make a silly mistake, say something amiss, and he looks at me as if he wants
to hurt me. He was . . . he was not gentle in the bedchamber. I fear the hand-fasting for what must come after."

By all the gods. There was nothing uncanny about this at
all, simply a naïve young woman drowning in a sea of shock
and cruelty and heartbreak. No wonder she kept saying the
wrong things. No wonder she seemed so ill at ease. She
must have been half out of her mind with distress.

"I'll go and talk to him," I said. "Right now. And if he
won't see me, I'll hammer on his door and shout until he
has to listen. You can't let him get away with this."

"No!" Flidais blanched. "Oh, please, no, Mistress Blackthorn! Nobody must know. He's the prince of Dalriada.
We're to be hand-fasted."

"You must tell someone," I said. "Not only me, but—
Lady Sochla, or—or Master Oisin, before he leaves Winterfalls." Her situation was dire. Oran ruled over the entire
district; he was the king's only son. Like Mathuin, the
prince doubtless felt he could do anything he chose. As for
why he had bid me spy on Flidais, and spun me that tale
about her, I could not begin to guess his reasoning—and I
no longer cared to. Perhaps, like Mathuin, he played cruel
games to amuse himself.

"No! I can't tell! And you mustn't either!"

"But, Lady Flidais," I protested as my mind raced ahead, trying to find answers for her, "you cannot marry a man who has shown such disregard for your feelings. You cannot wed a man you are afraid of. What sort of life would that be for you?" Even as I spoke, I reminded myself that this kind of thing happened all the time. Flidais was at least being offered marriage, where Mathuin had taken his victims casually and abandoned them without a second thought. But Flidais should not have to bear the full weight of this; Oran should be held to account.

"I need this marriage," she said now. "Oran will be king one day. My family needs it; you know their situation, Mistress Blackthorn. I cannot just pack up and walk away. I would disgrace everyone back home. Besides, there is nowhere to go."

I thought of Lord Muadan and his wife; no, if they sheltered her they would offend Oran's father, who was Muadan's overlord. I considered Lady Sochla, a woman with a great deal of common sense; but she was Oran's aunt, close family, and although she had her own home, it was at Cahercorcan. Druids? A Christian nunnery? For the life of me I could not imagine Flidais seeking refuge with either. One did not lightly flee a marriage with a king's son, however badly he had acted.

"Lady Flidais," I said, playing for time, "where did these assaults occur? I know Lady Sochla was not at Winterfalls as chaperone then, but were you not safe here in the women's quarters?"

Flidais pointed to something I had not noticed before: a second door in the bedchamber, half-concealed by a silken hanging. "That doorway leads straight into Prince Oran's quarters. It is not bolted; he could come in any time he wanted, though he would not do it with his aunt in residence—her chamber is next door to mine. But . . . it was not only here, in this room. There were times . . . he would take me by surprise, in other places. When we were out walking, or had stopped to rest while riding."

"Who else knows about this?" Surely Oran could not have kept such gross behavior secret from his entire household. Could it be that they all knew and were prepared to condone it? What had I walked into when I agreed to help the man? "Deirdre and Nuala?"

Flidais shook her head. "Nobody. Only Mhairi."

"And the prince's man," said Mhairi. "Donagan. He must know. At the time, he was sleeping in an antechamber to the prince's quarters; he moved out soon afterward, and you'll have noticed that he and the prince are no longer the best of friends. But even if he doesn't think much of his master's behavior, Donagan won't talk. He's been with the prince a long time and he'll protect him at all costs."

Donagan. The perfect manservant, the prince's childhood friend. My skin crawled; I wanted out of this place. "You can't let them get away with this," I said. "It's not right."

"This marriage will give me a home and a future." Flidais lay back on her pillows. "It will help protect my family in these difficult times. Many folk would say the price I have to pay for that is not too high."

"You should not have to pay any price at all. This could mean years of unhappiness."

"My lady thinks," said Mhairi, "that should she provide Prince Oran with a son, the situation would change for the better. He would, at the very least, be less . . . demanding."

It was a great deal to assume from the available evidence. On the other hand, I remembered the prince speaking of his parents and how badly they had wanted him to marry; there was, no doubt, considerable pressure on him to produce an heir. "If you don't want help in getting away," I said bluntly, "why have you chosen to tell me this? Why confide in me now?"

"I thought . . . I thought he had asked you to spy on me. He's been so angry since . . . since Lady Sochla came, and he couldn't . . . And the way you looked at me, the questions you asked . . . I did not think he would invite you to stay here only because your house burned down. There must be more suitable lodgings in the village."

It was a flash of the old Flidais, the one I had not much cared for. I must set that dislike aside; it had nothing to do with the current situation. Sometime I would tell her the whole story. After what I had just heard, I'd have no problem breaking my promise to Oran about secrecy. But not tonight. She was simply too tired.

"I wasn't thinking clearly," Flidais went on. "My mind has been all at sixes and sevens since that first night. I cannot settle to any of the pastimes I enjoyed before—reading, writing, walking, playing with my little dog . . . I have a confession to make to you, Mistress Blackthorn. You will hate me for this." Her voice was a whisper. "I can hardly make myself say it."

"Let me help," I said, guessing. "The headaches were never real, except perhaps for the time of your monthly bleeding. They were an excuse to hide from Prince Oran, so you would not have to face him, conduct conversations that were difficult for you, pretend in front of guests that everything was going well. Yes?"

"I felt so ashamed," Flidais murmured. "I still do."

"You have nothing to be ashamed of. Unlike your betrothed." How many women, I thought, faced with a situation like this, would be prepared to speak up? To make a stand against those who oppressed women? It did not matter if the oppressor was a prince or a common man, the offense was just the same. Such acts would never stop unless they were publicly exposed and punished under the law. As I had tried to do with Mathuin of Laois. And look where that had got me. How could I push Flidais to tell this story, when I had been thrown into that man's lockup for speaking out about his offenses against women? If it hadn't been for Conmael, I'd still be in there, and so would Grim.

"You asked why we told you the truth," Mhairi said. "We thought you would find out, with your sharp eyes and your tricky questions. We thought you would tell other folk, and the story would be spread about, and the prince would be angry with Lady Flidais and punish her."

Gods! This was all back to front and upside down, a woeful state of affairs. Flidais was choosing a future of abuse and fear, and I could think of no way to dissuade her. I had no alternative to offer her. "You're quite sure you don't want this made known? You really intend to go ahead with the hand-fasting?"

"Yes," Flidais said. "I have no other choice."

"Then I don't believe there's any way I can help you."

"Oh, but there is," she said, sitting up again. "There

might be. Do you remember when we asked about what you did as a wise woman, the potions and cures? If you could . . . Do you think you could . . ."

"What Lady Flidais wants to ask," said Mhairi, "is whether you know how to make sure she conceives a son. As soon as possible." Whatever I might think of the woman, I could not fault her for plain speaking.

"If anyone can tell me that, it will surely be you, Mistress Blackthorn," Flidais said. "Oran wants a child. It would be so much better if our firstborn was a boy. I have failed to please my betrothed in so many ways—you must have heard how sharply he spoke to me at suppertime, not even pretending to be kind—but if I could do this, I know his attitude would soften."

I hesitated. There was no way I knew of to be sure of a son. A woman could improve her chances of conceiving a babe by eating certain foods, taking a particular tonic, being mindful of the moon's waxing and waning, and so on. But that child might be boy or girl; there was no telling until it was born. I did not want to give Flidais this bad news. She was distressed and weary, and it was growing late.

"I'll think about this awhile," I said. "You should sleep, Lady Flidais. And you, Mhairi. You are very loyal to your mistress."

Mhairi gave me a tight nod.

"How long do you need?" Flidais asked. "Do you not know the answer?"

"As I told you some time ago," I said, "it's unwise to rush these things. They can be complicated, sometimes perilous. And far from clear-cut. I understand the urgency, my lady, and I ask only for a day or two. Now I will bid you good night. Make sure you take the sleeping draft; it should bring you rest without bad dreams."

Shaking, shaking until my teeth rattled. *Where is she? Where is the miller's daughter?* A gauntleted fist to my right cheek, smash! *Where is she? Speak up, slut!* A blow to the left cheek, thud! *Use your tongue or we'll cut it out for you, a little bit at a time!*

It hurt to speak. The words wouldn't come out right.

Gone. Gone where you'll never find her. My aching jaw, my bleeding mouth and muzzy head turned the words into a string of nonsense. I had to stand straight. I had to look brave. But everything was wavering and swirling around, and I wanted to be sick. *You're a thug and a bully and an abuser of women,* I tried to say. *And so are your men, because they follow your lead. You are not fit to be chieftain. The dung heap is too good—*

Slam! The floor was hard under my face. Something thudded into my ribs. All I could see was black. *Filthy slut's only good for one thing.* Mathuin's voice. *Throw her in the lockup with the men. Maybe by morning she'll be ready to tell a different story. If she survives that long.*

Pain, leering faces, dark corners. Shadows, filth, shame. Under it all, a cold fury that never went away. One day I'd bring him to justice. I'd hurt him as he'd hurt all those women. I'd burn him alive as he burned my sweet boy, my lovely man. I'd stick my knife in his chest and twist it, and I'd watch him suffer and die. When I got out of this stinking hole, I'd make him pay.

The door creaked open. They were coming! I crouched down beside the pallet, arms wrapped around myself. Waited for the clang of Slammer's stick on the bars.

"Blackthorn?" A woman's voice, slurred with sleep. "You all right?"

"Shut up," growled another woman.

My heart hammering, my body all cold sweat, I blinked and opened my eyes on the long chamber full of sleeping women. Wrenched myself back from the dream. The stink of that place still clung close, the screaming, the mindless dark. "Sorry," I murmured. "Nightmare." As indeed it was; not only the unfinished business I had left behind but the unsavory mess I now found myself mired in. Why in the name of the gods had I suggested to Flidais that I might be able to help? There was no answer for what she wanted. I was not even sure I'd want to share it with her if there was—her decision to appease the man who had abused her sickened me, even as I understood that hers was a pragmatic and, at heart, an unselfish choice. If she did make the best of this marriage, she would be helping her family back home, the family that was facing no lesser enemy than Mathuin of Laois.

Flidais would conceive a child without my assistance; she was young and healthy, and so was the prince. And if I stayed here in a misguided attempt to support her, I would be hard-pressed to keep up the pretense that nothing had changed. Surely, the very next time I met Oran, the look in my eyes must give me away.

Around me, the women were quiet again. I lay on my back staring up at nothing and making a plan. A simple plan that I would enact at first light. Forget Conmael. Forget the season. Forget the long miles to Laois. I had traveled in wind and rain and cold before and I could do it again. I had set out for Winterfalls with nothing but the rags on my back. I would leave the place with little more. For the one thing that really mattered, all I needed was my rage.

33

ORAN

The morning after I helped Oisin tell his transformation story, I took Bramble for a long walk around the farm, hoping the exertion would set my thoughts in order. Blackthorn had told me to wait; not to press her for news. But as the day of the hand-fasting drew ever closer, I was struggling to make pretense that nothing was amiss. I could not play the eager betrothed with Flidais. I could barely manage to be civil with her. And Blackthorn's were not the only pair of sharp eyes in the household. My folk knew me well. They had observed my falling-out with Donagan. They felt the unrest that had engulfed us all. When Donagan was not avoiding me altogether, he watched me, and I saw on his face that he was judging me. Aunt Sochla frequently asked me if all was quite well; she had known me since the day I was born, and not much escaped her. Aedan, Lochlan, Niall, even Eochu seemed careful of me, as if I might be about to expire from some disease. This was not the healthiest way to view an impending marriage. If Blackthorn did not come up with something soon, I feared my private business would become public knowledge.

The walk did nothing but stir up my anxiety. I decided to seek out Blackthorn as soon as I got back to the house, and never mind that it still lacked an hour or two until breakfast time. I strode down to the kitchen with Bramble trotting behind. With luck, the wise woman would already be at work in her makeshift stillroom, and I'd be able to speak to her without drawing undue attention.

Brid was preparing the day's loaves for the oven. As I greeted her, I glanced toward the stillroom and saw that the door was closed.

"If you're looking for Mistress Blackthorn, my lord, she's already gone out. Went off very early."

She must indeed have left early; I had been out since daybreak, and I had seen nothing of her. "Did she say where she was headed, Brid?"

"No, my lord, but she had a bag with her. Perhaps there's someone sick out on one of the farms."

Curse it. That could mean Blackthorn would be gone all day.

"Is she needed for Lady Flidais, my lord?" Brid asked.

For a moment I could not think what she meant. Then I recalled last night's fainting fit. I had barely given it a thought. "Lady Flidais is still sleeping, so I'm told," I said. "I believe all she needs is a good rest. As for Mistress Blackthorn, the matter can wait; there is no urgency." Oh, I was full of falsehoods today. Lying to the trusted members of my household sat ill with me; I was coming to despise myself.

Bramble was running around, getting underfoot; I'd best take her away. "What about Grim?" I asked. "Is he about?"

Brid's smile told me the unprepossessing Grim had become a favorite. "He'll be in for a bite to eat soon; then he'll likely be off to Dreamer's Wood to do some work on his house. And get some sleep. Night watch takes it out of a man, even a big strong man like him."

"When he comes in, please tell him I'd like a word before he goes off for the day. I'll be in the garden with the dog." I motioned in the general direction of Flidais's private garden. I'd have to take Bramble back anyway. After breakfast I'd be sitting down with Muadan and his councillors to discuss various matters before they traveled on to court.

"I'm sorry, Bramble," I told her when we were in the quiet of the little garden, I seated on the stone bench, she nosing about in the ferns by the pond. "I would find your presence reassuring. Other folk, however, would most likely differ. I'm afraid you must stay with the ladies today."

Not far off, someone cleared his throat. I looked up, and there was Grim. For a very big man, he walked softly indeed.

"Grim." I rose to my feet. "I did not hear you coming."

"Sorry if I startled you, my lord."

"Not at all." If he thought me foolish for conducting a one-sided conversation with a dog, he gave no sign of it. His manners had improved since our first encounter at the cottage. That felt strange, as I had been far more deserving of respect back then. Now I was guilty of being unkind, of telling lies, and of allowing myself to descend into near-panic. Some prince I was. "I wondered if you and Mistress Blackthorn had made any progress." I spoke in an undertone, trying to watch both the door from the women's quarters and the pathway back around to the main entry. "On the matter we discussed."

Grim gave me a look that said quite plainly, *I thought Blackthorn told you to wait.* But he did not say it aloud. "Been hard to talk to her. Busy, both of us. When she's got something, she'll tell me."

"And you?"

Grim shook his head. It might mean he had nothing to tell. But it might mean that he did know something but would not tell it without Blackthorn's approval. She had made it clear the two of them worked as a team.

"We are short of time, Grim," I said. "Perilously short. You do understand that, don't you?"

"I can count the days until full moon, my lord." Was there a hint of disapproval in the deep voice? It would be a mistake to underestimate this man.

"I'm sorry. I have not forgotten that Mistress Blackthorn asked me to wait."

Grim had crouched down to pat Bramble. She came to him delicately, allowing him to stroke her. "Friendly little thing," he said. "Reminds me of . . . never mind." He looked up at me. "Blackthorn's trustworthy. If there's a way out of this, she'll find it."

"I must exercise patience. I know that. Sometimes it's hard."

"Keep busy. That's my advice." He rose to his full, imposing height. "Not that you'd be wanting advice from someone like me, but there it is. Will that be all, my lord? Just that I'm off to the cottage soon, got a bit of work to do before the rain comes."

"Go, by all means. Ask Brid to give you some breakfast first. Night watch, then a day's work out at Dreamer's Wood—you push yourself hard."

"As I said. Keep busy. Stops your head going in circles, tangling itself all up. Quiet times, they're hardest to get through. I'll be on my way, then."

The man was wiser than he looked. When he was gone, I delivered Bramble to Aunt Sochla, then went to my bedchamber, where garments suitable for a council meeting had been laid out in readiness, though Donagan was nowhere to be seen. I sat at my writing table and prepared some notes for my discussion with Muadan and the others. I wrote a letter to my father, which Muadan could take for me, in which I made some comments on the situation at Cloud Hill and suggested we take advantage of the presence of various leaders at the hand-fasting to hold an informal council. We could discuss the matter of Mathuin of Laois. If all those who had accepted invitations attended, it would be an opportunity too good to miss. Lorcan mac Cellaig, King of Mide, had sent word that he would be there, though as yet his party had not passed Winterfalls. Lorcan was kin both to my father and, by marriage, to the High King. His influence in the matter would be critical. My letter contained little by way of domestic detail; I did not trust myself to speak of Flidais or of the hand-fasting itself. *Your obedient son, Oran.* There, that was done.

I turned my attention to the next open council, now only days away. I made a new document: a list of those matters I already knew would be put before me. There were several, but none was particularly serious, which was good, as I hoped to end the council by midday, feed the visitors early and send them off by midafternoon. The folk of my household would be busy enough getting everything ready for our departure for Cahercorcan the next day without having to cope with large numbers of folk in the house until suppertime. We might, perhaps, leave one day later. Flidais would not be happy about that. Not-Flidais. False Flidais.

I scattered sand to dry the ink, then set the list to one side. I laid out a third sheet of parchment; dipped my pen once more. *Flidais*, I wrote, *where are you? I cannot believe that you are only a dream, a woman I have conjured up from tales and songs and wild imaginings. You were so real. Lovelier than the first dew on the grass; sweeter than the song of the thrush; truer than a druid's vow. Gentle, brave and wise. Full of love and wonder and promise. Where did you go? How can I find you?*

I turned my gaze toward the portrait that still hung on the wall above my writing desk, and Flidais looked back at me, steadfast, tender, perfect. "She isn't you," I whispered. "I can't believe it. Tell me where you've gone. Tell me what I must do." I closed my eyes and tried to imagine how Flidais—the real woman, not the travesty that had come to Winterfalls—would reply to my letter. *Dearest Oran, I am . . .* No, try again. *Oran, I know you love what I love: wild places, wild creatures, the beauty of the passing seasons, the wisdom of ancient tales. You must put your trust in what you love. Seek answers there.*

Someone knocked on the door. I started in surprise; I had been lost in my imaginings. More likely, if she could see me now, Flidais would ask me how I had the gall to write such tender words when I had burned her letters.

"Come in!"

Donagan, his features perfectly schooled. "It's time you changed for breakfast and the meeting, my lord." He eyed the clothing I was wearing, garments snatched at random for my early walk. "You wish me to assist?" Since our rift, he had mastered a detached tone; it sent a chill through me.

"You know quite well I can dress myself," I said, failing miserably to make a joke of it. "There's a letter here to my father; you might convey it to Muadan's chief councillor to carry to Cahercorcan. And this list for the council. I'd like you to cast your eye over it. If you or Aedan have any items to add, please let me know."

"And that one, my lord?" Donagan had noticed the letter on the table, neither folded nor sealed.

I felt oddly calm. It seemed Grim's advice was sound; writing had steadied my thoughts. "I'll deliver this myself," I said, taking up the sheet and folding it once, twice, three times. And I made a silent vow. I would keep this letter within my garments, next to my heart, until I found my Flidais again and put it in her hands.

34

GRIM

Cottage is looking good. I make some fancy bits for the roof, creatures and the like. Old folk say they're lucky. Can't hurt, anyway. Owl at the forest end, cow at the field end, others along the ridge: fox, hare, hedgehog, squirrel. Hedgehog takes longest, lots of straw prickles to thread in. I'm putting the last of the creatures up when one of the lads from the brewery, Pátraic, arrives to give me a hand.

"Fine morning," he calls. "What do you want doing?"

I tie off the ends of the straw, fixing the hedgehog in place, then climb down my ladder. "Need a hand with some inside work. Couple of beds, worktable for Blackthorn, shelf or two. Timber's all cut to size, pegs shaped, just need to put them together. Your friend coming today?"

"He's got a job for Iobhar. Busy all day."

We get started on the work. Pátraic's a talker. By the time we're done with the first bed, I know all about who's been coming in and out of Iobhar's brewery and what they've been saying since last time I saw him. The lad's job, when he's not here helping me, is keeping an eye on folk's horses while they're drinking their ale or haggling with Iobhar over how many coppers he's charging for his goods.

We get started on the second bed, which is mine, though I don't tell Pátraic that. If he bothered to look, which he doesn't, he could work it out from the carving I've done along the side. Blackthorn twigs on one bed, with thorns and blossoms. Fierce-looking hounds on the other. Joke, that. Heard folk call me her guard dog more than once.

Morning's passing. Rain's holding off for now. Thought Blackthorn might come over today, gather herbs, stay for a chat. Be good to talk; it's been a while. Want to tell her what Donagan said, ask her if she's found out anything. But she doesn't turn up. Called away to someone sick, maybe, or busy in the house.

Second bed's all done. Looks fine. We stop for a bite to eat. Brid's given me supplies, and Pátraic's brought a crock of ale. We sit out on the step, looking over the garden, and behind that, the fields between Dreamer's Wood and Winterfalls. Clouds are filling up the sky; I can feel the damp in the air.

"What's it like, working in the prince's house?" Pátraic asks through a mouthful of bread and mutton. "Are the folk there friendly?"

Not sure how to answer this. "Some," I say. "Had a few problems, but it's sorted now. He seems a good fellow. Prince Oran, I mean. His people like him."

"What about her?" asks Pátraic. He means Lady Flidais. Feels wrong to be talking about her. Disrespectful. I'm about to tell him so when I see the look on his face. He's looking as if he's got a secret to share, the kind of secret the Winterfalls men-at-arms would be sniggering about over their ale. Don't want to hear it, but if it's about Lady Flidais, I have to let him talk.

"Haven't seen much of her," I say. "Been on night duty. Seems a nice lady. Why?"

"Nice lady, you think? You'd be surprised."

"I would?"

He leans closer, drops his voice to a whisper. "Saw 'em in the stables at the brewery, up against a wall, him and her, at it like ferrets. Or not ferrets, maybe, but you catch my drift. She was on her knees, giving him a suck, going at him as if she knew what she was doing. Funny thing was, it was her wanting it, not the prince. He was arguing with her, trying to push her away. Stupid, eh? What man in his right mind would turn that down?"

I'm too shocked to say anything, so I just sit there pretending to eat.

"Makes you wonder, doesn't it?" Pátraic goes on. "About the prince, I mean. Maybe he's one of those men that like other fellows. There's that serving man of his, Donagan, always hanging about."

Has to be a mistake. That's my first thought. Lady Flidais? Young, highborn and betrothed to the king's heir? Hardly. Even if she fancied a bit of that, she'd never be so foolish as to do it in a stable yard where anyone could— and did—see them. "Have you told anyone else?" I ask.

"Not a soul. Been tempted, once or twice. Wondered if I was imagining things at the time. But I wasn't. I heard him say, *Stop it, Flidais!*"

This is something Blackthorn needs to know. So I need to think fast and ask the right questions. "Bit of a surprise," I say. "When was this? Didn't think Lady Flidais rode out much."

"A while back. After they were betrothed. The prince was in the village to have a drink with the fellows and talk about the next council. He brought Lady Flidais with him."

"Mm. Might be best if you don't tell anyone else. Seeing as the lady has to live here, I mean. Might make some folk think badly of her. Or of him."

"Mm-hm. More ale?"

"Nah, better get to work on that table."

We finish the table, then Pátraic has to go back to the brewery. Still no sign of Blackthorn. I wonder if I should go to the prince's place and find her, tell her the snippets I've heard. They don't add up to much. Though when I think about it, Pátraic's unlikely tale fits with what Donagan said about the prince not being worldly-wise. What doesn't make sense is Flidais doing what he says he saw her doing. A lady who was going to be queen one day wouldn't act like that, out in the open. Would she? The prince did tell us she wasn't the woman he was expecting. He wouldn't have been expecting her to do *that*. There's a time and place for these things, and it's not in the stable yard of a brewery, before you're even properly wed.

So, head over to the prince's now? Could be a waste of time. Blackthorn might still be out doing whatever she went out to do. If it's a childbed, it could take all day and some of the night. If it's on one of the faraway farms, just getting there and back would take a while. And I've got work to finish here.

I'm yawning. If I don't catch some sleep I'll be good for nothing. There's enough of the day left for me to lie down in the outhouse for a bit, then finish the shelves and get back to Winterfalls before dusk. Plenty of time.

Got a pallet in the outhouse with a bedroll all ready. Sleep in there most afternoons. It's pretty dark even by day, and at first when I go in I don't spot anything different. Then I go to lie down and there it is: Blackthorn's red kerchief, neatly folded and sitting right in the place where I'd be laying my head. My heart gives a big thump. She's been here already. Been and gone long ago. She didn't have a rest and leave her kerchief by accident. Not set out the way it is. The red kerchief says one thing loud and clear: *Goodbye*.

For a bit I can't think straight. Don't know whether to scream or curse or cry or go rushing off in all directions. Have to make myself breathe, slow down, try to work out the puzzle the way she would. No time to think about why she'd up and go like this, when we're just getting settled and there's a job on hand. What I need to think about is where. I stuff the kerchief in my pouch and head outside. Black Crow save me, what if she had a horse? She could be miles away by now. Left Winterfalls forever. Broken her promise to Conmael. There's only one place she'll be headed for, winter or no winter. Laois. She's gone to face up to Mathuin. And if she doesn't want to be found, there'll be no finding her.

I throw my head back and bellow like a wounded bull. "Conmael, you bastard! Why in the name of the gods didn't you stop her?"

Last thing I'm expecting is an answer. But here he is, come from nowhere, standing right next to me all wrapped up in his big swirly cloak. On his own. Not sure if that's good or bad.

"Why did I not stop her?" he asks, in a way that says I'm far too stupid to talk to the likes of him. "Surely you know by now that Blackthorn is her own woman. If she wants to go, she'll go. If she wants to throw her life away, that's precisely what she'll do."

I want to grab the fellow and shake him up and down a few times, even though all he's done is say what I was thinking myself. But there's nobody else to help me, so I hold back. Count up to five in my head. "If you thought that," I say, "why did you get her out of Mathuin's lockup?"

He laughs. I want to kill him. "You're wasting time, Grim," he says. "You'll never win a battle of wits with me. If you want her back, go after her."

"You planning to help or just stand about watching? I don't know where she went."

"That way." Conmael points southward. His fingers are long and pale, with silver rings on them.

I want to ask him how he knows, and whether he saw her, and when, but he'll only say I'm wasting time. "She went early," I say. "And she's good at covering her tracks. Doubt I'd find her."

"What, giving up before you've even begun?" His brows lift in scorn. "And you the devoted hound who guards her every step? She'd be disappointed in you."

"If you won't help," I growl, "then I'll be on my way."

"Did I say I would not help? I don't recall that. What help do you require?"

I hate the mongrel. Always thought his kind weren't trustworthy, and he's done nothing to change my mind. But the day's slipping away and so is Blackthorn, so I swallow my pride, what there is of it. "A horse," I say. "Strong enough to carry her and me. And if you know how far she's gone, tell me."

Happens just like in an old tale. Conmael clicks his fingers, and there's a horse in the garden. Storm, one of Scannal's draft horses, with a blanket saddle and a riding harness on.

"Miller mightn't be well pleased," I say, but I'm already slinging my bag on my back, getting ready to mount and go.

"She might be far south by now," said Conmael. "Or not. If I were you I'd take the track toward Silverlake."

I frown at him. "That's not south, it's east."

"All the same. That is where I would go first."

I give him a straight look. I'm scared of the fellow, but I speak out anyway. "Why don't you go?"

He smiles, thin-lipped. "Oh, she won't listen to *me*."

Can't even start to work that out. "You sure you want what's best for Blackthorn?" I ask. Could be he's tricking me, sending me on a wild goose chase, making sure I don't catch up with her, even on Storm.

"If I did not," says Conmael, "she would be dead, and you would still be in Mathuin's lockup. Now go."

35

BLACKTHORN

South. Mathuin. Justice. The words were in my mind when I passed by our cottage and thought of Grim, and how I had not told him I was going. I left the red kerchief and kept on walking. I muttered the same words when I reached the crossroads: one track going south toward Laois and my enemy, the other branching off east toward Silverlake. Ness was still there; her recovery had been slow. I chose the southern path and walked on. *South. Mathuin. Justice.*

I made good progress. The morning was not far advanced when I came up through a beech wood and stopped to drink from my water skin. I hadn't brought much. Most of my healer's supplies were still in the prince's house. My bag contained a change of clothing, the water skin, a couple of bannocks I'd grabbed from the kitchen on the way out. My notebook, which could not be left behind for idle eyes to read. My good knife, my flint, a supply of dry tinder. Rolled on top, a blanket from the prince's household. I felt no guilt in taking it. With luck, I'd be far on my way before anyone realized I wasn't coming back.

Sooner or later Conmael would catch up with me, ask me why I'd broken my word. Perhaps make good his threat to throw me back in Mathuin's lockup, though I wondered,

now, if he would really do that. Supercilious meddler that
he was, he did appear to have my welfare at heart. The
mood I was in, I hardly cared anyway. His instructions were
impossible. Use my talents for good and say yes to any request for help; that had made a sort of sense when he'd first
set it all out. But when one of the folk who'd asked for help
would not stand up against the man who'd betrayed her
trust—indeed, planned to marry him—and the other was
that very man, courteous and charming on the outside, a
cold-hearted abuser of women underneath, how could I do
as Conmael wished? I could not help Flidais if she was not
prepared to help herself. As for Oran, he was a lying rat,
and I'd rather walk on hot coals than do a thing more for
him.

I'd promised myself I wouldn't look back. But as I hitched
my bag onto my shoulders again, I caught a glimpse of the
view. This hill overlooked grazing fields, and beyond them,
a mile or two to the northeast, lay an expanse of water,
gray under the overcast sky, with a settlement straggling
along its edge. Silverlake, where we'd confronted Branoc in
his bakery. Silverlake, where Ness was still lodging with the
family who'd taken her in. Where Emer, who might be a
fine healer one day, still stayed by her friend's side.

South. Mathuin. Justice, I told myself, wanting to turn
away, wanting to head on south, but hesitating all the same.
Mathuin was an abuser of women, whose callous, unthink-
ing assaults had left a trail of broken lives behind him.
Branoc's crime was the same, and even if he'd had only one
victim, her hurt was no less for that. I was going south to
make Mathuin face up to his ill deeds. A grand mission, far
grander than sorting out a lying prince's tangled betrothal.
But I owed it to Ness to visit her one last time before I left,
to acknowledge her strength, to offer her . . . what? Wise
advice? There wasn't much wisdom in me right now. I was
full up with Mathuin and my anger. But I could at least sit
down with Ness and listen. Silverlake was just over there,
not far at all. There would be time.

I found a way down the hill between the birches and
headed across the fields. I'd call in and see Ness briefly,
have a word or two with Emer, and be on my way again.

There was only one person likely to come after me and I'd made sure I had a good start on him. Besides, he'd be expecting me to go on south. Grim would be all right, I told myself. He had work at Winterfalls. He had friends; folk liked him. He could live in the cottage. He'd be better off without me.

I hoped Ness would be a little better today. Her body had healed quickly, with the resilience of the young. But last time I'd been here, she'd still been waking in the night, screaming. She'd still, sometimes, been wetting her bed like an infant. And although she'd talked to me, and talked openly, about what had happened to her, it had seemed to me part of her was absent, as if she had left something forever in that dark place of her captivity.

I came in to Silverlake. At Mór's house, where Ness was staying, there was nobody about. I knocked on the door, then entered, as was my custom. "Anyone home? It's Blackthorn."

"Through here!" Ness called from the inner chamber. The door to that room stood ajar, and light spilled from within. I walked through and stopped short. Ness was sitting on the edge of the bed, fully dressed, with a shawl around her shoulders all patterned with birds and flowers. Her cheeks were rosy, her eyes bright, and over her dark hair she wore the red kerchief that was almost, but not quite, twin to mine. On a stool by the bedside, holding her hand, sat a long-legged young man, dark-haired, thin and rather solemn looking, clad in a working man's clothing brightened by a vivid blue neckerchief. As I came in the youth rose to his feet but kept Ness's hand in his.

"Mistress Blackthorn, how good to see you!" Ness said. Her smile lit up her face; she seemed transformed. "This is Abhan. His folk are camped on the other side of the lake, not far away. They came in last night."

"Mistress Blackthorn," said Abhan, "it's an honor to meet you. What you did for my girl—I can't thank you enough."

He was all courtesy. Just like Prince Oran. Men were full of lies. I managed a nod.

"We're going to be married," said Ness. "As soon as we can. We'll be traveling south when Abhan's folk move on.

I'll miss you, Mistress Blackthorn. And Emer. But we'll be back next autumn with the horses."

Too fast; this was happening much too fast. "Where is Emer?" I asked, with cold disquiet running through me.

"Didn't you see her? She's helping Mór bring in some sheets. It's going to rain later."

So Emer was not far away; this was less improper than it had seemed at first. That didn't mean I liked the fellow turning up here and, within a day, persuading this frail and damaged girl not only to marry him but to leave everything behind and head off with the travelers. Thanks to her father's silver, Ness was a wealthy woman now. A good catch for a lad like this, even after what had been done to her.

Abhan was watching me, his expression as grave as if he could read my thoughts. "Mistress Blackthorn," he said, "might I speak with you alone?"

"By all means. We'll step outside a moment." Ness's smile had faded. I owed her an explanation. "You have no kinsfolk," I said. "You've been through a dark time, Ness, very dark. You and Abhan—you're young, both of you. Since your father cannot talk to him about this, I will do it. I need to make sure you'll be properly looked after and well provided for. To put it bluntly, I need to be convinced your decisions are your own, and not those of a man who would exploit you."

"Mistress Blackthorn!" exclaimed Ness. "How can you say that? Abhan is my sweetheart; he has been since I was young. I love him. He loves me. My father gave us his blessing; he only asked us to wait. Abhan wants only what is best for me."

"Then you have nothing to be concerned about," I said, "if he and I take a little walk and I ask him a few questions."

It was darker outside; the clouds were building. I'd best be on my way soon. "Come, we'll walk," I said, and the young man fell into step beside me, moderating his long strides. Once we were away from the house, I said, "I don't have much time. Which is regrettable, since we're talking about the rest of that young woman's life. First tell me this: how do you propose to look after Ness, provide a safe home, keep a roof over her head and food on the table, and ensure she need not work herself half to death just to make ends meet?" I made no mention of Ness's inheritance.

"I'm eighteen years old, Mistress Blackthorn. A man grown. I have my own cart, bought from my earnings in the horse trading business, and my own pair of cart horses. Tinker and Treasure, they're called. I travel with my whole family: Mam, my brothers and sisters, my aunties and uncles and cousins. We follow the same pattern every year. Spend spring and summer in the south, come north in the autumn. I know my trade; I make good sales and my dealings are always fair. I can provide for Ness." When I said nothing, he went on. "I know Ness has funds of her own now. But she won't be needing those for the everyday. What we thought . . ." He hesitated.

"Go on." I could not find fault with anything he'd said so far. I hoped this odd feeling I had was not disappointment.

"The prince . . . Emer told me what he said at the council, when that fellow, the wretch who hurt Ness, was brought to account." Abhan's voice was uneven; his jaw tightened. "She said the prince was very fair. She said that he was kind to her, and that he told the folk they should have seen earlier that something was wrong. She said he spoke well of Ness. What we thought, Ness and I, was that we would go to Winterfalls for his next council and ask to talk to him in private. Get his advice about Ness's payment. We want to put it away safe somewhere."

"For what purpose?"

"In case she changes her mind," he said simply. "Not about marrying me; she says she'll never do that. But if she doesn't take to the traveling life. It's not for everyone, Mistress Blackthorn. Some folk can't be happy without a nest, same place to rest their head every night. And though Ness says she'll be fine as long as I'm there, she hasn't tried it yet. If she's not content with it, we'll use some of her money to buy a place and settle. I can turn my hand to a few things. I'd find work."

"Really? Is it not just as hard for a traveling man to settle in one place as it is for a girl like Ness to take to life on the road?"

We had reached a wall that marked off the bottom of Mór's garden. Beyond lay a field with sheep grazing. Abhan stopped walking and faced me, his eyes as clear as the water of a pool in springtime. "I'd give my life for her, Mistress Blackthorn, I swear it. Settling down, going to work as a farrier or groom, I'd do it in a heartbeat. But Ness says she'll be fine on the road. She likes my mam and my sisters, and she says going south will make it easier to put what's happened behind her."

I could not argue with this. He sounded, and looked, both utterly sincere and remarkably practical. I could not make myself believe he was lying. As for seeking advice from Prince Oran, a man who really did know how to lie, it was quite true that the prince had spoken with fairness, wisdom and courage at the council; he had supported both Emer and Ness all along. On balance, I had no reason to think he would give bad counsel on the matter of Ness's funds.

But that was only half of it. "Ness has met your family?" I asked, heading into the more difficult part carefully.

"Yes, Mistress Blackthorn. They came over to visit her today, Mam and the two youngest. My eldest sister's tending to my grandmother, who's unwell. But, of course, they all know Ness from before."

"Before?"

"She and I—we've been sweethearts awhile. Ness always came over to visit when we were in the district. She and Emer. Mam loves the two of them; said she wished we could take them both back south with us."

"How long will you be staying in Dalriada this time, Abhan?"

"We'd want to be gone by next half-moon, or the roads will be all mud. I have some business to do first, and of course Ness and I must be married before we go."

Now came the crux of the matter. "You know she's been badly hurt. You know that man imprisoned her, abused her, took her by force, left her with scars both of the body and of the mind. Deep scars, Abhan."

"I know." His gaze remained steady and sure.

"I'm not sure you can know, not fully. You're young."

"I've been head of my family since my da died three years since, Mistress Blackthorn. I'm a man. Ness has talked to me about what that fellow did to her. She's told me the story. And we've spoken about getting wed, and what it would mean." He paused to draw a long breath. "I made her a promise. Said we wouldn't do anything until she was ready. Just lie in each other's arms, nothing more."

"You have good intentions, Abhan. What if you can't keep yourself under control?"

"I can, Mistress Blackthorn. If I couldn't, I wouldn't be a fit man to marry Ness. I can wait. I can give her as long as she needs."

We started back toward the house. I could see Mór and Emer now, going inside with a big basket of linen.

"You don't believe me," Abhan said.

"I believe you mean what you say. I'm not so sure about your ability to carry it out. What if Ness is never ready for the two of you to lie together as husband and wife? What if she cannot bear your children?"

"She means everything to me, Mistress Blackthorn. I want her to be happy. I want her to feel safe. I never want her to be afraid again. Ness is a strong girl; a brave girl. She wouldn't have got through this otherwise. Between us, we'll make a good life. It may not be the life some folk would choose, but we'll be content." After a little, he added, "You don't know me. I understand you'd be doubtful. You could have a word with Mam. She'd love to meet you. Ness and Emer told her all about you. It's not far, just over the other side of the lake. We were going to walk over anyway, me and Ness and Emer."

"Isn't that a bit far for Ness?"

"She says not. She and Emer have been going out every day. Emer says fresh air and exercise are good for Ness. Will you come?"

He was a charming young man. So was Prince Oran. They said all the right things, the two of them. Gave folk no reason to doubt them. Who was to say Abhan might not, on his wedding night or even earlier, take it into his head to act just as Oran had toward Flidais?

"I'll be honest with you, Mistress Blackthorn. There's another reason I'd like you to visit the camp. My grandmother is poorly. This cough has settled on her chest and she can't shake it off. And she's old. Remembers the wise woman who lived at Dreamer's Wood before you. Holly, was that her name?"

A pox in it. Now I'd have to go with him. Not because of my vow to Conmael, which I'd broken already, in intention if not in deeds. But because, despite everything, I wanted to hear that story, the one about Dreamer's Pool and the pigs, and this old woman might know it. "All right," I said, "but it needs to be quick; I've other things to do with my day, what's left of it." Nobody would look for me in a travelers' camp. I'd keep this as short as I could, and head off straight afterward.

The travelers had made their camp on a grassy sward near the lakeshore. At the far end were the horse lines, where folk were tending to a large number of animals. Closer at hand, the carts were drawn up in a half circle. Most of them had covers, so folk could sleep inside, protected from the weather; some were almost like little houses on wheels. These folk favored bright colors. Their clothing filled the area with patches of red and yellow and blue, as if a flock of exotic birds had alighted there by the water.

In the half circle an open hearth of stones had been built, and a fire burned there, with a three-legged iron support over it, and a big cook pot hanging from a chain. Groups of men and women sat around it talking, working at crafts, passing the time of day. As we walked into the circle a tall woman in a green shawl came forward to greet us. She had such a look of Abhan—the lanky build, the lean face, the steady eyes—that she must surely be his mother.

We were swept into a tide of welcome. She embraced first Ness, then Emer, then me, whether I liked it or not. Then with one arm around Ness and the other around Emer, she bore us away toward one of the covered carts, set at a little distance from the others.

"We'll give you a brew soon. Ness, you need to sit down after that walk, here." A blanket on the grass; a soft cushion for Ness. A couple of girls, silent and shy, brought everything without being asked. Obviously Abhan's sisters; they were like peas in a pod, this family. "Now then," said Abhan's mother, "make yourselves at home. Emer, will you take Mistress Blackthorn in to see Mother?" To me, she said, "My mother's ailing. Abhan will have told you. Emer made her a draft to ease the cough, and that's helped a bit. It's kind of you to take the trouble, Mistress Blackthorn. We're honored by your visit."

What could I say? Most certainly not that I was only here because I'd feared her son might be less than the good man he appeared to be. And not that I was in too much of a hurry to spend time with the old woman. "Good work, Emer," I said. "What brew did you make up?"

"A decoction of black spleenwort, sweetened with a drop of honey. I thought of milkweed root, marshmallow root . . . but I didn't want to try those without asking you first. I thought they might be too strong for an old lady."

Since she'd been in Silverlake, Emer had been making tonics for Ness, gathering herbs in the woods by the lake and using Mór's kitchen as a stillroom. It pleased me that she was keeping up the skills I'd taught her. "Good," I said. "How long has the old lady had the cough?"

"A full turning of the moon, as they traveled north. Deep in the chest. A rattling sound, and it hurts her. They've moved her cart away a bit, so she'll have more quiet."

I was expecting a frail old person like the crone in Winterfalls whose deathbed I had attended. The woman in the cart, lying on a bed of cushions, was old in body only. From her wrinkled face shone forth a pair of dark and penetrating eyes, lively with intelligence.

"Climb up, then," she ordered. "Not you, Emer, I don't need a crowd. Just you, wise woman. Let's have a look at you." As if she was the healer and I was her patient.

I climbed up; settled myself on the cushions beside her. The cart was neatly fitted out, with a bench built into one side, various bags hanging from pegs, a shelf here and there, a place for a jug and cup. "My name is Blackthorn," I said. "But I think they told you that already."

She was taking a thorough look at me. "They did, and more besides. Young Abhan, he's a good lad. Good through and through. He'll look after the lass well. No need to trouble yourself. But you will, of course. Seen too much of the bad, taken its toll. Can't trust."

"Your name wouldn't be Holly, by any chance?"

She roared with laughter. The sound became a splutter,

then a wheezing cough. I lifted her to sit, filled her cup and helped her take a mouthful of what must be the brew Emer had mentioned. "Holly? Me?" she gasped as the spasm subsided. "That would give her a good laugh if she was still here. No, lass, I'm no wise woman, just an ordinary traveling wife. A mother and a grandmother."

I gave her my own searching look. "More than that, I suspect, since you seem to know more about me than anyone here could have told you."

"When you're as old as I am, you learn to look inside. You learn to see what can't be seen. If you were as old as me you wouldn't need to ask questions about Abhan. You'd know at first glance that he's a good man, steady, brave, wise beyond his years. But something's filled you up with doubts."

It was uncomfortable to hear, the more so because it was true. I had seen that Abhan was a good man; that he truly cared for Ness and she for him. I had seen that his family loved her and would look after her. If he was less than he seemed, would they all have rushed to welcome us as they did? But still a faint doubt lingered.

"Not every man is a liar," the old woman said. "Some of them, yes. Not all of them. There are good men out there, men who respect women, men with the courage to stand up for what they believe in. Men who'll be gentle with a newborn babe. Men who'll defend family and land and country with their dying breath. Don't tell me you've never known a man like that, because I won't believe it."

"Stop right there," I said. "I was asked to drop in and check your state of health. Who I might or might not have known, and whether they were good or bad, has nothing at all to do with that. Now tell me about this cough." I bent my head to listen to her chest. "Breathe in, as deep as you can . . . that's right . . . Now let it slowly out. Does it hurt when I tap here? Here? Are you sleeping well?"

The old woman submitted to an examination. When this was done, she adjusted her shawl and looked down at her folded hands.

"Emer's draft will help relieve the pain," I said quietly. "And ease the cough a little." I hesitated.

"But I'm dying anyway," the old woman said. "I know

that, lass. I've been hearing the flap of Morrigan's wings this full turning of the moon and longer. If you could keep me going long enough to see the lad wed, that would please me well."

I'm not staying. I could not bring myself to say it. "I'll give Emer instructions for something that may help; a draft that's stronger than the one she's been using. I believe you'll still be here for your grandson's wedding. Sheer force of will goes a long way to keeping a person alive."

"Hah! You'd know that, I imagine."

A vision of Mathuin's lockup went through my mind in all its pitiful squalor. "That, and anger," I said.

"I don't feel angry. I just want to know things are set right." She stopped to cough again.

"I want that too," I said. "I'm sorry I can't stay. But Emer's a good girl, she's learning her craft, and she'll help you."

"How can she learn if you won't stay?"

I shrugged. "She'll manage."

"Oh yes? Wise women aren't abundant in these parts, so I hear. You're the first one since Holly passed on—that's what Emer told us."

It seemed the whole of Silverlake knew my business. I shouldn't have told this old woman that I was leaving. "I have a question for you."

"Go on then, ask it."

"You knew Holly, long ago. Did she ever tell a story about a place called Dreamer's Pool, over near Winterfalls, and pigs?"

The old woman smiled. "She did. Folk didn't like to hear that tale. It scared them. They wanted it forgotten. Seems they succeeded all too well."

"Could you tell me the story now?"

"I need to piss. Need to get down."

I would have helped her, but she waved me away with sudden impatience, calling for her daughter. In the confusion that followed, I found myself out of the cart and seated on the spread-out blanket between Ness and Emer, while Abhan's mother and sisters assisted the old woman to climb down and go off somewhere to relieve herself. She could walk; indeed, she moved with an ease that belied her apparent state of health.

"She's very unwell," I said to Emer. "There's not much you can do but ease her symptoms. I'd suggest the mallow root with milkweed root, in an infusion. But make it weak, and stop straightaway if it doesn't agree with her." I set out the quantities and method for her; she had a good memory, and could be relied upon to get it right.

"What about later?" Ness asked. "When we're away from here and on the road south? She'll still need the draft, won't she?"

I could not bring myself to say it outright. I glanced at Emer, hoping her intuition would serve her well. I would not have an opportunity to speak to her alone and tell her the old woman's time was running short indeed. "No need to worry about that yet," I said.

The day had darkened still further; was that a drop of rain? I did want to hear the story. It had teased at me for a long time. I did want to know if there was a secret to Dreamer's Pool. On the other hand, if I did not move on now I'd probably get soaked before I reached a spot to camp for the night, and that was not a wise way to start a long journey. Besides, now that Flidais had revealed the truth, sordid and mundane as it was, what was the point in entertaining the idea of some kind of magical transformation? Flidais was the way she was because Oran had hurt and frightened her. Not that she had ever been the woman of those sweetly romantic letters. I had sympathy for the girl's plight, but I could not believe she had written them herself. Oran's brutality toward her had perhaps been born, in part, from disappointment. She cannot give me what I expected, but at least she can give me *this*. The whole thing disgusted me. So, forget the pig story, whatever it was. Get up, make my farewells and move on. *South. Mathuin. Justice.*

"Brew?"

The voice was unmistakable. And there he was, standing beside our blanket with a steaming cup in his hand. How such a big man could move so softly I had never been able to understand.

"What are you doing here?" I snarled, scrambling to my

feet. A pox on the man. It hadn't been easy to summon the will to walk away: to set everything behind me, the cottage, my healing work, Emer with her thirst for knowledge. For a while, at Winterfalls, I had felt as if there might be a purpose beyond Mathuin of Laois. Doing good, as Conmael had wanted. Helping folk who needed me. Until Flidais had shared the wretched truth, I had been starting to feel almost comfortable. But she had told her story, and the old anger had stirred, and I had made my choice. *South. Mathuin. Justice.* Not the prince's trumped-up mission, but my own, which mattered more than anything. More fool I, then, that so soon I'd let myself be drawn off the path, and I'd wasted too much time, and now here he was.

"Might ask you the same," Grim said, putting the brew in my hands.

"I don't have time for this."

"We can walk while you drink it, if you like. Which way are you going?"

"What do you think?" I snapped.

"I'd have said south. But Conmael said to look here, so here I am."

Conmael? What in the name of the gods was going on?

"Excuse me," I said to the two girls. "I need to talk to Grim in private." Without waiting for a response I strode off toward the shore, with Grim following behind. The hot brew slopped over onto my hand, making me curse.

"Here," Grim said, fishing out a handkerchief and passing it over. "Want me to carry it for you?"

"No, I do not! How in the name of the gods did you get here so fast?"

"Borrowed a horse, in a manner of speaking. One of Scannal's."

I would not even ask about Conmael; that was one complication too many. "I'm going south, on my own. You know why. Nothing's changed."

We had reached the water's edge. I stopped walking, wishing he had not come, wishing I did not have to listen to him, wishing I did not have to explain. Knowing that if anyone could make me weaken, it would be him.

"Something must have changed," said Grim. "Had a mission, didn't we? For Prince Oran?"

"Hah! A pox on Prince Oran, the lying mongrel!"

He just looked at me.

I told him the story, how Flidais had confided in me, how it had all made sense once she had explained that Oran was two men in one, the courteous, poetic nobleman by day and the crude, selfish abuser by night. How Flidais, whom we had believed to be some kind of imposter, was in fact a victim. How she had asked for my help, but was not prepared to help herself. "Don't you see," I said at the end, "it's the same mission as Mathuin, in a way, bringing to justice the men who do this, making their crimes public. I can't do that here because it's not what Flidais wants, she needs the marriage for her family, but I can do it in Laois. I should never have given up on it—"

"You're forgetting," Grim said. "But for Conmael you'd be dead."

"I can't stay in Winterfalls, Grim. Not now that I know the truth. I can't stay while that man is ruler there and everyone believes him to be such a model of virtue. The very sight of him would sicken me. And I can't help Flidais with what she really wants, which is to bear him a son and heir."

Grim was staring at me as if I'd gone stark raving mad.

"What?" I growled.

"She told you that load of rubbish and you believed it? What about the way the prince stood up for Emer? The way he spoke at the council, telling folk not to judge Ness? What about the story he told us? How can all that be lies? His folk worship the ground he walks on. Folk who've been in that household since he was a little lad."

"All men are liars. He's a particularly good one. Now I'd best be getting on."

"Lady."

The name stopped me short. I waited, not saying a thing.

"Don't want to speak out of turn. Don't want to upset you. Hard to say this."

"Spit it out, Grim."

"What Mathuin did to you, to your family, that's made you deep-down angry. Doesn't matter where you go, what you do, there's red rage burning inside you. It won't die down until Mathuin pays for his sins. Only thing is, it can get in the way of seeing clear. It can make you deaf to the truth."

"Bollocks! What would you know?" But even as I snapped at him, the white-hot certainty in my heart, the passion that had seen me turn my back on Winterfalls forever, began to feel the cool touch of doubt. Men might be liars. But Grim would never lie to me.

"What if Prince Oran's told the truth," he said, "and Lady Flidais has spun you a story?"

"Why would she concoct a tale like that? If she wanted my help to conceive a son, why didn't she ask when I first moved in there?"

"Got a few things to tell you. Will you listen, at least?"

"All right, but make it quick."

He told me a story about Donagan, how the fellow had confided in him by night, saying the prince was not very worldly-wise, which Grim took to mean that Oran was inexperienced with women. How Donagan wanted to help the prince but couldn't because of something that had happened between them.

"Mm-hm," I said. Donagan was the most loyal servant the prince had; of course he would stick up for him. "They said—at least, Mhairi said—that Donagan knew about it all along. Had to, because he used to sleep in the antechamber next to Oran's bedroom."

"Used to," said Grim. "But moved out by choice. Now sleeps in the men's quarters."

"That proves nothing except that he didn't like what Oran was doing."

"Another thing. The men were talking, and they said Ciar, the girl who was drowned, was . . . ready with her favors. Liked a bit of fun."

"Men's talk. It means nothing except that they have no respect for women."

Grim shuffled his feet. "What I said. About being angry. You're letting it get in the way. You need to listen."

"I don't *need* to do anything but pick up my bag and walk away."

"Going to rain soon."

"All the more reason to get on with this. Anything else to tell me?"

"Only something I heard today, from one of the brewery lads." A story came out, an unsavory little tale, about

Flidais and the prince on a day when they'd gone into the village to talk to the people there. It was deeply implausible. "I was thinking," Grim went on. "When the prince talked to us about Flidais being different from what he expected. He seemed to think there might be something uncanny about it. This sounds crazy, but—could they have sort of—changed over? Ciar and Flidais? When they were in the water, I mean?"

"I'd been thinking along the same lines," I said. "And what you've just told me adds weight to that theory. But, if it's true, if this is a transformation, maid to mistress and mistress to maid, it means the real Flidais is dead. There's no happy ending to this. Besides, why would the false Flidais—if she is false—tell that story about the prince assaulting her? Nobody was casting suspicion on her. If she was holding out for the hand-fasting, hoping nobody would guess there was something wrong before she was safely wed, all she had to do was keep on pretending." Even as I spoke, I remembered that Prince Oran had asked me to spy on Flidais; that I had sat among those women writing in my little book and trying to pick up clues. Flidais had seen me watching her. She and Mhairi had been unsettled by my questions. She had known I doubted her. She had probably known the prince doubted her, especially after he and Master Oisin told that story about a pool, and magic, and a transformation. So she had taken steps, not only to convince me she was no liar but to make sure I did not do Oran's bidding any longer. She had persuaded me neatly that she was no pretender, but a real princess and a future queen. "A pox on it," I muttered. It was becoming apparent that I'd got this badly wrong. I'd acted as no wise woman ever should, letting the weight of things past blind me to the truth. When Flidais had told me her story, I'd been so incensed on her behalf that I'd thrown logic out the window. And if it hadn't been for Grim, I'd have headed on south without ever realizing what I'd done.

"Not like you to give up," said Grim.

"What if I told you I don't care? What if I picked up my bag and headed off right now?"

"Then I'd say you'd forgotten to check the sky. Be pouring soon."

"But if I did? Would you still try to help the prince? Solve the puzzle on your own?"

He looked at me in silence for a bit. In the blockish face, the small eyes were sad. "Nah. Couldn't. Do what I did before. Pick up my own bag and follow after. You can't stand up to Mathuin on your own."

"Then you're a fool," I said. Black Crow save me, the man was pigheaded. I remembered the night when he'd got soaking wet and lingered on the fringes of my camp like a huge forlorn ghost. My eyes were prickling. Were these tears? Impossible.

"Bonehead," Grim said, nodding.

Curse it! I turned away, scrubbed my cheeks, said, "Too late to head back for Winterfalls now, even with this borrowed horse of yours. And there's an old woman in this camp who knows a story about Dreamer's Pool. We'd best ask these folk if we can stay here overnight, go back in the morning."

"Mm-hm." Not a word of *I told you so*. "Horse'll be fine. I left him with the others, couple of lads keeping an eye on him. Couldn't believe it. Conmael just snapped his fingers, and there Storm was."

I'd have to ask some time. "Conmael. He was at the cottage?"

Grim shuffled his feet again; looked away over the lake. "I saw the kerchief, knew what it meant. Couldn't hold everything in, shouted a bit, his name and an oath or two. The fey, they've got magic at their fingertips. They can do whatever they want. Made me angry. He should have stopped you."

"Nothing would have stopped me. Not even threats of seven years turning to eight or nine. Not even the possibility that Conmael could get me thrown back in Mathuin's lockup. I've already broken my promise."

"Don't know about that. Yelled his name and there he was, right next to me. Came out of nowhere. Knew you were gone without being told. And knew where you'd be, though I didn't believe him. Told him I didn't have a hope of catching up on foot, and he conjured up the horse. Don't trust the fellow, don't know what his game is, but this time around he was useful."

"Grim. Thanks. For coming after me." It was hard to get the words out. "And sorry."

"Just doing my job." His tone was gruff. "One thing you could do for me, if you want."

"What's that?"

"Think of something to tell Scannal tomorrow about his horse."

36

Abhan's folk make us welcome. Food, drink, a spot by the fire. The old woman's been sleeping. Don't expect her to come out, but after supper she does, and the folk settle her on a pile of bedding, with Emer on one side and me on the other. Good ale, roast meat, music too — a whistle, a bodhran, a fiddle, a little harp. Some of the lads and lasses dance. The rain holds off, only a drop here and there. Feels like the place knows there's a party and doesn't want to spoil it.

I can breathe again. No need to race off south. She's coming home. Going to sort it all out. I hope. She doesn't like being wrong; doesn't like folk to tell her so. Doesn't like being stopped in her tracks. Mathuin, his crime, burning her man and her little one, that's so vile I can hardly think about it. But her man, Cass, he wouldn't want her taking Mathuin on all by herself. If he was here, he'd tell her getting herself killed won't bring him and Brennan back. All it'll do is give Mathuin another victory. Not something I can tell her. Deep down, she knows. But sometimes, when the past catches up, you just can't stop yourself.

The old woman tells the story, and an odd one it is. A couple of fellows take a herd of pigs into Dreamer's Wood to forage. This is before the time when folk know the place is dangerous. Before they know strange things can happen there if a body isn't watchful. So, while the pigs roam about, the two fellows stop by the pool to eat their bread and cheese. It's a warm day and they start to feel sleepy. One of them says what a pretty spot it is, sun coming down between the leaves, dragonflies over the water, birds calling up above. The other one says, *Yes, isn't it?* Then there's a great crashing and smashing on the bank above the water, and in falls their prize boar, that was going to make their fortune someday. It's gone in deep, and it hasn't come up.

I'll go in, says the first man. *No, I'll go in, I'm a better swimmer,* says his brother. *You stay here and make sure none of the others follow.* He jumps in and swims out to the spot where the boar has sunk without a trace, and he dives down to find it. The first brother waits and waits, pacing along the bank and back again, thinking they're drowned, his brother and the pig both. Then up they pop, the two of them, swim back to the shore and scramble out in a spot where the bank's lower.

Seems like a happy ending for all concerned. But no; something's wrong. The brother who went in the water can't talk anymore. Opens his mouth and all that comes out is grunting sounds. And the pig's scared out of its wits, standing on the shore shivering and shaking. Some of the sows wander over to take a look, sniff the boar and back off quick. The first brother has to lead his brother home by the arm, the fellow's so confused. And the swine are acting terrified, jumping around and squealing. None of them wants to be anywhere near the boar.

By the time the old lady gets to this part of the story, Blackthorn and me are eating up every word. Just as well most of these folk won't know the tale of how Ciar drowned in Dreamer's Pool, or they might be putting two and two together the way we are. Emer knows; we'll have to warn her not to talk.

Well, the tale goes, everyone thinks the second brother has lost his wits. They think falling into Dreamer's Pool has turned him crazy. Nobody thinks much about the pig. A pig's a pig, after all. Seems the boar can't do what he's supposed to do with the sows anymore. But he can provide a midwinter feast for the whole village. So he's put in a sty by himself and fattened up.

Villagers think it's a bit odd the way the first brother goes and talks to the boar every day, as if it was his best friend. Even odder the way the boar seems to be listening. Seems both brothers had their wits addled that day. Word goes around that nobody's to set foot in Dreamer's Pool. The water's cursed. A fey place.

One day, around dusk, the first brother takes the second brother, the half-wit, by the hand and leads him out to the sty where the boar's being kept. He opens the gate and lets the pig out, and the three of them walk all the way to Dreamer's Wood. The moon's full and by the time they get there the pool's shining with a strange light, so you can almost see the magic.

How's he going to do it? Doesn't want to set foot in the water himself, somehow has to get the two of them in. The boar understands what he wants; it wades in straightaway, then swims to deep water, a big speckled bulk in the moonlight. But the second brother, he doesn't want to go in. Scared stiff. Plants his feet on the shore and pulls away from his brother as hard as he can, once he sees what's happening.

First brother goes in up to his ankles, praying that he won't be changed. Calls his brother the way he used to call the boar. *Hoooo-piggy-piggy! Hooooo-piggy-piggy!*

Second brother shivers and shakes. Tight as a bowstring in his brother's grip. Won't go in.

First brother's got a secret weapon. He fishes it out of his pocket. Throws it out into the pool, into the deep water. Lump of fresh cheese. His boar would do anything for cheese.

Second brother runs forward, snorting. He's in to his ankles, his knees, his hips. He's diving under, he's gone.

First brother backs up onto the shore, checking his feet to make sure they haven't turned into trotters or something worse. Waits with his heart in his mouth. Nobody's told him this will work. It's just the only thing he can think of to set this right. You can't eat your own brother for the midwinter feast.

Long wait. He's thinking they've both drowned, and he'll get charged with murder, when there's a thrashing and a splashing out there and ah! There's the boar swimming back to shore and oh! There's the second brother coming after, gasping out, *Morrigan's curse, it's freezing in here!*

The boar gets out first, shakes himself, rolls around in the dirt a bit, snuffles and grunts as pigs do. The brother comes next, and the first thing he does is hug his brother and say, *Thank you, Brother, thank you! Oh gods, I'm never setting foot in this place again as long as I live!*

First brother gets out the rest of the cheese from his pocket and gives it to the boar, and they all walk home. He doesn't put the boar back in the fattening sty, but out in the field with the sows, who greet him like a long lost hero. By the next day, that boar's doing what he's supposed to do with the ladies, and folk start talking about roasting a sheep for the midwinter feast. As for the second brother's sudden return to himself, everyone welcomes it, but nobody talks about it. The brothers don't tell the whole story to many. Only the local wise woman, and their mother, and later their wives. But after that day, folk go carefully in Dreamer's Wood. And they make sure they never set foot—or trotter—in the water of Dreamer's Pool.

It's a good tale, if odd, and the old lady tells it well. Has to stop and cough now and then, and folk wait for her to take a drink and collect herself. Sounds too poorly to be out of bed. But it's plain she wants to be here by the fire, family all around, sharing the story. Comes to me that if I was dying, this is how I'd like to go. Love, music, family, tales. Not much chance of that.

Blackthorn's been looking at me on and off during the story, and me at her, both of us trying to work out if it's any help to us. Later on, when the traveling folk are abed and the fire's died down, we talk about it. They've moved things around to make space for us in a cart. Given us blankets. Rain's come at last, so we can't sleep beside the fire.

"Looks as if our theory's right," Blackthorn says. "Maid and mistress changing bodies when they went into Dreamer's Pool."

"Why would she tell that story right now? Isn't that a bit odd?"

"I asked her to tell it. When she said she knew the last wise woman, the one before me. I knew there was an old tale about the pool, something about pigs, but nobody else remembered it. Grim, this isn't much help. Maybe it shows that Ciar and Flidais switched over. But one of them drowned. Taking Flidais for a nice little swim in Dreamer's Pool can't bring the dead girl back. As for odd, this is no odder than Conmael telling you I'd be at Silverlake. How could he know what I'd do?"

"Knows you better than you think. That'd be my guess. Knew you'd want to see Ness again before you left. And Emer."

Too dark to see Blackthorn's face, but I bet she's grimacing at that. "I'm not the good person you think I am, Grim. I'm a messy tangle of doubt and hate and anger and bitterness. If Conmael thinks he can make me into something different, he doesn't know me at all."

I don't say anything. She's got it wrong. But no point telling her that. She won't believe me.

"Grim?"

"Mm?"

"We need a plan. It's not long until full moon and the prince's council. And after that they'll be riding off to their wedding and it will be too late. But pushing Flidais into Dreamer's Pool isn't going to achieve anything, even supposing we could convince her to go back over there. What do we do? Tell the prince the story we heard tonight and say we can't do anything more? Tell him Flidais and Mhairi lied to me? Confront Flidais with what we suspect? None of those will do any good. Maybe we should suggest he marries her anyway, since the woman of his dreams is dead."

I'm thinking hard. "You could ask Conmael," I say. "Since he seems to know all sorts of things he shouldn't know. He might have the answer, if there is one."

"A pox on Conmael," says Blackthorn, so quiet the rain nearly swallows it. "We're solving this ourselves. We need to talk to someone who was there that day, when Ciar was drowned."

"You were there."

"Not at first. By the time I reached the pool she was lying dead on the shore. I want to know exactly how it happened. We're missing something, and it's not pigs and cheese."

"Couldn't you ask Flidais's ladies? Not Mhairi, the other ones?"

I remembered them weeping and wailing over Ciar's body. "I don't think they'd be very helpful. Besides, there's always the chance one of them would tell Flidais or Mhairi that I'd been asking questions again."

"The guards," I say. "Lady Flidais's men-at-arms. Not the friendliest bunch, but I know them now. Think I could get one of them to tell me the tale. Young Eoin, he talks about it sometimes. Scared him. He's the one went into the water to fish Ciar out that day. Probably lucky he came out a man and not a newt or a frog." Morrigan's britches, the more I think about this, the odder it gets.

"That's your job for tomorrow, then," Blackthorn says. "The start of a plan. Ask him, but don't be too eager, we don't want word to get back to Flidais that we're poking around again."

"And your job?"

"Convincing the lady that I still believe her lies. Playing for time, until you bring me an answer."

Next morning we take Storm back to Scannal's. I tell the miller I found his horse wandering over Silverlake way, and it was too late to bring him home safely. Scannal's a bit surprised, as you'd expect, but he seems all right with it.

Turns out I can't talk to Eoin that day, or the one after, because Domnall's organized some kind of training to keep the lads from Cloud Hill busy, and they don't come in from that until suppertime. Can't talk about it after supper in the men's quarters. Too many of them around, no privacy, can't take him aside without drawing attention. And then I'm on duty.

Stroke of luck on the third day. I'm working at the cottage, slapping limewash on the inside walls of the lean-to, when Eoin and Seanan—that's the fellow whose skull I nearly broke for him—turn up asking if I want help. Seems Domnall's given them the day off. Every time something useful happens now, I ask myself if Conmael's behind it. Stupid. Luck, that's all this is.

Seanan takes over the limewash, and I go outside with Eoin to start on a new drain. Planning to do most of the dig-

ging myself, and get him talking while I work. We mark out
the spot with sticks and twine, fetch a couple of spades from
the outhouse. Ground's sodden. It'll be a muddy job.

We chat about the training they've been doing with
Domnall. It's tired the men out but they're happier. Keeping busy suits them. We talk about the weather, which is
dry today, so far at least. Eoin says he's noticed some big
trees are down in the wood, must've fallen on that night of
wind and heavy rain. He says it looks as if they might stay
where they lie, if what he's heard about Dreamer's Wood is
right. So, easy as easy, we get around to what I want him to
talk about.

"Why's that?" I ask.

He leans on his spade, takes a quick look over his shoulder, up toward the wood. "Nobody likes the place. Don't
know how you can live so close. There's a strange feeling
about it. As if anything might jump out and grab a fellow."

"Mm," I say, digging my spade in. "There's a few old
tales about the wood. That pool, too. Must've been hard for
you when the girl—what was her name, Ciar?—had her accident. Heard you tried to save her. Bit of a hero."

"Just doing my job. Trying to keep the womenfolk safe. I
can't understand how she drowned so quick. Soon as we saw
she was in trouble, I went straight in. And I swim fast. But she
was gone by the time I reached her."

"Did your best." I wait a bit, then say, "Seems odd, Lady
Flidais wanting to go swimming. Nearly at Winterfalls
and all."

"Lady Flidais is not your usual sort of lady. Gets these odd
ideas sometimes. Folk at Cloud Hill are used to it. For all her
fancies, she's a good lass, kind and thoughtful. Or was."

I keep on digging.

"Funny, she never said thank you. For me trying to save
Ciar. Not a word. Not like her at all, she used to make a
point of thanking us for every little thing, knew all our
names and our wives' names and how many children we
have and where we all come from. Sweet girl, not what
you'd think a chieftain's daughter would be like. What happened that day—it's sort of soured her. She doesn't seem to
care anymore." His cheeks go pink. He gives me a sideways
look. "Shouldn't have said that. Disrespectful. But . . . it can

be hard here. The fellows are restless, you'll have seen it. Worried about Lord Cadhan, wanting to get home. And not happy with . . . you know."

"How did it all happen, that day?" I ask. "Wondered sometimes if there were, well, *things* in the wood, fey or the like. Wouldn't mind hearing the story. Only if you want to tell it, of course. Why don't you take a break, and I'll do this next part?"

Eoin's happy enough to sit on the wall and watch me working. And bit by bit the story comes out. How they had a choice of ways to Winterfalls, and Lady Flidais wanted to go through the wood because of something in a letter. How she bade them stop when they came to the pool; how she seemed entranced by it, saying it was so beautiful it was like a poem all in itself.

"Then she said she'd like to bathe, and who was going in with her? The other ladies didn't want to, but Ciar was always up for a challenge. Lady Flidais told us to get down and rest the horses a while, and turn our backs while she and Ciar had their swim. So we did, and there was some splashing and laughing, and then Deirdre screamed, and Nuala yelled out, 'I can't see them! They've gone under!' and when I turned around, there was nothing out there but some ripples. Got my cloak off, bent down to pull off my boots. When I stood up, there was Lady Flidais, swimming back, and there was the dog scrambling out on the other side. But no sign at all of Ciar."

You know those times when you come out of a tunnel or a cave or a dark place, and suddenly there's daylight and a view like you've never seen in your life before? This was like that. Sent my head into a real spin. Had to work hard not to let out an oath. "A dog went swimming too?"

"Lady Flidais's terrier, Bramble, you know the one. Wouldn't be parted from her. Like a shadow. Back then, anyway."

"What happened next?"

"I went in, being the strongest swimmer out of the escort. Ciar was under the water, couldn't see her at all. Found her quite quick, though, dragged her out, laid her down on the shore. Domnall tried to squeeze out the water, get her breathing again, but no. Mistress Blackthorn came not long after that, had a look, said it was too late. Never seen anyone drown so fast."

I'm full of wanting to rush back to Winterfalls and tell Blackthorn. This is the answer. That little dog, that scrap of a thing that sits on Prince Oran's knee and toddles around after his aunt, it's . . . Danu have mercy. All this time. Starts all kinds of questions in my mind, too many questions.

"Sad story, Eoin," I say, putting my back into digging. "But you couldn't have done any more for her."

"Weighs on me a bit," Eoin says. "Lovely girl, Ciar, a bit wild, not the sort you'd take home to meet your mother, but full of life. Too young to die."

"So you brought her back to Winterfalls, and she was buried there."

"Prince Oran arranged that. Ritual, prayers and so on. All of us were there to see her buried. All of us but Lady Flidais. Feeling poorly; a big shock."

A big shock. Well, it would be. How would it feel, finding yourself in someone else's body? I try to imagine myself as Donagan, or as the prince. Morrigan's britches! Doesn't bear thinking about. Worse than that, she'd be seeing her own body put in the grave. Enough to turn anyone a bit odd. I know one thing. If it was me I'd tell the truth, even if folk thought I was crazy.

We get the work done, then have some food and drink, and when the fellows need to go back to Winterfalls I pack up and go with them. Forget sleep for today; I've got to see Blackthorn. Hoping she can think of a plan. Seems impossible to me. Why would Flidais—Ciar, I suppose she is—agree to take another swim in Dreamer's Pool, when the weather's cold enough to freeze a man's bollocks off, and she knows Blackthorn's suspicious, not to mention the prince? Can't see Oran forcing her to go over there and throwing her in. And even if he does, what happens if it doesn't work? Charges of murder, that's what. But Blackthorn's clever. She'll find a way.

37

*B*ramble. *Flidais.* I stared at Blackthorn, wordless. I saw on her face that she expected me to challenge the theory, to argue that such things simply weren't possible. To tell her that although I'd suspected strangeness of some kind, this went beyond belief.

"I knew it," I said when I had found my voice again. "I knew she wasn't gone, I knew she was still here somewhere." I wanted to run out right away and find Bramble, to hold her close, to keep her safe until . . . What Blackthorn proposed was both wonderful and terrifying. I could barely bring myself to consider it.

"It's only a theory at this point," the wise woman said. We were in my council chamber, she and I, with the door closed behind us. Grim had been half-asleep when they came to find me; she'd sent him off to rest. "Acting on it would be extremely risky. If we were wrong, there could be most unfortunate consequences."

I was shivering from head to toe, so full of feelings I thought I would burst apart. What if Flidais had retained her human understanding, what if she had understood every single thing I had said to her? "When can we do this?" I asked, and my voice shook like a terrified child's.

"*If* we do it," Blackthorn said, "it must be done with

great care. It must be carried out exactly to my instructions.
You don't dabble with magic carelessly, even if you're a
prince. And you need to be fully aware of what this could
mean for everyone concerned."

"Yes. Yes, of course."

"First, then, you must make peace with the lady. Be
kinder to her; make believe you've accepted that she's having a few difficulties, and that you've realized you should
stop being so critical and help her through them. Don't
thaw too suddenly, though, or she'll be suspicious. A smile
here, a kind word there, no snubs or reprimands. Can you
do that?"

My cheeks were hot with embarrassment. "I'll do my
best. Better than before."

"Good. Now I have a question for you, and you may not
like it."

"Go on."

She hesitated. "My lord, you and your betrothed—you
have lain together already, yes?"

Now my face must be red as a strawberry. "Why would
you ask that?"

"Because Lady Flidais told me you had. And because
the plan will not work if she is still untouched."

"We ... well, yes, but ... not since my aunt came to Winterfalls. You are not suggesting ... ?"

"That you do so again? Indeed not," Blackthorn said.
"What you must do is convince her that should a good opportunity arise, you would not be averse to lying with her
once more before you are hand-fasted."

"I don't know if I ..." Shame overwhelmed me. How
much had Flidais—the woman who was not really Flidais—
told her? And who exactly had shared my bed on those
nights of tangled passion? The beautiful, tantalizing body
had been that of my sweetheart; the fierce and determined
person within had been Ciar. Gods, if only I could erase
that time!

"You must," Blackthorn said. "If you want Flidais back,
you must do exactly as I say. Including this, difficult as it may
be. Convince her, between now and the evening of your
council, that you've realized you've been unfair to her. That
you've judged her too harshly. That you still love and desire

her, and that you're eagerly awaiting the hand-fasting. I don't care how you do it, but be subtle and be convincing."

"Very well. I will do my best."

"And one more thing," says Blackthorn. "She doesn't know the story about the man and the pig. She doesn't know this has happened before, or how the spell was undone. She has no reason to suspect Bramble was part of it. And she mustn't find out. So you should treat Bramble just as you did before, my lord."

"I understand. The evening of the council, you said? We cannot do this any earlier? That would leave no time for a second attempt; we would be leaving for Cahercorcan the next day."

"It should be at full moon. A time of magic and mystery, tides and changes. There will only be one chance."

"How can I persuade her to go to Dreamer's Wood? What if she refuses? I do not wish to have her conveyed there by force."

"You can leave that part of it to me," said Blackthorn. "Just be advised that, at some point between now and the council, the lady will put an unlikely suggestion to you. When she does, make sure you say yes."

"I see." That was a lie; I did not see at all, but I understood this was my only hope.

"Take Donagan into your confidence," Blackthorn said. "Grim says he can be trusted, and Grim is a good judge of men. Tell him as much of the truth as you think he can stomach. In particular, make sure that when you do ride out to Dreamer's Wood, the escort you take is Donagan and nobody else."

"Donagan is leaving my service after the council."

"You might prevail upon him to stay for one more night, my lord," said Blackthorn. "I wager he'll have changed his mind by the morning."

38

I fed her the idea piece by piece. A sudden revelation, straight after I'd told her there was no sure way to conceive a boy, would surely have had her suspecting a trap. So, while I went to talk to her and Mhairi every evening, what I told them was that I was studying the lore, going over all the charms and spells I knew of and speaking to the old folk of the district, one by one, in case there was something useful that I didn't know. I hoped to have an answer for her soon. Soon.

She was impatient, just like the prince. I guessed that she feared discovery before they were wed, and knew that if she could say she was with child, or might be, Oran would feel obliged to stand by her even if the strange truth came out. As for what would happen to her if my plan succeeded, I shrank from it even as I knew that we must do this for Flidais's sake. To pretend we did not know what Ciar had done, to let her continue as Flidais, marry the future king and condemn the real Flidais to remain in her current form would be a coward's way forward. Besides, now that I had told the prince, there would be no doing that. I'd agreed to help Oran, and Oran wanted his true Flidais back. He'd hardly hesitated before he said yes to my proposal. He was a man of some intelligence; he must realize what it could mean for him, for all of us, if this went wrong. High stakes. My instincts, and Grim's, had better be right.

I tried not to feel sorry for wretched Ciar, who had found herself in a terrifying situation and had lied to get through it. The first lie, that she was Flidais, I could almost understand, though I hoped that if it had happened to me, I would have been braver. But the later lie, about Oran abusing her — that I found unforgivable. So many women were hurt by men and found themselves powerless to make it stop. So many had no voice. Ciar had used me. She had heard me speak strongly at the council, when Branoc's case came up, and she had found the key to turning me against the prince, so that I would cease spying. She must have believed I was close to finding out her perilous secret. I despised her for that lie. That did not stop my belly from churning at the thought of what lay ahead. I would add this to the burden of guilt I already carried.

Waiting until full moon to do it meant enduring more days of pretense, more days of anxiety. But full moon would best fit the story. And it would give Oran time to soften his attitude toward her. Besides, we had to wait until a few days, at least, after her moon-bleeding ended. So I went out every morning, in what I hoped was a convincing pretense of seeking answers, and I came back to tell her I'd heard a whisper of a story, something that might possibly work, only I needed to talk to one more old woman, or perhaps two more, and they lived in a valley a long walk to the west . . .

Often I went no farther than Dreamer's Wood. Often I spent the morning helping Grim with the last touches on the house, or warming water on the new hearth to make a brew, or planning a tidier way to store my materials when we moved back in. The way the work was going, we'd be doing so around the time Oran and his bride rode off to Cahercorcan for their wedding. If they did. If this happened. If all of us were not charged with assault or murder or using dark magic for evil ends.

One morning I went right into the wood, taking Grim with me. Dreamer's Pool lay quiet under the leafless trees.

Pale mist wreathed the leaden water; no birds sang. The air was chill enough to freeze your bones.

"Feels like the place is holding its breath," said Grim, who sometimes surprised me with his words.

"Mm. As if we're being watched. Never mind that. We need to walk through this; make sure we've got it all worked out." At the eastern end of the pool lay the level stretch of shore where Eoin had pulled Ciar out of the water. If the tale of the boar was true, that would be the spot where the animal had plunged in after the lump of cheese. It was surely also the place where Flidais and Ciar—and, I assumed, Bramble—had waded in to swim.

I imagined Grim and myself trying to drag a screaming woman into that uninviting water; trying to immerse her without ourselves risking a transformation. Impossible, even supposing Donagan and the prince were prepared to help. And what about Mhairi? Flidais was hardly likely to ride out here without an attendant. "We won't be able to lead her in," I said. "She'll have to be pushed."

"Up there," Grim said, pointing. "See where the bank rises along that side? Deep water below, I'd be guessing."

Morrigan's curse! I couldn't think of a less appealing spot. "She'd have to be mad to agree," I said.

"Been up there once before," said Grim. "Come and take a look. Might be all right."

We climbed around the bank, followed the rise, clambered with difficulty between the young birches and through the tangle of undergrowth. Up on this side, it was hard to get a clear view more than two strides ahead even by daylight. I muttered a prayer, thinking that what we were planning was likely to disturb whatever spirits dwelled in the place, and that they were surely dark and devious ones. A spider goddess, maybe, or something that liked to pop out unexpectedly, cackling. Gathering herbs in Dreamer's Wood was all very well; I always did so with respect, offering the right words, taking only what I needed. But this felt perilous.

"See?" said Grim as we came out of the thicket, and there it was, sudden and surprising amid the tangle of growth: a patch of greensward, level and soft, surrounded by sheltering ferns, and just enough room for two people to lie down comfortably together.

"This has been here all the time?" How had I not found it before? *Conmael, you meddler*, I thought, but did not say it.

"Mm-hm. Good spot to sit and think. That's if the strangeness doesn't get to you. Careful!"

It was a sharp warning. I halted and looked down. At one end of the sward, the ferns masked a sudden drop to the waters of Dreamer's Pool. In this spot, the bank stood more than the height of two men above the surface, and it was sheer. There would be no easy scrambling out. The place might have been created just for our purpose. "Danu save us," I muttered. "But what about getting up here? It'll be dark."

"Path," Grim said. "Over there. Come in that way, saves the scramble through the trees."

"You might have mentioned that before I got all these scratches." My heart was pounding, and not only from the climb. "I don't know what scares me more: the thought that it won't work, or the thought that it will."

"Just one thing," said Grim. "What if it rains that night? She won't be wanting to come out here if it's soaking wet."

"It won't rain."

He gave me a straight look. "Conmael?"

"If Conmael chooses to help, that's his business. I'm not asking him for any favors. I'll make sure the rain holds off." I'd been able to do it, long ago; natural magic, the kind that lets you use what is already present, the power of earth, air, fire and water, to help you in times of need. Small tricks, maybe, but deep ones. Whether I could summon that skill again was yet to be seen. I might need to have a word with the spider goddess, or the hole-dwelling surprise spirit, or the shade of Holly, if she lingered close by. I would need all the help I could get to make this work. Only not Conmael's. I was in enough debt to that supercilious know-it-all already.

"If you say so," said Grim with perfect confidence.

I let five days go by before I told Flidais the story. I judged that still left long enough for her to pluck up her courage and put the proposition to Oran, and for him to make a convincing show of reluctance before agreeing to it. That evening I tapped on her door after supper, and Mhairi let me in.

Flidais was examining two gowns laid out on the bed. One was deep violet-blue, with a lilac overtunic trimmed with fur. The other was pine green with a yellow tunic elaborately embroidered in leaves and flowers.

"For your hand-fasting, Lady Flidais?" I could not have been less interested. But I'd been practicing saying the right things, using the right tone.

She straightened, turning to face me. "Do you have anything for me? Any news yet?"

"As it happens, I do, my lady. I met some of the traveling folk—you'll have heard that they're camped near Silver-lake at present. There's a very old woman among them, whom I was asked to tend to. And it turned out she'd known the wise woman who once lived in my cottage, Holly, her name was." The lie would be more convincing if I kept it as close as possible to the truth. Flidais was not going to visit the travelers to check my story. She was not going to ask anyone about it; the matter was far too personal, and she had too much to lose. Besides, we had only a few days left.

"And?"

"She told me a story everyone else has forgotten. A strange bit of lore, to do with Dreamer's Pool."

Flidais shivered, wrapping her arms around herself. "That place! I don't even want to think about it."

"You might need to, my lady." I tried for a kindly tone. "Because the story I heard was that if a woman wants to be sure of conceiving a boy, she should lie with her lover at Dreamer's Pool under a full moon. The crone said folk knew about it in Holly's day, and so many of the local women put it into practice that it could be hard to find a private spot in the wood, especially on the full moon nights of summer. But Holly's dead and gone. She's forgotten by most folk in these parts, and it seems this wisdom died with her." Flidais was staring at me, utterly silent. One thing was plain: this had caught her attention completely. "Of course," I added, not wishing to seem too enthusiastic, "this is hardly the best time of year for it. If you wanted to try, it would be wiser to wait until spring."

"Sounds like an old wives' tale," said Mhairi. "Are you sure you're not making this up, Mistress Blackthorn?"

"Why would she do that?" Flidais, at least, was captured by the idea. And Flidais was the one who mattered. "Mistress Blackthorn, do you mean it has to be by night? In the dark? What if it's cloudy and the moon can't be seen? What if it's raining?"

"I would take it to mean you should do it at a time when the moon can be seen in the night sky, my lady. Clouds—I do not think they would make a difference, provided the position of the veiled moon could be judged. As for rain, I have been in Dreamer's Wood in wet weather. The trees provide quite good shelter, even at this time of year. You would certainly need to wear a woolen cloak and take a warm blanket to lie on."

"I cannot believe you're considering this, my lady," Mhairi said. "What if you catch your death of cold, just before the hand-fasting?"

"It's not up to you to decide!" Flidais snapped. She must be strung tight indeed to lose her temper with her trusted maidservant. What had these two been before the transformation—fellow servants or close friends? Mhairi could not be ignorant of the full truth, surely. She must be Ciar's accomplice in the deception.

"Of course," I went on, "if you delayed this until after you returned from the hand-fasting, it would spare you from having to lie with the prince again for a little longer. I do not imagine Prince Oran is in such a rush to father a son that you need do this now, before you leave for Cahercorcan. The weather is indeed inclement."

"Exactly," said Mhairi. "It's a foolish idea. Besides, how could you possibly convince Prince Oran to go along with it? Full moon—that's the day of his council. It's the day before we ride off to court."

"I'm doing it," Flidais said. "And you'll support me, Mhairi, if you know what's good for you. I will persuade him. He's been a little kinder, these last few days. And of course he wants a son. His whole family are hoping for that. Lady Sochla hints about it all the time."

Mhairi had gone white. A threat, that had been. Stay on my side or . . . what? You'll lose your favored position, or be packed off back to Cloud Hill? If Mhairi did know the truth, Flidais was foolish to threaten her. Should she choose to tell, Mhairi had the power to create utter chaos.

"Flidais," said Mhairi, not even bothering with *my lady*, "if you do this, *everyone will know*."

The words hung in silence for a moment, frightening in their implications.

"Know what?" asked Flidais in a shaky voice.

"That you and the prince have lain together," said Mhairi. "That you've anticipated your wedding night. That's no way to start a marriage to the king's son."

I breathed again. "Maybe not," I said, "but there's a way of doing this and keeping it quiet. May I tell you?"

"Of course. Mhairi, fetch the mead. Bring a cup for Mistress Blackthorn. And let us all sit down."

We sat. Mhairi, now tight-lipped and silent, poured mead for the three of us.

"Now tell us," said Flidais, "how can this be done?"

I set it out for her. First she must work on the prince in private, telling him the tale about Dreamer's Pool, playing the part of a starry-eyed young bride desperate to give her new husband a boy. She must persuade him to try this at the next full moon, which was the night before they were to leave for court. She must ensure they took only one attendant each: Mhairi for her, Donagan for him. Yes, it might seem odd to the household that they would ride out at dusk. But we could invent a story to explain it. Prince Oran was known for his interest in the natural world, the fields and woods and lakes of the district and the wild creatures that lived there. Perhaps he might want to show his betrothed a white owl he'd glimpsed in the wood, or simply share with her the beauty of the landscape under the full moon. Or I, in my role as wise woman, might offer a special full moon blessing for the happy couple. The explanation would only be needed if someone happened to ask. Donagan could make the practical arrangements, such as having horses ready.

"I imagine," I said, "from what you have told me about his behavior, that the prince will be eager to avail himself of this opportunity. It will be hard for you to go through with this, my lady, after what he did to you. I understand that, and I salute your courage. Keep your thoughts on what you will gain from it, and say a word to the ancient guardians of Dreamer's Wood, who provide the magic that makes such things possible." Gods, if my old mentor could hear me she would be horrified. This was a travesty of a wise woman's counsel.

"Thank you, Mistress Blackthorn," said Flidais. "You are so kind. I'm sorry I judged you harshly when you first came here."

"I'm used to it," I said, rising to my feet with my mead barely begun. "Now, if I may, I'll leave you to your deliberations over the wedding gowns. Who did the embroidery on the yellow tunic? It's very intricate."

"Beautiful, isn't it?" said Flidais with a crooked smile. "It was Ciar."

39

Blackthorn's unlikely plan fell into place with a curious ease. It was as if a force beyond the human had sprung into being, sending us hurtling toward what might be triumph or catastrophe. It sent my mind back over old tales of wonder and enchantment, and the price that could be exacted if a man or woman meddled unwisely with nature's mysteries. I did not feel in the least wise, only strung tight with the knowledge that if this succeeded, my Flidais, my own, dear Flidais, would be returned to me on the night of the full moon.

I managed to dissemble. So much hung on this, I could not afford to make the least blunder. So, when Flidais — Ciar — came to me in private and told me, with blushes and hesitation, a very strange tale about Dreamer's Pool, I heard her out. Then I told her, gently, that I feared it was no more than an old wives' superstition, and that she should not get her hopes up when she was likely to be disappointed. Later, she came to me again, and when she put her arms around my waist and leaned her head against my chest, I made myself stroke her hair and speak words of tenderness. I told her I had not been myself lately; that the added responsibility of a marriage, and perhaps children, on top of my role as heir to the throne, had for a little while felt too weighty to bear, especially since my falling-out with Donagan. I told her I was sorry, and kissed her on the lips. And I felt such a confusion of emotions that I wondered how she could possibly believe my lies. But it seemed I played my part well enough.

As for Donagan, he listened to me, which was as much as I had hoped for. He listened while I told him the old tale of the brothers and the boar and explained what it might mean, and he listened while I told him what I had not told Blackthorn: the shameful and bitter story of how false Flidais had come to me by night, twice, and how I had let desire be my master. When I was finished, he said, "I know," and poured me a cup of mead. And when I asked him to come with me on the night of full moon, and to arrange horses for four, and explained what he should say if anyone asked why we were riding out at such an hour, he said he would do it. He did not tell me whether he believed the plan might work and I did not ask. I simply accepted what he offered and felt my heart ease a little.

It was as well there were no grave matters to be heard at the council, for my mind was leaping here, there and everywhere. Donagan helped, as did Aedan, keeping the proceedings moving along, asking the questions I forgot to ask, making suggestions when I had none. Ciar sat beside me, demure in a gown of russet brown with her hair in a plait down her back. She smiled and nodded, contributing little. The mood was muted, and the council concluded early.

Our departure for court in the morning would require a great deal of work. I let the folk of the district know that after the next council we would have a feast, with music and dancing. We provided mead and oatcakes, then sent them all home. The folk of the household busied themselves with packing up and preparing for the journey. They were too busy to think of asking awkward questions.

The most difficult moment, for me, was encountering my aunt, with Bramble, in the hallway. Aunt Sochla asked if I was planning to take the dog with me to Cahercorcan or leave her here at Winterfalls.

"I know Lady Flidais has lost her enthusiasm for the creature," she said. "If you prefer, Bramble can ride along with me and I will house her with my other dogs. It will be a shock to her at first, I imagine, but she'll cope. Bramble

may be happier there, Oran. Your father's court is full of
hunting hounds and the like. And Flidais . . ."

It was as much as I could manage not to gather Bramble
up and hug her close, bear her away and open my heart to
her somewhere in private. Which was, in fact, not so very
different from what I had already been doing from time to
time, before I knew anything about her true nature. "Thank
you, Aunt," I said. "We've decided to leave Bramble here
until we return. Aedan and Fíona will make sure she's
looked after. She has many friends at Winterfalls, don't you,
lovely girl?" I bent down to caress her soft head. She licked
my hand. Her bright eyes seemed to me full of knowledge;
of truths that could not yet be spoken. If tonight's endeav-
our did not work, if it was a disastrous failure, my heart
would shatter in pieces.

"Very well, Oran." I could see Aunt Sochla was disappointed. "If you change your mind at any time, just let me
know. I always have room for one more. Especially a well-
behaved little soul like Bramble. It really defies belief
that . . ." She let her words trail off. "Ah, well, I have a great
deal to do. And the morning will be chaotic. It might be
best if Bramble went to Aedan and Fíona's cottage tonight,
don't you think? The departure is sure to disturb her. Why
don't you take her now?"

"Of course." Whether my aunt sensed something odd,
or whether this was another of those turns of events that
made me suspect uncanny interference in our affairs, there
was no doubt it was convenient. "I will. And . . . thank you
for being here this last while, Aunt Sochla. Your presence
has provided a welcome dash of common sense. And you
have been kind to Bramble."

"Kind but firm," my aunt said. "Makes them feel safe.
Does wonders for their behavior. Good-bye, little one."
She turned on her heel and walked off without another
word. I suspected my formidable kinswoman was holding
back tears.

I broke my promise to Blackthorn. I went to my bedchamber, with the dog at my heels, locked myself in, and
sat on the edge of my bed holding her. Stroking her. Whispering to her of what was to come, and how she would
need to be very brave, and how I knew she would be when

the time came. Explaining that she would have to leave me now, but that soon we would be together again. For the rest of our lives. Perhaps she understood my words; perhaps she retained her human awareness while she was in canine form. If she could not understand, she was at least soothed by my tone; her neat, small form was warm and relaxed against me. "Soon," I murmured. "Soon this nightmare will be over."

Then I sent for Grim, and he took her away.

Before dusk, we rode out to Dreamer's Wood; Ciar and I, Donagan and Mhairi. All of us were quiet. The day was chill but dry, and the fields were fading to purple-gray in the last light. The horses' breath made little clouds in the freezing air; the sound of their hooves was muffled on the muddy track. It seemed to me the others might hear the pounding of my heart, which felt like the wild drumbeat of a charge to battle.

"Are you warm enough, Flidais?" I asked.

"Fine." She was wrapped in a thick woolen cloak with rabbit fur around the hood, and looked utterly charming, her cheeks pink with the cold. *Let this not fail*, I prayed. *Let Blackthorn not be wrong about this.*

The wood lay in stillness, shadowy, forbidding.

"We'll tie up the horses by Mistress Blackthorn's cottage," I said to Donagan, who knew every part of the plan.

"Nobody home," he observed as we rode up to the little house, which had been expertly repaired and looked, against the gloom of the wood, almost reassuring in its neat homeliness. "Never mind. Should be enough light from the moon, and I don't imagine you'll be very long."

"Who knows?" I said, attempting a smile. "Let me help you down, Flidais. Careful now."

The next part was awkward. Blackthorn had told me where to go, and both Donagan and I knew the wood well enough to find the place. But with our purpose being so intimate, it did not seem quite right for me to suggest that he and Mhairi come with us all the way.

"I'll walk you in, my lord," said Donagan, staunch as ever. "Don't want to leave you and the lady in the wood all alone; doesn't feel right. Mhairi and I can wait at a distance, down by the water. I have a flask of mead to keep the chill out."

"Thank you, Donagan." Ciar was nervous now; when I offered her the support of my arm, I could feel her trembling. "All right, my dear?" I wondered at my own capacity for deception.

"Mm. Only, being here brings back that day. When Ciar was drowned. This is a strange place." And, after a moment, "We don't need to go down there, do we? Where they brought her out of the water?"

"No, my lady," said Donagan. "There's a much better place up on the other side of the pool. It's sheltered and grassy. Let me show you."

It was dusk, and as we climbed the path the full moon appeared beyond the network of bare branches, casting a cool light upon us. An owl gave a sudden eerie call, disturbing the quiet of the wood. From farther off, another answered.

"This place scares me," said Ciar.

"My lady," put in Mhairi, who had been unusually quiet, "you need not do this now, tonight."

Ciar turned on her. "Don't think to tell me what I should or should not do! Why would I come all the way out here only to lose my courage and go running off home again? Keep your opinions to yourself!"

"Through here," Donagan said, parting some foliage to show a narrow pathway. Ahead lay the place Blackthorn had chosen, a soft patch of greensward amid the proliferation of ferny undergrowth. "I will lay my cloak down here"—he did so—"and, my lady, you might wish to pass your own cloak to Mhairi. And we will leave you in peace awhile."

The moment was here; the wood seemed to tremble. Ciar and I stood side by side on the sward. The others had retreated to the path. Night was descending fast; the moonlight on Ciar's perfect features—Flidais's features—turned her to a silver goddess.

"Ciar!" said someone softly from behind her.

"What?" Ciar turned, then sucked in her breath; she had just given herself away.

Blackthorn stepped forward from the shadows, somber-faced. She was clad in a voluminous woolen cloak. She put me in mind of some old goddess of the wood, come to deliver judgment.

"What are you doing here?" Ciar's tone was shrill. I put my hand on her shoulder and she started, looking up at me. "Oran, what is this?"

"We know the truth about you," I said. "That you are Flidais in outward appearance only; that when you went swimming in Dreamer's Pool that day, you were somehow changed. Your response when Mistress Blackthorn called your name is proof in itself."

"What can you mean? That's nonsense! It's ridiculous!" Then, to Blackthorn, "I never trusted you! I knew you were up to something! I knew it the moment you and your big oaf came to live in the house! You've lied to me, haven't you? That story about the wood and what it could do for me, you made it all up just to get me here! But why? Why?"

Over on the path, Mhairi burst into tears. "Ciar, just tell them the truth! This has gone on too long. Please put a stop to it."

"You accuse me of lying, Ciar," said Blackthorn with commendable calm. "And yes, I did tell a story to bring you here tonight. But you have spun a mighty web of lies. It's time to start telling the truth, as Mhairi so wisely advises. Much of it we've guessed already. And I imagine that if you are not prepared to tell us the rest, your maidservant will do it for you."

"This is rubbish! What do you think this is, some fairy tale?" Ciar tried to wrench away from my hold, intending I knew not what—it would hardly do her any good to run. "Let go of me! It's not true!"

"Then tell us what is true," I said. "Perhaps Mistress Blackthorn has it wrong. If that is so, you should have no trouble agreeing to put it to the test."

"Put . . . what do you mean?"

"There's an old story about Dreamer's Pool," Blackthorn said. "I heard it from the traveling folk not long ago." She told the tale she'd shared with me when first telling me of her plan, a story about a pair of brothers and a prize boar. "So, you see, we know how to reverse the charm," she added at the end. "It should be easy."

"No! You can't do that!" Ciar was struggling now; I had

her by both arms, but fear can give a person strength, and I was hard put to hold her.

"Let me, my lord." Here was Grim, walking in from the other side, closing his great arms around Ciar. Perhaps realizing how futile it would be to fight against such a giant, she became still, save for her hard breathing.

"Tell us your story, Ciar." Blackthorn's tone was level, but the look on her face would have struck fear into anyone. "Do as Mhairi suggested; she, at least, has the wisdom to know this pretense can go on no longer. If the prince himself knows you are not Flidais, then how can you continue with it?" After a moment she added, "It must have been frightening for you, that day. It must have seemed impossible, unbelievable. And yet there you were."

"You can't prove anything," Ciar snapped. "Try telling that story and folk would only laugh at you. Look at me, I *am* Lady Flidais! Nobody would believe you!"

Donagan and Mhairi had moved in closer. All of us were on the sward, above the waters of Dreamer's Pool. If Ciar was strung tight, so was I. I could hardly believe we would go ahead with what Blackthorn had planned. It felt something akin to committing murder. Even as the longing to have my Flidais back filled my heart, the knowledge of what must come lay like a cold stone in my belly.

"We don't plan to tell the story," Blackthorn said calmly. "If we do as the man in the tale did, with his brother and the boar, there will be no need for anyone else to know."

"You can't make Ciar go into the pool again." Mhairi's voice was hushed with horror. "It's not like the man and the boar. Flidais is dead, drowned. There's no changing back."

I made to speak, but Blackthorn gave a little shake of her head.

"We have a plan," she said. "But we want Ciar's story first. Whatever happens, whatever we do, it should be based on truth. There's a powerful magic here. Only a fool mixes lies and magic. Ciar, tell us. What happened that day?"

Ciar stared at Blackthorn, her chest heaving, her eyes wild. She said not a word.

"Mhairi, why don't you tell us?" Blackthorn asked after a little pause.

"After the drowning," Mhairi said in a wisp of a voice, "she told me—"

"No!" Ciar's voice was like the crack of a whip. "I forbid you to speak! Have you forgotten what I said?"

A silence, then.

"No," said Mhairi, lifting her chin and straightening her shoulders. "But I'm not covering up for you any longer. After I'd helped you for so long, ever since you told me on that first night what had happened to you, when I said Mistress Blackthorn was sure to work out the truth soon, even if Prince Oran didn't, you said you'd send me straight back to Cloud Hill in disgrace if I didn't do what you wanted. You said you'd tell everyone I'd stolen your silver bracelet—the one Lady Flidais's mother gave her when she left home. You said you'd make sure nobody would ever give me a position again."

Another silence; a telling one.

"I was scared," said Ciar. She did not look at me, or at Mhairi, or at Blackthorn, but fixed her gaze on the middle distance, and I wondered if she was seeing that day unfold in all its shocking truth. "Scared by what happened to me. Scared to tell, because nobody would have believed me. I thought I could do it. I thought I could be Lady Flidais; I'd spent a whole year with her, listening as she prattled on, watching as she played with wretched Bramble or admired wildflowers or fussed over her letters and her books. What was I supposed to do that day, when I hardly knew myself what had happened? I came out of the water, and there was my own body lying on the shore, drowned. I thought I was dreaming. I thought I'd wake up any moment. But I didn't. What I did—it felt like the only choice."

"Black Crow save us," muttered Grim.

"So you took your mistress's place," Blackthorn said with a mildness I suspected was deceptive. "You lay with her sweetheart, only days after you arrived in his house." I felt myself flush with mortification; just as well the place lay half in shadow. "You would have married the prince; you would have become lady of a great house, and in time, queen of Dalriada."

"I could have done it," Ciar said, looking up. Now there

was a hint of defiance in her voice. "I may not be a chieftain's daughter, but anyone can run a household and bear children. And I know how to please a man in bed, most likely better than Flidais ever would have." She fixed me with her gaze. "Prince Oran can attest to that; he wasn't exactly reluctant."

"That's enough!" snapped Donagan. "You'll speak to the prince with due respect!"

"You!" retorted Ciar. "If you're so shocked, why did you turn a blind eye to it? You must have known."

"Enough," said Blackthorn. "I don't suppose anyone's behavior has been entirely beyond reproach; that's for each of you to come to terms with. Just now we are only concerned with you, Ciar. Why did you lie to me about Prince Oran and what he had done to you? Why did you accuse him of rape, or something close to it?"

Ciar scowled. "You were always there, asking questions, looking at everything, writing in your wretched little book. I was sure you'd find out, if you didn't already know. I guessed he—the prince—had asked you to snoop. I'd have had to be blind not to realize he'd started to suspect me. And poxy Bramble didn't help. That dog took against me from the moment I came out of the pool. I talked to Mhairi about the best way to put you off the scent. We'd heard you at the council, seen how angry you were about that girl, what was her name? And you'd spoken out in the sewing room about men having too much power over women and not being properly answerable for what they did. If you believed Prince Oran had abused me, then you wouldn't want to help him anymore. That was what we thought."

"I'm sorry, my lord." Mhairi was weeping again. "I didn't want to, but . . ."

"But she threatened you," Blackthorn said. "It can be hard to find the courage to stand up for what you know is right. You've done it now, at least. A bit late, maybe. But not too late."

"Too late for what?" asked Ciar. "I'm not going back in that water. If that was Flidais in my body, she's dead. There's nobody for me to change back into. You can't do this. It would be murder." The terror was back in her voice;

she looked from one of us to another, her face white in the moonlight. Grim shifted his grip.

"You know," said Blackthorn, "I don't believe it would be. If this concerned only yourself and Lady Flidais, maybe. But there weren't only two who went into Dreamer's Pool that day. There were three." She pushed back her concealing cloak and there, in her arms, was Bramble.

Ciar stared, not understanding. Mhairi was quicker. "You mean — are you saying Lady Flidais has been alive all this time? That she's in Bramble's body?"

"So I believe. And so Prince Oran believes. If we are right, a terrible injustice has been done, and there is only one way to fix it."

Ciar let fly a stream of curses. She was fighting against Grim's hold.

"It seems hard," said Blackthorn. "It is hard. But we cannot leave things as they are. Lady Flidais is the innocent in all this; she is entirely without blame. If I'm wrong, then both you, Ciar, and the dog will emerge from the pool unchanged, if a little cold, and it will be up to the prince to decide what comes next. If I'm right, then . . ."

"No!" shrieked Ciar. "No! That can't be Flidais, it's only a dog!"

"Then you have nothing to fear," said Blackthorn.

"You can't do this!"

"Just watch us," said Blackthorn, her voice like iron. She stepped toward the drop, and my heart quailed. The water was so cold, and Bramble was so small.

"Now, Grim," said Blackthorn.

He picked up the struggling Ciar as if she weighed no more than a babe, walked to the edge and, without a moment's hesitation, cast her bodily over. There was a splash, and my heart clenched in shock. This was real. We were actually doing it. I, the prince of Dalriada, was here in the woods in the dark, a willing party to what might be an act of murder.

"Oh gods, oh gods!" muttered Mhairi.

And now Bramble, so tiny, so delicate, so trusting. I wanted this with all my heart, and yet I could not bear to see Blackthorn cast her in.

"Don't — " I began.

Bramble wriggled, twisted, half fell from Blackthorn's

arms. Like a streak of moonlight, she bolted toward the drop, leaped off and was gone.

"Morrigan's curse!" murmured Donagan.

I strode toward the edge. Strong hands gripped my arms, holding me back—Donagan on one side, Grim on the other. I teetered on the brink, staring down as the cold light revealed only widening ripples on the dark water.

"Down to the shore," said Blackthorn. For the first time, her voice was less than perfectly steady. "Quickly."

We ran, tripping over tree roots and sliding on the carpet of damp leaves in the deceptive light. We ran all the way to the place where the waters of Dreamer's Pool lapped a flat stretch of shore, the spot where someone had lain dead on the fateful day when Flidais first came to Winterfalls. We stood there, Blackthorn and Grim, Donagan, Mhairi and I, staring out over the water, waiting. *Perhaps she cannot swim*, I thought. *Perhaps Bramble cannot swim.* But I did not say it. None of us spoke a word.

Time passed. Too much time. Donagan moved to the water's edge and started to take off his boots.

"No," I said. "If anyone's going in, it should be me."

"Wait," said Blackthorn. "All of you wait."

Out in the dark water, something stirred. Ripples spread out, catching the moonlight. She rose, spluttering and gasping, her dark hair like a mermaid's over her shoulders, her eyes huge and shocked in her deathly white face. She struggled a moment, hampered by her long gown, then struck out toward the shore. There was no knowing, yet, which woman had emerged from the pool.

Another disturbance, another head coming up, this time Bramble's. She swam as a dog swims, untidily, following her mistress in. Without any awareness of having moved, I was at the water's edge. The woman waded to the shallows, shuddering with cold. Her gown clung to her, revealing plainly the lovely form beneath. The body I had enjoyed for two long nights in that time of utter madness. I felt my face grow hot.

The woman halted in knee-deep water, staring at me. She moved her hands to cover herself, one across her breasts, the other lower down. It was Flidais. Without a doubt, it was my lady.

"Prince Oran." Blackthorn put something in my hands.

A cloak. Flidais's fur-lined cloak. As my beloved stepped up toward me, I reached to put it around her shoulders.

"Oran," said Flidais through chattering teeth, and it was the loveliest sound I had ever heard. "My love, my dear, I'm sorry. I'm so, so sorry you have had to go through this." She reached up a hand to brush my cheek. "Don't weep, beloved." She was crying too; tears flooded down her perfect face. "It's all my fault," she said. "If I had not taken it into my head to swim that day . . ."

"Morrigan's britches!" murmured Grim. "Who'd have thought it?"

Bramble was crouched on the shore, wet through and shivering. Donagan attempted to pick her up, then cursed as she sank her teeth into his hand.

"I'll take her," Blackthorn said. "She knows better than to bite me. Now, it's freezing cold, and Lady Flidais needs to get warm straightaway. You'd best come to our cottage, sit by the fire awhile and have some food and drink before you go back to Winterfalls." She glanced at Mhairi. "You'll all have some matters to consider."

"Thank you, Mistress Blackthorn." Wrapped in the cloak, sheltered by my arm, Flidais sounded steadier now. "We owe you far more than we can ever repay. You've taken a great risk in order to right this wrong. And yes, it is indeed cold; a sojourn by your hearth fire would be most welcome." She gazed up at the moon. "We have been fortunate, I believe. Fortunate that whatever spirit dwells here has looked on us with kindness tonight. We should be mindful of that."

"We will return here, my love," I said. "Say prayers. Make offerings."

"But not tonight," said Blackthorn, "or Lady Flidais risks perishing from cold, not to speak of this dog. The spirit won't require that, I'm quite sure of it. Let's go and find that warm fire, and perhaps a jug of mulled ale." She bent to gather up Bramble. "Try to bite me," she said, "and I'll set a curse on you. Fancy life as a slug or a beetle? I thought not. Grim, lead the way."

40

GRIM

They talk and talk. I make a brew and another brew, and keep the fire burning high. Blackthorn takes Lady Flidais to the lean-to to remove her wet clothes, and the lady sits by the hearth with my blanket wrapped around her, over the prince's cloak. Her and Prince Oran, they've only got eyes for each other, though they thank us, and they thank Donagan, and they listen while Mhairi fills in some parts of the story that haven't come out yet. For instance, how Ciar had thought that if she was with child, the prince would still wed her even if he found out the truth. How she'd slipped into his bed a couple of times, trying to make this happen, until Lady Sochla came and she'd had to stop.

When Mhairi says this, the prince is ashamed. Scarlet in the face, can't look at Flidais. But she says, quite sweetly, "I know, Oran. I saw and heard a great deal during that time; I understood it in ways a dog could not."

Because yes, she's been Bramble, or Bramble's been her, all this time. Three-way switch, like Blackthorn thought. The one who drowned that day wasn't Ciar and it wasn't Flidais. It was the dog. Lady Flidais, the real one, is sad about this, says she loved Bramble dearly, and if she hadn't taken it into her head to go swimming that day, Bramble would still be here. Prince Oran tells her he knows Bramble can never be replaced. But when she's ready he would love to help her choose another little dog. Maybe a pair of them.

Bit shy with each other, those two. Must be odd for them. He's lain with Ciar, only she was in Flidais's body. And the dog, that is, Flidais, has heard Ciar bragging about it to Mhairi. But the lady, the way she is now, hasn't lain with any man. She's the highborn, untouched bride of a future king. Could be awkward, you'd think. But a blind man could see they're fond of each other. And though Lady Flidais is a quiet, courteous sort of girl, she's not afraid to speak up for herself, that's plain. Could be the two of them will do all right.

I make another brew, and we eat what food there is at the cottage, which isn't much. Donagan's brought some honey cakes and cheese in his saddlebag, as well as the mead, so we finish those off as well, though Flidais and the prince don't eat much. Too busy gazing into each other's eyes and whispering in each other's ears.

They're supposed to be off to court in the morning, the prince, his lady and a bunch of other folk, and it's getting late. Prince Oran asks Flidais if they should leave it a few days, put off the hand-fasting till she's recovered, and she says no, best if everything goes to plan. That way nobody else needs to know what's happened, ever. And they won't be starting their marriage with all sorts of weird tales being whispered. As for Mhairi, Flidais tells her she'll need time to work out what's best, but she's pleased Mhairi told the truth at the end, and for now she can stay provided she keeps her mouth shut and makes herself useful. The first way she makes herself useful is taking off her gown and tunic so Flidais can wear them on the ride back. Mhairi gets an old shirt of mine to put on over her shift, with a cloak on top. Blackthorn bundles up the lady's wet things for Donagan to carry.

We stand at the door and watch them go. Moon's high now, lights the path home for them. Donagan's a good man. He'll make sure they get there safe.

Blackthorn and me, we'll stay here at the cottage now. Go over in the morning and pick up our bits and pieces from the prince's place, borrow some supplies from Brid, maybe wave farewell if they're not already gone. But no going back to stay there. Didn't need to say so, either of us. Just knew.

The place is toasty warm. I bank up the fire, find a couple more blankets. Glad we got the repairs done. I sit on my pallet, reach down to take off my boots. Something growls and snaps, nearly taking my hand off. "Dagda's bollocks!"

It's the dog, Bramble. Or not Bramble, because this is Ciar. Maybe it's fair, though it seems cruel. She kept quiet about the spell on Flidais, and now the same thing's happened to her. Seems she doesn't think much of being a dog, and plans to let everyone know it.

"Thought they'd taken her with them," I say, lifting up my feet so I can get the boots off and keep my fingers. "Walk her over there in the morning, mm?"

The dog bolts out from under my bed, skitters across the room. Dives under Blackthorn's bed, right to the back. Two eyes in the shadows. She whines.

"She'll be staying here," Blackthorn says, offhand. "Lady Flidais may be a softhearted girl, but it's too much to expect her to hold on to the creature. And Oran wouldn't want it—I'm quite sure of that."

"Just put her out the door and forget about her." Told a lot of lies, Ciar did. Made a lot of folk unhappy. "Can't understand why you'd want to keep her."

"I have to." Blackthorn lies down on her bed, shuts her eyes, pulls her blanket over her. "Hear that whining? If that isn't a cry for help, I don't know what it is."

Morrigan's britches! Blackthorn's going soft about a vicious, noisy little monster like that? And here I was, thinking how peaceful it's going to be here, all neat and tidy, everything where it should be, and me and her settling in as if it's a real home. I was feeling good. Almost happy. "You have to? Why?"

"You know," Blackthorn says, sounding half-asleep. Been a long day. A big, big day. "Conmael. My promise."

"Didn't think that fellow made you promise to give a home to stray dogs, even ones that used to be human." Use her gifts only for good and stay away from Mathuin for seven years, those were the two parts of it. Nothing about dogs.

"Not dogs in particular. Cries for help. Remember, I

have to say yes to folk who ask me to help them. Even if they don't say it in so many words. Even if they're folk like Ciar. It gets complicated sometimes. Difficult. But I've kept to it. And I'll keep to it even now Ciar's a dog. I can train her not to bite you."

I think about this a bit, then I wish I hadn't. I wish I'd never asked about the dog, because a shadow's come down over me, and my head's full of folk calling me Bonehead, and folk making fun of me, and Strangler dying just after I got him out, and Dribbles and Poxy lying butchered by the road. And before that, the dark thing, the terrible thing, and a load that'll be on my shoulders till I die. Thought I could put it behind me. Thought I could start again. That night, when she called me up to her campfire, when she said I could come with her, I thought it was because she wanted me. I thought she needed me around, even if it wasn't forever. That made me feel like flowers and sunshine and fresh bread. Like a starving cur expecting another kick, and getting a juicy bone and kind words. What she's just told me turns that upside down. She only took me on because of poxy Conmael and his wretched promise. She never wanted me. She never needed me. Fool. Bonehead. Soon as you think you've found something good, someone comes and takes it away.

Blackthorn's breathing quiet, like she's asleep. Shadows creep close, pressing into me. Can't stay. Not now. I get up, go out quiet-like, shutting the back door behind me. Path's been laid new, flat stones in a pattern. I pick up a few big ones and put them in my pockets. Shouldn't take many. Never did learn to swim.

41

BLACKTHORN

What a gift: a night's sleep in my own bed, in my own house. I felt as weary as if I'd spent the whole day haymaking or fighting a battle or hauling in fishing nets. The hardest part of it, the part nobody knew about, had been casting the spell to delay the rain. It was years since I'd gone down such a path; longer than I could remember since I had used the more arcane skills of a wise woman. I had done my best with the spell, and it had exhausted me. Whether the rain had held off because of me, or whether it would have been dry enough for Ciar to be coaxed up that path anyway, there was no way of knowing. Unless I asked Conmael, and he probably wouldn't tell me even if I did.

It was raining now, steadily, which did make me wonder. The rain fell on the thatch that Grim had restored so lovingly, and on the stone pathways he'd laid in place, making special patterns of his own devising, and into the water barrel he'd set up outside the back door. It fell on the little straw creatures he'd fashioned to guard the roof, and on the garden with its new planting of winter vegetables. And it fell over Dreamer's Wood, where tonight the strangest of scenes had played itself out. I listened to the rain, and to the snuffling sounds from the little dog under my bed, and felt myself drifting into a deep and peaceful sleep.

The dog barked, jolting me sharply awake. I cursed. If the wretched creature planned to keep that up, I'd be tempted to do as Grim had suggested and put her outside to fend for herself. "Mongrel!" I muttered, glancing across in the hope that Grim had slept through the noise.

He wasn't there. His blanket was in a tangle, his boots were on the floor, his cloak still hung on its peg. Gone to the privy, no doubt. Without that cloak, he'd get soaking wet. Fool.

I lay on my back, staring up at the rafters. Thinking over the day, wondering how the prince and his lady would cope with life at court, wondering how they would do as king and queen of Dalriada when the time came. From what I'd seen of her, Flidais matched perfectly the woman Oran had fallen in love with after reading her letters: sweet, courteous, scholarly, a little shy. But he was going to find that she was far more than that. That leap down into the dark water of Dreamer's Pool had been an act of true courage. And her measured treatment of Mhairi, after all that had befallen her, had been the response of a leader. They would, I suspected, do very well indeed. I found myself almost looking forward to watching them grow and learn together.

As for Ciar, the price she had paid for her actions had indeed been high; perhaps too high. That day in Dreamer's Wood she'd been scared—anyone would have been scared—and she'd made a quick decision. That decision had become, in time, simply too much for her to handle. An error. Reprehensible. But not a crime.

But I did not see, truly, what else we could have done. To deny Flidais the chance of a future would have been wrong. But to condemn Ciar to life as a dog, a short life most likely, when that first transformation had been beyond her control . . . it was hard. I had complied with Conmael's requirements. Oran had asked me for help, and I had helped him. I wished I could be sure that what I had done was right.

Where had Grim got to? He'd been gone far too long. I sat up, fully awake now and possessed by a creeping sense of wrongness. Just a sore belly, a touch of the gripes that was keeping him in the privy? But the boots. The cloak . . .

I got up, flinging my own cloak over the clothes I'd lain down in, and went to the back door. Stuck my head out into the rain and called out, "Grim? Are you all right?"

Nothing. Even through the steady fall, he should have heard me.

"Grim!"

Not a sound. What now? Go out looking and get soaked? Or stay indoors and build up the fire so he could dry out when he came back? Where could he have gone?

The dog was at my heels. She gave another sharp bark. A warning.

"What?"

She could not tell me, of course. But something was wrong. I knew it. I felt it in my bones. "Grim," I muttered, "why would you do this, you foolish man? What would draw you out into the dark on a day when everything's gone so well?"

And then, with a sensation like a plunge into icy water, I realized what it was. Remembered what I had said to him before I settled for sleep, about the dog and my vow to Conmael. Remembered that I had told Grim, long ago, about promising to use my gift for good, and promising to keep away from Mathuin of Laois, but not about promising to help anyone who asked me to. I'd been too ashamed to have anyone know I did not help folk out of the goodness of my heart, but only because I was bound to it. The first person I'd helped, after making that vow, had been Grim. Grim, a dark hulking shadow in those woods north of Laois; Grim, wet, cold, alone; Grim, not prepared to come to my campfire that night in case I ordered him to go away and leave me be.

Cursing, I went back for my boots, thrust my feet in, made for the door again. "Stay here!" I ordered, but did not wait to see if the dog obeyed. I ran. Into the woods, along the path, onto the branching way that led to the patch of greensward where Ciar had expected to lie with the prince and make a child. I did not shout his name. I did not shout *stop*, *wait*, or anything else. I simply ran, heart drumming, chest heaving, feet stumbling over stones and roots, for the moon was quenched by clouds now and the wood was in near darkness. Behind me, a faint light shone from the cottage, where I had left the back door open. In there our hearth fire still burned, lighting the way home.

Up, up the hill. Where was the spot? It was so dark I risked toppling over the edge to plunge into the water as

Ciar had. I might end this remarkable day as a fish or a frog or anything at all. *Grim, you fool, why would you do such a thing?*

The rain abated. For a moment, the veil of cloud parted and moonlight shone down, showing me the narrow entry, the patch of soft grass, and at the far end, standing on the very edge of the drop, the dark, still bulk of a man.

I froze, not daring to speak. Startle him and he'd go right over. Say the wrong thing and he'd jump. He'd commit himself to that pool, knowing what it could do.

There was a right way to go about these things. Speak quietly and calmly. Don't approach, keep at a slight distance, go on talking. I knew how to do it; I'd done it before, more than once. But all of a sudden my eyes were streaming and my nose was running and the words came out broken and unsteady and out of control. "Grim! Don't! Please!"

His whole body tightened. He was going to jump.

"Grim, you wretched man! Do as I bid you right now or I'll turn you into a fat rabbit and eat you for supper, I swear!"

He took a step back from the edge. Turned toward me. Muttered something.

"What was that?" My heart was thumping fit to leap out of my chest. "What did you say?"

"No good to you. Never was. Only took me on because you had no other choice. True, isn't it? Let me tag after you because if you hadn't, it would have been another year on Conmael's bargain."

I was right. This *was* all about Conmael's accursed bargain.

"True, isn't it? Don't lie to me. Don't honey-coat the truth."

"You're saying that to *me*? Have I ever lied to you, Grim? Have I? You're the one person I can't lie to. You're the one person who knows me too well to be taken in by it. Why do you imagine I asked you to come with me to confront Branoc that day, instead of waiting to go there with men-at-arms? Why do you think Conmael sent you after me when I was running away, instead of following me himself? Why do you think I needed you to stay at Winterfalls with me to solve the puzzle of Lady Flidais?"

"Don't know," said Grim. "Never did know, really. Just happy there was something for me to do. Somewhere for me to go. Somewhere near you. Thought you knew that, Lady."

"A pox on this. I'm wet, I'm cold, I've had enough of this wretched wood for one night. Will you come back with me? Please?" I held out a hand toward him. He stood there looking at me, like a big shambling bear that had lost its way. "I don't beg," I said. "I do have my limits."

"Thing is," Grim said, sounding more like himself, "you don't need me. You don't need anyone. Told me that early on. You like living on your own. Hoped if I made myself useful you might change your ways. Foolish. Wise woman and all, of course you don't want a lump like me around. Didn't take the hint. That's why they call me Bonehead."

"Bollocks. Stop being sorry for yourself. You know quite well you're capable at so many jobs everyone in Winterfalls wants to hire you. You can't be blind to the way folk warm to you. They trust you. They trust you to do a good job, an honest job. Nobody around here's calling you Bonehead or anything else of that nature."

"A man did, in the prince's house. I bashed his head on a table and nearly killed him. Get a red rage sometimes. Makes me do bad things. If you knew—"

"Enough! I've got enough ill deeds in my own past to fill a book. And now's not the time or the place for you to tell me about yours." I struggled for the right words. "Listen, Grim. Yes, it's true that when we met up, after Mathuin's lockup, I let you come with me because of my promise to Conmael. You didn't ask me for help any more than that dog did tonight. But cries for help don't always come in words. I knew what I had to do, and I did it."

He stood silent. His stance screamed, *I knew it. I knew you didn't want me.*

"But it's different now. I can't believe you thought otherwise. We're friends. We work together. We understand each other. We put up with each other. We know when to stay around and when to leave each other alone. We're a team, Grim. I'd never have worked out the truth about Branoc and Ness without you. And what about tonight? Have you forgotten I was going to turn my back on Prince

Oran and Lady Flidais and the whole mess, until you came out to Silverlake and stopped me? Without the evidence you gathered, I'd never have seen how wrong I was. Without the hard talking you were brave enough to give me, I'd never have understood how Mathuin was skewing my thinking." I drew a deep breath. "The fact is, I can't do without you. We're friends." It came to me, through a blur of tears, that we'd been friends since the wretched, lice-ridden days in Mathuin's lockup. Only, back then, I'd been too eaten up with bitterness to see it. In that place, we'd kept each other alive.

"Can we go home now?" I asked.

He took a step toward me. An awkward, stumbling step; he must be cramped with cold. I took one toward him and slipped my arm through his. "Home," I said. "Come on, you foolish big man."

We made our way back to the path, and down the hill beside the still waters of Dreamer's Pool, on which the moon now shone again, making a silver mirror. A white owl passed over in whispering flight, and a small creature cried out, deeper in the wood. Was that a cloaked figure I could see, shadowy under the birches? A pair of fey eyes under a dark hood, watchful as we passed?

By the back door, the little dog sat where I had left her, waiting for us. We went in. I hung up my dripping cloak; Grim stripped off his wet clothing in the lean-to and emerged clad in a blanket, conjuring a sharp memory.

I stirred up the fire. "Brew?"

"You sit down awhile. I'll make it."

"Let go that blanket to fetch herbs, and you'll show me a sight I really don't want to see right now. What I want's a friend, not a . . . you know."

"Take a lot to shock you," said Grim, managing a smile. "You fetch the herbs, I'll boil the water. Team, aren't we?"

Read on for an exciting excerpt from the next
Blackthorn & Grim Novel by Juliet Marillier,

TOWER OF THORNS

Available now from Roc

GEILÉIS

Rain had swollen the river to a churning mass of gray. The tower wore a soft shroud of mist; though it was past dawn, no cries broke the silence. Perhaps he slept, curled tight on himself, dreaming of a time when he was whole and hale and handsome. Perhaps he knew even in his sleep that she still kept watch, her shawl clutched around her against the cold, her gaze fixed on his shuttered window.

But he might have forgotten who she was, who he was, what had befallen them. It had been a long time ago. So long that she had no more tears to shed. So long that one summer blurred into another as the years passed in an endless wait for the next chance, and the next, to put it right. She did not know if he could see her. There were the trees, and the water, and on mornings like this, the mist lying thick between them. Only the top of the tower was visible, with its shuttered window.

Another day. The sun was fighting to break through; here and there the clouds of vapor showed a sickly yellow tinge. Gods, she loathed this place! And yet she loved it. How could she not? How could she want to be anywhere but here?

Downstairs, her household was stirring now. Someone was clanking pots, raking out the hearth, starting to make breakfast. A part of her considered that a warm meal on a chilly morning would be welcome—her people sought to please her. To make her, if not happy, then at least moderately content. It was no fault of theirs that she could not enjoy such simple pleasures as a full belly, the sun on her face, or a good night's sleep. Her body was strung tight with waiting. Her heart was a constant aching hurt in her chest. What if there was no ending this? What if it went on and on forever?

"Lady Geiléis?"

Senach tapped on the door, then entered. Her steward was a good servant, discreet and loyal. "Breakfast is ready, my lady," he said. "I would not have disturbed you, but the fellow we sent to the Dalriadan court has returned, and he has some news."

She left her solitary watch, following her man out of the chamber. As Senach closed the door behind them, the monster in the tower awoke and began to scream.

"Going away," she said. "For how long?"

"King Ruairi will be attending the High King's midsummer council, my lady." Her messenger was gray-faced with exhaustion; had he traveled all night? His mead cup shook in his hands. "The queen will go south with him. They will be gone for at least two turnings of the moon, and maybe closer to three."

"Who will accompany them? Councilors? Advisers? Friends and relations?"

"All the king's senior councilors. Queen Eabha's attendants. A substantial body of men-at-arms. But Cahercorcan is a grand establishment; the place will still be full of folk."

"This son of King Ruairi's," she said. "The one you say will be looking after his father's affairs while they're gone—what manner of man is he? Of what age? Has he a wife?"

"Prince Oran is young, my lady. Three-and-twenty and newly married. There's a child on the way. The prince does not live at Cahercorcan usually, as he has his own holding farther south. He is more a man of scholarship than a man of action."

"Respected by his father's advisers, those of them who

remained behind?" A scholar. That might be helpful. "Is he a clever man?"

"I could not say, my lady. He's well enough respected. They say he's a little unusual."

"Unusual?"

"They say he likes to involve all his folk in the running of household and farm. And I mean all, from the lowliest groom to the most distinguished of nobles. Consults the community, lets everyone have a say. There's some at court think that odd; they'd sooner he just told folk what to do, as his father would."

"I see." Barely two turnings of the moon remained until midsummer. After the long, wearying search, the hopes dashed, the possibilities all come to nothing, she had been almost desperate enough to head south and throw herself at King Ruairi's feet, foolish as that would have been. Common sense had made her send the messenger first, with orders to bring back a report on the situation at court. She had not expected anything to come of it; most certainly not this. Her heart beat faster; her mind raced ahead. The king gone, along with his senior advisers. The queen absent too. The prince in charge, a young man who would know nothing of her story . . . Could this be a real opportunity at last? Dared she believe it? Perhaps Prince Oran really was the key. Perhaps he could find her the kind of woman she had so long sought without success.

She'd have to ride for Cahercorcan soon—but not too soon, or she risked arriving before the king and his entourage had departed. It was the prince she needed to speak to, not his father. How might she best present her case? Perhaps this scholarly prince loved tales of magic and mystery. She must tell it in a way that would capture his imagination. And his sympathy.

She rose to her feet. "Thank you," she said to the messenger. "Go to the kitchen; Dau will give you some breakfast. Then sleep. I'll send for you later if I have further questions." Though likely he had told all he knew. She'd sent him to the royal household in the guise of a traveler passing through and seeking a few nights' shelter. There'd be limits to what a lad like him could learn in such a place. "Senach," she said after the messenger was gone, "it seems that this time we have a real opportunity." At last. Oh, at last! She had hardly dared to dream this might be possible. "You understand what this means?"

"Yes, my lady. You'll be wanting to travel south."

"I will, and soon. Speak to Onchú about an escort, will you? In my absence, you will be in charge of the household."

"Of course, my lady." A pause, then Senach added, "When do you plan to depart?"

"Not for a few days." Every instinct pulled her to leave now, straightaway, without delay; any wait would be hard to bear. But they must be sure the royal party had left court. "Let's say seven days. That should be long enough."

"When might I expect you to return, my lady?"

Her lips made the shape of a smile, but there was no joy in her. She had forgotten how it felt to be happy. "Before midsummer. That goes without saying. Prepare the guest quarters, Senach. We must hold on to hope." Hope, she thought, was as easily extinguished as a guttering candle on a day of spring storm. Over and over she had seen it tremble and die. Yet even now she was making plans again, looking ahead, seeing the way things might unfold. Her capacity to endure astonished her.

"Leave it to me, my lady. All will be ready for you."

Later still, as her household busied itself with the arrangements—horses, supplies, weaponry—she climbed back up to the high chamber and looked out once more on the Tower of Thorns. All day its tenant had shouted, wailed, howled like an abandoned dog. Now his voice had dwindled to a hoarse, gasping sob, as if he had little breath left to draw.

"This time I'll make it happen," she murmured. "I swear. By every god there ever was, by the stars in the sky and the waves on the shore, by memory and loss and heartbreak, I swear."

The sun was low; it touched the tower with a soft, rosy light that made a mockery of his pain. It would soon be dusk. There was just enough time.

With her gaze on that distant window, she began the nightly ritual. "Let me tell you a story."

BLACKTHORN

I sat on the cottage steps, shelling peas and watching as Grim forked fresh straw onto the vegetable patch. Here at the edge of Dreamer's Wood, dappled shade lay over us; the air held a warm promise of the summer to come. In the near distance green fields spread out, dotted with grazing sheep, and beyond them I glimpsed the long wall that guarded Prince Oran's holdings at Winterfalls. A perfect day. The kind of day that made a person feel almost . . . settled. Which was not good. If there was anything I couldn't afford, it was to get content.

"Lovely morning," observed Grim, pausing to wipe the sweat off his brow and to survey his work.

"Mm."

He narrowed his eyes at me. "Something wrong?"

A pox on the man; he knew me far too well. "What would be wrong?"

"You tell me."

"Seven years of this and I'll have lost whatever edge I once had," I said. "I'll have turned into one of those well-fed countrywomen who pride themselves on making better preserves than their neighbors, and give all their chickens names."

"Can't see that," said Grim, casting a glance at the little

dog as she hunted for something in the pile of straw. The dog's name was Bramble, but we didn't call her that anymore, only Dog. There were reasons for that, complicated ones that only a handful of people knew. She was living a life-long penance, that creature. I had my own penance. My fey benefactor, Conmael, had bound me to obey his rules for seven years. I was compelled to say yes to every request for help, to use my craft only for good, and to stay within the borders of Dalriada. In particular, Conmael had made me promise I would not go back to Laois to seek vengeance against my old enemy. I'd known from the first how hard those requirements would be to live by. But my burden was nothing against that borne by Ciar, who had once been maidservant to a lady. For her misdeeds, she had been turned into a dog. Magic being what it was—devious and tricky—she had no way back.

"Anyway," Grim went on, "it's closer to six years now."

"Why doesn't that make me feel any better? It doesn't seem to matter how busy I am, how worn out I am after a day of applying salves and dispensing drafts and giving advice to every fool who thinks he wants it. Every night I dream about the same thing: what Mathuin of Laois did to me, and what I'll do to him. And the fact that Conmael's stupid rules are stopping me from getting on with it."

"I dream about that place," Grim said. "The stink. The dark. The screams. I dream about nearly losing hope. And when I wake up, I look around and . . ." He shrugged. "The last thing I'd be wanting is to go back. Different for you, I know."

I wanted to challenge him; to ask if there weren't folk who'd wronged him, folk he might care to teach a lesson to. Or folk who'd once loved him, who might still be missing him and needing him to come home. But I held my tongue. We didn't ask each other about the past, the time before we'd found ourselves in Mathuin's lockup, staring at each other across the walkway between the iron bars. A whole year we'd kept each other going, a year of utter hell, and we'd never shared our stories. Grim knew some of mine now, since I'd blurted it out on the day fire destroyed our cottage. How Mathuin of Laois had punished my man for his part in a plot against injustice. How he'd burned Cass

and our baby alive, how he'd ordered his guards to hold me
back so I couldn't reach them. Grim knew the dark thing I
carried within me, the furious need to see justice done. And
Conmael knew. Conmael knew far more than anyone rightly
should.

"Pea soup?" Grim's voice broke into my thoughts.

"What? Oh. Seems a shame to cook them—they taste
much better raw. But yes, soup would stretch them out a
bit. I'll make it."

"Onion, chopped small," he suggested. "Garlic. Maybe a
touch of mint."

"Trying to distract me from unwise thoughts?" I turned
my gaze on him, but he was busy with his gardening again.

"Nah," said Grim. "Just hungry. Looks like we might
have company in a bit."

A rider was approaching from the direction of Winterfalls. From this distance I couldn't tell who it was, but the
green clothing suggested Prince Oran's household.

"Donagan," said Grim.

The prince's body servant; a man with whom we shared
a secret or two. "How can you tell?"

"The horse. The white marking on her head. Only one
like that in these parts. Star, she's called."

"You think the prince's man will be happy to eat my pea
soup?"

"Why not? I always am. Need to start cooking soon,
though, or he won't get the chance." Grim laid aside his
pitchfork and straightened up, a big bear of a man. "I'll do
it if you want."

"You're busy. I'll do it." Since I didn't plan on standing
out the front like a welcoming party, I headed back into the
house. Donagan was all right as courtiers went, but a visit
from a member of the prince's household generally meant
some sort of request for help, and that meant saying yes to
whatever it was, however inconvenient, because of my
promise to Conmael. The most reasonable of requests felt
burdensome if a person had no choice in the matter. If I
were to survive seven years, I'd need to work on keeping
my temper; staying civil. I only had four chances. Break
Conmael's rules a fifth time, and he'd put me straight back
into Mathuin's lockup as if I'd never left the place. That was

what he'd threatened, anyway. Maybe he couldn't do it, but I had no intention of putting that to the test.

Grim stayed outside and so did Donagan, whose arrival I saw between the open shutters. Once he'd tethered his horse, he leaned on the wall chatting as Grim finished his work with the pitchfork. That gave me breathing time, which I used not only to prepare the meal, but to put my thoughts in order. Step by small step; that was the only way I'd survive my time of penance. My lesson in patience. Or whatever it was.

Donagan had brought a gift of oaten bread. It went well with the soup. Dog sat under the table, feasting on crusts. Our guest waited until we had all finished eating before he came to the purpose of his visit. "Mistress Blackthorn, Lady Flidais has asked to see you, at your convenience."

Nothing surprising about that, since Lady Flidais, wife to the prince, had been under my care since she'd first discovered she was expecting a child. The infant would not be born before autumn, and thus far the lady had remained in robust health. It was typical of her, if not of Donagan, that this had been presented as a request rather than as an order.

"I can come by this afternoon, if that suits Lady Flidais," I told him. "I have one or two folk to visit in the settlement." This had to be more than it seemed, or they'd have sent an ordinary messenger, not the prince's right-hand man. "Is Lady Flidais unwell?"

"The lady is quite well. She has a request to make of you."

There was a silence; no doubt Donagan felt the weight of our scrutiny.

"Can you tell us what it is?" I asked. "Or must this wait until I see her?"

"I've been given leave to tell you. King Ruairi and Queen Eabha will be traveling south soon for the High King's council; they and their party will be away from Dalriada until well after midsummer. The king requires Prince Oran to be at court for that period, acting in his place."

My thoughts jumped ahead to an uncomfortable conclusion. Lady Flidais and the prince both loved the peaceful familiarity of Winterfalls. I was quite certain they'd rather stay here than go to the king's court at Cahercorcan, some twenty miles north. But although Oran was not your usual kind of nobleman, he wouldn't refuse a request from his father, the king of Dalriada. And where Oran went, Flidais would be wanting to go too. The two of them were inseparable, like lovers in a grand old story. If they needed to be at court for two turnings of the moon or more, that meant . . . My guts protested, clenching themselves into a tight ball.

Grim said what I could not bring myself to say. "The lady, she'll be wanting Blackthorn at court with her. That what you're telling us?"

"Lady Flidais will explain," Donagan said. "But yes, that is what she would prefer. Lady Flidais does not place a great deal of trust in the court physicians." He fell silent, gazing into his empty soup bowl. Grim and I stayed quiet too. There was a long, long list of reasons why the prospect of going to court disturbed us; not all of them were reasons we could share with Donagan or indeed with Lady Flidais.

"Inconvenient, I know," the king's man said eventually, still not meeting my eye or Grim's. "Your young helper would need to act as healer here in your absence. And . . . well, I understand this wouldn't be much to your liking." Now he glanced across at Grim. "Lady Flidais's invitation extends to both of you. Since it's for some time, there would be private quarters provided."

"Invitation," echoed Grim. "But not the sort of invitation a person says no to, coming from a prince and all."

Donagan gave Grim a crooked smile. I had come to understand that he had a soft spot for my companion, though what exactly had passed between them during that odd time when Grim and I had stayed in the prince's household I was not quite sure. I knew Grim had been in a fight and had hurt another man quite badly. I knew Donagan had helped get Grim out of trouble. So it was possible that Donagan realized how hard it was for Grim to sleep without me to keep him company—not the sort of company a man and a woman keep when they're wed, more the company of a watchful friend, the same as we'd had when we were in that wretched place together, before I'd understood what friends were.

"True enough," Donagan went on. "Still, I imagine you will say yes, not because you feel obliged to, but because Lady Flidais trusts you. And because you have her welfare at heart, as we all do."

It was a pretty speech. No need to tell him that if I said yes, it wouldn't be for that heartwarming reason, but because I was bound to it by Conmael. Court. Closed in by stone walls, surrounded by high-bred folk quick to judge those they deemed their inferiors. I imagined myself embroiled in petty disputes with the royal physicians, who could only resent Lady Flidais's preference for a local wise woman over their expert and scholarly selves. Court, where every single activity would be subject to some sort of ridiculous protocol. Morrigan's curse! I'd found it hard enough staying in the prince's much smaller establishment. Grim would loathe it. And what about Conmael and our agreement? He'd ordered me to live at Winterfalls, not at Cahercorcan. So complying with one condition of my promise would mean breaking another. A pox on it!

I rose to my feet. "Thank you for bringing the message. I have some herbs to gather before I head over to the settlement, but please tell Lady Flidais she can expect me around midafternoon." I thought I did an excellent job of sounding calm and unruffled, but the look Grim gave me suggested otherwise.

"How soon?" he asked Donagan. "When's the king leaving?"

"At next full moon. It's a long journey to Tara, made more challenging by the fact that Mathuin of Laois is stirring up trouble in that region. And the king will want Prince Oran settled at court before he leaves."

"Doesn't give us long," Grim said. His hands had bunched themselves into fists.

"You'll be offered all the assistance you need for the move. Horses, help with packing up, arrangements put in place so young Emer can continue to provide a healer's services to the community."

"Emer's been under my guidance for less than a year," I protested. "She may be quite apt, but she can't be asked to step into my place. It's too much to expect."

Donagan smiled. "I'm sure a solution will be found. Lady Flidais will discuss that with you. Now, I can see you are both busy, so I will make my departure."

When he was gone, we sat staring at each other over the table, stunned into silence. After a while Grim got up and started gathering the bowls.

"Court, mm?" he said.

"Seems so. But what if Conmael says no?"

"Why would he?"

"The promise. Go to Winterfalls. Quite specific."

"Then you tell Lady Flidais the truth," Grim said.

"What, that the wise woman she trusts with her unborn child is actually a felon escaped from custody? That the only reason I help folk is because I have no choice in the matter? That the person I answer to is not even human?"

Grim fetched a bucket, took a cloth, wiped down the table. He spooned the leftover soup into a bowl for Dog. "Thing is," he said, "she knows you now. She's seen what kind of person you are. She's seen what you can do. That's why she trusts you; that's why the prince trusts you. And you did get them out of a tight corner."

"You mean *we* did."

"Something else too," said Grim. "Escaped felons. We may be that, and if we went south we might find ourselves thrown back in that place or worse. But Lady Flidais is hardly going to take Mathuin's side. He's her father's enemy."

The thought of telling Flidais the truth—of telling anyone—made me feel sick. "Trust me," I said, "that is a really bad idea. What lies in the past should stay there. I shouldn't need to tell you that. Let word get out about who we are and where we came from, and that word can make its way back to Mathuin."

"Mm-hm." He poured water from the kettle into the bucket and started to wash the dishes. After a while he said, "Why don't you ask him, then? Conmael?"

"What, you think he's going to appear if I go out there

and click my fingers? I need to know now, Grim. Before I go and see Flidais."

"Mm-hm." He looked at me, the cloth in one hand and a dripping platter in the other. "What were the words of it the promise you made to the fellow? Was it *live at Winterfalls*, or was it only *live in Dalriada*?"

I thought about it: the night when I'd been waiting to die, the terrible trembling that had racked my body, the way time had passed so slowly, moment by painful moment, Grim's presence in the cell opposite the only thing that had stopped me from trying to kill myself. Then the strange visitor, a fey man whom I'd never clapped eyes on before, and the offer that had saved my life.

"I'm not sure I remember his exact words. One part of the promise was that I must travel north to Dalriada and not return to Laois. That I mustn't seek out Mathuin or pursue vengeance. Then he said, *You'll live at Winterfalls*. Or, *You must live at Winterfalls*. He told me that the prince lived here, and that the local folk had no healer. And that we could live in this house; he was specific about the details."

"Maybe you don't need to ask him," said Grim. "Isn't part of the promise about doing good? Looking after Lady Flidais, that's doing good. Sweet, kind lady, been through a lot. And her baby might be king someday. If it's a boy."

"Some folk might say a future king would be better served by a court physician."

"Lady Flidais doesn't want a court physician," Grim said. "She wants you."

"Why are you arguing in favor of going? You'll hate it even more than I will."

"Be sorry to leave the house. And the garden. Just when we've got it all sorted out." Grim spoke calmly, as if he did not care much one way or the other. His manner was a lie. It was a carapace of protection. He had become expert at hiding his feelings, and only rarely did he slip up. But I knew what must be in his heart. He had spent days and days fixing up the derelict cottage when we first came to Dreamer's Wood. He had labored over both house and garden until everything was perfect. Then the cottage had burned down, and he had done it all over again. I wasn't the only one who would find going away hard. "But it's not forever," Grim said. He tried for a smile but could not quite manage it. "Lads from the brewery can keep an eye on the place. Emer could drop in, make sure things are in order."

I said nothing. A lengthy stay at court would be miserable for both of us. We had a natural distrust of kings, chieftains and the like, based on our experience with Mathuin of Laois. That Oran and Flidais were exceptions did not mean a stay at Cahercorcan would be easier, since the king and queen would leave a good part of their household behind. We preferred to be on our own, Grim and I, which was why Conmael had suggested the cottage as a likely home for us. Conmael, a stranger, had somehow known that living at a distance from the settlement was the only way I was going to cope with being a wise woman again. At Cahercorcan, private quarters or not, we'd be right in the middle of things.

And there was another complication. The baker, Branoc, whom we'd helped bring to justice after he kidnapped and abused a young woman, was serving out his sentence as a bondsman to the king. He would be living in the household at Cahercorcan. I doubted Grim's capacity to be so close to the man without killing him.

"So, you going to ask him?"

"You mean Conmael?"

"Mm-hm. I know you don't much like the fellow. Me neither. But he's had his uses. And he did save your life."

I hesitated. If Grim was right, and the promise had been only to stay in Dalriada, then going to Cahercorcan would not be breaking my vow. On the other hand, if Conmael had bound me to stay at Winterfalls, then heading north would put another year onto the term of our agreement and lose me one of my four chances. That was a sacrifice I was not prepared to make.

"Brew?" asked Grim. "Ready when you get back."

"What makes you think Conmael will be there when I need him?"

"Came when I needed him, didn't he? The day you took it into your head to rush off south on your own."

There was no arguing with that. I had believed a lie that

day, and I'd let anger guide me, not common sense. Although there were times—more than a few of them—when I'd have preferred my own company to Grim's, there was no doubt that he had the ability to steady me, and that was not something to be lightly set aside. "I'll look. But he won't be there."

Also available from
Juliet Marillier

TOWER OF THORNS

Disillusioned healer Blackthorn and her companion, Grim, have settled in Dalriada to wait out the seven years of Blackthorn's bond to her fey mentor, hoping to avoid any dire challenges. But trouble has a way of seeking out Blackthorn and Grim.

Lady Geiléis, a noblewoman from the northern border, has asked for the prince of Dalriada's help in expelling a howling creature from an old tower on her land—one surrounded by an impenetrable hedge of thorns. With no ready solutions to offer, the prince consults Blackthorn and Grim.

Their quest is about to become a life and death struggle— a conflict in which even the closest of friends can find themselves on opposite sides...

Available wherever books are sold or at penguin.com
julietmarillier.com
facebook.com/ juliet.marillier

r0210

Want to connect with fellow science fiction and fantasy fans?

For news on all your favorite Ace and Roc authors, sneak peeks into the newest releases, book giveaways, and much more—

"Like" Ace and Roc Books!

facebook.com/AceRocBooks

twitter.com/AceRocBooks

acerocbooks.com